Dark Traveler

Peri Jean Mace Ghost Thrillers #9

Cover artwork by Book Cover Corner

Content Editing by Word Webber Press

Copy Editing by Julie Glover

Proofreading by Deborah Digrispino

ISBN Ebook: 978-1-947462-16-8

ISBN Print: 978-1-947462-01-4

First Printing, 2017

Rhodes, Catie.

Dark Traveler/ Catie Rhodes. — 1st ed.

Visit the author website: www.catierhodes.com

SERIES LIST

DARK TRAVELER

PERI JEAN MACE GHOST THRILLERS #9

CATIE RHODES

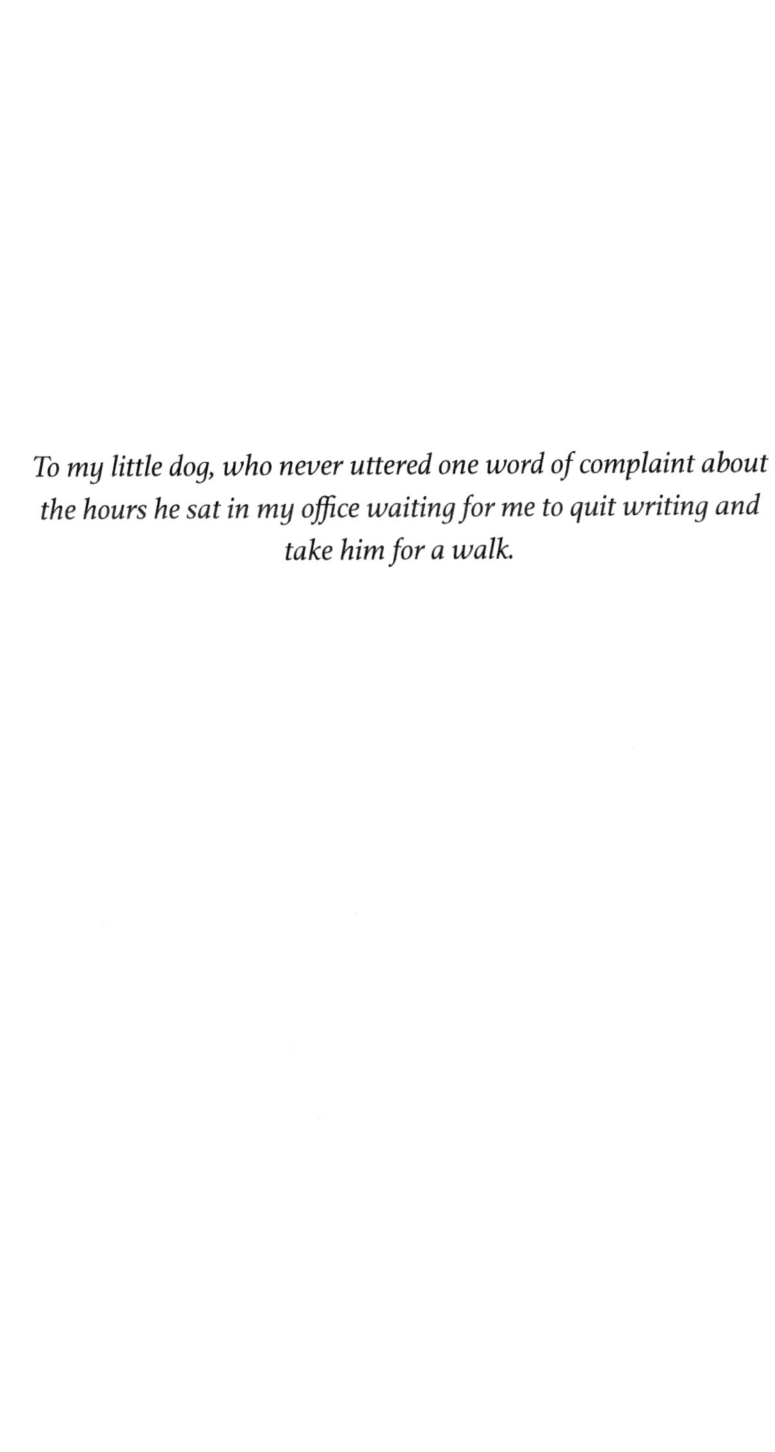

To my little dog, who never uttered one word of complaint about the hours he sat in my office waiting for me to quit writing and take him for a walk.

1

———

The dead lady whispered in my ear, "Tell him my wedding band is in the cookie jar on top of the refrigerator, but don't tell him his father killed me."

I broke my connection with the spirit and gave the cowboy across from me what I hoped was a mysterious smile. "Your mother says her ring is in the cookie jar on top of the refrigerator. And that she loves you."

"S-s-seriously? I been looking for that thing for the better part of a year now." The cowboy was young, early twenties at most. Lean, hard body in tight jeans. Sleeves of his western cut shirt rolled up to reveal tanned, muscled forearms. He'd have been cute if it hadn't been for his buck teeth. Less than two years ago, I'd have come on to him just to see what happened. But I'd changed since then. The cowboy leaned a little closer. "Lemme axe you something. Was that real? All them shadows moving behind you? The way the room got cold?"

I pushed away the defensiveness I felt when they asked

this question. They meant no harm. They were just responding to something they didn't understand. "I didn't see the shadows since they were behind me, so I don't know if they're real or not. As for your mother's spirit? Sure. She was real. Redhead, right? Pretty eyes?" I didn't mention the way the side of her head was dented or the gash on her face.

The cowboy's face paled beneath the smooth, tanned skin. "Yep. Died in a car wreck eighteen months ago. Somebody ran her off the road."

The hair on the back of my neck stood up, and a shiver rolled through me. I itched to tell him his father had something to do with it but knew I wouldn't. It wasn't my business. We never interfered with townies. It was the unspoken rule of Sanctuary, the traveling community of grifters and magic practitioners I helped lead. Instead, I'd close the transaction and let him go.

"Sir, are you satisfied that I answered what you came in here to find out?" I pushed the silver jar toward him.

He dug in his pocket but stopped short of getting out his wallet.

My stomach hardened. I'd had a few people try to cheat me. Here, surrounded by friends and family, all fiercely loyal, that kind of thing wouldn't fly. But the fights were nasty.

The cowboy cleared his throat. "I know the price you gave was just to contact my mother and find out where the ring was, but can you tell me if asking Harley to marry me is the right thing?" Those buck teeth made him look like a brown rabbit.

"Sir, I could take your money and tell you something, but I don't have the gift of precognition." I glanced behind me as though my great-uncle Cecil or his wife, Shelly, were about to rush out of the shadows and scold me for turning down money. That didn't happen. They were both busy with their own jobs.

The cowboy, eyes downcast, took out his wallet and peeled off the agreed upon amount, plus one dollar, and dropped it into the jar. The last of the big tippers.

I bit back a smile, thanked him, and followed him out, closing the flap of my tent and hanging up a "Be right back" sign. Summoning his mother's spirit had taken a bite out of my energy. She'd been a sad spirit, and she hadn't wanted to cross the veil. I needed a spike in my blood sugar if I wanted to last the rest of the evening. The freaks came out on Saturday night, which meant a chance to earn big money.

People moved past my tent, most barely giving me a glance. Finn, my cousin, called them sheeple. The rest of my family, still new enough to me to seem mysterious and exotic, called them townies. I'd resisted the classification but had gotten where I classified people within a few minutes of meeting them. Thrill seeker. Wannabe mystic. On the grift. Too stupid to live. On a Saturday night in the rural part of the Texas Hill Country, an hour minimum from any large city, Summervale Carnival was the best show for miles.

I stepped into the throng, determined to eat and feel more human. Hot, dry July wind ruffled my hair, drying the sweat on my face and powdering it with dust. A chaser of rancid grease and burnt sugar hit my nose. My appetite shrank. I lit a cigarette and strolled, coaxing myself to force down some kind of sustenance. Anything other than carnival food sounded good.

Sometime in my few months of traveling with the carnival, the honeymoon had ended. But Cecil had contracted Sanctuary to work the Summervale Carnival through Labor Day. We had our own little area in a hidden corner people seemed to find no matter how out of the way it was.

In addition to the spirit work, I sold spells that worked so well they scared the smart-ass out of the people who bought them. But money wasn't the only reason to be out here.

As long as Oscar Rivera's soul remained, he constituted a threat not only to me and my family, but to the world in general. Oscar Rivera, known as the Coachman, had been a nasty man and a nastier ghost. Neither my family nor I would be truly safe until I banished Oscar from the living plane. Otherwise, he'd eventually find a way to get revenge for the way I'd stomped his ass a few months earlier.

The search brought us to the Texas Hill Country because, in a vision, I'd seen Oscar hide his soul in what looked like a cavern. This part of Texas was known for its underground caverns. My best friend, Hannah Kessler, and I had been scouring newspaper archives and stories of old murders, trying to find a trace of Oscar during his human life. Our luck hadn't hit yet, but I held out hope it would.

I stopped walking, letting people stream around me,

and sucked in a deep breath of the dry Hill Country air. I tilted my head upward to stare at the sky. So huge, so many stars. Unfettered by the branches of tall pines we had in East Texas, the sky here opened up and stretched out into eternity. The summer heat was as unforgiving as a brimstone-preaching evangelist. But at night, like now, the stars seemed closer and sharper, like I could reach out and cut my finger on them. The energy flowed from them into me.

Tired as I was of Summervale Carnival, I wasn't tired of the Hill Country. This place grabbed me and held on tight. It had a different feel than East Texas, sort of an Old West vibe. The sight of actual cowboys on their way to work at nearby ranches captivated me. Germans had been the ones to settle much of this county, and their influence still colored the style of buildings and the local restaurants. And the country itself. Breathtaking. The land stretched out into hills and valleys covered by clumps of hairy looking grass and squat, gnarled trees.

My stomach rumbled. Accepting the inevitable, I stopped at a booth selling tropical punches made out of "100% real fruit." The owners sold moonshine out of the back of the booth. They'd said it came from a recipe in the family for three hundred years.

"Ms. Peri Jean." The female half of the couple who owned the booth passed me a cup of punch with a slice of pineapple garnishing the cup's edge. I dug for my money. She raised her chin. "Nope. On the house. That spell you sold us to increase our business really worked."

I nodded my thanks and cut back into the crowd, guzzling the drink. My tent and maybe more customers awaited. Before long, I reached the row of tents belonging to the traveling community of Sanctuary. Made of a heavy vinyl-coated material, the tents rattled and flapped in the hot wind.

A shadowy figure leaned out from the edge of one of the tents as though taking a peek at me. That cowboy's mother's ghost. I groaned.

Some of the spirits I contacted for money weren't so eager to go back where they came from. I had learned to deal with them in a businesslike way and to act confident.

Spirit, be gone. I drew on my magic and gave it a hard push. The spirit disappeared. I rejoined the throng of drunk townies, wild-eyed thrill seekers, and bored parents walking the dirt path through the makeshift carnival and walked past my family's row of tents.

I stopped at the sound of Dillon's husky smoker voice ringing out of the first tent. The sign outside read "Stop smoking with HYPNOSIS! $75 per person." A peek inside showed me she had a full house.

A Sanctuary member stood just inside the entrance taking a wad of money from a woman whose wizened skin made her look like an advertisement for quitting smoking. The Sanctuary woman, on the run from an abusive husband, raised her brows in question. I smiled, backed out of the tent, and peeked into the next one.

My cousin Jadine sat staring into a crystal ball. Inside the ball, a mist of smoke moved around. The sign next to Jadine read "See into the future. Ask Mistress Jade for a reading."

"Peri Jean, I need to talk to you." Jadine raised her head

and stared in my general direction. Her accuracy still amazed me, especially since she was blind.

"How'd you know it was me?" I stepped the rest of the way into the tent.

"Your soap. And you coughed a couple of times." Jadine took her hands off the crystal ball, and the mist stopped moving inside it.

"I think you like catching people off guard." I moved close enough to give her a playful nudge but didn't sit at her table. My butt was tired. "What's up?"

"I'm not sure I should tell anybody this." Something in her voice raised my drama antennae.

I'd sounded that way too many times not to recognize it when I heard it another woman's voice. "What is it?"

"Brad's asked me to marry him." A little smile hovered on her lips.

I swallowed my first response, which was incredulity. Brad Whitebyrd loved playing the field, loved thinking he was a ladies man. Had Jadine stolen his heart? I counted how many times he'd visited camp, even going as far as to work while he was among us. His actually doing work convinced me. "What'd you say?"

"That he'd have to ask Papaw. What do you think Papaw'd say if Brad asked for my hand?" I thought it over. Cecil would be brokenhearted that the only child he'd raised to adulthood thought herself ready for marriage. His heartbreak would come out in anger and admonitions.

I had my own misgivings. Jadine was only twenty-one. She really ought to date a bunch of guys and make a more informed choice.

But what did I know? I'd married young, divorced quickly, dated a bunch of guys, and still spent every night alone, the man I loved completely cut off from me. By choice.

"Peri Jean? Are you saying nothing because I ought to tell Brad no?" She clenched her hands in the lap of her brown, flowered dress.

"Just thinking." I came close enough to put my hand on her shoulder. "You're old enough to do what you want, no matter what I or anybody else thinks."

She grinned, and I thought I knew why Brad White-byrd would swear off bachelorhood for Jadine. She was gorgeous. "So you think Papaw won't get angry?"

"Oh, I didn't say that. He'll scream. He'll cry. He'll tell you not to do it." I giggled, and Jadine joined me. "But once he gets over it, he'll welcome Brad into the family. He's a pretty accomplished energy witch. Cecil will want him in Sanctuary after he thinks about it."

"I can see us being happy together." The look of hope on her young, untested face made me want to laugh and cry at the same time.

I'd have never told her she was wrong. Sometimes you just know when somebody's the right one. I'd leave the persuasive speeches to Cecil and Shelly. Jadine's adoptive parents, especially her mother, would probably drive her crazy. Shelly viewed her daughter as a princess and thought she'd marry a prince. Brad Whitebyrd was more like a spoiled frat boy.

"Will you go with Brad to talk to Papaw?" Jadine twisted in her chair. I knew this request came from Brad.

"Nope. If Brad's big enough to get married, he's big enough to do the hard stuff on his own." I leaned down and slowly pulled my cousin into a hug. She squeezed tight and let go of me.

"There's something else. I had a vision, a real one." Jadine plucked at the rayon of her dress.

My breath caught in my throat. This might be the break I needed, the thing that would make all these weeks with Summervale Carnival worth the effort.

"Something with Oscar Rivera?" I willed her to say yes. The worry about what I was going to do when I found his soul and could dispatch him was eating me up worse than just finding him and fighting him.

She shook her head, frowning. "It was a man asking about us, like he was looking for us. He was in San Antonio at that RV park where we stayed."

I quickly calculated. Our stay in the city of San Antonio had been two weeks ago. "What did he want with us?"

"I don't know. But he had a snake for a necklace." She made a face.

My guts twisted as I considered all the people or *things* that might wear a snake for a necklace and might be looking for me. Anybody from Sol, my contact across the veil, to a topside supernatural overlord and slave trader I'd nicknamed Mohawk. I turned my attention back to Jadine. "Tell me more about this man."

She shook her head so hard, her blond waves whipped back and forth. "That's it. Then the vision flashed to you. You had a hole right here." She tapped herself on a spot above and between both eyes. "Bright light was streaming out of it." Her breath came faster. "Those runes—the Coachman's runes—were floating around you, and they were glowing." She gulped.

I took a step away from her, freaked out by what she'd seen and unable to make sense of it. Sometimes Jadine's visions were symbolic. This one would take some thinking.

"I did a search on my phone for the part about the light coming out of your head." She gave me a sly little smile. I wanted to thump her. Brad Whitebyrd had probably taught her how to talk to her phone and make it talk back.

"Find anything interesting?" I did all I could to keep the amusement out of my voice.

"I found stuff about an evil eye and stuff about a third eye." Jadine shrugged. That was the extent of her knowledge, which was more than she'd have been able to access on a smartphone a few years ago.

"Okay. Thank you for letting me know. If you think that man is getting any closer, or if you somehow sense him here, come get me. Immediately." Feeling eyes on my back, I glanced at the tent's flap, only to see the shadow pull back quickly, as though to avoid detection. That was it. I'd banish this damn spirit as soon as I got away from Jadine. I turned to go. "Good luck with Cecil and Shelly."

Jadine blew me a kiss and went back to her crystal ball.

Outside I disconnected from the noise and stench and searched for the shadow. At first, I felt nothing, but that prickling feeling of someone watching me soon returned. I did a slow circle until I spotted the shadow. It hovered right at the end of my family's row of tents. I walked toward it.

With each step, my black opal necklace sent shocks of heat into my skin. The necklace, a gift from an ex-boyfriend's mother, magnified my natural gifts and warned me of nearby supernatural activity. The stronger the magic, the sharper the black opal's warnings became. The level of heat the gem was generating made no sense for an everyday ghost.

The shadow and I watched each other for several seconds. With no warning, it flew right at me, smacked into me, and knocked me off balance. Several people who'd been too close shouted as I slammed into them. I hit the dirt with a grunt and got up mad.

The mantle rolled over and woke up. It was ready to kick ass. Its power, my birthright, had been passed down through my family for no telling how many generations. Because of a spell put on me in infancy, I did not yet have full control of the mantle's power. But I was still a damn powerful witch and spirit medium.

I gently gathered the massive, shining power, coaxing it through the spell blunting it. My vision wavered at the edges. Pinpricks of magic stung at my skin. Still I let the power unfurl further, let it fill me.

I looked for the shadow again. It had backed away like a bull preparing to charge. It flew at me.

This time, I met it with a blast of power strong enough to knock me backward a few steps. The mantle's magic slammed into the shadow. I didn't so much hear the impact as I felt it. The air rippled against my skin. In a strong voice, I said, "Go rest. There's nothing left for you here."

The shadow backed away, slowly turned, and zipped into the dark night sky, becoming one with the inky expanse. I breathed a sigh of relief and tried to gather myself.

Slowly, the sounds of the carnival came back. I became aware of a few people staring at me. I glared until the last of them, a middle-aged man who thought it was his job to teach me a lesson by staring me down, turned and left.

Nearby, the bell on the strongman high-striker dinged. I'd argued against adding a high-striker, thinking modern people wouldn't pay to do something so silly. Seems I'd underestimated the pull of testosterone. I shook my head and walked toward my tent. Break time was over.

A familiar male voice raised in outrage. "That's not right. I hit that thing harder than that."

I stopped in my tracks, swallowed hard, spun around, and started walking toward the voice.

The game-runner, an unfortunate runaway named Early Ramey, shrugged. "Just a game, mister."

I crowded a little closer, heart slamming so hard I could barely breathe, and stood on my tiptoes. I didn't see the head of long black hair. My mind was probably playing tricks on me. Jadine's upcoming nuptials had me thinking of lonely days and nights stretching into infinity. The alone part wasn't the kicker. It was knowing that the perfect man, one I already loved, had slipped right through my fingers.

Then the familiar voice spoke again, and I locked eyes on the speaker. I'd been looking for the wrong man, the old Wade Hill. The one a few feet away was a different version altogether.

"But I'm trying to win a bear for this little girl here." Wade's voice hadn't changed any over the months since I'd last seen him, but he sure had. His black hair, which had reached down to the middle of his back the last time I saw him, had been cut very short.

The conservative cut was probably to compensate for where Wade's hair had been shaved around his head wound. The scar from the bullet that almost killed him looked a decade old instead of only a few months. Wade's sister and niece must have known something about healing too. Wade's beard, which had been a bushy mess hanging to his collarbone, was trimmed to hug the shape of his face. The lack of facial hair showed off a strong jaw and sexy, pouty lips. The broad shoulders and narrow hips were the same as ever—hot, hot, hot. I started toward him.

A hard hand closed around my upper arm and dragged me out of the dirt thoroughfare. I yelled, "What the hell?"

Whoever had ahold of me said nothing and kept on dragging me. They'd caught me off balance and had the upper hand.

I struggled anyway, elbows flailing, and yelled, "I'll beat the skin off your bones, shit brains."

No answer. I was jerked into the narrow space between two tents.

Fist cocked, I spun to face my attacker. The blond woman, many inches taller than me, wore skin-tight blue jeans, a black lace see-through shirt, and a wide belt made of metal hoops.

She put her hands up in response to my threat. "Don't you remember me?"

I dropped my hands and shook my head.

"Makes sense. We only met for a minute, and you were exhausted."

But we'd met. I cocked my head and tried to place the full lips and square jaw. There was something about the hair. It reminded me of an angel's halo.

She got tired of waiting and said, "Wade's sister, Desiree."

I got pissed again. "You made him leave without saying goodbye to me." Fury and hurt at the way Wade had left, with just a Dear John note, came roaring back. I stomped forward and gave Desiree a hard shove, intending to go out there and speak to Wade, to try to figure out if there was still anything between us.

She shoved back, harder than I'd expected. I stumbled backward and sat down in the dirt. Second time in one night someone had pushed me onto my ass. My face flamed, first with humiliation, then with anger. I moved to get up.

Desiree stepped forward to tower over me. "Just listen, okay? Then if you want to fight, we can." She held out a hand to help me up.

What the hell. First the giantess knocked me down, now she wanted to help me up. The two of us gave each other catfight eyes. But the fight drained out of me as quickly as it had come. I'd need to go through Desiree to get to Wade.

The first step was listening to what she had to say. I nodded my agreement and let her pull me to my feet.

Desiree watched me closely, maybe making sure I wasn't going to sucker punch her. When she finally spoke, her voice sounded heavy and tired.

"Wade said he told you about the reading, the one forbidding you two to be together. Is that right?" She crossed her arms over her flat stomach and stood with her feet at shoulder width.

I nodded again. "Your reading predicted great tragedy if we got together. In other words, you," I said, pointing one finger at her, "advised him to keep his dick in his pants when it came to me."

She rolled her eyes. "Close enough."

I crossed my arms and mirrored her stance. Desiree was taller and heavier. Worse, she probably knew how to fight as well as me. She'd beat my ass. But I was pissed enough to give her a good contest. I loved Wade, even after his weird exit from my life, and still wanted to take a chance with him.

"Your reading might be wrong." I raised my eyebrows.

Anger flashed behind Desiree's blue eyes, and her fist curled. "No, ma'am. My reading ain't wrong. Too much of it has come true."

The fruit punch burned sour in my stomach. "Like what?" I squeaked.

"Like my brother getting shot helping you rescue that girl." She licked her lips. "You saved his life, like you were supposed to. He loved you more than ever. The next thing is y'all would have a child together. Then my brother would die." Her voice broke, and she put her hand to her mouth and said nothing for several seconds. When she looked back up, tears brimmed in her eyes. She rubbed her index finger underneath one before it had a chance to ruin her makeup. "And another man would raise his child."

I shook my head, still not ready to believe. "But that's just one fate. Each person's fate changes every day, with every choice you make." That was what Mysti Whitebyrd told me, and I wanted to believe it.

She pressed her lips together. "Did yours? You been fated all your life to take on your ancestor's magic, to be a leader to your family. That change when your memaw had that spell put on you?"

I flinched. Wade had told her about the spell blocking me from accessing the full measure of Priscilla Herrera's mantle? That hurt worse than if Desiree had doubled up her fist and busted my nose. A lump worked its way up my throat. I swallowed against it, unable to speak.

Desiree's reading couldn't be right. Wade and I had a special connection. He always knew just what I needed, just how to help me. And I understood his sudden rages and how he sometimes got sad over nothing.

Desiree dropped her fighter's stance and came forward. Hands out, beseeching. "This man who'll raise my brother's child will be the way for you to gain access to all your power without losing yourself, but you'll make the wrong person mad. Hell, maybe you already have. And Wade'll die trying to save you."

"No. You're wrong," I whispered, tears streaking down

my face. This didn't sound like bullshit. It sounded so real. But Mysti's words kept coming back. "That doesn't have to happen. Our fate changes in response to the choices we make. Things could turn out good for me and Wade."

She hooked one arm around my neck, dragged me to the edge of the tent, and pointed. "If that loyal, sweet man out there was your brother, would you want to risk it?"

I thought about it. Part of me wanted to claw out this bitch's eyeballs. How dare she come between me and the man I loved? Another part of me cringed at the thought of getting together with Wade for real, enough to make a baby, and then losing him.

The bell on the strongman high-striker dinged. Wade's happy shout floated back to us.

Desiree smiled. "Thank goodness. That's my grandbaby he's trying to win something for. He's got her pretty spoiled."

This woman had a grandchild? She didn't look old enough. I had always calculated Wade's age at maybe five years older than me. How much older was Desiree?

She snorted at the look on my face. "Thanks for the compliment. But I'm older than Wade by thirteen years. My oldest son has a baby, and that's her out there."

We stared at each other. Of all the ways I'd foreseen myself getting into a fistfight over a man, a confrontation with the man's sister never occurred to me.

"So what are we gonna do?" The mirth went out of Desiree's face. "I guess I can't stop you if you're really determined. But, Peri Jean, he's finally getting over you." She stepped close enough for me to read the sadness on her face. "I know I'm being unfair. It's always us women who make the sacrifices, and it sucks. I see how sad you are, know you love my brother, and it breaks my heart. I know we'd love each other as sisters-in-law, but I'd rather have my brother."

Another tear tracked down my face. The bell on the high-striker rang again. One more, and he'd have his pick of the stuffed animals. I had to make up my mind soon, or Wade would come looking for Desiree and make my decision for me.

There was always a possibility Desiree was wrong. But her specific predictions scared me. Jadine saw the future. When she got specific like this, she was rarely wrong. Maybe Desiree had a similar gift. She must've had some powerful magic to heal Wade from his gunshot wounds. Why not the gift of accurate precognition too?

"Do you love him enough to let him go?" Desiree came close enough to put her arm around me. I wanted to elbow her in the ribs, maybe break a few.

"What's going on here?" Hannah stood in the opening between the tents.

Shelly, my great-aunt by marriage, stepped up next to Hannah, bleached blond hair fluttering in the hot wind. Shelly's dark eyes, cold as a rainy January day, focused on Desiree. She curled one hand against her side as though searching for a weapon.

I put my arm around Desiree, and she gave me the saddest look I'd ever seen. It said more than words ever could have. *We'd have liked each other. We're the same kind of woman.* I broke her gaze and spoke to Hannah. "This is Wade's sister. It's all right."

I stepped to the edge of the space between tents, leaned out, and watched Wade.

He now had Desiree's granddaughter seated on his shoulders. "Hold on," he yelled and lifted the mallet.

Desiree stood next to me, a soft smile on her face. "I remember when Wade was born. Mama and Daddy were just drunks. So I got to hold him all I wanted. I'd dress him up and take him places, pretend he was my baby." She laughed. "I can only imagine what people thought about a thirteen-year-old saying she had a baby." She put her arm around me again. "How I wish things were different, Peri Jean Mace."

I still didn't know if they couldn't be. But the thought of things ending up like Desiree said ripped open my emotions and salted them for good measure. I pushed my hand over my mouth as if that would quell the ache.

"I just want Wade to have a chance to enjoy his own grandchildren like I'm doing now." Desiree watched her brother slam down the mallet.

The bell dinged the third time. The finality of it made me want to scream and tear at my hair. My voice wobbled when I spoke. "Get him out of here. He knows all of us. He'll recognize somebody and know I'm here."

Desiree stepped around me but turned back to speak one last time. "I think he already does. He had that look on his face when he insisted we come here tonight." She shrugged. "Sometimes we can't resist tempting fate." With that, she walked off, hips swinging in those tight jeans.

More than one man turned to get a second look at her. She reached Wade and lifted her granddaughter off his shoulders. The three of them picked out a huge, pink bear with a purple bow tie.

Wade stuffed the bear under one thick arm and took the little girl's hand. She tugged him toward the main part of the carnival, yelling and pointing.

Desiree turned back to look at me one last time. I swiped the tears off my face and stood up straight. She nodded, turned, and walked away.

Shelly took my arm and spoke in her brisk Northern accent. "Let's get away from these prying eyes. This isn't anybody's business but ours."

Hannah nodded and led the way to our row of tents. Face set and on the edge of angry, she threw one glance toward Wade and Desiree. Neither saw the look she gave them. Good thing. It might have made them mad enough to fight.

2

———

Hannah went inside the face painting tent where she worked every time the carnival was open. I followed with my head hung low. Nobody needed to see my makeup tracked all over my face.

Shelly stayed next to me, a maternal hand on my back, and led me toward the back of the tent where there was a separate room set up for privacy.

In her mid-sixties, Shelly had a body as nice as mine and dressed to show it. Tonight's outfit was a loose salmon tank top, which showed off firm arms and allowed occasional peeks at her surgically enhanced boobs, a pair of tight, white Capri pants, and high-heeled sandals.

Something more sinister lurked under Shelly's high-gloss outer shell. If my suspicions were correct, Shelly and Cecil had dropped the dime on Shelly's first husband to the cops and got him killed. She'd been on her own since she was thirteen and always had one scam or another going.

Most nights she wandered the carnival, talking to random men and leading them back to our special corner. But some nights, she hung out a sign offering "love advice." She always had a long line.

Finally in the safety of the back room, I flopped down in a metal chair, put my hands over my face, and let the shame roll over me.

"How much did y'all hear?" My voice sounded muffled behind my hands, and I felt like a teenager having a tantrum, so I dropped them.

"Enough to get the gist." Shelly's clipped accent made it sound like she was telling me off, but I'd learned it was just her way of talking.

Hannah nodded agreement. She held a lighter to the tip of one of her long, skinny white cigarettes. She handed it to me and lit another one. The novelty of watching Hannah smoke after all the times she'd bitched about me doing it took away some of the sting of Desiree's rebuke.

Smoldering cigarette in one hand, Hannah fixed her gaze on me. I didn't see much sympathy in it, but I saw understanding. "You knew it was over anyway, right?"

I nodded, tears burning my eyes and a sob building in my throat.

"Hon, I get why you're upset. Really I do." Shelly softened her voice. "But just liking someone, even loving them, doesn't make them the right person for you."

I hung my head, already sick of this conversation even though it had only just started. Shelly had no idea who was the right person for me and who wasn't.

Shelly leaned forward, squinting at my face. "Oh, but I do know who's right for you. You forget, I give love advice."

Shelly claimed to be an empath, capable of seeing a couple's compatibility. Privately, I wondered if it was a scam. Cecil had told me his wife had a scam for every occasion. He even warned me not to let myself get pulled into any of them. I'd taken his advice seriously and stayed away from Shelly's booth. Maybe I shouldn't have. Shelly might have told me to give up hope on Wade months ago. Or not. Shelly Gregg was a grifter all the way down to her bone marrow.

"I can see that speculative look on your face. Even through all that raccoon makeup. What I do isn't just a scam." Shelly held her cigarette to her mouth and took a casual drag. "I introduced Dillon and Finn. Finn's aura showed that he was about to meet someone. We stopped in this little town in Alabama. I met Dillon in a coffee shop. Knew she was the one right away, even if she was too young for Finn. I introduced them. Finn tried to wiggle out of it, but..." Shelly shrugged her thin shoulders and smiled. It made her look fifteen years younger.

What was this supposed to have to do with Wade and me? I tried to keep a look of polite interest on my face.

Shelly gave me a shrewd wink. "What this has to do with you is that I saw your aura, and I saw Wade's. There's a strong connection there, but not the lasting kind."

Rage built in my chest. I didn't want to let it out at Shelly. We had a good relationship so far. It wasn't worth it to sour it over Wade. After what Desiree told me, I was scared to get within ten feet of him. But I still didn't want to let the idea of him go.

Shelly watched me. I'd have sworn she knew exactly what was going on in my head. She was that good at reading people. "Just keep an open mind. Don't let old wounds cripple you."

That went against my beliefs. The wounds I'd survived had taught me things, made me stronger. I held on to them to keep me from repeating the same mistakes. "The past is my armor. I have to keep it close so I'll never forget."

"Learning from mistakes is one thing. Carrying them around like luggage full of souvenirs is quite another. Forget him." Shelly flicked ashes off her cigarette and blew them away, staring at me the whole time. Her meaning couldn't have been more clear. *Clear Wade out of your mind, out of your heart.*

I opened my mouth to argue but snapped it shut. Wade had made his decision when he wrote that Dear Peri Jean Mace letter and hightailed it out of my life. Hearing Desiree tell me why it would never happen broke my heart into a million pieces, but it solidified things. Wade and I were done. Nothing I said or did would change it.

Shelly watched me, her dark eyes intent on something around my head. "Your aura shows that now would be a good time for you to drop the rock and start again. My advice? Go for it with the next man who seems interesting. You never know what you'll find."

It didn't matter what Shelly thought or said. I couldn't imagine myself liking another man enough to even bother with a ten-day ugly bumping marathon. Forget any new relationships.

Hannah watched me think. She knew me better than anybody. She smoked the last of her cigarette and stood. "Let's drop it for now. I've got some stuff I want to show you."

I sat up straighter, glad for a change in the subject. "Did you find anything about Oscar Rivera in Austin?"

Shelly and Hannah had taken a day trip to Austin, ostensibly to shop, while the workers had been setting up Summervale in its current location. They must have done a lot more than shop.

"I've been talking to a girl online who does ghost tours in Austin. She'd written an article for her blog about something that intrigued me. She agreed to meet me for coffee." Hannah turned to a file cabinet in the corner, slid open one of the drawers, and dug around in it. "She gave me a few ideas. I ended up having to make copies out of a reference book they had at the library, but look at these." She handed me a sheaf of pages. I leafed through them.

The first one was a copy of a page-sized picture. At first glance, all I saw were a bunch of people dressed in dusty looking clothes and staring straight ahead like they were having their mugshots taken. But then I recognized Oscar Rivera's thick lips and sloe eyes.

"Holy shit. It's him." A shiver worked its way down my spine. I set the page aside and skimmed over the entry associated with it.

Oscar Rivera was named as William Burkehardt in the picture. This Burkehardt started a church in Austin catering to wealthy widows interested in spiritualism. He presented it as exploratory Christianity, but one of the members of the order said they did a lot of trying to contact the spirit world and even tried a crossroads-style meeting to attract spirits.

One weekend, the entire membership—about ten women—disappeared. It was thought Oscar, or William, had spirited them away to get their money. They were looked for but never heard from again.

The member quoted in the article, which was based on an old news story, said the disappearance happened while she was out of town but that she had already lost interest in the group before she left. Burkehardt scared her.

I tried to hand the papers back to Hannah.

"There's one more," she said.

I flipped to the last page. It was from an article dated a year after the disappearance of Oscar and his harem. It was a copy of a newspaper article about a murder. I skimmed through the details, noting the name of the victim. It matched the one member of Oscar's church who hadn't disappeared. She'd been hacked to death with some sort of long blade and then mutilated. The bones had been taken out of one leg.

"The runes," I whispered.

During my fight with Oscar Rivera several months earlier, I'd become acquainted with a set of runes he'd created out the bones of his victims. Each rune, smaller and thinner than a domino, had been carved with a particular symbol. The symbol represented a deal Oscar had made for immortality with a creature from the dark outposts.

Each rune carried the life force of the victim it came from. The life force contained in the runes allowed Oscar's corporeal body to live without the effects of age or disease. Because of the runes, Oscar walked among the living.

But every bargain with a creature like the one Oscar dealt with has a loophole. Oscar's loophole had been that his corporeal body, while it could not get old or sick and die, could be killed. Oscar had pissed off the wrong witch —an ancestor of mine—and got his corporeal body killed.

His consciousness, the evil that made him Oscar, went to where he'd hidden his soul. No longer able to walk among the living, and unwilling to join the ranks of the dead, Oscar had languished there with his trapped soul. Until the wrong person had found one of his death runes and summoned him back.

Oscar's second walk among the living had ended in a fight with me. I'd sacrificed so much to send his awful, evil consciousness back to his soul. As far as I knew, he was still sitting in that cave with his soul, waiting for another moron to find one of his death runes. My goal was to find the box where he'd hidden his soul and forcefully banish it to the dark outposts before Oscar could make his way back among the living.

Hannah's voice cut into my thoughts and made me jump. "How much you want to bet a piece of every single one of those missing women is in that bag of runes you have?" Hannah wrinkled her nose.

Gross. I wrinkled my nose. "That makes me wish I

could throw them away. But Samantha said the wheel and the runes were my key to finding where Oscar hid his soul."

"You made any progress on that?" Shelly knew the story and seemed to have a working understanding of it.

"I tried a few of the divining spells in Priscilla Herrera's grimoire, but nothing happened." I stopped and reconsidered. "Oh, the runes got hot with magic and I could hear people screaming, but I didn't see anything useful."

"What about the wheel?" Shelly asked.

The wheel had been gifted to me by Priscilla Herrera's daughter Samantha—the witch who'd killed Oscar's mortal body. Of course, Samantha was already dead when the gifting happened. But I still thought it counted as a gift.

My biggest problem with the wheel was that I couldn't quite understand its purpose. Therefore, I didn't know its function or what to do with it. Realizing both Shelly and Hannah were watching me with puzzled looks crinkling their features, I said, "The only time I've seen the wheel do anything is when Sol crawled out of it and killed people." I paused, enjoying the horrified looks on Hannah's and Shelly's faces.

"So it's a summoning device." Shelly spoke with confidence. But then she always sounded that way.

I shrugged. "I've tried a few of Priscilla's summoning spells on it. It just stays cold and dead."

Jadine's vision of me with the runes returned to my memory. The image still didn't connect to anything I knew. I needed more information.

"Who would know about the wheel?" I muttered out loud.

"The only person I know is Mysti Whitebyrd," Hannah said, "and I can't believe the two of you haven't beaten the topic to death."

We had. I gave her a shrug and a nod.

"What about your problem accessing the center of our family's power?" Shelly raised her pencil-thin eyebrows. "The mantle, I mean. Could that have anything to do with your inability to make the wheel and the runes work together?"

I grunted in answer. I didn't even want to think about that stupid spell. It made me tired.

"Have you done any more work on removing the spell?" Not one to beat around the bush, Shelly also wouldn't drop a topic just because it made me uncomfortable.

I shook my head. "I don't know what to do. Cecil mentioned a man he knew who might help. But honestly, I'm a little afraid of what he'll do to me. When Sol ate a hole in the spell to let some of the mantle out, I thought I was losing my mind from the pain."

Hannah, who'd endured more physical and emotional pain than just about anybody I knew, stared into the face painting tent, face haunted.

Shelly spoke up. "I tend to believe the power we need is within us from the start. There is a way to remove that spell yourself. Didn't you say it was a form of scar tissue, made up of the bad things you've endured?"

I nodded.

She pointed at me. "Think about what we were just saying about leaving the past behind and blazing a new road into the future."

"But..." I didn't know what my argument was, but I did know it wasn't as simple as shrugging off all the bad I'd endured like a too-hot coat.

"No, not yet." A man's cry came from right outside the tent. I recognized the voice right away.

Before I could react, Shelly shouted, "That's my Cecil," and raced out of the tent. Hannah and I hurried along behind her.

———

Cecil stood off in the middle of the dirt midway, one hand clapped to his chest, sucking in deep, moaning breaths.

"No, Jackson. Not yet," he managed between pants.

Shelly ran to her husband's side and grabbed his arm. "Somebody call an ambulance," she yelled. For Shelly to want outside help, she had to believe Cecil was really dying.

I whipped out my phone, but Hannah gripped my wrist.

"He's not dying," she said. Her caramel eyes locked on my darker ones. For a second I relived the horror of saving her after a suicide attempt. Her re-entry into the land of the living came with a talent. She predicted deaths. The irony of it hurt my soul. I gave her a grateful nod, and she let go of me.

Still holding my phone, I approached Cecil. His frightened gaze latched on to mine.

"Peri Jean, do you see Jackson's ghost?" He pointed at a man standing a few feet away, mouth hanging open in shock at the scene. The poor man clutched a picture in one hand.

"That man's not a ghost, Papaw. He's alive like us." I advanced on the man. "Are you Jackson?" I yelled, expecting the man to back up. He stood his ground, head lowered like an animal, staring out at me from narrow glittering green eyes.

"No. I'm not Jackson. My name's Tanner Letts. My grandfather was Jackson." Tanner's voice, a rough purr, stopped me from coming any closer.

The sound of that voice did something to my body. Made it hot all over. Suddenly, I didn't want to argue with Tanner any more. I wanted to go somewhere and splash cold water on my face.

Tanner walked toward us, steps soft and rocking, like a big animal on the prowl. "Should I call the paramedics?"

His concise way of enunciating words, of speaking every syllable, marked him as not from Texas or the South. An outsider in every possible way. Just what we needed.

I looked at Cecil for the answer. Only he knew if he still felt like he was dying. Sweat covered my uncle's face, had dampened his white dress shirt, and made it stick to his chest.

"No. I thought Tanner here was his grandfather's ghost. Jackson always said... well, it's silly." Cecil put his arm around Shelly and leaned on her.

"Tell us, honey." Shelly stared at her husband, probably worried he'd keel over with no warning.

Cecil cleared his throat. "Jackson Letts was my best friend throughout boyhood. The last time we spoke, Jackson and I agreed that whoever died first would come fetch the other when it was their time to die so we could walk into the afterlife, the next great adventure, the same way we'd done things as young men." Cecil's voice quaked on the last word. Tears flooded his eyes. He tried to laugh. "My heart's been so bad the last couple of years...I just thought..."

"I'm sorry, sir." Tanner stepped forward and handed Cecil the picture he'd been holding this whole time.

I crowded in, brushing against Tanner. Those jewel-colored eyes met mine again. I tried to ignore him and looked at the picture. It showed Cecil as a very young man, maybe early twenties, standing next to a man who shared Tanner's narrow chin and wide cheekbones. Both Tanner and Jackson sported broad, bar-fight noses, though Jackson's was more crooked.

Tanner caught me staring. I glanced away, cheeks heating. World's Biggest Tramp goes to Peri Jean Mace. Five minutes earlier I'd been crying my eyes out over Wade, thinking I'd never get over him. Thinking any other man would be a weak substitute for Wade. Why was I even bothering to assess Tanner Letts? He was probably a loser anyway.

I caught Hannah watching me. She raised her eyebrows and shrugged. I could practically hear her thoughts in my head. *Let it go. Move forward or be trampled by everything else moving past you.* I ignored her and pretended to be fascinated by the picture.

"You were good-looking, Papaw." I nudged Cecil. He laughed and shook his head, already getting his color back. I took the opportunity to check out Tanner some more.

Long brown hair brushing his shoulders. Muscular thighs encased in black jeans so faded they were gray at the thighs and white on the knees. Tight T-shirt with a faded emblem I couldn't quite read. Facial hair trimmed to the perfect length, not quite stubble, not quite beard. Mr. Rock-n-Roll.

Then I noticed the necklace. Jadine's vision of the man looking for us came crashing back. The necklace wasn't a snake. It was a plain silver chain looped through a silver ring. The ring was a snake eating its own tail. Ouroboros. Close enough.

Especially when the other part of the vision had me with a hole in my head and wading in the Coachman's runes. Tanner better have some good answers about why he was here.

"You're the one who's been looking for us." I faced Tanner. The black opal pinged to let me know there was something magical about him. I didn't care what it was right then. He'd been tracking us, and he'd better have a damn good reason why.

"Of course I've been looking for you." He tried to laugh it off, but he widened his stance. The cat getting ready to pounce.

"Move," Finn yelled at the people who'd surrounded us.

For the first time, I took in the curious faces. "Show's over," I yelled. "Go back to having fun or go home. My uncle just had a scare."

The people moved enough for Jadine to push her way through. Finn followed right behind her. I pulled Jadine to me, made her stand next to Tanner, and whispered, "I think this is the man from your vision. He's here looking for Papaw, and he has an ouroboros necklace. Can you sense anything?"

Jadine held one hand toward Tanner, fingers reaching. She wanted to touch him.

Tanner backed away, muscles in his arms tensing. "What is this? I'm just here to talk to Cecil Gregg. I don't want trouble."

Finn stepped behind Tanner and gripped both his arms. Tanner twisted in Finn's grip, easily slipping out of it. He bent both knees and held up his fists.

"I don't want to fight you people. I'm just..." Tanner glanced at Cecil, the intimidating eyes no longer confident. Now they almost pleaded.

Cecil motioned for us to get away from Tanner. "You kids stop it. Give him some room."

Tanner backed into me, his long hair brushing my face. The scent of his shampoo filled my nose, clean and manly. I shoved him back toward Finn. Tanner spun, already rearing back to hit, but stopped himself with an obvious effort. We glared at each other. The bright lights gleamed golden on his not-quite-beard, and sweat glossed his sun-bronzed skin. I forced a frown onto my face.

"Tell us what you're up to." I tore my gaze off him and glanced around for Finn's wife, Dillon. She could use her gift of persuasion on Tanner. Get him to tell us anything we ever wanted to know.

"Everybody stand down," Cecil shouted. "Tanner is the grandson of the best friend I ever had. He'll be heard with respect."

Finn and I backed away, hands up in surrender. We exchanged a glance. I pushed a thought to the forefront of my mind. *Jump him if he runs.* Finn, a telepath, nodded his understanding of my command.

"This is not how I pictured this." Tanner, having regained his cool, kicked at the ground with one of his worn-out, square-toed boots.

"Life is rarely how you picture it. Start talking." My eyes met Tanner's again. I narrowed them to let him know I meant business. Tanner did the same.

Cecil put his hand on Tanner's arm. "Just relax. Peri Jean here—she's my niece and Sanctuary's enforcer— seems a lot meaner than she is."

Cecil shot a glare at me, its meaning clear. *Back off and let this guy talk.* Even though I didn't want to, I took a step backward.

Watching me, Tanner tucked a lock of hair behind one ear. His neck, smooth-shaven, looked soft but strong. A current of desire ran through me, made my jeans too tight. My lips parted. Tanner's nostrils flared, his tongue going to the corner of his mouth.

He took his eyes off me and spoke to Cecil. "Fine. I've had a bad couple of years. Lost everything."

His voice, rough and soft all at the same time, seeped into me as though he was touching my body.

Tanner danced foot to foot, uncomfortable, but still fluid with each movement. "When I was getting the last of my stuff out of my house —what I didn't have to leave after the bank foreclosed—I found a box of pictures. That one was in it." Tanner gestured at the picture Cecil still held. "I remembered all the times my grandfather told me about Sanctuary, how he said it was a place where you go when you need somewhere safe."

Tanner's story pierced my heart, stirred up the beginnings of sympathy. No. I did not want to sympathize with this guy. He needed get the hell out.

I couldn't quit looking at him, and looking at Tanner felt like a betrayal to Wade. It wasn't that Tanner was pretty. The wide cheekbones and the brawler's nose kicked him out of male model territory. But it didn't matter. Tanner's kind of magnetism ran deeper than pretty. And those eyes. They made my stomach flip-flop.

That was when I decided Tanner couldn't stay with Sanctuary. Because if he was around, it was going to make me have thoughts I didn't want. I wanted to mourn the loss of any possibility ever with Wade on my own terms. I formulated my no and glanced at Cecil.

My uncle wore a wide grin, and his dark eyes glowed with excitement. Before I could tell Tanner to hit the road, Cecil said, "We'd love to have you, son."

Tanner swallowed and stood very still, breeze fluttering long strands of his hair.

I thought fast. "Wait a minute. Let's talk about what kind of trouble Tanner's in. Is anybody after you?"

Tanner's broad cheekbones darkened. "Just bill collectors."

I nodded, sympathy overriding my basic need to send Tanner packing. "Yeah, I've been there." I jumped at my own words, frantically searching for another reason Tanner couldn't stay. It came like magic. "If you've lost everything, what are you staying in? We don't do motels. We've all got RVs."

"Tanner can stay with Shelly and me," Cecil broke in. "Jadine can bunk with you, Peri Jean."

Tanner shook his head. "No, sir. I'd never ask that. The last two things I own are an old camper and the truck my dad used to use to pull it."

Cecil slipped his arm over my shoulders. "Tanner's great-grandparents helped my parents found Sanctuary. They and their children, one of which was my dear friend Jackson, were here from the beginning. Surely we can consider Tanner a legacy member and give him a chance."

My cheeks flamed. I knew I was being played, and there wasn't a damn thing I could do about it. I gave a grudging nod. Cecil took his arm off me to shake hands with Tanner. Tanner watched me as he shook hands with my great-uncle.

I couldn't look away. Those eyes. Damn it. Just damn it.

3

____

I stomped toward my tent. Even arguing with people about whether or not they really wanted a love spell was better than standing around acting like it was okay that Cecil had allowed a weirdo that nobody knew into our group just because he'd been friends with the weirdo's grandfather.

"Wait," Hannah called from behind me. I waited until she caught up to begin my rant.

"I can't believe Cecil just let this Tanner nerd in. Especially after he gave me such a hard time over the fire-eater family." That had been a sore spot for me. I'd liked the family of fire-eaters and thought they'd make a good addition to Sanctuary. We had too many people who depended on the runoff from those of us who actually had marketable talents. Cecil had vetoed me, claiming the fire-eaters looked like trouble.

Hannah said nothing. I glanced over to see a smirk on her face. I stopped.

"Don't you think we should have checked out Tanner

more?" I heard the high-pitched exasperation in my voice, felt it in the acid on my stomach. I wanted Hannah to be on my side.

Hannah's smirk grew into a grin. "I think you checked out Tanner enough for all of us." She raised her eyebrows. Hannah's recent bad experiences with men kept her out of the dating pool. But she still noticed and rated every good-looking man.

"Oh, good grief," I muttered to let her know now wasn't the time.

"Don't you try that with me. I know you well enough to detect interest." She laughed.

"He's a loser." I stomped toward my tent. At least it was one place I was in charge.

"I don't think Tanner's a loser." She trailed after me. "Something bad happened in his life, sure, but I think he's decent."

I barely heard her. I was too busy staring at the man coming out of my tent.

"Hey!" I took a few running steps toward the guy, trying to decide if I recognized the gray hair and the emaciated body. I didn't think I did.

But maybe this guy was ill and wanted to check on a healing potion. I made them from recipes in Samantha's grimoire, which I'd recently obtained, and they worked. The guy might also be up to no good. Either way, I wanted to find out, maybe take out my annoyance with Tanner Letts on him.

The guy never acknowledged me. He picked up his pace, hurrying toward a crowd of yelling, jostling teenagers. Maybe I did recognize the way he walked, but I couldn't quite place it. I watched more carefully, noting a flash of silver at his feet. I focused on his cowboy boots. Duct tape. The guy had duct-taped his cowboy boots together. Damn. That was pretty dire.

I hurried toward the crowd of kids, but they picked that moment to stop in the middle of the path leading through the tents and start talking and giggling. By the time I picked my way through them, the man was gone.

Hannah peeked out of my tent. "Peri Jean? You better get in here, girl."

I changed direction and rushed into my tent.

The drawer where I kept Oscar's bone runes hung open. The runes covered the chair where I sat to do business, just hovering on it, sort of jittering. Oscar's special brand of evil, tinged with his hate, baked out from the runes. As we stood watching, the runes dropped to the floor and began to spin lazily. Hannah skittered backward, trying to get away from the evil.

I stood my ground, letting the haze of horror radiate over me. Jadine's vision of me surrounded by Oscar's runes came back. That was two in one night. First Tanner, now this. But I still didn't know what it meant.

I inched closer to the runes scattered on the dirt floor. "Were the runes already stuck to my chair when you came in here?"

She nodded. "And the room already felt the way it does now."

The guy I'd seen, Mr. Duct Tape Boots, must have done this. I fumed, wishing I'd caught him. I'd have made him eat that duct tape and thank me for the nice meal. Occupied with my anger, it took several seconds to realize nothing had been tampered with except the runes. Odd. There were items in my tent that looked far more valuable than the runes. Besides, they'd been tucked out of sight.

"Is anything missing?" Hannah still held her hands over the runes in a warding off gesture.

I glanced around but saw nothing other than the runes scattered on the floor. I shook my head at Hannah and bent over to see what was going on.

How had the runes stuck to the chair? The only magic connected to those runes belonged to Oscar Rivera.

Oscar was supposed to be powerless in his soul prison. He shouldn't have been able to manufacture enough magic to make the runes stick to the chair. Had the guy we saw coming out of the tent done this? I hadn't gotten any magical pings off him. And the black opal usually let me know, as it had with Tanner.

I lit a cigarette and paced back and forth, rubbing my temples and muttering to myself.

"Do you think the Coachman—I mean Oscar—is trying to get another coven to summon him?" Hannah stared at the scattered runes, a sick expression on her face.

"Sure, if he can manage it. But..." I gestured at the runes. "How could that guy have known the runes were here? It's not like I had a sign saying, 'Contact a Crazy Motherfucker with These Runes.'"

Hannah frowned at the runes and chewed her lip in thought. "Didn't you once tell me it's possible Oscar had caches of these runes stashed in places where he murdered people? That guy we saw could have found more of Oscar's runes somewhere else. And Oscar might have sent him. Right?"

I groaned in answer. Leave it to Hannah to bring up an even more horrifying scenario. Oscar had been a prolific murderer. Logic said there were way more runes than the ones in my possession. But I had held out hope those runes didn't exist. "There's nothing we can do now, other than tell the others to keep an eye out for Mr. Duct Tape."

Hannah walked over to the mess of runes, picked up the muslin bag I kept them in, and tried to use the edge of her phone to sweep them into the bag. The runes slid over the dirt floor, away from Hannah. She dropped the bag and backed away.

I sent a text message to everybody in my family about Mr. Duct Tape. Then I got a folder out of the buffet where the runes had come from and tried sweeping the runes into a pile. They ran from me as well. Impatient, I grabbed at one. Soon as my fingers touched it, a flash of evil shot through me. My heart stuttered, then ached. My vision of the living world faded.

A woman runs down a hallway, screaming. Blood streams from a gash on her cheek. Footsteps pound behind her. Oscar Rivera gains on her, teeth bared in a bloody slash, an axe gripped in both hands.

The intensity of the vision rocked me on my feet. I gripped the back of my chair and pushed myself out of it. Reality bled over the vision, and I realized I'd missed whatever Hannah had said. "What?"

"I didn't say anything. It was this awful sound..." She

cut off her words and pointed at the flap leading outside. "Hear it?"

"Hooooo." The sound came from outside and sounded like an engine winding down or maybe a very strong wind whistling around large structures.

The sound drilled into my head, its wrongness scraping against my nerves. I left the runes where they lay and stood.

It came again. "Hooooo."

"What is that?" I asked Hannah.

She shook her head.

"Hooooo." This time it was closer.

My black opal woke up and gave me a little shock. The stone began to heat the skin on my chest and ping me at intervals.

"Hooooo." The sound raised the hair on the back of my neck.

The black opal's pulses of magic came closer together, almost like an extra heartbeat. The table where I performed séances began to shake.

"Hooooo." It was right outside the tent now.

I walked to the flap, knees so weak I could barely keep my balance. But I had to see.

"Don't go out there." Hannah had backed herself against the wall, as far as she could get from the runes and the awful sound.

"Stay here." I walked outside.

Our little thoroughfare off the midway was nearly deserted. It was almost time for the carnival to close. Several yards away, I caught a glimpse of Tanner's long hair as he walked next to Cecil, who seemed to be explaining something. They both glanced at me.

"Hoooooo." It came from all around me.

Cecil looked up at the sky. He'd heard it too. Tanner followed Cecil's movement, eyes wide in confusion.

The air changed. The hot wind that had been rushing through stopped. A heaviness replaced it, pressed against my skin. My teeth throbbed, and an annoying hum filled my ears.

"Hoooooo." The sound came from above me.

I raised my head and stared at the sharp stars and inky sky. They looked normal to me. Then everything changed.

Far above, a blob appeared. It shot toward me, growing bigger as it came. Its sound came with it. "Hoooooo."

It flew closer, and I recognized the shadow from earlier. Only now it was three times the size it had been. It raced toward me, the sound growing louder and louder.

I stood rooted to the spot, the ringing in my ears so loud I could barely think.

"Run!" came Cecil's shout. It snapped me out of my trance. I looked around for the source. Cecil cupped his hands around his mouth and shouted again. "Run, baby, run!"

Next to him, Tanner stood open-mouthed at the spectacle.

I took a few steps toward the main part of the carnival and glanced back at the shadow. It shot forward and brushed against me. The world flashed black and gray.

I kicked it into high gear and ran for my life.

4

I rounded the corner into the main carnival midway running wide open. Funnel cake booths and games of skill and chance flew past. People standing in line stared. Some pointed me out to their friends.

I pumped my legs as hard as I could and raced for the attractions. People littered the fence next to the Ferris wheel. Screams came from somewhere nearby, probably the zero gravity ride. I went past them all with no idea where I was going. I just knew I didn't want that shadow to pull me off the carnival grounds.

The "hoooooo" sound chased me. It was like someone sucking wind and hollering at the same time. Not too creepy, unless it came from the larger-than-human shadow behind me.

My thighs ached and shivered. They wouldn't hold out much longer. My lungs screamed for mercy. Hannah and I smoked way too much. If she'd quit, I would too. I shook off the foolishness and ran harder. I had to figure this out and do it fast.

Problem was, I didn't even understand what happened. That cowboy's mother's ghost turning into this shadow didn't make any sense. The dead lady had seemed so normal, even with the bashed-in head.

Black dots swam at the edges of my vision. My body was on the verge of collapse. I had to get somewhere I could rest.

A row of tents with inside attractions was coming up. Some spirits couldn't cross into structures. Maybe this one was one of the unlucky ones. The Hall of Mirrors was first. Not the greatest place to elude a spirit, since they liked mirrors, but I was out of go-juice. I swung around the line and barreled through the door.

"Hey!" yelled the ticket taker. "I don't care if you work for the carnival. You can't go in free."

I pretended not to hear and ran into the dimly lit enclosure. The Summervale Hall of Mirrors sported a medieval fantasy theme, the mirrors framed in elaborate gilt. Overhead lights flashed off the mirrors. My fatigued vision interpreted it as a strobe effect. It made my head swim. I stopped and put my hands on my knees, struggling to breathe. The sound I made didn't sound too different from the shadow's "hoooooo." Maybe we deserved each other.

As I caught my breath and began to feel normal again, I listened for the "hoooooo" and didn't hear it. I began to relax.

The first scream came from within the Hall of Mirrors.

High-pitched, teenage, female. A teenage boy yelled, "Holy shit! What is that?"

Then came a grown woman's voice. "You can't be in here dressed up all horror-like. This attraction is for little kids too." She was trying to sound big and tough, but fear quivered at the edges of her words.

The cowardly part of me, the part Priscilla Herrera always criticized, considered finding the emergency exit and slipping out. The shadow was just a spirit and would likely go back to its realm at dawn. But I couldn't do that. It would be an asshole move. Even though I considered myself a die-hard butthole, I didn't think I'd crossed into asshole territory yet.

I trudged toward the sound of the disturbance. One question plagued me. Why had they seen the spirit? The reason I saw them made sense. But normal people didn't usually see spirits.

I followed the sound of a child wailing through the maze until I found them. The woman knelt on the floor next to a little boy old enough to have lost one of his front teeth. Tears streaked down his red face.

"There's somebody dressed like a scary witch." The woman, whose voice I recognized from earlier, was still trying to be a badass for her kid. Her wide, fear-filled eyes and the way she clutched her child gave away her terror over what she'd seen.

That told me she didn't regularly see ghosts or spirits. There had to be a reason, but I was too rattled to hit on it. Best thing I could do right then was get this woman and her kid out of here so I could deal with this nasty ghost without an audience.

"Yes, ma'am. I apologize on behalf of Summervale Carnival. That person is playing a prank. We'll remove them right now. Go back outside and ask for a refund." Unable to believe how calm I sounded, I helped the woman up and pointed her in the right direction.

Something moved behind me. I turned and faced the shadow. At first, I saw nothing but a ripple in reality. But then I glanced at one of the mirrors. I saw what the townies had seen. And it was ugly.

A scream worked its way up my chest. I opened my mouth to birth it into the world, but nothing more than a hiss came out of me. "No," I whispered and backed away.

The shadow advanced on me, its features taking shape now that I had glimpsed its true form in the mirror. That told me the being was from the dark outposts and likely not a spirit in the sense of ghosts and specters. This thing was a puredee monster. And now that I had seen it, it would never let me un-see it.

The monster's greenish-gray skin was either covered in slime or had a slick, rubbery looking surface. Its eyes, with no iris, consisted of a huge black dot in the middle of the eyeball. The creature's sunken mouth opened and let out another "hoooooo." This one rattled the mirrors in their frames.

I backed into one of the mirrors. It shook with the impact. I pushed against it, wishing I could scoot through the wall.

The creature took another step toward me, hunching at

the waist to lean closer. Its hooked nose reached almost to its thin slash of lips. A pointed chin curved away from its body.

The creature wore no clothes. Deflated looking breasts lay flat on her bony chest. Both her head and her sex were covered with thin, greasy black and gray hair.

The thing reached out one hand to me. The sight of that hand scared me weak. Bony fingers, three times as long as mine, covered with inches-long, sharp, black fingernails, grazed my face.

I pressed myself against the mirror, barely feeling its cool, hard surface. My breath came in wild gasps, each one followed by a grunt. My brain lost its ability to reason and only sent one message. *Run. Run. Run. Run.*

Running was a good idea. I pushed away from the mirror and tried to duck around the monster. She closed one hand around my arm, squeezing so tight the bones of my forearm ground together. With a flick of her arm, she slung me back.

My head slapped the wall. A thump reverberated through my head. Dull pain spread from the point of impact. The blow scrambled my thoughts further. Somewhere, very far away, a raven cawed. I couldn't remember why that was important.

The black opal pinged. But I didn't know what that meant either. I couldn't do anything but try to escape from the monster. It raised one bony foot, tipped with long black nails matching the ones on its hands, and swung it toward my legs. Her kick forced my legs out from under me. I toppled to the dirt. The creature straddled me and pushed me onto my back.

The black opal sent ping after ping into my chest. Finally I remembered I was a witch. The raven's caw came again. This time, my brain spit out the information I needed. Orev. This raven was my familiar. Orev had roosted for the night somewhere too far away to get here in time. But he still wanted to help. The next caw echoed through my head. *The mantle*, it said. *Find your power.*

I reached for the mantle and grabbed on to it, panicked and pulling too hard. The spell blocking me from the mantle's full power required finesse if I wanted to get around it. But right then, I was beyond anything but animal panic. The mantle screamed against the tissue of the spell. Pain lanced through my magical core. I loosened my hold and pushed a jolt of magic into the creature.

I waited, expecting a howl of rage or pain. Nothing happened. The monster showed no reaction at all. I called forth the power again, this time drawing energy from the dirt. I let my magic surround the creature and then pushed her away from me.

"Go home, spirit." I no longer believed it was a spirit, but in my panicked state, no other words would come out.

The creature acted as though I had done nothing. She used her claws to rip my T-shirt down the middle. She pushed both sides open almost gently.

"Peri Jean?" Hannah's shout came from somewhere within the maze.

I wanted to call out to her, to beg her to help me, but it would endanger her. I bit down on the shout and called to the mantle again. I'd used too much power the first two times. This time, it hurt to take hold of my magical ability.

Desperate, I endured the pain and pushed the power at the creature. This would be my last time. My back bowed as I pumped all the power I had into the blast of pure fire and sent it into the creature.

This time, she jumped a little and tilted her head to stare at me. She ran one claw along my cheek. I jittered as it scratched down my skin.

"It's too late. Your fate is sealed." Her voice, thickened with some accent I didn't recognize, rumbled like water slurping down a clogged drain.

She leaned back. With one razor-tipped finger, she punctured the skin right underneath my collarbone and laid it open. The pain went beyond a cut or scrape. It felt like a strip of hot metal branding me. I screamed, body bucking and writhing underneath my captor.

Footsteps raced toward us. Hannah, red-faced and sweating, careened around a corner. She took in the monster, mouth going slack, eyes widening. Then her eyes hardened, and she dug a brown vial of my holy water out of her pants pocket. She popped off the cap and splashed it on the creature.

The creature turned to glare at Hannah, showing teeth the color of rotted meat, and hissed. Other than that, she showed no reaction to the water. The monster slashed at my chest again. This one hurt more than the first. I howled, vision going gray at the edges. Cold sweat broke out over my body.

"Do something," Hannah screamed at me.

I tried to answer, to tell her I'd used up all my power and it had done almost as much good as pissing into the wind, but all that came out was a sick croak.

The monster turned to Hannah. "Hooooooo" issued from her.

Hannah raced forward and shoved at the monster. The thing flashed out one of those horrible spidery hands and grabbed Hannah by the leg. She shifted her weight off me, and I scooted out from under her.

"Hooooooo." The monster threw Hannah across the room. She hit the wall of mirrors, and the whole maze shook. Hannah slid to the floor and stared at the monster with a dazed expression on her face.

A blast of cold came from behind me. Priscilla Herrera said, "Make her see herself in the mirror. Do it now, or you'll both die."

Trying to keep an eye on the monster, I backed up, reached as far as I could behind me, and grabbed the edge of the nearest mirror. It rattled against the wall, held by some hook or stay I couldn't even see. I yanked harder.

The monster began making her noise. "Hooooooo." It sounded like a jet engine winding up to take off into the wild blue yonder.

"What are you doing?" Hannah picked herself up off the floor, rubbing at a skinned elbow.

"Showing Miss Ugly her reflection," I hollered back.

Hannah got on the other side of the mirror. We both lifted, and it came off the wall. We turned it so it was right in front of Miss Ugly.

She stopped hoooing and cocked her head, studying

herself. Then she let out a bellow louder and more appalling than anything else she'd done so far. It sounded like a dinosaur trying to shit a skyscraper. All the mirrors cracked and crashed to the floor, glass tinkling.

I threw my arms up over my face and hoped Hannah had the sense to do the same. The sound of falling glass stopped, and it hit me that Miss Ugly had shut up too. I took down my arms. Miss Ugly had gone, hopefully for good. My chest throbbed where the monster had scratched me with her filthy fingernails. I glanced over at Hannah. She still had her arms over her face.

"You okay?" I asked.

She took down her arms and nodded, blinking fast. "Where is she?"

"Gone, I hope." I looked at all the broken mirrors, thinking of the belief that breaking a mirror earned you seven years bad luck. If it was true, I had an eternity of bad luck coming. Figured.

My chest began to sting as well as throb. Liquid dripped from the wound. I tried to pull the edges of my T-shirt back together, but they hung open like a vest.

Hannah stared at the sore, nose wrinkled and lip curled. "That's bad. Really bad."

Cold blasted through the room again. Priscilla Herrera stepped out from behind one of the partitions where mirrors had once hung to create a confusing maze.

"Come with me. Samantha needs to talk to you." She motioned at the wall, and a dark hole opened.

I stared at the hole, making no move to go toward it. Priscilla had proved herself trustworthy, but she didn't much care if she scared or hurt me. I didn't have much more tough girl left in me that day. But if I refused to do what Priscilla said, she might not help me again.

"Where are you going?" Hannah moved toward the dark maw.

"To the other side." I glanced at Priscilla and motioned to Hannah. The ghost rolled her eyes but nodded. I approached Hannah and held out one hand. "Wanna go?"

Together, Hannah and I stepped into the darkness.

The blackness only lasted a second. Then Hannah and I stood in the woods across the meadow from Samantha Herrera's house.

Samantha was my great-great-grandmother and Priscilla's daughter. She'd been the last truly powerful witch to come from Priscilla's genetic line until I came along.

Samantha had died long before I was born. She now lived across the beautiful, sun-dappled meadow in front of me in a stone cottage on the edge of a grove of graceful oaks in a totally different dimension.

"It's day here." Hannah breathed in the cool air.

"I think it always is. Come on." I led the way though the meadow, wading through the Indian paintbrush and bluebonnet flowers.

Hannah walked alongside me, gazing with wonder at everything. "This is the afterlife?"

"It's Samantha's afterlife. But she created this place

before she died. She calls it her hiding place." I pointed at a butterfly the size of a bird, and Hannah gasped.

Something large crashed through the woods behind us. We turned but saw nothing. I tugged Hannah in the direction of Samantha's cottage. We got to the stone courtyard, where I'd last had tea and cookies with Samantha, but found it empty.

"Peri Jean?" Samantha's voice came from inside the cottage. "Get inside now. Hurry up."

I hurried to the plain wooden door and worked the iron latch. The door swung open. The smell of baking cookies drifted out to meet us.

Samantha's fat, white cat streaked between my feet and leapt onto a worn chair before either Hannah or I could even get inside. I tried pulling my T-shirt together again and stepped inside.

"I'm in the kitchen," Samantha called.

We wove around the living room furniture, all worn but clean, and followed the smell of warm sugar into the kitchen. Samantha took a sheet of cookies out of the oven and set them on the counter. She turned to me, smiling, but took one look at the mess on my chest and let out a little scream.

"How bad is it?" I lowered my chin, but the wound was too close to my head. I wouldn't be able to see it without a mirror.

"It's oozing clear liquid. That means it's deep." Samantha grabbed a muslin towel off the counter and came to dab at my chest.

Priscilla's voice came from behind us. "I told you she'd

been hurt, but you never believe how serious things are. Everything's a game to you."

I twisted away from Samantha's ministrations to find Priscilla at a small table, a cup of tea and a plate of cookies in front of her. Hannah gasped at the sight of the proud, tattooed lady, pointed, and said, "That's Priscilla Herrera." She turned to me for confirmation.

I nodded. Samantha gripped my arm and made me face her again.

Hannah edged closer to the ghost. "I can't believe I'm seeing you."

Priscilla finished her cookie and brushed the crumbs off her hands. She pointed at a chair next to her and spoke to Hannah. "Sit here."

Hannah wandered over and did as she was told, still staring at Priscilla.

Samantha took the towel away from my wound and went back into the work area of her kitchen. She took a container off a shelf and poured brownish liquid into a bowl. Motioning me to the table, she followed me with the bowl and a new towel. I sat in one of the chairs.

Samantha dipped the edge of the towel into the dark liquid and pressed it to my wound. The burn of the wound, which had ebbed to a sustainable roar, leapt back to high flame. I screamed and tried to push her hands away.

"No," she muttered. "Let's clean it good. Tell me what attacked you."

I suspected the question was to keep my mind off the fire burning in my skin. "She was homely as an outhouse."

I described Miss Ugly's rubbery skin, hooked nose, and long, sharp fingernails. "I used up all my magic on her, and it didn't matter a bit."

Samantha, face pale, stood and went back into her kitchen. She took a canister off a high shelf and came back to the table. She pulled the top off, and a sour smell wafted out.

"Please no," I moaned. The stuff smelled like it would hurt worse than the brown liquid.

Ignoring me, Samantha took something that looked like wood chips out of the canister and began mashing it into a paste. She scooped up the whitish paste, which still had a nose-stinging odor, and applied it to my chest. I tensed, waiting for the burn. Instead a heavenly numbness crept through the skin. I moaned and leaned back in the chair, letting my eyes drift closed.

"What is this stuff?" I whispered.

"White willow bark." Samantha wrapped a handful in one of her linen napkins and pushed it at me. I put it in my pocket. She took her first aid supplies back into the kitchen. "The monster that attacked you—and she is a monster—left a mild poison in you. This should draw it out."

"Then you're familiar with what attacked Peri Jean?" Priscilla's voice rose in anger. "And you sat there playing with herbs?"

Samantha spun around. "Mother, having hysterics will not change what's happened. But to answer your question, yes. I know what Peri Jean encountered."

I sat straighter. "You know Miss Ugly?" Priscilla snorted at my name and muttered an insult under her breath.

"Miss Ugly?" Samantha raised her eyebrows and let out a laugh.

"Go on and laugh. This is all very funny," Priscilla called at her back.

Samantha took her time preparing a tray with two teacups and a chintz teapot. She walked carefully back to the table, poured both Hannah and me tea, and motioned for us to drink. Hannah hesitated.

"You have to. Otherwise you can't stay." I sipped my tea to let her know it was okay. Actually, it was more than okay. The tea tasted dainty and delicate.

Hannah took a cautious sip and nodded her thanks to Samantha, who sat down at the table with us.

"Let's talk about this creature you met," she said, her face so grim I knew I was about to hear some awfully bad news. "The first thing is that your magic isn't going to affect Miss Ugly at all. She has more magic than any creature I've ever heard of. "

Samantha glanced at Priscilla, asking a silent question.

Priscilla shrugged. "I can't advise you on whether or not to tell Peri Jean all you know. But the more Peri Jean knows, the more likely she is to survive this. And our family needs her to survive." Priscilla and Samantha stared at each other a long moment, some unspoken under-standing passing between them.

"Miss Ugly prefers to consume her kills. She absorbs their magic. This is why she's so strong." Samantha grimaced and took a sip of tea. "These marks she made on you are her signature. They season your meat to make it more palatable."

My mouth hung open, a cookie halfway to it.

Samantha pressed her lips together. "Miss Ugly has not yet completed the signature. She does it over the course of three visits. Your meat will be ready at the third visit."

"Gross." It was the only word I could think of, but my feelings went beyond that. My skin tightened at the idea of those ugly, rotten teeth tearing into my flesh.

"Whatever you do, don't let her make the third mark. It will weaken you so that she can take you back to her lair and cook you. She prefers her food cooked." Samantha glanced at me, mouth turned down, then at Priscilla who gave her a mysterious nod.

"That's it." I snapped my fingers. "I'm tired of these loaded glances between you two. Tell me what's going on."

Priscilla raised her chin and looked down at me. "You have a destiny to fulfill. Your death at this point would create complications."

I sat back in my chair and stared at my lap. It wasn't that I might die. Oh, no. It was all about stuff I needed to do. I let out a disgusted grunt.

Samantha ignored my reaction and said, "As I told you, magic won't work. Neither will weapons. This creature is unstoppable."

"Nothing is unstoppable." Priscilla raised her voice. I glanced at her and was surprised to see true anger contorting her features.

Samantha straightened. "Mother, until you began making contact with Peri Jean, you dwelled in the realm of the lost. You've not experienced everything on this side of the veil."

"I may not know exactly what Miss Ugly is." Priscilla sneered at using the nickname. "But I know every creature has a weakness."

Samantha ignored Priscilla and pushed a cookie jar at Hannah. "Take a cookie, please. You too, Peri Jean."

Hannah nibbled on the edge of her cookie and then began eating it. She took another.

"What else?" I ate one last cookie and brushed the crumbs away.

Samantha sighed and sort of slumped in her chair. "This is the bad part. Miss Ugly is used by the dark beings that rule this side of the veil. She settles debts and metes out punishments and vengeance. She is their assassin, their mercenary. They use her because she is unstoppable, impervious to most magic, and she never quits."

It all sounded pretty grim. "Can we find out who sent her after me?" If I knew who sent Miss Ugly, I could make them call her off.

Samantha nodded. "There's a...man who comes by to sell me things. He knows all the gossip."

"Can you send for him?" After the way Samantha called this creature a man, I wasn't sure I wanted to meet him. But if I could find out how to get rid of Miss Ugly, it might be worth it.

"He won't be back for another day. The two of you can't stay that long. I'll speak with him and get back in touch with you." Samantha stepped away from the table and went to look out the window.

The room grew silent. Hoofbeats pounded in the distance. Other than that, there was no sound other than the rush of wind in the treetops.

"You're going to have to leave soon, Peri Jean, before it becomes known that you're here. But I have one last thing to tell you about Miss Ugly. It might help you." Samantha turned away from the window to face me. "She makes a good assassin to these beings because she's single-minded. Distract her from her purpose when possible." She walked across the room and pointed to the hearth. "I don't like to ask company to leave, but you must go. If something in this realm is after your life, you're not safe in this place."

Hannah and I walked to the hearth. I glanced back at Priscilla.

She shook her head and motioned me to go. "We will find out what we can, both about Miss Ugly and about who sent her to kill you. We'll be in contact."

The darkness within the hearth wrinkled, and the smell of frying corn dogs drifted out. Hannah hooked her finger through the belt loop of my blue jeans, and I ducked into the hearth.

Going back to the realm of the living felt like falling.

5

———

Hannah and I crossed back into our world through the same space in the wall. We found my family frantically searching the Hall of Mirrors. The looks of fright on their faces gave me a good dose of guiltiness.

Shelly and the ticket taker screamed in each other's faces, both of them ready to fight. Leon Blackfox, owner of Summervale Carnival, hovered next to them, patting the air with his hands, trying to defuse the situation.

Finn spotted me first and ran for me. I let him fold me into his arms even though my open shirt rendered me half naked. Over his shoulder, I caught Tanner watching the whole scene, open-mouthed and wide-eyed.

I let go of Finn and leaned around him to snarl at Tanner. "Still eager to join us?"

Without speaking, he pulled off his faded T-shirt and held it out to me, head turned away. I snatched it, face flaming and muttered a thank you.

Leon, who had a thing for Hannah, rushed at her. "Are

you all right, Hannah? Do you need me to take you to the hospital?"

Hannah flinched away, grabbing Finn, who was nearest her, by the arm.

He faced Leon. "We're all right, dude. Hannah's fine."

Leon slunk away, still giving Hannah sidelong glances. I almost felt sorry for the poor man. Good-looking, well-dressed, and financially solvent, Leon probably had no idea why Hannah dodged him at every turn. Had she not been so adamant about not dating, and had I not understood the reason so well, I'd have teased her until she pulled out her hair.

The drama died down, and the carnival closed for the night. The members of Sanctuary got in their cars and left. Some workers stayed with the carnival at night. Not Sanctuary. We always camped at an RV park, separating ourselves even from the normal carnies.

On the way to my truck, I noticed Tanner climbing into a vehicle with Cecil, Shelly, and Jadine. They drove into the dark night. Someone turned back for one last look at me. My gut told me it was Tanner. I wanted to shoot him the finger but was so tired I couldn't even work the remote to unlock the door. Hannah ended up driving us back to the RV park.

She parked my truck in front of my camper, slid out, and came around to make sure I could climb out without falling on my face. "Want me to spend the night with you?"

I shook my head. The pre-Michael Gage Hannah would have argued.

This one simply nodded and said, "We need to fortify your camper with iron. Maybe that'll keep her out."

My frustration built. "How will iron work if the holy water you pitched on her didn't?"

Hannah thought it over. "I'm not one hundred percent sure it will, but it might. We're talking about two different animals. Holy water is blessed. That's sort of magic. But iron is alchemy. Might be more like poison ivy for Miss Ugly."

She had a point. Tired as I was, we went around to the other members of Sanctuary begging for iron. It was worth a try. Miss Ugly meant business, and I didn't have any better ideas.

I hit the jackpot with an older couple, one who'd been with Sanctuary since they were first married many years ago. They offered me a box of old, iron horseshoes they'd scavenged from somewhere or other. Hannah and I hefted them back to my camper.

"So...if Tanner asked you out, would you go?" Hannah grinned at me across the box of horseshoes. I bared my teeth at her, ready to kick her in the ass just to see if it would make her shut up.

The mere mention of Tanner Letts made me think about the way he moved, about the intensity behind his eyes. I shoved off the thoughts. I was mourning Wade, dammit. Tanner Letts wasn't even good enough for a rebound tryst.

"Well?" Hannah pressed.

"No. I wouldn't go. Quit worrying about that nitwit and

come on. This box is heavy." I walked faster. She followed, shooting me satisfied smiles.

We set the box in front of the camper. Hannah grabbed several horseshoes. "I'll put these around your RV's other side."

I got my own handful of horseshoes, but my phone began playing the old Stevie Nicks song I had assigned to my friend and magical mentor, Mysti Whitebyrd. Dropping the horseshoes to the dirt at my feet, I took out my phone and saw Mysti was requesting a video call. I accepted and smiled as Mysti's face appeared in the window.

Unlike Hannah's striking redhead beauty, Mysti's beauty had more of a girl-next-door vibe. Her plain light brown hair and perky nose let her hide in plain sight. But her eyes, piercing and intelligent with surprising sensitivity, made her hard to forget.

"Good to see you, sister. How's the job in Canada?" I couldn't quit smiling despite the bad night. Next to Hannah, Mysti was my best female friend.

"The norm. People always wait too late to call in help." She turned away from the phone and glanced behind her. In the silence, a woman was screaming. Had Mysti stopped working and taken time out to call me? That wasn't good.

"What's going on? Are you and Griff okay?" I didn't need more bad news tonight.

"We're okay. I'm more concerned about you. I heard you had quite the night." Mysti peered at the phone as though the little camera could give her a true idea of my well-being.

I tried to sound tough. "You talking about Miss Ugly?" Mysti nodded, and my knees weakened. "How'd you hear?" I sat at the wood picnic table in front of my RV. Each RV space came with one. I had a cheap, plastic ashtray on mine and now lit a smoke.

"I've been talking to ghosts. Samantha—your great-great grandmother?—contacted me just a few minutes ago. Both she and Priscilla are frantic." Mysti's darting eyes indicated the ghostly visit had unsettled her. It gave me the heebie-jeebies too.

Mysti could contact the spirit world, but it wasn't her specialty. It took effort and skill. A spirit, especially one like Samantha who had a bond with me, would not contact Mysti by choice. Especially not after telling me she'd be in touch. Something was wrong.

"Do I even want to hear this?" I propped my phone up on the ashtray and dragged hard on my cigarette.

"Probably not, but you need to." Mysti licked her lips, something she always did when nervous.

I nodded. "I'm not ready, but go ahead."

"The dark beings have barred Samantha or Priscilla from contacting you. Samantha says they'll probably stop her from contacting the living world at all once they figure out she contacted me." Mysti paused for air.

The ball of nerves in my stomach began rolling around, sending painful tendrils of anxiety through my body. My shoulders tightened. "How can they do that?"

Mysti shrugged. "I can only guess. Samantha has used her hiding place to somehow surpass the spirit realm. She exists in much the same way the dark beings—like your friends Sol and Bub—exist. But that's their world, and they're more powerful than Samantha. She's bound by whatever rules they impose on her."

"Sol and Bub aren't my friends." The two monstrous beings scared me, made me do things I didn't want. We weren't friends. At all.

"But you understand the distinction I am making, do you not?" Mysti's voice sharpened. This let me know that she was scared more than anything else could have.

Cheeks heating, I nodded.

"Good," Mysti said. "According to Samantha, the dark beings, which I sometimes call chthonic beings after the Greek myths, are greatly amused at your plight. They are taking bets on whether or not you'll survive this thing you call Miss Ugly. Neither Samantha nor Priscilla may interfere."

"But what am I supposed to do?" My voice rose. Footsteps crunched in the dirt, and Hannah came to the edge of the camper to watch me.

"You'll rely on your own wits and gifts." Mysti raised her chin. She wouldn't coddle me. There wasn't room for it this time.

I gestured with my cigarette. "But how? Samantha said magic won't work on Miss Ugly."

"I don't know, dammit." Mysti's voice rose. Hearing the frustration there somehow helped. I wasn't alone, neither in my feelings nor in my ignorance.

I took a deep breath and held up the T-shirt Tanner had given me back at the carnival. Mysti gasped at the design taking shape on my chest.

I gave her a wan smile. "Samantha said this is Miss Ugly's signature. She intends to eat me like food. This mark seasons my meat and makes it more palatable for her."

Mysti began nodding before I finished. "Is that Hannah I see standing in the background?"

I twisted in my seat to see that Hannah had snuck up behind me. She and Mysti waved at each other.

Mysti continued. "I want Hannah to take a good picture of that mark and send it to my phone. There are several beings that use a signature to mark people they claim. What else can you tell me about Miss Ugly?"

I told Mysti about how I hadn't been able to see Miss Ugly until I glimpsed her in the mirror and how she'd run when shown her own reflection. Then I said, "She made an awful sound. Like this, 'hoooooo.'" I recreated the noise by moaning while sucking in my breath.

Mysti's face went still. "Let me do some checking and get back to you tomorrow."

"No. You know something. Tell me now." I leaned into the camera until all Mysti probably saw was a little fraction of my face.

She shook her head. "I don't want to misspeak. Let me have my due diligence. We'll discuss it tomorrow."

I leaned back. This was my life we were talking about. Fear of death aside, being cannibalized topped my list of Unappealing Ways To Die.

Mysti continued as though the matter was settled. For her, I suppose it was. "For now, remember that it's unlikely she'll come for you in daylight hours."

I made a show of rolling my eyes. "Gee, it's only six hours to daybreak. That'll be real easy."

Mysti stared me down. It worked, even long distance. "If she shows up, try iron."

I nodded. We had that covered.

"Samantha had one last thing to say." Mysti sounded like she was running down a mental checklist. Knowing her, she probably was. "She said you cannot die yet. You have business yet to complete."

Business yet to complete. Like my life wasn't even my own. Like having a happy life didn't matter. "What the hell does that mean?"

Mysti shrugged, and it wasn't one that invited more discussion. "I have one more matter to discuss with you. It's completely unrelated, but it might take your mind off this mess." She tried to smile and almost made it. "You game?"

"Okay." I wasn't really game, but I never told Mysti no. She'd been too good to me.

"I woke up this morning with you on my mind. When I drew my daily tarot card, I concentrated on you." She paused, and a secret smile, one I usually only saw when she talked about Griffin Reed, her lover and business partner, snuck onto her face. "I drew the two of cups."

Tarot interested me, but I hadn't yet mastered the technique for intuiting the meanings of the cards. I shook my head to show her I didn't know the significance.

"Cups as a suit deal with your emotions and relationships. The two of cups means that new relationships should be rewarding. Have you met someone new?" She smiled again, and her meaning hit home.

"You mean a romantic relationship." I slumped. Not Mysti too. I didn't have time for this. Not with Miss Ugly trying to feast on my flesh.

Mysti somehow read my thoughts. "It doesn't matter if it's a good time. The universe doesn't work that way."

Hannah leaned in. "She did meet someone new tonight. Her panties are on fire for him, but she's in denial."

I spun in my seat to glare at Hannah. "You little red-topped turd."

Hannah gave me wide-eyes and innocence. "I'm just talking about what I see."

I ignored Hannah and told Mysti about running into Wade and Desiree.

Mysti's smile faded at my story. "True or not, it's obvious they both believe it. There's nothing further you can do. Let it go."

"But Desiree is full of shit, right?" I needed Mysti to say she was so I could go back to pining for Wade.

"The universe gives you signals when it's time to move forward," Mysti said.

"But I..." I wanted things to go like I planned just one time.

"You'll know what to do when the time is right. For now, stay alive through the night." A particularly high-pitched wail came from behind Mysti. She glanced behind her.

"You have to go, don't you?" The idea of the next few hours without her scared me more than it should have.

"I do, but I'll be in touch soon." She blew a kiss, and the screen went dark.

"Let's go take that picture of your mark so you can send it to Mysti." Hannah led the way into my camper. We turned on the brightest lights and took a grim photo with my phone. I sent it to Mysti.

Hannah got herself a cigarette out of my pack.

"I thought you were quitting." She really needed to, but I'd smoked so many years there was no way I could lead by example.

Hannah ignored what I said about quitting smoking. "Even Mysti is saying Tanner might be worth your time." Her grin was almost like the ones she used to have before Michael Gage attacked and brutalized her. It reminded me how far she'd come these last couple of months, and I couldn't help returning it.

"Why don't *you* go out with Tanner?" I sat down at my table and gave Hannah a smarty smile of my own.

"I'd never step on your toes. You were practically salivating." She ran her tongue over her lips and made an exaggerating slurping sound.

I pointed at the door. "Isn't some silly romance novel calling you over there at your place?"

She pretended to pout. "Sure you don't want company?"

"If you're going to talk about Tanner Letts, no," I said with mock ferocity. She walked out the door laughing.

I don't know when I went to sleep or how long I slept, but I woke up thinking a summer storm was blowing through. Snuggling back down into my bed, I waited for the soothing sound of the raindrops to start tapping on the camper's metal roof. A warning hovered at the edge of my consciousness, but my sleep-fogged brain didn't want to latch on to it.

"Hoooooo." The noise snapped me out of my doze and into full awareness.

I climbed out of my bed and crept to the window over the kitchen sink. Lights affixed to tall poles cast a yellowish glow over the still sleeping campground. Dawn hadn't broken. It was close, but no cigar. I peered into the half-darkness, muscles already rigid with fear.

"Hoooooo." The noise came again, this time giving me a direction to look for Miss Ugly. I refocused. Her hunched-over form lurched toward the camper.

My mind scrambled for defenses. I remembered the iron horseshoes. *Please let them work.* I remembered watching Hannah put the horseshoes around the back of my camper, remembered the feel of the box in my hands as I prepared to put them around the camper's front side. I let out a little moan of fear as I realized my mistake.

I didn't set the horseshoes because Mysti had called right then. I talked to her about Miss Ugly, but then she mentioned that stupid two of cups. Hannah took the opportunity to start blabbing about Tanner Letts. None of it really mattered except for one thing. I'd come to bed without putting out the rest of the horseshoes.

I dug through my witch pack, finding only sea salt and holy water. Hannah had tried holy water on Miss Ugly back at the carnival with no result. There was no need to waste time trying it again. My fingers closed over a tiny jar of salt.

"Hoooooo." Miss Ugly's howl came from right outside the camper now. If she was going to come in here with me, I had only seconds.

I went to stand in front of the door. Flutters of fear ran through me like painful electrical currents. The black opal got in on the act, pinging to warn me of the nearby magic.

Orev's caw joined the ping. He'd roosted somewhere near my camper and was now awake. Together we'd fight Miss Ugly. The idea of having more magic on my side bolstered my confidence. I braced myself and got ready to battle.

The door blew open. Miss Ugly stood backlit in the doorway, hideous as ever. "Hoooooo," she moaned.

My legs weakened, but I pulled myself together, took a step toward her, and tossed the salt in her face.

She didn't even react. One long-fingered hand flashed out and grabbed my ankle. She yanked me off my feet and dragged me out of the camper. I landed on my tailbone and let out a yelp. Pain radiated up my spine. I lay there looking at the starry night for just a second and then blocked any thoughts of pain. Now wasn't the time to hurt. It was time to fight.

"Orev," I yelled. "Come now."

The flapping of many wings filled the air. My fear abated. Orev had not only come, he'd brought friends as he sometimes did. I had no idea where he found willing ravens at night or how he convinced them to help a human. Right now, it didn't matter.

Orev swooped toward Miss Ugly's head. She shooed him away as though he was no more consequential than a fly. He catapulted backward, but came right back. Miss Ugly turned from me to wait on the next attack.

Caw. Caw. Caw. Orev wanted to peck out Miss Ugly's eyes. Having seen him kill a snake once, I knew his vicious side and urged him forward.

A ripping sound came from above, blasting my eardrums. Wind whipped against my skin. It pushed at me with enough force to sway me on my feet.

Orev flapped harder, but the wind suspended him in midair, a few feet above Miss Ugly and me. Something held him back. He cawed in frustration.

The ripping sound came again. The wind roared harder and pushed Orev away from me. Soon his black feathers blended with the night. A blast of white flashed far above.

Orev's angry caws filled my head, but he was farther from me now than he'd ever been on this plane. Had the dark beings that barred me from Samantha now taken my familiar? How dare they? Hot fury flooded my skin and curdled in my stomach. Tears burned my sinuses. I wanted to kick and scream, have a tantrum. Orev was mine.

Miss Ugly turned back to me and said, "Hoooooo."

I snarled at her and showed her my fist. She yanked me

off balance and started walking, dragging me along behind. I kicked at her. A few kicks landed. She ignored them.

Hannah boiled out of her camper and launched herself at Miss Ugly, throwing wild punches.

"No," I shouted at Hannah. There was no way I could protect her, not now. If Hannah tried to save me, she'd only get herself hurt.

Miss Ugly used her free hand to squeeze Hannah's wrist. Hannah's eyes filled with agony. Her knees crumpled, and she let out a squeal. Miss Ugly slung Hannah out of the way.

"Not you," Miss Ugly grated at Hannah. "Only the thief. Not you."

Thief? Huh? This was all so crazy.

Hannah rolled to her feet and ran to the box of horseshoes. She snatched one, pressed it into my hand, and shouted, "Remember what Mysti said."

Miss Ugly dragged me toward the nearby woods. One fist gripping the horseshoe, I attempted the mother of all stomach crunches and swung it at Miss Ugly. The iron missed the monster by a few inches. Having short arms sucked. I gripped the horseshoe tighter, determined to have another chance to use it.

Meanwhile, sharp rocks cut into my bare legs, scratching them raw. Moonlight made the larger limestone boulders lining the path glow in the dark night. I grabbed for a larger one, wrapped the arm holding the horseshoe over it, and held on for dear life. Miss Ugly nearly pulled my leg off my body. The feeling reminded me of a kid pulling a wing off a bug. I let go of the boulder and let myself be towed, the horseshoe gripped in my fist clanging against rocks.

The darkness changed, became thicker, deeper. More there but less of this world. I sat up straight. Miss Ugly was taking me into the dark outposts. *No.* If I went in there, I might never come out.

I kicked as hard as I could, ignoring the way Miss Ugly's claws punctured my skin as she tried to hold on. I dragged my other foot on the ground to slow our progress. It didn't do anything but jab rocks into my bare heel.

Miss Ugly dragged me between two thick trees, standing like pillars at the entrance into the next dimension. Then I was in the place where red and yellow stars littered the sky, and the air felt alive.

The rocks on this path were sharper. Glowing eyes watched from either side. Mad laughter floated out to me, teasing chill bumps out on my skin. My body, already tense, began to tremble.

Miss Ugly would finish her mark on my chest and kill me. Nobody would ever find my body because Miss Ugly would eat me.

Of all the things I could have felt, pissed topped my list. This wasn't fair. I had no way to fight this thing, and bigger, meaner things were betting that it would kill me. I gave my leg another hard kick.

Miss Ugly ignored me, continued dragging me down the rock-stubbled path. Light, either from a campfire or a torch, flickered through the trees. *More people. Maybe rescuers.* I opened my mouth to call out, but then I remembered the things I'd met here in the dark outposts. They might be worse than Miss Ugly. I clamped my jaw shut. Miss Ugly seemed to be taking me to them.

Miss Ugly pulled me into a clearing with a fire blazing at its center. Any hope I'd felt at finding creatures who'd help me, human or not, withered. Nothing lived in this corner of hell. Firelight danced over a ring of half-buried human skulls marking the edge of the clearing. A human-sized black cauldron hung over the fire. Steam rolled off the liquid bubbling inside it.

"No," my voice rasped out. "Don't do this. Let's bargain."

"No bargain for your kind," Miss Ugly mushed out. She let go of my leg and straddled me in one move. She cut my sleep shirt down the middle. Through my fear, I realized she'd ruined another shirt. That irritated me. Clothes didn't grow on trees.

The anger cleared my head. This was it. My last chance. I slapped at Miss Ugly with one hand and reared back the hand holding the horseshoe. *Here it comes, baby.* I let the thing fly at her head. But lying down like I was, the blow barely packed any wallop. It just bounced off her head. I dropped the horseshoe. It clanged to the ground.

Miss Ugly grabbed both my wrists in one giant hand and pushed them to the ground over my head. With the other hand, using her index finger as a drawing instru-ment, she again punctured the skin on my chest. I thought I heard the pop when her nasty fingernail broke the skin. The new wound poked the old one, and they both sang soprano. I let out a yell that ended in a sob. A tear streaked out of one eye and slid toward my hairline.

"Please. Isn't there something I can do for you? A way to buy forgiveness?" Sobs shook my voice. They shamed me, but I couldn't help myself. This had to be the worst possible way to die.

Miss Ugly raised her head, contemplating my question. Samantha had suggested distracting her. Was it working?

I spurred my mind to think of another question. "Can't we make a deal?"

Miss Ugly opened her mouth to answer, showing off teeth that glowed slick and dark in the firelight. Her grip on my hands loosened. One of my hands slipped out.

I didn't give Miss Ugly a chance to answer. I just snatched the horseshoe out of the dirt and rammed it into her open mouth as hard as I could.

She leapt off me and staggered toward the fire, slumped and yelping in pain. Her agonized moans gave me a nasty thrill. The smell of smoldering flesh drifted across the clearing, sweet like barbecue.

The iron must have been burning the inside of her mouth. Miss Ugly fell to her knees, back arched like a cat trying to cough up the fur balls of its ancestors, and heaved. I hoped she'd fall into the fire or choke to death on the horseshoe, but I didn't dare wait around to see what would happen.

I crashed through the squat trees. Their gnarled, bony branches grabbed at me like extensions of Miss Ugly's hands, cutting ruts in my skin. Sharp rocks stabbed the bottoms of my feet as I found the path. The rocks ground in and hurt more than I dreamed anything could. I kept running, the thick air clogging my lungs.

After a short distance, I stopped and tried to get my bearings. The trees Miss Ugly had dragged me between had to be somewhere around here. The mad laugh came out of the bushes again. Fear prickled the back of my neck, but I held my ground. The way home had to be close, but nothing in the silvery moonlight looked familiar.

"Peri Jean?" Hannah's shouts came from the other side of the veil.

I didn't answer but ran toward the sound of my best friend's voice, praying it wasn't some sort of trap. The two trees forming an archway into the next world came into sight. I raced for them, sure Miss Ugly's spindly fingers would close around my arm or leg just before I got out, and leapt back into our world.

Hannah raced to me and grabbed me in a hug. "Here she is," she yelled.

Footsteps crashed toward us. Members of Sanctuary melted out of the woods. Some held flashlights. Others brandished actual weapons. The sight of them worried me. I'd rather they just let Miss Ugly take me away. The idea of them risking their safety for mine didn't sit well.

Dillon and Finn, my cousins, rushed to me and grabbed me in hugs. Dillon was the first to see the blood streaming from the new scratches on my chest and to notice my shirt hanging open.

She jabbed Finn with her thumb. "Give her your shirt."

"Why?" her husband whined. Then he saw my bare chest and stripped out of his shirt without another word.

My cousin's shirt smelled of his cologne and eau de kid. I breathed deep and reminded myself I couldn't wig out in front of the members of Sanctuary. They whispered among themselves, glancing at me with expressions varying from excitement to fear.

I held up my hands for silence. "Thank you for your help tonight, for risking yourselves on my behalf." As briefly as I could, I explained what I knew about my situation. "Hopefully this problem will resolve itself before tomorrow night. Until then, run if you see that thing. You can't win a fight with it. So just save yourselves."

People nodded and mumbled among themselves. Two men stepped forward, arms around each other. I'd had to fight Cecil to let a same-sex couple join Sanctuary, but I had hit it off with Gus and Noah right away. That they deconstructed and put on Victorian era séances for a living only sweetened the deal.

"W-w-what's going to happen to you?" Noah asked.

"Nothing." I didn't sound convincing at all. "I'm going to figure out a way to get rid of the monster. She won't be back."

Kenny Johnson, a man who'd once tried to exile my family from Sanctuary, stepped forward. "Who's in charge if you get killed?" His eyes flitted over my cut-up legs and filthy feet.

I didn't like Kenny on the best of days and didn't have the energy to fake goodwill toward him. "Not you."

Without another word, I trudged back to my camper where I had Hannah take a new picture of the scratches on my chest. I sent it to Mysti with an explanation of what happened. There was no reply.

"Where is Cecil?" I asked nobody in particular.

"He, Shelly, and Jadine aren't back yet," Finn answered. "They went off with that new guy. Letts? Isn't that his name?"

My whole body flushed. I didn't want to talk about, or think about, Tanner Letts. Maybe he'd decided against joining Sanctuary and would just move on.

My phone buzzed with a return message from Mysti. "The monster won't be back tonight. Too close to daylight. Rest. I'll do some checking and send you a message later." I set down the phone and tipped my head back, wishing I could scream at the ceiling. But I didn't want to listen to it and figured none of my guests did either. I opened my eyes and tried to smile at the people crowding my little camper.

Dillon made a face at my chest. I glanced in the bathroom mirror and groaned. Blood was soaking through Finn's T-shirt. I moved to take it off. Dillon shook her head, still making the same face. "Give it back after you clean it."

I slumped and nodded.

"What are you gonna do?" Finn sat down at the table and began spinning my cigarette lighter with one hand.

"Hell if I know," I snapped.

Finn winced away from my fury.

I forced myself to calm down. "That monster thinks I stole something from her. I've never seen her in my life. She won't even discuss a bargain."

Finn stood from the table and motioned at Dillon. "We'll get it figured out."

I shook my head. "I meant what I told everybody else. Try to stay away from it. You'll only get hurt."

"I'm not just leaving you to get eaten alive." Dillon's eyes got bright and fierce.

"She's going to cook me first." My stomach gyrated at the thought.

Dillon paled. Finn dragged her out of my camper. Hannah left with them, throwing me a sympathetic glance. They piled horseshoes at my door, the heavy objects clunking against the aluminum door, in case Miss Ugly came back. I crouched underneath my table, holding a butcher knife that wouldn't help me a bit if Miss Ugly returned.

6

I jerked awake to a god-awful racket that sounded like the world crashing in on itself. Butcher knife gripped in my fist, I hunkered lower underneath my camper's table, waiting for Miss Ugly to take me away again.

Awareness crept into my mind, chasing away the sleep, bit by bit. My bleary eyes recognized the daylight streaming through the windows. Relief flooded through me. Miss Ugly was gone until sundown. But then what?

I crawled out from under the table, wincing at my sore muscles screaming. The skin on the backs of my legs and on my feet sang with a million scratches and cuts. My neck had a catch in it that flared up every time I turned my head. The noise came again. This time I identified it as another RV rumbling along the little dirt lane in front of my camper. Back throbbing from the cooped up way I'd slept, I climbed over the table's bench seat and peeked through the blinds.

An ugly, eyesore camper, 1970s vintage from the look of

it, backed slowly into the spot next to mine. A faded two-toned blue and white pickup truck with a matching camper over the bed pulled it. I squinted to see who was in the truck.

Sunlight glared off the windshield, so I couldn't see who was inside. Irritation burned away any residual fear I carried over the encounter with Miss Ugly.

What was this? I'd rented the spot next to me for extra privacy. Hannah was about the only super-close next-door neighbor I could stand. And she was bad enough.

I shucked off last night's clothes in front of the bathroom mirror and did a double take at the mark Miss Ugly had scratched onto my décolletage. Puffy, raised edges, crusted over in some spots, skin red and angry around it. I dabbed at it with a cool cloth, whimpering as I did so.

The truck's engine shut off and backfired. I snapped back into control. No way would I let anyone see me hurting. My pride might never recover. I dragged on a pair of cut-off denim shorts that were only moderately dirty and a clean peasant blouse Hannah insisted I buy. Showtime.

I slammed out the door and kicked on the flip-flops I kept next to the steps. Hannah had wandered out of her camper, probably to bear witness to the drama. She pulled one of her long, skinny cigarettes out of the pack and lit it, rubbing the sleep out of her face.

"I stayed up watching your camper, but I guess I fell asleep." She shrugged in apology.

"Good thing Miss Ugly decided not to take another run at me. I slept under the table waiting for her." I smiled at the look of shock on Hannah's face and pointed at the formerly empty space.

"I thought you rented the space next door." She ground one fist against her eye and shook her head.

"I did. If the RV park rented it out, I'm going to have their asses." I stomped to the other side of the trailer, spotted Cecil, and hurried to him. "What is this?"

He turned to me and gripped both shoulders. Holding me at arm's length, he looked me over the way Memaw would have. "I am so sorry we were still out when that monster attacked you. Are you okay?" He spun me around, clicking his tongue at the scratches up and down the backs of my legs. "Dillon said that thing cut you again last night? Where is the mark?"

I plucked at my blouse. "It's under here. With the other cut. Mysti said it's the monster's signature."

"Horrifying," Cecil muttered. "I have to wonder if full control of the mantle would make you powerful enough to send it away." He didn't give me a chance to reply. "I haven't forgotten about the man who might be able to help you remove the spell blocking the mantle. It's just going to take time to find him. Meanwhile, I'm not sure what to advise you to do."

"I don't know what to do either. I stopped Miss Ugly last night by shoving an iron horseshoe into her mouth. Eventually, my luck will run out." The problems compounded in my mind until they were a wall of chatter, slowly chipping away at my sanity. I pushed away my problems with Miss Ugly and gestured at the camper. I could do something about this right now, at least. "What the hell?"

Cecil put both hands up, palms out, and I knew we had a problem. "Now honey, we talked last night about Tanner joining Sanctuary as a legacy member. You agreed. Remember?"

I glanced at the camper again. The truck's beat-up-assed door screeched open. Tanner Letts slid out, muscles flexing underneath the material of his worn cargo pants.

Dragging my gaze off him, I leaned close to Cecil and lowered my voice, not sure why I cared if Tanner heard me. "But I didn't agree to him bunking next to me."

"The park's full. This is prime tourist season, sugar." Cecil threw a smile over his shoulder at Tanner, who had started plugging the camper into electricity, water, and sewer.

I went over my strategies for winning this argument. Complaints about lack of privacy wouldn't work with Cecil. He'd roll his eyes at me. He thought me renting the extra space was stupid anyway. The best claim I had was financial. "But I paid to rent that spot out of my own pocket."

Cecil came closer and lowered his voice to a whisper. "Tanner doesn't have a cent to his name, honey. He needs our help. This is part of how we take care of each other."

I allowed myself another quick look at Tanner. His ragged clothes and his worn-out vehicle attested to a dire financial situation. That argument lost, I raised my eyebrows at my great-uncle. "And what kind of financial trouble is he in? Who does he owe? Are they going to come down on us?"

I'd presented all these arguments the night before, and Tanner had answered my questions, but I believed him about as much as I believed any desperate person. He came to us because he needed Sanctuary, just like the name promised. What kind of heat did Tanner Letts have trailing him?

The man himself glided around his camper, surefooted and efficient. He occasionally tucked a lock of hair behind one ear and glanced at his surroundings. Those intense green eyes met mine, and he raised one hand shyly. I nodded in return. Yep, this guy was in some kind of trouble. Or he was trouble himself.

"Tanner's problems are his story to tell. I've heard it and think it's genuine." Cecil fixed his dark eyes on mine. It hit me that Tanner camping next to me was a done deal, no matter what I said. The look in Cecil's eyes said he was pulling rank, and I'd better not get my nose out of joint over it. He gripped one of my arms as a further signal that he meant serious business. "Get to know Tanner. Maybe he'll tell it to you once he trusts you."

Shelly sped up in the golf cart she and Cecil towed behind their state-of-the-art motorhome. She shouted a cheerful greeting to Tanner, hurried over to us, and gave Cecil a hug. He kissed his wife's cheek. They exchanged the kind of smile people who've been together a long time give each other, one full of secrets and stories, love and laughter.

My anger ebbed watching them. I envied their easy

togetherness, the concern they showed for each other, and the ways they complemented each other. Not everybody finds that level of companionship. With the door closed firmly on a relationship with Wade, I highly doubted I'd ever get close.

"I checked with Kenny," Shelly told Cecil. "He did have an extra tent. It's one of those silly striped ones, but Tanner can have his own setup tonight rather than being in with one of the other businesses."

"What's he do?" In spite of myself, I watched Tanner's graceful movements, shying away each time he caught me staring.

"Tanner, like the rest of his paternal family line, is a finder of artifacts." Cecil followed my gaze and gave me a smile that made me blush to the roots of my hair. I turned my back on Tanner, ignoring both Shelly's and Cecil's chuckles.

"What's that mean, and how does it equate into him needing his own tent?" I'd had to buy my own tent and decided to splurge on a custom made one with the design of a night sky, a Ouija board, and a crystal ball on it. It set me back some serious dollars.

"Tanner sells arcane items. A lot of good luck charms, but some of his stock has magic." Cecil said the words seriously, but mischief danced in his eyes.

I couldn't believe him. I'd been attacked the night before, twice, and here he was acting like I was at a single's bar. Gross. Well, he could act silly if he wanted to. Any relationship I had with Tanner Letts was going to be all business. "What kind of artifacts do you mean?"

I had been talking to Cecil, but Shelly spoke up. "Last night he showed us a good luck charm with nine pieces on it, each one with a different purpose. The little spade was supposed to help you retrieve stolen items. I don't remember what the others did."

Interesting. But I pretended it wasn't. "And they're supposed to actually work?"

"It's like the rest of our businesses." Cecil shrugged. "Some of it's genuine, some for show."

I let Tanner's new role in our group sink in and watched him some more. He wandered over to us, eyes on me, wiping his hands on his jeans. I turned my back to him.

He spoke to Hannah, his rough purr of a voice raising the hair on the back of my neck. "You're Hannah, right?"

Hannah turned her million-watt smile on him. "Yep. Hannah Kessler. And you're Tanner, the guy who has the magical items. When do I get a look?"

Tanner smiled and held one arm out showman style. "They're in the camper on my truck. Come on over."

Hannah bounced over there as though she wasn't wearing a silky dragon kimono and house shoes. Tanner leaned into the truck and moved a few things around. Hannah, who had the talent of acting believably interested in anybody, exclaimed over them and asked questions.

"Go on." Shelly gave me a nudge. "You didn't see him watching you?"

I shook my head. Double negative. No to going over there and no to seeing Tanner watching me.

Cecil came closer. "Shelly's told me what happened

yesterday with Wade's sister. Do you want Kenny to keep an eye out for them, kick them out if they come back?"

The idea appealed to my inner teenager more than it should have. That alone told me the right answer. "No. Don't do that. Desiree's not a danger. Neither is Wade. If they need us, they need us." Shame at the scene with Desiree flashed through me, heating my skin.

Shelly came closer but stopped at putting her arm around me. She'd been raised in the Northeast, and her version of comforting and motherly was less touchy-feely than the version I'd grown up with. Right now, prickly as I felt, it worked.

"I know you wanted to be with Wade, sweetheart. I've seen the way your face lights up when you talk about him." She cast her voice low, speaking directly into my ear. "Remember what we talked about last night? Don't sit around mourning Wade. Any man who doesn't want to be with you isn't worth it."

I nodded and swallowed hard. "I'm going to lone it for a while. Maybe forever."

Shelly and Cecil exchanged a glance. He raised his eyebrows. She shrugged. Cecil turned his attention back to me.

"Shelly and I know you're fine alone, but you've got a lot on your shoulders. It never hurts to make friends."

Shelly cupped her hand around her mouth and cut her dark eyes at Tanner's fine form. "Especially when they look like that."

I glanced at Tanner and Hannah, already laughing and becoming friends. Maybe they'd fall in love, and I wouldn't have to worry about whether he liked me. Something that felt more like disappointment than I cared to admit took root in my chest.

"There's something else you may not understand." Cecil came closer.

Hearing the change in his voice, I took my attention off Tanner and Hannah. "What?"

"Now that you've taken on the center of our family's power—the mantle—your gifts will be passed to one of your descendants. Not anybody else's." He had lowered his voice almost to a whisper.

"How do you know?" When I didn't want to believe something, the easiest thing to do was challenge it. It was way better than considering the implications of what Cecil suggested.

"I heard my mother and her mother, Samantha, talking about it enough times." Cecil had spots of red high on his cheekbones but otherwise looked determined to deliver this message. I glanced at Shelly for reassurance, hoping she'd override this announcement, call it old-fashioned or anti-woman. The sympathy on her face suggested I wouldn't have her on my side.

"Now that you're not going to get together with Wade, you need to think about stuff like this." She tried to smile. "I know it sounds incredibly old-fashioned, like kings passing on kingdoms. Papaw hasn't wanted to be this blunt about what you'll eventually need to do." Shelly patted Cecil, and he cleared his throat, face turning redder than ever. "But you need to face this part of your duties as the center of our family's power." Shelly carried our raven tattoo as well, hidden beneath her shirt on one shoulder.

"It doesn't have to be tomorrow, and it doesn't even have to be Tanner," Cecil said quickly. "But you'll want to choose well. My personal suggestion is to find a man who has his own gifts, so your child will have a better chance of being magically inclined."

And Tanner fit the bill. They had it all figured out. Find Peri Jean a man. Get her knocked up. Then everybody'll be happy. The whole thing annoyed me. I decided to play my trump card. "I thought y'all knew I can't get pregnant."

Shelly's face dropped in shock, but Cecil only nodded. "In our world, anything can be fixed. And you know this. You have destiny, Peri Jean. Don't let that fact escape you."

But have a child with a man I didn't even know? The idea was old-fashioned and silly. *Isn't the idea of romance silly as well?* It didn't even exist until fairly recently. Before that, people got married and had children together to merge fortunes and continue family lines. What was so different about me needing to pass on my gift?

Gift. The word struck a blow in my subconscious. When had I started thinking of the things I could do that way? Maybe I didn't. I could have just picked up the word from Mysti. More horrifying than my change of heart over my talents was my dampening outrage over needing to have a child to pass on those gifts. A long time ago, I'd wanted one.

Maybe having a child outside the concept of romantic love would work better for me. My relationships all crashed and burned. In the case of Wade, it never even got off the ground. Either I was the wrong woman, or they were the wrong men.

Despite all my reasoning and logic, I still fumed inside. But I couldn't get angry at Cecil and Shelly. They weren't suggesting I run over there and jump Tanner. They wanted me to keep my options open. Unable to face them anymore, I walked over to where Tanner and Hannah stood, still talking. They quieted as soon as I came close.

"I'm going to make coffee." I spoke directly to Hannah. Then to Tanner, I said, "Come get me tonight after you get set up. I'd love to see your shop."

Without waiting for his response, I marched toward my camper. Hannah's light footsteps came behind me. I held open the camper's door.

Hannah gave me the most annoying grin and said, "He's a really nice guy."

"Don't say another damn word about Tanner Letts." Because I was attracted to him. *Of all the stupid damn things.* My heart couldn't take another round of hurt, but loneliness had a way of pushing me to do stupid things.

———

Hannah did what I asked and said nothing more about Tanner. We fixed coffee and ate little cups of Greek yogurt while we waited for it to brew.

"Cecil mentioned the spell blocking the mantle again." I scraped the last of my yogurt out of its little plastic cup and licked it off the spoon.

"Has he found the man he thinks can help you?"

Hannah gathered up our trash, dumped it, and poured two cups of coffee. We both lit cigarettes.

"No. He just said he hasn't forgotten about it." I sipped the dark brew, savoring the way it felt on the back of my tongue.

"I'm sort of wondering if you even need magical help getting the spell off. It's made of your bad memories and broken dreams, right?" Hannah rolled her cigarette between her fingers, something she'd been doing instead of wringing her hands.

"Yes. Each of us, including you now, has a magical core. The spell caused a type of scar tissue to form around mine. That scar tissue keeps me from fully accessing my power." I paused for a sip of coffee.

"Holy moly. Imagine what you'd be able to do with it gone." Hannah stared at me with a kind of awe in her eyes that made me uncomfortable.

I shrugged off what she'd said. "From what I saw when the Coachman trapped me inside the spell, yes, the scar tissue is made up of bad memories and broken dreams." I opened the blinds on the window looking out on Tanner's camper. He'd either gone inside or walked off. I caught Hannah watching me.

She winked, but when she spoke, she said nothing about Tanner. "After everything that happened to me last year, and then this year, I've done a lot of thinking about how I perceive myself in light of..." She swallowed hard and waved one hand to describe a horror most people couldn't imagine.

"You have nothing to feel ashamed of," I said, anger

heating up.

"I know that. But those words are easy to say. They're a lot harder to internalize." Hannah's voice had risen in impatience. She took a couple of deep breaths, and her caramel-colored eyes calmed. "Here's what I wanted to get across. One of the big things I figured out in all my soul searching is that I decide how I feel about me on a day-to-day basis. It's all on me, all my choice."

I nodded my understanding but did not interrupt.

"If I let myself start thinking negative things, it gets easier and easier to fall into darkness. Before I know it, I've had a nasty day, full of bad thoughts. But doing stuff like making myself talk to Tanner, reminding myself I'm perfectly safe with him, helps create positive paths of thinking." She watched me, vulnerability naked in her eyes. She'd laid herself out to me, told me how her mind worked day to day. The least I could do was take her seriously and try to understand.

"That makes sense. So you're saying that maybe I could kill the scar tissue by not allowing those bad memories to control my present day life?" It made a kind of sense. Hannah had been saying similar things to me all along, especially about letting go of Wade. The problem was, I didn't think I could do it. Those events and the pain that went with them were buried deep, so deep that I didn't know who I'd be without them. The thought scared me.

"I'm not saying you have to do it this second. But just think about it." She drained her coffee cup and stood for a refill. "When the negative beliefs you learned from those experiences arise, try to let go of them. Think about good stuff instead. It might starve the scar tissue." She grabbed my cup and poured in a little fresh coffee to warm it up.

I nodded my thanks and took a sip. "I'll try it next time I'm aware of thinking about the bad parts of life."

"That's the problem you're going to run into." Hannah lit another cigarette. "You've lived with your scars for so long they're embedded in your subconscious. You're not even aware you're reacting to them."

I lit my own cigarette. Get two smokers in a room together, and they'll smoke every cigarette they've got. "You're right. Some of those memories are so old that I don't even remember the actual event."

"Do you ever wonder if your mind could have overblown what happened? All this time, your feelings have been building, and whatever hurt you might not have been that big of a deal in the first place." Hannah sipped her coffee, staring at something I couldn't see.

My phone blared out Mysti's ringtone. It saved me from having to spout off some unhelpful but well-meant platitude to Hannah in exchange for her genuinely good advice. "It's Mysti, and she wants to video chat again. Come over here so she can see you too."

Hannah raised her head, eyes dead and cold for a split second, and then smiled. I accepted the video call wondering where Hannah went when her eyes dulled. Maybe it would be best if I didn't know.

Mysti's face appeared on my phone's screen. She'd put her brown hair up in a messy bun with a lace ribbon trailing down onto her shoulders. She beamed good morning at us. "You had a second visit from Miss Ugly last night?"

I nodded. "She cut more marks on my chest and dragged me through the woods. You should see the backs of my legs." I told Mysti about Miss Ugly taking me into the dark outposts, how she seemed to have a lair there, and about the cauldron bubbling over the fire.

Mysti listened with her nose wrinkled in distaste. She glanced at some papers next to her and shook her head. "Did you see anything else?"

"The clearing had a row of skulls set into the ground, sort of making a ring." The yellow light flickering over the bones flashed behind my eyes. I'd be going back to that place if I couldn't get rid of Miss Ugly. And it would be the last place I saw. I checked the clock on the stove. Twelve hours to sundown and Miss Ugly's return.

Mysti's voice broke into my thoughts. "Did you see a house made of bones? It would have been on a platform of some sort."

"No. But that doesn't mean it wasn't there. The only light came from the fire." If the house existed, and I bet it did, whose bones was it made from? The people Miss Ugly cannibalized? The whole ugly scenario played again in my head. Something new occurred to me. "That monster called me a thief."

"She what?" Mysti's voice sharpened and raised a little.

"She called me a damn thief. Like I'd want any of her crappy stuff." It had just occurred to me to be offended by the accusation. I'd been too scared before.

Mysti picked up a sheaf of papers and glanced through

them, frowning. Finally she began to nod. "I can't make any promises on the accuracy of what I'm about to say. It's not like there's a directory of these creatures."

"Where do you get your information?" Hannah nearly shoved me aside in her eagerness to speak to Mysti. I'd thought her love of research and puzzles died in the wake of her ordeal with Michael Gage. This was the first real interest she'd shown since then.

Mysti answered excitedly. "The only human accountings of the chthonic beings, which Priscilla Herrera simply called dark beings, are limited to mythology and folklore as source material. It's important to remember two things." She held up two fingers. "One: humans only see what these beings want them to see. Two: these beings evolve with human imagination. They're capable of just about anything. Their greatest desire is for us to need them."

The room fell to silence at the chilling reality of Mysti's words. No real record of how to defeat Miss Ugly or how get rid of her existed. We'd have to give it our best guess. One wrong step would end with me being served as human pot roast.

"So what do you think we're dealing with?" I stared at my mentor's face, searching for just how bad this was. I had a feeling it was about a nine on a scale of ten.

"What you've said about Miss Ugly fits the details of some of the wild woman of the woods, or witch of the woods, folktales. Cannibalism. Weird noises. There's a Slavic folktale where the creature lives in a house of bones. I advise you to read a few of them." Mysti tipped her chin at me. "Samantha is right in what she told you. You cannot out-magic this creature, nor can you fight her with magic. My contact in the dark outposts..."

"Oh no. What did you have to trade for information from one of them?" The dark beings, or chthonic beings as Mysti called them, always wanted to offer favors to humans. Any trade would be to their advantage.

"Actually, my contact owed me a little something." Mysti's chilly smile wrapped freezing bands around my chest. Not for the first time, it hit me that my mentor had a whole, secret existence in the magic world, probably one I didn't want to know much about.

Mysti's smile faded as she began talking again. "My contact said that Miss Ugly often believes her victims have stolen something from her. So that's why she called you a thief."

"Could I theoretically bargain with her to return whatever she thinks I've stolen?" The idea sounded like a good one to me.

"Maybe. She's known to reward good deeds, although her idea of a reward and yours might not mesh." Mysti nodded. "Has she said anything else?"

I thought hard. Miss Ugly had said more, but I'd been too scared to latch on to it. Whatever she'd said made me think of a spool of thread for some reason. Had she threatened to tie me up? I gave up. "She said more, but I don't remember it now."

"When you do, text it to me." Mysti held my gaze through the camera, asserting her authority even across the miles between Texas and Canada.

"What aren't you telling me?" I tried using the same

tone of voice on Mysti that I used on members of Sanctuary. She barely responded.

"Let's not worry about it right now. For now, let's talk about the last piece of information I have for you. And my contact did charge me for this, so please appreciate it." Mysti played with the strip of lace coming off her bun, the only indication she'd ever give of sour nerves. "The Coachman sent Miss Ugly after you."

"Oscar Rivera?" I shouted the words.

"How?" Hannah's yell blasted into my eardrum, making it rattle.

Mysti acknowledged our outrage with a tired sigh. "The Coachman, or Oscar, is cut off from the living plane, but he's not cut off from the dark outposts." She shook her finger at the camera, a habit she'd picked up from me. "He can contact anybody in the dark outposts he wants."

"So what do I do now?" It didn't sound like there was much I could do.

Mysti gave me an apologetic smile. "You need to contact Oscar."

The idea sent a bubble of burning anxiety through my stomach. I shook my head. "I can't."

Mysti cocked her head at me, eyes narrowed. "What did the runes allow that coven to do a few months ago?"

My cheeks heated at the rebuke in her voice. I mumbled the answer, feeling like a first grader who'd just caught her teacher's bad side. "Summon Oscar."

"And who has those runes?" Mysti softened the rebuke with one her smiles.

"Me." I was too embarrassed to smile back. I should

have known this. Mysti couldn't be with me every second leading me along.

"Now this is dangerous. Oscar siphoned a lot of power off you back when the two of you battled. If he's wheeling and dealing in the dark outposts, he managed to conserve some of it." She paused and checked some papers next to her.

"If Oscar has a little power left over, does that mean he could escape into the world?" My scalp tingled as I began to sweat.

"He wouldn't do that," Mysti said. "What he really wants is to possess you. He's smart enough to know that would not only carry him further but allow him to get really, really powerful before he went off on his own. Understand?"

I nodded, body tightening at the memories of Oscar inside me, manipulating memories to distract me while he stole power.

Mysti pressed her lips together and gave me an apologetic look. She didn't like making me hurt emotionally but probably considered it a form of tough love. "You'll have to safeguard against losing control of him…"

An idea flashed in my mind, something I'd wanted to try but hadn't needed to yet. "I've got an idea on how to do this, using my stang."

Mysti drew back, and a mischievous grin split her lips. "You have been studying. Good job." She point one finger at me. "But listen. Oscar's not going to cooperate. He will likely tell you to eat it. You're going to have to get clues from whatever he says. So listen carefully."

"Maybe I can offer him something in exchange for calling Miss Ugly off." As I said the words, I realized how stupid and childish they sounded. Oscar would never bargain with me. It was all his way or the highway. He had his vision of perfect. Anything that didn't fit wasn't acceptable.

I cringed at the thought, realizing it described me too. If I ever got out of this, I might have to rethink my all or none position.

An alarm went off on Mysti's side of the conversation. "I hate to end this so abruptly, but I need to get moving. We should wrap up this job tomorrow. Or be dead. I'll fly straight into the airport at San Antonio."

I forced a smile, no easy feat considering my dread for contacting Oscar. But Mysti deserved it. She would do anything to help the ones she loved. And all I did was take and take. "Maybe I should fly out there, if I get this straightened out, and help you and Griff."

Mysti raised her eyebrows. "Only if you want to see the real version of the thing people consider a werewolf." She clicked off with that.

7

———————

I wouldn't summon Oscar in my camper. Not where I lived. I'd never allow something as evil as Oscar Rivera access to my home. He'd taint it. I saw only one other option.

"I'll do the summoning in my tent at the carnival," I told Hannah.

"You can't do it alone." Hannah had her long arms crossed over her chest.

"You can't help." I mimicked her posture.

She answered by jerking my witch pack out of the closet next to my bed and holding it tight in one fist. "You can't stop me."

Tired of the argument before it had even gained traction, I gave up. "We need more than just the pack."

My witch pack had expanded to an oblong cedar chest with a triquetra for protection burned into the lid. Hannah and I hauled it out from the storage space underneath my mattress by its rope handles and put it in my truck along with my witch pack.

The carnival wouldn't open until mid-afternoon. I drove through the empty dirt lot and parked the truck in front of the grouping of RVs and tents where many of the workers stayed.

A few of them came out to see who was here. Leon Blackfox, owner of Summervale Carnival, joined them. Soon as he saw Hannah, his face lit up.

"How are you today?" Leon had his long black hair pulled into a ponytail, and his bronze skin glowed in the midday sun. He had packed his lean body into tight jeans and wore expensive cowboy boots.

He was worth a second look. And a third. Maybe even a fourth. But he was interested in Hannah, not me. And she wasn't ready.

Hannah gave Leon a vague smile and hurried away from him. Leon's shoulders rounded, and he frowned.

"Need help?" He spoke to me this time, probably hoping I'd include him.

"No, thanks" was my answer. Though Hannah teased me about Tanner Letts, I wouldn't mess with her about Leon. She was hurting emotionally. It would be cruel.

Leon made a sour face and went back to his RV. The other workers watched us pass by, curiosity etched onto their faces, but asked no questions. They probably thought I was setting up for some blowout of an attraction. If only they knew.

With my witch pack slung over one shoulder, Hannah and I hauled the cedar chest between us. My guts boiled at what we were about to do, and the smell of my own fear drifted up to me, chemical and sour. But I just didn't know what other option I had at this point. We got into my tent, and I flipped on the lights.

Because I did other magic work and summoning in the tent, it had to be cleansed. I pulled my censer out of the cedar box and filled it with a couple of inches of limestone sand, found in an area not far from here where I'd felt an old, sacred presence. On top of the sand, I placed one charcoal disk and used a long match to light the edge. Sparks flew from it.

Hannah skittered backward, hand to her chest. "Is that him?"

"No. This is just for the ceremonial cleansing." While the charcoal got hot enough for incense, I set out the other things I'd need.

Oscar's runes went on the table. Using rubber kitchen tongs, because I carried the silly belief the evil wouldn't conduct through rubber, I arranged them in their own circle. Evil rose from them like stink off an open sewer pipe. This wasn't the first time I'd attempted to work with them, but their ugliness never failed to surprise me. I set a bowl filled with holy water next to the runes. I'd be using the runes as a doorway, and I needed a way to close that once I finished. Soaking in the holy water would break any connection Oscar managed to forge between his prison and the topside world.

I set my stang on the chair, away from the runes but still convenient to me, careful not to get the deer antlers, which served as prongs tangled in anything. The rest of the summoning would be done on my own steam. As I worked, I couldn't help stealing glances at Orev's perch. He often summoned with me, and I missed him.

The raven familiar hadn't shown his beak since he was plucked from the sky while I fought with Miss Ugly. He wasn't dead. I'd feel that. But what if whoever took him decided not to give him back? Sorrow ached in my chest. Even though he wasn't a person, Orev had become my friend. I wanted him back. A tear welled in my eye, blurring the perch.

I pulled my focus back together, taking deep breaths. Orev would have to wait until later. He was alive and in no distress for right now. I'd have to leave his whereabouts there. This task of summoning Oscar had to be my entire focus. It was too dangerous not to. If his spirit got into me, I was in deep trouble. Hannah's voice cut into my thoughts.

"Do we need to cover the floor?" Hannah had watched me do a few spells since she'd been traveling with us. I occasionally used an old Persian style rug as a decorative floor cover when summoning. Spirits liked ceremony.

"I need the dirt this time." I lifted the stang to show Hannah. Its power lapped gently against that of the mantle. She eyed it warily, gaze lingering on the deer antlers. I set the stang back down.

The charcoal finally glowed fiery red. I placed white sage on top of it. Smoke flooded from the incense. I let it die down. Then I placed more incense in the censer and capped it.

I shook my hands the way Brad Whitebyrd taught me to do, releasing my insecurities and my misgivings. Today was harder than usual. I'd foolishly coasted on the belief that I'd neutralized any danger from Oscar until I was ready and able to deal with him. This was turning out not to be true. I wasn't as strong or as in control of my abilities as I'd thought. There was still such a long road for me to travel, one lined with the bones of those who failed on the same path. One wrong move, and I'd become roadkill right along with them. I shook my head to clear the negative thoughts. The black opal heated against my skin. It was ready, and so was I.

"This is it," I told Hannah. "Run now or stay for the show." I lifted the censer. White sage smoke undulated from it.

Hannah glared to let me know she was offended by the implication that she might leave out of fear. I nodded my understanding and moved the censer up and down. The smoke drifted, caressing and curling over my bare arms.

I began my chant, concentrating on letting go of my own negativity and pushing any other negativities out of this space.

"Impurities of this place drift away on the air

Negativity float away like water."

I moved about the space as I spoke, swinging the censer, which let out a steady stream of smoke. I let smoke drift into every nook and cranny, and even released it at the ceiling.

"Smoke, chase it all way and cleanse me

Cleanse this place

Let impurities become one with the earth, gone forever."

A low hum built in the tent. The smoke took on weight,

pressing against my skin, swirling low to the ground to tickle my ankles.

Light flashed, bright and blinding. A chilling heat burned through the room and me, filling me with the whitest of light. A strong wind from nowhere rushed through and pushed out the incense smoke.

My heart picked up speed. The cleansing had worked, but this was the strongest physical result I'd ever seen. The results I usually saw dealt more in a change of energy.

I glanced at Hannah to make sure she was still okay and saw a possible answer to the increased activity. She had her eyes closed and her hands clasped beneath her chin as though in prayer. Had she done that thing with the light? Hannah's connection between life and death was new to both of us. Her knowledge of death, of spirits leaving the living realm, could have accelerated the process. But I had no real way to know.

"Now it's time for the circle. Once it's up, stay inside, no matter how scary things get." I picked up my stang. Its power moved through me and kissed the mantle. The two energies curled together, golden as the rays of afternoon sun. I gathered my power.

Mysti had expressed surprise at my desire for one of these, but the stang had called to me at a Witch's Feast of Lights she'd dragged me to. The guy selling it didn't have a stitch of magic in him. The stang, however, had enough to go around.

A little taller than me and topped with removable deer antlers to create many forks, the slick, oiled piece of wood was covered with protection and earth symbols. The stang would act as a representation of the world tree.

The top part, the antlers, offered protection above, in the heavens. The middle of the stang, where my hand rested, represented my part of the world, the living realm. The bottom of the stang, which I'd drive into the earth, extended the circle of protection into the lower realm where the roots of all things on the topside dwelled.

My studies had suggested this type of circle would be tighter and stronger than what I normally did. This was the same research Mysti had praised me for doing. Though her praise felt good, I chose this method because, like the stang, it spoke to something deep in me, in the place where my magic lived. And I hoped it would be strong enough to keep Oscar out of me.

I pointed the stang at the dirt floor and turned my body sunwise as I spoke.

"Lord of the fire
Lady of the earth
Daughter of the water
Son of wind
Hear my call
Witness my works
Keep me safe
Let not evil roam past this circle
Let this circle seal now."

I drove the stang into the hard dirt at my feet. It should have been a struggle. That dirt was hard enough to bow the stang, even break it with enough force. But the energy from the earth nearly pulled the stang from my hand and sucked it into the ground.

The circle went up around us. In it were shadows shaped like tree leaves and branches. They curled around us, protecting and sheltering us. I let my energy flow in silent thanks. It answered with a rustle of leaves and the smell of resin.

Now for the worst part. I had to call Oscar. I stood over the table where I placed the runes. They'd moved themselves from the circle in which I'd placed them into the shape of the symbol carved on each rune. The symbol on the runes themselves, usually black, glowed with a jumping fire.

I put all the power I could behind my voice. "Oscar E. Rivera, I summon you to into this realm. We have business to discuss."

At first, nothing happened. I got ready to speak again. About that time, an ugly, menacing energy rose from the runes and rolled around the circle, testing its boundaries. The runes chittered on the table and emitted the smell of rotting meat. Red mist, like blood vapor, rose from the runes. Within it, a human shape formed.

Oscar's thick features emerged slick and shiny in the mist. He had his hands clasped underneath his chin the way Hannah had a few minutes earlier. Slowly, he raised his head to stare at me. Then, without warning, he launched himself at me.

The circle I'd made to contain his spirit stretched toward mine. My throat closed. My mind raced back over everything I'd done, looking for the mistake. I shook off the thoughts, concentrated on the angry spirit coming toward me, and waited for him to break his circle.

But before Oscar's circle could break, it slammed into my special circle. The impact shook the room. Cold fear spread over me. *Hold. Please hold.* A sound like wood rubbing together, a nerve-grinding flat squeak, rattled my eardrums. Oscar's circle flew back into place, Oscar along with it. My circle pushed it there and then spread over it to hold it down.

Oscar launched himself at the invisible wall a few more times. Each time, red mist flew from him, and he became a little less substantial. Finally he gave up and glared at me, emanating hate and violence. The red mist collected around him again and made him look solid.

I licked my lips and took a trembling breath. "I know you sent that creature to assassinate me. Let's negotiate a truce to our conflict." I tried my best to sound strong and brave like Priscilla Herrera, even though I felt naked and weak without her and Orev.

"Speak it." Oscar Rivera, known in folklore as the Coachman, must have taken voice training in his human life. Or maybe he'd had a natural talent. Either way, his rich melodious voice was pure seduction. It could have convinced the most saintly of humans to commit mayhem and make bad decisions in his name.

"I'll help you cross into the spirit world, taking your entire soul with you. Your isolation will end. You can reunite with people you knew in life. Haunt as a ghost. If you seek it, you can find peace." I used my Priscilla Herrera voice to speak the words I'd been mentally practicing since I'd decided to contact Oscar.

The offer was a good one. Oscar Rivera's actions, both in life and in death, were those of a tormented soul. Crossing over would allow him to leave behind the chaos and hate on which he'd thrived for more than a century. Remembering Mysti's warning of Oscar telling me to eat it, I tried not to get my hopes up too high.

The seconds ticked past. Oscar's shimmering form gave no indication of hearing. Fear scratched at my already fragile confidence. My mind raced back over my actions, searching for the step I'd forgotten. But I'd done everything I knew to do.

"Did you hear me? I've made you an offer." I let the words come out of my diaphragm the way Priscilla Herrera did.

Oscar Rivera lowered his head. His form twitched a couple of times. Then it began to shake, his shoulders hitching. Oscar threw back his head, flung his arms wide, and screamed laughter at the ceiling of my tent. It left a fine spray of red mist on the material. I puzzled at it. This wasn't right. Oscar shouldn't have been able to manifest physically at all. *Uh oh.*

My chest tightened, and my throat closed. I had jacked this up royally, but damned if I had any idea how. Hannah edged closer to me until our bodies pressed together.

"I don't want to cross over, you moron. I'd lose everything important." Oscar's voice shook the contents of my tent, vibrated in the dirt at my feet, and buffered against my skin.

"Then what will you take in exchange for calling off your assassin?" I didn't know what Oscar called Miss Ugly. Assassin was as good a name as any other.

Oscar smiled, his slick, bloody teeth glimmering in the low light. A chill rolled through my body. I grabbed Hannah's hand. Her trembling fingers curled around mine.

"You want to bargain?" He cocked his head at me.

"Within reason, yes." Unable to muster the Priscilla Herrera voice this time, I sounded like a rabbit caught in a snare.

Oscar laughed again. This time, he got over it faster. "Even if I could call off my assassin, which I cannot, there's only one thing I want from you." He paused, maybe waiting for me to ask what. I said nothing. I knew if I spoke, my voice would tremble. He sneered at me. "I want your death for what you and your ancestor did to me. Then I'll rise again and make things go the way they should have in the first place. My followers would have ruled this nation and the world had it not been for Samantha Herrera and for you."

Oscar was wrong. His foolishness and arrogance would have always done him in, but we never see our own failings or how impossible our tightest held dreams are. Oscar, mad in both life and death, thought his goal achievable, and it drove him just like any other, saner man's desire.

"Look at you." His laughter came back, doubling him over and shaking him where he stood. "You don't even know that your fate is now entwined with my assassin's and nothing can ever change it. She owns you now." He stared at me, his blood-slick features impossible to read. "You're too stupid and stuck in your ways to figure out how to get away from her."

Wait a minute. Had Oscar implied there was a way to escape Miss Ugly? He wouldn't help me, so there was no reason to ask what he meant. Mysti'd hoped he'd give me hints about what was going on. Was this one?

"Let me ask you something, Peri Jean Mace." Oscar's voice lulled me, caressed my senses. "Have you had any visitors lately? Faces from the past?"

Only Wade. The hurt bubbled up, almost overpowering the fear.

Oscar studied my face. "Not Wade Hill, fool."

I jolted. Had Oscar read my mind? My skin tingled as fear made my heart pump even harder.

Oscar cocked his head, lip curling as though he was staring at a particularly interesting piece of shit. "You didn't recognize him, did you? Don't worry. He'll be back." Oscar wiggled his fingers at me. His form turned back to red mist and slithered back into the tiles.

I hurried to the table and swept the tiles into the holy water. The evil still emanated from them, but I no longer felt Oscar's vile presence. My heart slowed. In control again, I spoke aloud to Hannah the thing that had bothered me most.

"Oscar read my mind. He knew I was thinking about Wade." My voice shook.

Hannah said nothing. She stood in the spot where I'd left her, fingers twitching, too shocked to move.

I kept talking anyway. "Oscar shouldn't have known

what I was thinking. I broke the connection he forged with me when I killed the coven that summoned him a couple of months ago."

Hannah shook herself. "Maybe he read your mind because that's what ghosts do."

She might have been right. I took the stang out the dirt, breaking the circle, and said, "I guess they do."

But Oscar knowing my thoughts teased at the edge of my brain like a fish who nibbles at the bait but won't take the hook. My gut said there was something to it. I just didn't know what.

————

Hannah and I spent the next couple of hours cleaning out my tent. We burned more white sage incense to get rid of any spiritual filth Oscar left behind. I used my homemade spiritual cleanser on the table, chairs, and my stang. I checked my phone's clock often, counting down the minutes until Miss Ugly returned.

Hannah gestured at the bowl of holy water holding Oscar's runes. "What do I do with this?"

I walked over to her, hand out, and peeked into the bowl, sort of the way you look in the toilet bowl before you flush. The symbol on one of the runes glowed fire, distorted by the moving water. It winked out almost as soon as I noticed it. I gasped and almost dropped the bowl. Hannah clapped both her hands to the bowl's sides to keep it from falling.

"What happened?"

"One of the runes was glowing red. Same as when we were talking to Oscar." Stress squeezed my ribcage. This had something to do with Oscar knowing about Wade. I didn't know why I thought that other than my gut said so. It all fit together, but my mind couldn't grasp the connection.

I dressed the runes with my special banishing oil just to make sure I'd closed the door between me and Oscar.

Sounds of people arriving and setting up around us drifted through the tent's thick material. I checked the time. Only a few hours until dark.

Hannah put her hand over my phone's display. "Stop looking. You're only making it worse."

"Maybe, but I don't know what I'm going to do when Miss Ugly comes back." I pushed the phone into my pocket.

"What are you more afraid of? Dying and changing into new energy or being killed?" That scary emptiness had come back to Hannah's eyes.

A few months earlier, a chthonic being had preyed on both of us, scratching open our shadow sides. Hannah's had been a darkness leading to self-destruction because of what Michael Gage did to her. Mine had been a lack of fear of death because I secretly hated my life. Those who don't fear death take chances because life has no true hold. Now that Hannah had asked the big question, the unspoken hung between us.

My answer came out in a near whisper. "Being slaughtered for food."

"You won't feel it anymore once your heart stops beating," she whispered back.

"Should I give up?" The idea pissed me off. I didn't back down to anybody or anything. It was my nature. My eyes locked on Hannah's, and the answer was there. *No. Don't give up. Fight to the death but don't fear it.*

I took a deep breath. My mind stopped running in circles. "I have to find out what she thinks I stole. That'll at least buy me time."

Hannah nodded. "And I'm here to help."

"Sure is quiet in here." Tanner's rough voice came from the tent's flap.

Hannah and I moved away from each other as though we'd been caught doing something forbidden. And I suppose we had. It's a given for humans to fear death. Those who don't are looked upon as mad or unbalanced.

Tanner wore a thin white linen shirt, the sleeves rolled up enough to display dark forearms corded with muscle. His suntanned skin stood out against the white. Those intense eyes pegged me from across the room.

"Hey. What's up?" My libido was one thing that was up. *Whore,* I said to myself. It hadn't even been a full day since seeing Wade and having Desiree give me the facts of life. How could I turn the corner on Wade so quickly? *Because it's been a done deal for months now,* answered a less judgmental part of my brain. And I had been lonely a lot longer than that.

Tanner tweaked a part of me that had lain dormant for too long. He wasn't pretty the way Dean had been, but he wasn't rugged the way Wade had been either. Tanner's odd leonine features made him someone people looked at twice but maybe shied away from. He had an inner badassery. It showed in the way he moved, in the fierce gleam of his eyes. But there was vulnerability too, in the way he'd tuck his hair behind his ear or glance down at his worn shoes.

"If you still want to see my shop, I just finished setting it up." He licked his thin, bow-shaped lips. My inner tramp wondered what those lips would feel like pressed to mine. Or on my body. I pushed the thought away.

"Sure." I glanced at Hannah, silently inviting her.

She shook her head. "I'd better get over to the face painting tent. See ya, Tanner." She brushed past him and walked out without a backward glance.

"So it's just us?" Tanner's eyes darted around the tent, never settling on anything for long. He fingered a hoop hanging from his belt.

I came closer. "Unless you'd rather wait until it's not."

"No." His laugh sounded like a dry bark. His smile was more genuine. He motioned me to follow, and I did.

Tanner's tent, the red and white striped one Shelly turned up her nose at, was wedged between a lady who read Lenormand cards and a guy who sold handmade animals made out of wire. His specialty was scorpions. Both vendors, husband and wife, called greetings to me.

Tanner held open the flap of his tent for me to pass through. My shoulder brushed him. Electric attraction spiked through me. Shelly had been right. There was something between us. The big question was whether I wanted to do something about it. The answer didn't come, so I stepped into the tent and looked around.

Tanner had arranged his wares in a collection of glass cases I recognized as belonging to Kenny Johnson, Sanctuary's unofficial security team and gofer. I walked slowly in front of the cases, taking in the items. I had no idea what purpose any of them had. This was something I could talk to Tanner about so we could break the heavy silence between us.

"Cecil said you locate magical items." I raised my voice on the last word to let Tanner know it was a question.

"Well, the items sort of find me. Might as well do something with them." He crossed his arms over his chest. I couldn't help noticing the bulge of his biceps underneath the thin white linen of his shirt. Then I noticed his hands. Scarred just like mine. A fighter. Was that the source of his financial problems? I turned back to the glass case.

"What's this?" I pointed at two stacks of weathered two-dollar bills.

I didn't hear Tanner's footsteps on the dirt floor of his tent, but suddenly he stood next to me. His scent invaded my nose, and his body heat kissed my skin.

"Which one?" His voice had more sharp burrs than it had a second ago.

"The two-dollar bills. What do they do?" I tapped the glass.

Tanner leaned across me and pointed to the stack on the left. "The ones on the left are bad luck." He moved his finger over a few inches. "The ones on the right are good luck."

I pivoted slightly so we were facing. This close, his eyes mesmerized me. Animal passion lurked in their sparkling depths. "Why both kinds of luck?"

"Just depends on who the person is and what they believe. Some people consider two-dollar bills bad luck. But some consider them good luck." Tanner pulled out his wallet and showed me a bill compartment, empty except for a lone two-dollar bill. We exchanged a smile, but I glanced away quickly, still feeling guilty over even being attracted to Tanner. Was I really this fickle?

"Wanna know why I put the bad luck ones on the left?" Tanner lowered his chin, never taking his eyes off mine. The nostrils on his barroom brawl nose flared.

I nodded, afraid I'd say something really stupid if I spoke.

Tanner tapped the glass over the left-hand stack of bills. "Centuries ago, left-handedness was considered evil. So I put the bad luck bills on the left side as a private joke."

I smiled and walked to the end of the counter. Tanner followed, explaining the uses of white heather, acrylic-encased four-leaf clovers, evil eye talismans, and the meanings of a small selection of Catholic medals. The pile of dimes near the end intrigued me. I leaned close to the glass, trying to pick up magical vibrations.

"Mercury dimes. Or Winged Liberty Head dimes." Tanner still hovered close enough for me smell the soap he used. "Some people drill a hole in a dime and string it around their ankle as sort of a magical metal detector. If the coin turns black, it means somebody's doing bad spell work against them."

"Does it work?" I thought not since my black opal didn't react to them.

Tanner shrugged and winked. I knew the wink. People bought our wares, paid us for séances and witch work, because they *wanted* to believe. "People also buy them for SATOR work. You know, from Germanic folklore. The dimes are also used for money-drawing spell work."

Tanner stopped talking. We stared at each other, and the silence got big again. Every beat of my heart boomed in my ears. He broke the stare and moved to the last glass cabinet. This one contained only two items, a brass cornucopia and an ankh so old I couldn't even tell what kind of metal it was made of.

"Right now, these are my high ticket items. The cornucopia was supposedly hexed by an otherworldly being. It'll fill with whatever its owner needs at the time." He smiled at me. "And before you ask, I don't know if it works. The price for using it is too high."

I bet I knew the kind of creature who had turned it into magical item. Those dark beings seemed to be everywhere now that I knew about them. They'd been around since the beginning of time, using people for amusement, and most never even knew they walked among us. I shivered.

Tanner frowned at my shiver, reached out a hand like he might touch me, but then dropped it. "The ankh belonged to a powerful sorceress or sorcerer. It's a gateway to the divine."

"What do you mean?" I leaned close to the glass, black opal shocking me with magic.

"Supposedly it can be used to cross into..." Tanner

paused and frowned, seeming to search for the right word. "Other realms. I discovered it in a pawnshop. The pawnbroker sold it to me for a song. He was scared of it. Said one of his employees had taken it in back to catalogue it, and the guy went missing. They never found any trace of him. He was just gone, and the ankh was lying there on the floor." Tanner fingered a hoop hanging from his belt again. Up close, it looked sort of like a keychain, but the pieces of metal on it weren't keys. Was this the thing Shelly mentioned, the shovel that found stolen items?

We were at the end of the display. Tanner still stood close, almost hemming me in. I should have pushed around him and left. But I didn't want to. The metal on the hoop jingled as he fingered it.

"What's that?" I pointed at the hoop.

"Nine irons amulet. Good luck and protection." Tanner stood so close now the shadow of whiskers on his upper lip, dozens of black dots, were visible. "Items similar to it have been found in Viking ruins, but they were also popular in the 1800s. This one's new, but the blacksmith made it from reclaimed iron." He unbuckled his belt, slid off the amulet, and handed it to me.

I bounced the amulet in my hand, testing the weight. Heavier than it looked, its magic crept up my arm. Each piece of metal on the hook was attached by a hole at its top end.

"Know what they represent?" Tanner lips curved into a smile.

I shook my head. His hand closed around mine, linen

of his shirt brushing against my arm. Chill bumps rose on my skin.

If Tanner noticed, he didn't let on. He used a finger to lift the circle-shaped piece of iron. "This is a pan. Heat it to ward off enemies. The saw and axe protect you from evil spirits." Tanner's voice rolled over the descriptions like sultry dark coffee. Something imported with a sensuous bite. His light touch resonated in every part of my body. Sweat broke out on the nape of my neck. He touched another two items and raised his eyes to mine. "The plow coulter and plowshare soothe sleepless children." He moved his finger again. "The shovel and spade will help you recover lost or stolen property."

"That makes sense. They can dig up whatever you've lost or stolen." As soon as I spoke, I regretted it. My logic sounded stupid. But Tanner smiled and nodded. I searched his eyes, his posture, for signs he was interested. He turned his attention back to the amulet of nine irons. The next charm was a cross.

Tanner held it between his thumb and forefinger. "This is to bless holy water and keep spirits away." The final charm was a horseshoe nail. Tanner tapped it. "For good luck."

We were so close I heard his inhales and exhales, felt the puffs of humid breath on my overly sensitive skin. Our eyes met again. This time I was the one who glanced away, Wade's face foremost in my mind. The way he lit his cigarettes. The tattoos on his arms. The way he'd told me he loved me a few times.

I turned away from Tanner, still hyper aware of him at

my back, and focused on a framed picture he'd set on the edge of the glass cabinet. The casual picture, taken on rocky terrain and overlooking hills spreading into the distance, showed a shorter-haired Tanner. He posed next to a pretty blond woman. Two dark-haired girls stood in front of them, obviously their children. One of the girls, a teenager, must have been born when Tanner was pretty young, or he was a lot older than he looked.

So this was Tanner's problem. An ex-wife demanding alimony and child support. Maybe college for the older girl. If Tanner didn't pay, police could get involved, raid Sanctuary. I turned back to Tanner, almost relieved to be able to walk away from him before I made a fool of myself.

He stared at the picture, eyes glossy. "My wife and daughters. They died in a car crash eighteen months ago." He swallowed hard and shook his head. "I never go anywhere without a picture of them." He choked on the last word and turned away from me.

My cheeks heated at my uncharitable thoughts. I'd discovered his secret, though not how he'd become poverty stricken, and now I regretted it. Tanner stood stock still, his back to me. I didn't know what to do, or if I should do anything. I tiptoed toward the door.

When I got there, I blurted, "Thanks for showing me your shop," and nearly leapt out.

8

———————

I trudged toward my tent, awash with regret. Running off like that couldn't have been more insensitive. But what else could I have done? Men usually didn't want to hang their emotions out in the wind for all and sundry to analyze and try to fix.

Then why had he lost his cool in front of me? Maybe he felt guilty about whatever attraction he felt to me just like I felt guilty over my attraction to him. Tanner's wife wouldn't be back. But that didn't mean he'd gotten over her. He might never move on.

If he was stuck on his dead wife, didn't that let me off the hook with Tanner? Nothing would ever happen. Wade Hill could remain front and center in my emotions, the great love who got away. Tanner Letts could be an amusing piece of eye candy I never made a move on.

Good. That's settled. I smiled to myself, ignoring the sharp pang of disappointment way down deep where I hid the real me from the world.

A few feet away, Finn stood fast-talking a young couple. He was likely using his telepathic abilities to swindle them. I gave him a knowing wink just to show myself there was nothing to be disappointed over.

Finn's dark eyes settled on my face. Light fingers tickled my brain as he rummaged through my thoughts. I tried to push away the thoughts of Tanner, but a smile broke out over Finn's gaunt face and he gave me a lewd wink. I showed him my middle finger and ducked into my tent. What I saw stopped me cold.

A man squatted in front of the old, shabby painted buffet where I kept my magical implements out of sight. His cowboy boots, so worn the only color they had was the dirty strips of duct tape holding them together, stuck out beside my séance table. I recognized those boots.

I quickly sifted through my memory and placed them from the previous night, right before Miss Ugly attacked for the first time. The man I'd caught coming out of my tent. He'd hurried away when I called to him.

His walk had seemed familiar last night. The way he knelt seemed familiar tonight. I studied the back of his mostly gray hair. His emaciated shoulders moved underneath his T-shirt as he rummaged in my cabinet. Still unable to place him, I took out my cell and texted Finn. One word summed up the situation. "Intruder."

Then I blocked off the man's exit. I kept a set of brass knuckles in my back pocket while I worked. The most I'd had to do so far was show them to a nitwit who tried to leave without paying. Now I slipped them onto my fist, ready to fight. "The fuck are you doing in here?"

The man spun around. Even from the distance between us, I could see his eyes were bloodshot. The deep, dark quarter moons underneath them looked like something on a corpse. But he wasn't dead. He might have been close, but not just yet.

He smiled, showing teeth that had a line of black between each one. That was when I knew him. Tim. My ex. The man who beat me until I miscarried our child because he thought I owed him money.

When I'd last seen him, he'd had a rock-n-roll messiah mane of hair with a matching beard. The beard had been so soft and shiny under my fingers. I glanced at his hand to see if he still wore the ring that had hurt so bad the night he beat me. It was there, gleaming in the dim lights of my tent. My stomach tightened, and bile crawled up the back of my throat.

"Get out," I said from between clenched teeth.

Tim stood, glancing at the brass knuckles on my fist, and raised both hands. The chemical smell of his sweat hit me. "Hey. 'Member me?"

"Get out." My breaths came in hard gasps.

"Listen, I ain't here for trouble." He took a slow step toward me. When I'd known him before, the drugs hadn't had time to eat away his body, only his soul, and he'd been a healthy weight. Now his jeans flapped around his emaciated legs, and his arms looked like pickup sticks.

I backed toward the flap of my tent. *Damn it, Finn. Can't you get your ass in gear?* He knew "intruder" meant to come quick. I'd been having so much trouble the last few days, he should have been on high alert for me anyway. What was he up to?

Tim closed the distance between us, arms outstretched, his body odor nearly gagging me. I doubled up my fist and tried to make myself swing it. It hung uselessly at my side. My knees went rubbery, and my head swam.

Tim pulled me into a hug, pressing his disgusting, stinking body against mine. The first tear leaked out of my eye and slid down my face. I still couldn't move. He let go of me and leaned back so he could look in my face, still baring those awful rotting teeth.

"My gorgeous ex. Thought we'd never meet again." He squeezed my shoulders for emphasis. "'Bout a month ago, back when y'all was in Gonzales, I seen you. But when I went after you, you'd already gotten away. Did a month of asking around, looking for you."

Remembering Jadine's prediction, I glanced at Tim's neck. Sure enough, a serpent tattoo, faded by time and sunlight, crept out of his shirt and onto his neck. I'd thought Tanner was the one she'd seen, the one I should watch out for, but it had been Tim all along.

For some reason, that calmed me. "What do you want, Tim?"

He made a mock pout, which would have been charming when I was in my early twenties and stupid as a pile of poo. Now it just looked creepy. "Why I gotta want anything?" he whined. "Why can't I just want to catch up?"

"You don't look for somebody for a month just to catch up. And you sure as fuck don't go nosing through their things." The eff-word gave me some of my swagger back. I shrugged Tim's filthy hands off me and got a few steps away from him. He tried to crowd in on me, and I held up my brass-knuckled fist. He nodded and put up his skeletal hands in a warding off gesture.

"All right. I wanted to do this nice, but I'm just gonna be blunt. Last time we talked, it was about money." He tilted his head and gave me a parent-to-kid glare.

"Talked? Is that what you call beating me until I had a miscarriage?" My voice raised with each word until I was screaming so hard it hurt. Tears flowed freely down my face.

There was no way I could express, in a way his fried brain would understand, what that miscarriage had done to me, besides making me infertile. He could never understand what it had been like to meet Finn's daughter and realize she was the spirit of our lost child, a child lost because of Tim kicking and punching me.

"You had a miscarriage? Was it mine?" The asshole actually looked worried.

That did it for me. I actually heard my self-control snap. I raced toward him, rearing back the fist with the brass knuckles and letting it fly as hard as I could. It hit Tim's jaw, and a spray of spit came from his mouth. But he knew how to fight too. He doubled up one fist and rammed an undercut into my sternum.

The air whooshed out of my lungs in one long stream. My knees went loose, and I sank to the floor, lungs aching, bowels burning. I tried to catch my breath. Nothing happened. I glared at Tim, lips pulled back from my teeth, and tried to hit him again. I couldn't work my arm.

"That last time we talked, you owed me money." He knelt on the floor next to me and grabbed a handful of my hair to drag my face toward him. "You still owe it."

I wanted more than anything to argue with him, but I couldn't even catch my breath, much less talk. So I did the next best thing. I pulled on the mantle. It was tired from summoning the Coachman, but it came willingly enough. I imagined dozens of red wasps covering Tim's face. Then I pushed the power into them.

He winced as the first phantom bite stung his skin. Then he let out a yelp as another one hit. He let go of me and slapped at his face. I poured more power to it. Tim ran around the room, slapping his own cheeks, and crying out.

In the back of my mind, I heard Mysti's sweet voice. *It comes back times three.* I didn't give a shit right then. I sent fire into the stings. Tim's cry was as pretty as an opera.

While I enjoyed Tim's plight, I concentrated on getting my breath back. I'd give Tim a beating that would mark him the rest of his short life. Even if I had to cheat with magic. I took a shallow breath. My stomach roiled. I forced myself to take another and rolled onto my knees. Tim was still busy with his phantom wasps.

Finn, sweat-faced and gasping, rushed into my tent. Kenny Johnson came in behind Finn carrying a crowbar. So that's where Finn had gone, to get our flunky to do the dirty work. Good. Kenny was a dirtbag.

Finn glanced at me. "Are you all..." The light fingers touched my mind, and Finn's sentence broke off. His head slowly pivoted to stare at Tim, his eyes widening. Finn's face reddened, and rage contorted it. My skinny cousin let out an animal yell and rushed Tim.

Tim, still occupied with getting whatever was stinging him over and over again off his body, didn't see Finn coming. My cousin threw a wild punch at Tim's head. Tim staggered backward and fell on the dirt. The sudden jolt broke the simple spell.

Tim rolled to his feet. In one smooth motion, he went around Finn and snatched the crowbar from Kenny. It all happened so quickly that Kenny barely reacted until it was too late. He backed away from Tim. My ex-husband advanced on Kenny, weapon raised to hit.

"Peri Jean, I know you found that treasure and got plenty of money from it. You gonna give me some of that money." He glanced at me for just a second, the old hatefulness bright in his eyes.

"Let's fight for it." I took a step toward him, fist doubled up, not caring if this was the last five seconds of my life.

"Peri Jean, let us handle this." Finn came up behind me and grabbed at my arm. I spun around and pointed one finger at him. He backed away until he bumped into Kenny. The two men glanced at each other, both not sure what to do. Well, I knew what to do.

Tim let out an incredulous laugh. "Come on then. I'll beat you like a little bitch. You thought the other time was bad?"

"I think you're in such bad health that I can whip your sorry ass. What's wrong with you? Hep C from those ugly fucking tattoos?" I circled Tim, knees loose to dance away when he swung. "Or did you end up in prison getting your asshole stretched? I heard you can get asshole disease in there." Tim winced. I went in for the kill. "You might be big enough to beat up a woman, but I bet you were everybody's little butthole bitch in the pen."

That was enough. Tim took a running step at me and swung the crowbar. It arced toward me, and I don't think my heart even pumped an extra time. I took a step backward.

Someone rushed up behind Tim and delivered a series of fast punches to his back. Tim staggered and tried to turn around.

Tanner Letts grabbed Tim's wrist and brought it down on his knee. The crowbar clanged on the dirt. My ex-husband reached into his back pocket.

Tanner didn't give him time to get out whatever he was going for. He reared back one fist and let it go, pivoting his whole body as the punch unfurled. It slammed into Tim's temple. Tim glared at me as his legs folded underneath him. He hit the ground. His head bounced once, and his eyes closed.

I ran over and kicked my ex in chest. It felt so good, I did it again. And again. I think I would have stood there kicking him all night had Tanner not dragged me off him.

Tanner, barely breathing hard, spun me where he could look at my face. I flailed in his grasp. If I could get back to my loser ex, I'd kick him to death.

Tanner grabbed both shoulders and shook me hard. "That's enough."

My teeth clicked together. I stopped struggling.

Tanner loosened his grip and stared into my eyes. He softened his voice. "He didn't hit you in the head?" I shook my head. Tanner turned to Finn and Kenny. "You two were going to let her fight that guy? Are you crazy? He'd have killed her." Tanner turned back to me. "And you. Even with him sick, he'd have hurt you. Do you have a death wish?"

I pushed Tanner's hands off me and muttered, "I had it under control."

The shock and shame went off Finn's face. He turned to Kenny and jerked a thumb at my ex-husband. "Get this piece of trash out of here."

Kenny shuffled over to Tim's still form and tried to sling the man over his shoulder. "I can't do this by myself." He grunted with the effort and finally dropped him back on the floor.

Finn rolled his eyes. "You can't carry him out of here like that during business hours. The three of us'll have to act like we're ejecting him. Tanner, you up?"

Tanner didn't answer right away. He leaned over my table staring at something. I went over and found Oscar's runes scattered all over the dirt floor. The gold-colored wheel Samantha had given me, the one that was supposed to help me find Oscar, lay beside them. Tanner pointed one finger at me. "Stay here while I help them. I want to talk to you about this stuff."

"You don't tell me what to do," I shot back.

Tanner spun and walked away from me, shoulders squared. Mad as I was at him for not letting me do things my way, I still noticed the shape of his butt as he brainstormed with Finn and Kenny on how to get Tim out of there. They finally agreed on a plan and dragged Tim toward the door.

I ignored them all and squatted over the scattered runes and the wheel. It was obvious Tim had come here for them, which meant he could be working with Oscar. But how? When I looked up again, my asshole ex was gone.

Good. I needed to get myself together. My position in the community of Sanctuary didn't allow for meltdowns.

———

I sat down at my séance table, hands still shaking. Tanner had said he wanted to talk about the runes. I didn't want another close encounter with him, but I needed his expertise with arcane items. Something was going on, and I needed help understanding what.

Besides, I might not have to face Tanner alone. Word of what happened would spread soon, and my tent would fill with concerned family and friends. I leaned my head forward and took deep breaths, concentrating on slowing my heart. My anger at the whole situation ebbed. Guilt stepped into its place.

Tanner had been right about one thing. I could have gotten myself killed, and it would have been because of my fury. The poor man didn't deserve the sharp end of my attitude. His pain over his losing his wife and daughters had to be unimaginable. I'd lost friends and family. It had been bad enough. But losing both your children and your life partner? I shied away from the thought. It was too much to contemplate. My mind, still agitated, jumped straight to what had happened with my ex.

Tim's finding the runes made no sense. Earlier, Hannah and I had put the runes back in their muslin bag and placed that in a black wooden box. I'd placed the box at the very back of the shabby chic buffet's bottom drawer. Tim had come in here looking for the runes.

He couldn't have known about them on his own. Someone must have sent him. It made sense that someone was Oscar Rivera. But how had he and Tim hooked up?

Tim had been in my tent the night before. Could he have taken a rune then? Sure. He could have dropped one or two in his pocket as he stood when I first confronted him. If he'd done that, Oscar would definitely be in contact. He'd even help Tim act against me.

I let out an irritated grunt. This wasn't helping me figure out a damn thing. Might as well clean up Tim's mess.

I stood, got out my rubber tongs, and began picking up Oscar's runes. My black opal gave me a few shocks to warn me of their magic. Then it went cold, so icy it made the skin on my chest ache.

I counted the runes, dropping each one in the muslin bag after I counted it. There were a total of sixteen. But this was the first time I'd counted them. There was no way to know if Tim took one or not. I used the tongs to put the muslin bag back into its black box and placed the box back in the buffet.

Samantha's wheel lay where Tim had left it, gleaming

in the dull overhead lights strung through the tent. My black opal gave me a sharp ping.

The wheel didn't look like a magical object at first glance. It just looked like a dull, tarnished metal disk. The only magic I'd ever seen it perform had manifested after making a deal with Sol, my chthonic contact in the dark outposts.

Realizing Tim had rifled through the cedar chest to get the wheel and that he might have damaged things I actually treasured, I hurried over and opened it. The smell of cedar enveloped me. I closed my eyes, took a deep breath, and blew it out my mouth. The familiar ritual comforted me, and I looked on the contents of the cedar chest with calm eyes.

Nothing seemed to be missing. Things were a bit moved around but not what I'd expect for them having been burgled.

A throat cleared behind me. Recognizing Tanner's husky purr, I took a deep breath and forced calmness into my mind. Then I turned.

Tanner looked as though he hadn't been doing anything more strenuous than taking out the trash. Which I suppose was exactly what he had been doing. In a funny way.

"He gone?" I asked.

Tanner nodded and came further into the tent. He reached into his back pocket and withdrew something. Metal caught the light. He came forward and set it on the table. "I pulled this off your ex-husband before we sent him on his way."

I got to my feet, expecting to see a rune or two, maybe some magical item I hadn't yet realized missing. Instead I found myself looking at a buck knife.

Tanner calmly raised the knife and flipped open the blade. He picked up one of my business cards. "May I?"

I shrugged. With careful precision, Tanner shaved an even sliver off the edge of the business card. He set the knife and the card down and settled his eyes on mine. They burned with intensity. "I stopped you from attacking him because I could see he was about to pull a weapon. You were so angry that you were acting without thinking. I've done a lot of fighting in my life. That's a deadly combination."

And here I'd thought Tim might have just beat me to death. My new friend, Tanner, had saved me from getting stabbed. I eyed the knife curiously, wondering how long it would have taken to die if Tim had stabbed me. Raising my head, I said, "But you risked yourself to help me."

Tanner shrugged. "Cecil explained how important you are to this community. If I want to stay, I have to respect that."

Dying still didn't frighten me like it should have, but Tanner had done me a good turn. And after I'd so callously brought back the sadness of his loss. I owed him big.

"You saved me. As far as I'm concerned, you've earned your place among us. Stay until it doesn't work for you anymore." I knew Cecil wouldn't disagree with me. He wanted Tanner here. Some of his reasons still made me uncomfortable, but there were other, good reasons to have Tanner around.

Tanner flushed at my pronouncement and shifted on his feet. The display of humility didn't work on this compact, powerful man. He took a step closer and leaned down so we were at eye level. "I have to admit something here. What I did, helping you, was for selfish reasons too."

"Oh?" I couldn't manage more than the one word, not with Tanner so close, his warm scent surrounding me.

"Yeah." His tongue teased the corner of his mouth. "I want a chance to get to know you. You're like nobody I've met so far."

My face heated along with the rest of my body. *Change the subject or do something stupid.* I got control of myself. I pushed the knife at his hand. "Do you want the knife? Maybe for a souvenir?"

Tanner picked it up, considered it, and slipped it into his back pocket. "I came back in here to talk about..." He trailed off.

I entertained the possibility of him closing the space between us and pressing his lips on mine. My body heated as I thought about how his mouth might taste.

Tanner took a step forward. His arm brushed against one breast. My nipple hardened, tingles shooting through me. Wade's face appeared in my mind. I loved him. How could I even sort of want Tanner to kiss me? But I did.

Instead of kissing me, Tanner leaned around me and stared at the floor. He jerked back and raised his eyes to mine. "Where'd it go?"

"Huh?" I'd been so sure we were about to engage in a

little slobber swapping that I didn't even know what he meant.

"The stuff that was on the floor." He enunciated very clearly, his lack of a Southern accent pronounced.

"Oh." Face on fire, I turned to the cabinet and took out the black box. I opened it, removed the muslin bag, and scattered the runes on the table.

Tanner backed away, hands up, mouth turned down in disgust. "No. The wheel."

I left the runes scattered on the table, went to my cedar chest, and took out the pouch holding the wheel. Turning, I found Tanner right behind me. He'd approached without me hearing again. I jumped in surprise and dropped the pouch. Tanner caught it before it was even halfway to the dirt floor.

"May I?" He had his finger on the rawhide drawstring, but the question in his green eyes indicated he'd do nothing without permission.

I nodded. "All yours."

Tanner went to the table but stopped and stared at the runes scattered over it. His face puckered as though he'd smelled something rotting. Suddenly, I smelled it too. I hurried to the table, used the tongs to sweep the runes back into their bag, put the bag in the box, and put away the whole mess.

The odor lingered, as did the pall of evil. Grabbing a bundle of white sage, I lit it and distributed smoke over the table to cleanse it. Those runes seemed to get nastier every time I dealt with them.

Tanner absently nodded his appreciation and sat down

at the table. His fingers gently worked the rawhide, loosening it enough to remove the disk. Touching the disk as though it might break, he pulled it out of the bag and set it before him on the table.

The contrast between this gentle man and the fierce warrior who'd beaten my useless ex-husband fascinated me. I sat down across from him, stuffing down all the questions that came to mind. I had a feeling I'd gather more if I let him take the lead.

"This *is* it," he muttered.

"What is it?" The wheel had saved my life but at great personal cost. After seeing Tanner's cornucopia and ankh, I didn't see why he'd be so impressed. It was the same sort of magic.

"My ability is not just finding items of power," Tanner said, gaze still fixed on the disk. "I can tell what an item will do if I get close enough to it. Do you know what it does? What it is?"

I was absolutely not going to admit how little I knew about the disk. "I've seen this disk used once." In a vision, but it still counted. "And I've used it once myself. It helped me kill a bunch of people."

Tanner frowned. But then he started to nod. "That makes sense in its way." He raised his head and met my gaze.

My body tightened. "Why don't you tell me what you know about the disk?" We weren't getting anywhere bandying about, and Tanner might give me a hint for how it could be used to discover where Oscar hid his soul.

Given recent events, I needed to immobilize Oscar more than ever.

"For starters, I wouldn't call it a disk. It's a wheel. More specifically, it's the wheel of life."

I thought about that. Samantha had called it a wheel. But Tanner's calling it a wheel of life gave me an immediate reference.

Mysti had an expensively framed poster on her wall with the words "wheel of life" printed on it. The poster listed the eight seasonal festivals and had stylized graphics for each one. My favorite, Beltane, showed a group of figures dancing around a maypole. Mysti said the wheel and its symbols represented the constant movement and cyclical changes of the year. She also said it represented our journey through life. Imbolc was the beginning, Samhain, the end. Tanner watched me, those amazing eyes probing into me.

When he spoke, his voice was soft, reflective. "No matter what else happens in Texas, seeing the wheel of life makes the trip worth it."

I tilted my head. Wasn't it just another arcane object?

Tanner shook his head as though I'd asked the question aloud. "The wheel of life is legendary. Nobody I ever spoke to knew if it was a myth or real. And if it had once existed, if it still did." So this was why he held it like something breakable. He was in awe.

I was still confused. "I thought the wheel of life was more of a calendar than a magical object. Mysti never mentioned anything magical about it." I bit off my words, too aware of how stupid they made me seem.

Tanner turned the wheel over and back quickly. The eight-piece pie shape etched itself into the metal. "But you've seen it do this? You had to've if you used the wheel."

"Yeah, I've seen that." I watched the wheel warily, waiting for it to open in the middle and for waterlogged hands to appear and start pulling to get out.

Tanner traced the pie shape. "These represent the seasons of life, the phases of life." His eyes sparkled. It was as though he'd woken up after a deep sleep. "The sorceress who can manipulate those seasons and phases may bless or curse anybody she chooses. Their fate is in her hands."

No wonder he was in awe. Power like that would come at a high premium. What Tanner said about the wheel fit with what I'd seen it do. Both Samantha and I had called down divine intervention in the form of Sol, a chthonic being, to snuff out the fates of dangerous people.

Tanner gazed at the wheel. "This is capable of great and terrible things. The consequences of using it for less than honorable purposes are too horrific to comprehend." He glanced up at me. "Only the most powerful of witches could use this without summoning a more powerful entity to help. You said you made the wheel work?"

Tanner stared at me the same way he'd stared at the wheel, with an awe that almost bordered on adoration. That I couldn't tell him I was a super-powerful witch disappointed me. Then I caught myself. Why did I care if I impressed Tanner Letts?

"I had to summon a dark being to help me do what needed doing." I shrugged and raised my eyebrows. Then I began explaining myself again, in spite of my declaration of not caring. "Both my life and the life of Dillon and Finn's daughter depended on it."

"That's a damn good reason. If it comes down to you or someone else, make sure you're the one who makes it out. Always." Fierce light burned in Tanner's eyes. It was the same way he'd looked when he'd punched out Tim.

"Since that night I killed those people, the wheel has been dormant. Maybe it decided we weren't a good match." I let out a humorless laugh. If that was the case, I'd never be able to use the wheel to find Oscar's spirit. Or I'd have to bargain away more of myself to the dark beings than I was willing.

"Nah. You just haven't figured out how to make it work." Tanner said the words the way a man does, with absolute confidence in their truth.

I found myself telling Tanner about the mantle and the spell my own grandmother had put on me to keep me from my gifts. I went on to the story about how Sol, a chthonic being, had eaten through the spell tissue but said I still had to get rid of the rest before I accessed my true power.

Tanner listened, a frown line deepening between his eyes. "Then we get rid of the spell. Because I have a strong feeling this wheel is just waiting for you to figure out how it works." He handed it across the table to me.

I took it, wanting to tell him my fears about removing the spell, how I wondered what of the real me would be left. But I couldn't find the right words. I didn't want to whine in front of this haunted yet tough man.

Outside the tent, a familiar sound started up.

"Hoooooo."

Miss Ugly. Dark must have fallen, and she'd come to collect me. The fears and insecurities I'd been battling all day rose up again to smite any confidence I'd managed to hold on to.

"Hooooo." Closer than ever.

Tanner half rose from his chair. "Is that what I think it is?"

"If you're thinking about a monster who has come to kill me, you'd be right." I delivered the pronouncement in the same way I might have said I needed to get back to work. "She's convinced I stole something from her. I'm going to try to find out what it was and see if she'll give me a chance to find it."

Tanner's eyes widened. "What do we do?"

"You run." I pushed back my chair and stood.

"Don't you tell me to run." Tanner glared at me. "I've never run in my life, and I'm not going to start now."

I gripped his arm, too aware of the charge passing between us, and tried to pull him toward the tent's flap. He locked his legs and used his weight to throw me off balance.

"Hoooooo." So close the wheel clattered on the table.

"Tanner, it's going to be too late. Get out." I let go of his arm and pointed at the flap.

He shook his head. I wanted to argue some more, but the tent's flap blew open. Miss Ugly flew toward me.

"Hooooo." The sound rattled my eardrums.

Somewhere underneath it, I heard Tanner's scream. He should have left when I told him.

9

I stepped in front of Tanner, wanting to help him the same way he'd helped me. He didn't deserve whatever Miss Ugly might do to him.

Tanner pushed me aside and assumed a boxing stance in front of Miss Ugly. His first punch hit her in the chest. The second one slammed into her long, hooked nose. The punches had no effect.

She raked her claws across Tanner's chest, laying open shirt and skin. Blood soaked into the ruined white cloth. Tanner staggered backward, eyes full of pain but also burning with hate. He tripped over his own feet and sprawled on the dirt floor.

Miss Ugly advanced on me. I backed to the other side of the tent, hoping I'd lead her away from Tanner. She followed, a line of saliva dripping from her mouth. Was it from eagerness to skin her teeth into me? I nearly gagged.

"Hoooooo." Her awful sound made the tent sound like a wind tunnel.

I clapped my hands over my ears and walked backward, not sure exactly what to do. My heels connected with my cedar chest of magic items. I'd forgotten to look behind me. What a genius move.

The impact knocked me off balance, and I sat on the thing with a hard thump. The impact jarred me so hard I bit my tongue. Pain radiated out from it.

"Wait a minute." I held my hands out in front of me.

"No more minutes. You are mine." Miss Ugly's teeth, awful green and black clumps, flashed. I imagined those teeth biting into my cooked flesh. The idea froze me in place. Miss Ugly's swampy, mildewy smell filled my nostrils, burning my sinuses.

My mind ran crazy circles, trying to remember what it was supposed to do. A question? Yes. There was some question I was supposed to ask Miss Ugly. Now if I could only remember it.

Tanner ran over. He'd taken his nine irons amulet off his belt and picked the cross out of the jumble of charms. He pushed the cross against Miss Ugly's flesh. It sizzled where the cross touched it.

Miss Ugly let out a ground-shaking howl and clapped her hand to the side of her face. Her bony shoulders heaved. A sound similar to sobs came from her, and she curled away from us, using her free arm to guard her head.

Tanner held out one hand to me. I let him pull me to my feet and climbed out of the corner where Miss Ugly had trapped me. My mind went back to normal programming. I had been going to ask her what she thought I'd stolen.

Tanner gave me a light tug to follow him. I took a big step around Miss Ugly. I'd rather be as far away from her as possible when I asked her my question. I'd think better. Just as I went past, she pulled her hand away from her cheek. Burned flesh stretched with it and tore off. The smell of seared meat hit me.

That and the look of that rubbery skin pulling away from her face sent my stomach into a tailspin. I scrambled, trying to get away. She whipped forward and closed the hand with the burned skin stuck to it on my bare forearm. The burned flesh still sizzled from its contact with iron, popping against my skin. My stomach hitched.

"Do something," Tanner yelled. For a man who hadn't wanted to give up a few minutes ago, he sure looked pissing-his-pants scared now. Eyes eating up his face, tanned skin faded to a sickly yellow, his panicked breathes tore out of him.

I was supposed to ask Miss Ugly something. What? A few seconds ago, I'd known what to ask. But the feel of Miss Ugly's flesh on mine had clawed it away.

"Thief," Miss Ugly growled. "Thief must be punished."

It came then. "The man who said I stole from you lied. I don't have anything of yours." I tried to yank my arm out of her grasp. She pulled me closer like she was going to lay a kiss on me. I shrank away from her, but she held me where I had to look into her ugly face.

"Thieves always lie." The smell of her breath coated the inside of my nose. I gagged, then took a few breaths and got myself under control.

"I'm not lying. Oscar Rivera is the liar." I gave my arm another yank.

Tanner, still holding on to my other hand, tugged me. Miss Ugly gripped me tighter. Tanner, teeth bared, bent his knees and put his whole weight in the tug of war.

"No," I yelled. "You're going to pull my arm out of socket." Tanner relaxed some of the pressure but tightened his grip on me.

Miss Ugly cupped my chin with her free hand. "If you come without a fight, I'll kill you before I cut you up to cook you."

Images, each more horrific than the last, flashed through my mind. I begged Tanner, "Please don't let go."

"I won't." Tanner repeated himself several times, eyes locked on mine. "I will not let you go."

Hannah ran into the room. "What's this I hear about your sorry ex…" She trailed off, eyes widening as she took in my visitor. Her brain snapped back into gear quicker than mine had. "Ask her a question, Peri Jean."

I stared at Hannah. "Huh?"

Hannah hurried over to stand behind Tanner. "When she had you pinned last night, you escaped after asking her a question. Maybe it'll work again."

I was so panicked, I could barely mold my thoughts into question form. "If it doesn't work, do what it takes to get me away from her."

"I'll help Tanner pull," Hannah said.

I turned back to Miss Ugly, that combination of frying meat and swamp rot shooting up my nose. "What did I steal from you?"

Miss Ugly shrank. It wasn't by much, but the length of her fingers shortened by half.

I got myself together and did it again. "What did Oscar tell you I stole?"

Her fingers shortened to normal human length, and her body shrank to eye level with me. I gave my arm a good hard yank and got it away from her.

I ran at Tanner and Hannah and pressed myself against them. We all held on to each other as Miss Ugly examined her newly reduced fingers.

"I am your fate. You cannot escape. If not this night, then the next." But her voice sounded smaller, weaker. Could I kill her? I was afraid to try.

"Even though I didn't steal from you, I'm willing go get whatever is missing. Return it to you." Rivulets of sweat streamed down my back, one right after the other.

Miss Ugly came toward me, her lips puckering. "Hoooooo." Her eyes bugged out so far it looked as though they'd pop out on their stalks. Her face wrinkled and seemed to pull backward. She grew several inches.

"No, no, no," Tanner chanted beside, his arm tightening around my waist.

"What was stolen from you?" I yelled the question, and Miss Ugly shrank again.

She stopped in her tracks, cutting off her 'hoooooo' in mid *o*. "It is hours to daylight. You can't continue this way. If you do not come now, I'm going to eat you alive."

There was no way I'd go with this thing so she could turn me into steak tartare. "What did I steal from you?"

Miss Ugly shrank so much, she was barely taller than me.

This time I didn't give her time to respond. "What did I steal? Tell me."

She shrank again, now shorter than me. If she got small enough, maybe she'd wink out of existence. Maybe. But she'd be back again tomorrow. In my pause, she grew back a few inches of height. I spoke quickly. "What do you need me to find?"

She shrank again. This time a howl, one I recognized as frustration, came from her. She bared her rotten teeth at me. "You stole my lantern."

I fired out another question. "If I get back your lantern, will you leave me alone forever?"

She shrank at my question, now the size of a grade-school kid. Her head hung, and her sides heaved. She was tired. Had to be.

I begged the universe to let her say yes to my proposal. If the dark beings were taking bets on whether I could survive her, there must be some clever way of beating her. Maybe I'd found it.

"I reward a good deed with a kindness." Her voice, now thin and weak, was barely audible.

That was no kind of answer. She wasn't promising to quit coming after me. She was simply promising kindness. Kindness to her might be giving me a choice of the apple she put in my mouth as she roasted me.

"But will you..." I began the next question. This might reduce her to baby-sized. The next one after that would make her too tiny to see. Even if she came back tomorrow, I'd be rid of her for one night.

She shouted over me, her voice small and squeaky. "I cannot promise more than a kindness. Our fates are married."

She rushed forward, the ugliest troll in the world, and launched herself at my legs. Within seconds, she'd climbed up my body, grunting and making slobbery sounds, against my skin. I shuddered with revulsion.

I pushed at her with all my might. My hands just slid off her rubbery skin. Tanner grabbed Miss Ugly's short little legs and tried to yank her off me. She dug in her claws, ripping at my skin. I screamed in pain. Tanner let go and backed away, face set in desperation.

Shelly burst into the tent, her mouth open in shock. Cecil crowded in behind her. He took one look at my predicament, and his mouth opened with a scream that the roaring in my ears prevented me from hearing. He clutched his shirt and fell to his knees. Shelly dropped next to him, frantically pulling at him, trying to see if he was okay. They couldn't help.

Miss Ugly had wrapped herself around my torso like a deranged toddler. She lifted herself up. With one sharp fingernail, she pricked me on the forehead between my eyes. That done, she popped out of existence.

One other part of Jadine's vision came back. She'd claimed to see me with light streaming out of a spot between my eyes. Everything in her vision was coming true, and I didn't know what to do about it. I sagged, sobs of frustration just begging to be let out into the world. Tanner held me up with one arm, but his knees wobbled.

"It's okay," I mumbled and let my legs fold. Tanner eased me to the dirt floor and plopped down beside me. I barely reacted to his presence. I was too busy thinking how I'd probably be spirited away to be eaten the next night.

10

I closed my eyes. What could Miss Ugly have meant by her lantern? I didn't know much about her. All I knew had to do with eating. Maybe I should just wrap myself in a bow tomorrow night and meet Miss Ugly with a bottle of hot sauce. But I wouldn't. I was too angry at Oscar and at Miss Ugly herself. I wanted to fight them as hard as I could.

Hannah staggered a few feet away to sit down. She closed her eyes. "That was intense."

I nodded and rocked back and forth on the dirt floor. My skin tingled from the blood still rushing through my veins. My cheeks felt numb. Gray dots danced on the edge of my vision.

"Don't pass out." Tanner nudged me with one hand. "You gotta figure out how to find her lantern."

He didn't have to keep reminding me. It wasn't as though I'd forgotten. I groaned and hung my head.

Normally, I'd ask Priscilla Herrera what Miss Ugly

wanted. Priscilla wasn't nicey-nice, but she always helped. Now she couldn't. She'd been blocked.

Orev had been taken away just like Priscilla, and I had no idea how to get him back. The thought pissed me off. Orev probably could have shown me a great deal of insight into Miss Ugly. But not now.

Wade had been my security. The man who always knew what to do and whose loyalty would keep him in my corner long after he should have gone home. Besides, if Miss Ugly took a bite out of me, he'd heal it. Easy. But he had been gone for months.

I wished for the past, wished for things to be the way they had been even a week before Miss Ugly showed up. It hadn't been great, but it had been better than this. But yesterday was gone forever.

I pulled my thoughts off myself and glanced over at Cecil. He'd taken his hand off his chest, but sweat poured down his face.

Too weak to get up and go to him, I said, "Papaw, are you okay?"

He nodded. "Just a little shock, that's all. Shelly and I came by to ask about your burglar. We did not expect to see that thing climbing up your legs."

Maybe Cecil could help. "You've now met Miss Ugly. She thinks I stole her lantern. She said she'd reward me with kindness if I gave it back." Saying what I had to do aloud only made it sound more impossible.

When was the last time I woke up in the morning and didn't have a bunch of crazy stuff hanging over me? Back in Gaslight City. Back when Memaw was still alive. Back in the lost past. Pining for the past now, or trying to live there, would get me eaten. I needed to let it go but couldn't.

"What is that spot on your forehead?" Shelly got up from Cecil's side and approached me. She leaned down to stare at me.

"It's a cut that monster made on her." Tanner leaned back on both hands.

Shelly pulled a tissue out of the pocket of her tight slacks and dabbed at the cut. She examined the dot of blood on the tissue, made a face, and dropped it in my lap.

"You know what I thought it was, just for a second there?" Shelly got my chair from beside the table and sat down, crossing one leg over the other as though we were at a dinner party.

I shook my head, too tired to answer, and not sure I cared at this point.

"A third eye." She waited for a response, but nobody moved. We were all too tired. "When I was a teenager, after my mother threw me out, I lived with a very nice family as their maid. One of the other maids, an older Italian lady, believed she had a third eye." Shelly put her fingers to her forehead to demonstrate. "She was always going on about her third eye showed her this or that. I figured she just listened at doorways. I ran away later that year and forgot about it. But when I saw that mark on your forehead, it all came rushing back."

I thought about my magic, the part of the mantle not blocked off from me. Was a third eye part of that? I had no idea, nor did I have a clue how it would help me. Before the trouble with Miss Ugly, I had always depended on Priscilla to tell me what to do next.

But now Priscilla wasn't here. I'd have to research the lore on the third eye myself. That would be the only way I'd get any kind of idea. Was this how things worked for Mysti?

I got out my phone and did a search on third eye folklore. "This says the third eye allows vision beyond ordinary sight. Religious visions, chakras, precognition, out-of-body experiences."

Nobody spoke. I read a little more. Nothing resonated or sounded like it was within my abilities. Experience had taught me that the supernatural manifested differently for each person. I closed out the tiny web page in frustration. Miss Ugly might not have even been trying to point out a third eye. She might have meant she intended to eat my brains first.

Hannah's voice startled me out of my thoughts. "I got curious about the Slavic folklore that Mysti mentioned and did a little research." Hannah watched me, waiting for me to say I remembered what Mysti said.

I shrugged. I had put it out of my mind as soon as the conversation was over.

"The folklore character is called Baba Yaga. The folk-tale is actually Russian in origin." Talking about this had Hannah sitting up straighter, a light in her eyes that I rarely saw anymore.

I tried to stay focused.

"In this story, Baba Yaga lived in a house with a porch

made of bones. The house's lock was made of human teeth, and the house itself sat on a huge chicken leg." Hannah, more excited than ever, talked with her hands.

I hated to discourage her but had to speak up. "I didn't see Miss Ugly's house. All I saw was the clearing where she had her cauldron set up."

"With the skulls around it." Hannah nodded, not discouraged in the least. "The most popular folktale about this Baba Yaga stars a beautiful young girl named Vasilisa the Fair."

"Am I Vasilisa the Fair?" I grinned, caught Tanner watching me, and ducked my head. How could I possibly be shy with this guy? He'd saved my life twice today. I glanced back up. Tanner winked at me. I swallowed hard.

Hannah, seeing the whole exchange, smiled wickedly at me. If I had been closer, I'd have kicked her. Hannah continued, "I think Vasilisa was blond, probably taller too. In the story, Vasilisa's mother is dead, and her father has married an awful woman who has two daughters older than Vasilisa."

"This sounds like Cinderella," Tanner said.

"It does have some of the same elements." Hannah nodded. "But in Vasilisa the Beautiful, the father leaves her with the wicked stepmother and the two lazy stepsisters. The story takes place in a time when electricity does not exist. The family has to keep one candle lit so they'll have something to light the other candles from."

"Sounds dire." I glanced at Tanner, and we exchanged a secret grin.

Hannah rolled her eyes. "Anyway...one of the lazy stepsisters puts out the last candle. The wicked stepmother sends Vasilisa to Baba Yaga's hut in order to get light from Baba Yaga. When Vasilisa gets there, Baba Yaga holds her prisoner and makes her do chores in exchange for the light. I'm thinking maybe the light mentioned in the folktale is the lantern Miss Ugly wants from you."

Lantern. She'd finally mentioned a lantern. This had to be it. I sat up straight. "You're finally going to talk about the lantern?"

"Yep. Once the chores are done, Baba Yaga gives Vasilisa a skull on a stick with burning coals inside, and that's her lantern." Hannah dug around on my table until she found my cigarettes. She lit one with relish, throwing her head back and jetting smoke at the ceiling.

"I want one of those," Cecil said in a weak voice.

"Not just no, but hell no." Shelly stood, marched over to her husband, and motioned him to get up. "I'm going to get Papaw something cool to drink. If you young people need us..."

She didn't finish the sentence. Instead, she pulled Cecil to his feet and nearly dragged him out of the tent. Hannah and I raised our eyebrows at each other. Shelly must have gotten more serious about Cecil not smoking.

"Let me get this straight." I reached for the cigarettes, and Hannah gave them to me. "Miss Ugly's is really Baba Yaga, and Baba Yaga's lantern is a skull on a stick."

Tanner began shaking his head before I finished asking the question. "Baba Yaga is the name of the character in the folktale. Everything said in the folktale may not be how Miss Ugly is choosing to present herself to you right now."

I remembered what Mysti had said now. The folktales reflected some scared person trying to process what they'd experienced and warn others. I digested what I knew. "So what now? Do we go find a skull and a stick? Stick 'em together?"

"I doubt it's that simple." Tanner got up, brushed the dirt off his nice-looking behind, and went to stand near the door.

"I tend to agree with Tanner," Hannah said.

"Where did Vasilina leave the skull lantern in the folktale?" I was getting frustrated.

Hannah giggled. "It's Vasilisa, not Vasilina."

Tanner laughed. "I like Vasilina."

"That's because you're a man." Hannah rolled her eyes. "In the folktale, Vasilisa carried the skull lantern back home. Fire came from its eye sockets and burned her stepmother and stepsisters to ash. Vasilisa buried the skull in the garden and went on to marry a rich dude."

"Then all we need to do is fly to Russia, find where Vasilisa lived, and excavate her garden?" I dragged on my cigarette, enjoying the banter in spite of the night's horror.

Tanner, still standing by the flap leading outside, laughed. "No. You both forgot something. Finding magical items is what I do. Let me set some things up next door, and I'll come back to get you." He lifted his shirt off his chest and examined the scratches left by Miss Ugly's fingernails. He squirmed with discomfort.

"There's mild poison in Miss Ugly's fingernails," I said. "You're feeling its effects right now." I used Tanner's injuries as an excuse to stare at the bare skin of his chest peeking through the rips in the torn shirt. If they gave out awards for insensitivity, I'd have won the Olympics.

"You clean those cuts up before you do anything else," Hannah said.

"He can have some of the healing salve I made from those recipes in Samantha's grimoire." I stood and rummaged in the cabinet I'd caught Tim burgling a lifetime ago. I took out a metal tin with a screw-on top and took it over to Tanner. "Now this stuff works. So clean the wound good before you put any on. Wait a minute. I have something for that too." Scolding myself for letting Tanner's physique rattle me, I went back and got a handful of the white willow bark Samantha sent home with me. "Use this to draw out the poison and the pain."

Tanner took everything I gave him, an odd, almost sad look of gratitude on his face. "Thank you," he finally said and ducked through the flap.

When he was gone, I pulled out a small mirror and began doctoring my own wounds, too tired of the stress and the constant threat to do any more than a half-assed job. The old Hannah would have flitted around me, trying to help. This one watched through amused eyes.

"Change your mind about Tanner yet?" Hannah put the cigarette between her lips and gave it a pull.

"Shut up," I muttered.

She laughed long and hard.

———

For what seemed like the zillionth time that day, Hannah and I straightened my tent. She got a bundle of white sage and walked the room distributing the smoke. Though I had been doing more personal business than working the last couple of days, this room was the place where I generated income. I needed it to be as free of negative influence as possible.

My phone buzzed with a text from an unknown number. *This is Tanner. I'm set up. Ignore the closed sign on the door.*

"How did he know my number?" I said aloud, trying to remember when I gave it to him.

Hannah turned so red she looked like a cherry with hair.

"Girl." I shook my head at her and showed her a doubled-up fist. I texted Tanner back. *On the way.*

Though Hannah hadn't seen what I sent, she said, "I'm not going with you. You and Tanner can handle this alone."

I shoved my phone back in my pocket. "You know what? I'm sick of people trying to force me and Tanner together. Poor guy's still mourning the loss of his family." I told her about Tanner losing his wife and daughters in a car accident.

She stayed quiet while I spoke, seemed to be listening. But then she said, "It's never the right time. Live each moment the best you can. You never know when your whole world's going to get turned upside down and you have to start building it again." She walked toward the door.

I tried again. "Come on. It'll be an adventure, get the old adrenaline pumping."

"I'm going to go paint a few faces." She turned to leave. I opened my mouth to beg. She shook her head. "Remember how you told me that part of your reason for deciding to move out of Griff and Mysti's house and travel with your family was that you were a third wheel with Griff and Mysti?"

Understanding flooded me. I nodded that I got her point and let her leave without further protests. Then I made a call on my phone.

Shelly answered on the first ring. "What is it?"

"I'm going to be out of my tent for a bit. Would you send someone to sit in here?"

Shelly paused for several seconds before answering. "You think your ex is coming back?"

"I wouldn't put anything past him." I left my tent and put the closed sign on the flap.

"I'll have somebody over there in two swishes of a cow's tail." Shelly liked trying out Southernisms. The down-home expressions mixed with her clipped Yankee accent made me laugh. After the night I'd had, the laughter felt good. Shelly laughed with me. "I thought you'd like that."

We said our goodbyes. I hung up and walked toward Tanner's tent, trying to talk myself out of liking him too much. He'd come and then he'd go, the way they all did.

The smell of unfamiliar incense came from Tanner's

tent. As he'd commanded, I ignored the closed sign and went inside. Smoke hung low in the small enclosure.

Tanner had emptied one of his glass cases and now leaned over it. He'd changed shirts and wore one of his tight, faded T-shirts. He raised his head and tucked a lock of his long, brown hair behind one ear.

"Sorry about the incense. I know it's strong, but horseheal helps me focus when I'm using my scrying mirror." He held up an oblong piece of shiny black rock.

Immediately attracted to the item, I moved forward, peering at it through the smoke.

"It's obsidian," Tanner said in response to my interest. "This one belonged to Jackson, my grandfather. The one who was friends with Cecil?"

I nodded to let him know I followed and came close enough to see that the extent of his pageantry was his black mirror and a smoking bowl of incense. "Before we get started, let's talk about a problem I foresee."

Tanner put his hands on his hips and nodded.

"Baba Yaga is a Russian folktale. That's far, far away from here. I don't even speak the language." My mind helpfully dredged up more reasons we couldn't go out of the country on a whim. Passports were first in line. I had never even applied for one.

"You mentioned that back in your tent. The reason I interrupted you is we likely won't have to travel across the world." Tanner pulled a small striped, woven blanket from the back of the cabinet and set the scrying mirror on top of it.

"Can we somehow summon the skull lantern to us?" I tried and failed to think of a workable scenario.

Tanner smiled, and it was completely charming. I smiled back. We stared at each other for several useless seconds.

"I've heard you call the beings from beyond the veil chthonic beings," he began.

"Yeah. I got that from my friend Mysti Whitebyrd. I also call them dark beings." The latter name came from Priscilla Herrera's grimoire and my conversations with her spirit.

"Jackson, my grandfather, lived in California a good forty years, and he never lost his Texas accent. I loved him for that, and I loved his name for the dark beings. It was boogers." Tanner's grin broadened.

Wade had also called the dark beings boogers. The memory stabbed at my heart, waking up the heartbreak. I smiled at Tanner anyway. What was that saying Hannah kept spouting? Fake it until you make it.

Tanner came around the counter to stand close to me. "Let me tell you what I've managed to learn about boogers over the years, some from my own experience, some from Dad and Grampa."

This was the most I'd seen Tanner talk, and the most confident he'd seemed since I met him. I liked it too much.

Maybe sensing my openness to him, Tanner cocked one elbow out and leaned on the counter. "You've mentioned mythology and folklore as a source for information about boogers. Mythology and folklore are surprisingly universal. You can find the same types of stories and the same themes in different corners of the world."

It hit me then. Much as I was enjoying this side of Tanner, I couldn't help blurting out my realization. "Boogers can meet up with humans anytime and anyplace."

Tanner nodded and pointed at me. "You got it. So Miss Ugly has likely played out different versions of the Vasilisa story all over the world since the dawn of time."

"If we have the right story, and if that was her." Worries crowded in, reminding me this could all be for naught. Miss Ugly might have been talking about something else altogether.

"Don't go there." Tanner shook his head and put his free hand on my arm. It was warm and sent sparks of desire through me. Tanner startled and removed his hand. He'd felt it too. "We have a limited amount of time until tomorrow night, and we have to act on the intelligence we've been able to put together."

"You're right. We have to just do this and see where it takes us." I turned to the scrying mirror. "I thought you said items called to you."

"That's one way I find them, yes. But they have to be in close proximity for that to work." Tanner lit the bowl of incense next to his mirror. "This method requires having a bit of the item's maker available to me." Tanner pointed at his chest where Miss Ugly scratched him. "Even though I did what you said, some of her poison likely got in my system. It'll help us find her skull lantern."

"What do I need to do?" I reached for the mantle and

felt it fluttering like a candle flame. It was tired from the show I'd put on with my crummy ex-husband and even more tired from the encounter with Miss Ugly, but I had a little more to give before I had to recharge.

"Cecil told me you can lend your energy to people. I need all the range I can get on this." He pointed to the scrying mirror.

"It's easier with family, but I can lend you power." I stiffened as I remembered how it worked. "I'll have to touch you."

Tanner stilled at that and gave the picture of his family a guilty glance. I understood. Neither of us were ready to move on from the pain of our pasts.

"I can put my hand on your shoulder," I said quickly, not quite able to articulate the idea that it didn't have to be sexual. Both Tanner and I would have probably incinerated from embarrassment at the suggestion.

Tanner smiled, blushing at the same time. "I can probably stand that."

I grabbed on to the mantle's smooth edge, letting its power drop over my vision. The black opal pulsed with each of my heartbeats, growing warm as I let the mantle manifest. The world of Tanner's tent took on a glow. The smoke from the incense turned bright white and seemed to have tracers connected to it.

Around Tanner moved a shifting nimbus. A closer look revealed the faces of Tanner's wife and daughters. Their spirits protected Tanner, watched over him. I moved closer, and the woman's ghost changed her face into a long, ugly horror mask with hollow eye sockets.

My first instinct was to recoil, and I let myself do it for a second. But I knew from experience I had to face my own fears because they weren't going away. I gathered my strength, pulled on the earth energy from the ground at my feet, and accessed the part of me that was made to communicate with the spirit world.

I reached out to Tanner's dead wife, tried to soothe her, to assure her that Tanner needed me for what he was about to do. She rushed at me with the likely expectation I'd run. I stood my ground and tapped into her emotions, something I'd been able to do ever since I could remember.

Her anger and sadness about the way things had ended for her and her daughters washed over me, so understandable and raw it almost became my own. But I had learned to stay on top of that too. I opened my heart to her, let her see my good intentions, my lust for Tanner, my hurt over Wade, my fear that my life would never be anything I truly loved, all of it.

Tanner twisted to face me. "Are we doing this?"

I waited for his dead wife's answer. She'd either step aside or make me fight her. I didn't want to do that, but I would do what it took to find the skull lantern. She glared at me with suspicious and jealous eyes but stood down. I stepped forward, put my hand on Tanner's shoulder. He jumped at my touch. I pumped the power of the mantle into him.

Tanner leaned over the obsidian scrying mirror and slowed his breathing. The lights strung through the tent buzzed, brightened, then flickered. I pushed more of the mantle into him. He let out a pained grunt and stiffened. At the same time, the mark of Miss Ugly's signature on my chest flamed to life.

I glanced down at the front of my shirt to see it smoking, light glowing beneath it. Tanner was at the wrong angle for me to see if his wound glowed as well, but the sweat dampening the back of his shirt gave me a good idea something was causing him intense pain.

I leaned around Tanner's body, now sharing his gift, and watched the black obsidian scrying mirror. Images swirled in it. Faces, places, even animals. Finally it settled on a neon light, the kind you see over a bar. I could only see two of the letters, an *o* and an *n*.

Tanner's shoulder tightened underneath my hand. His body quivered with effort. The view on the scrying mirror began to pan out. More and more letters of the sign became visible. So did tables with people sitting at them, enjoying pitchers of beer and mystery drinks in smudged glasses. Finally, the whole sign was visible. It read, "Welcome to the Pale Horse Saloon." As we watched, it flashed blue, then red, then white.

Tanner began to tremble hard, sweat rolling down his face. The view panned out further until we saw the whole room. At the very back, a set of eyes glowed in the darkness.

Tanner made the view zoom in on those eyes. We got close enough to see it was a skull on what looked like a silver-embossed walking cane. A light glowed from it, but no candle or other source was visible.

Tanner panned out again. I searched for people

guarding the skull lantern or for anybody who might give us trouble. Everybody seemed too focused on having a fun night out getting soused, and nothing else.

The panning out stopped with a jolt, as though we'd hit a wall. Tanner's knees bent as he strained to direct what we saw. But our view didn't budge. The image winked out.

11

———————

Tanner released the tension in his muscles. His dead wife's face appeared, wanting me off her husband, worried I'd hurt him. Understandable. I let go and stepped back.

Tanner turned to me, shaking his head. "I'm sorry. It was like something just blocked us. I've never had that happen."

"Don't apologize." I already had my phone out, tapping in "Pale Horse Saloon." Immediately, I got a match for Pale Horse, Texas. The word saloon appeared in the preview. "Hey, come here. I think we got it."

Tanner came to stand next to me. This time, I knew enough to search for the presence of his lost family. Though I could no longer see them because I wasn't tapping the mantle, they hovered nearby, insuring Tanner would never take a step without their presence hanging over him. I tamped down the attraction to him, tried to keep it all business, and had a harder time than I'd expected.

"Can you see?" I asked Tanner. He reached two fingers out, enlarged the text on the screen, and nodded. I tapped on the entry for Pale Horse, Texas. It turned out to be an article in an e-zine devoted to creepy sites in Texas. It read:

Pale Horse, Ghostly Rider
by Louisa Mora

Pale Horse, Texas is a ghost town built on top of a ghost town. It became a ghost town again only eighteen months after being rediscovered by investment prodigy Dane Whitlock.

Whitlock discovered Pale Horse, Texas when he won the historic Hill Country estate, Rosen Ranch, once owned by cattle tycoon Alton Rosen, at auction.

The text broke to show a picture of a pristine rock mansion shadowed by ancient oaks. Winding sidewalks cut through the manicured yard. A "For Sale" sign was stabbed into the lush grass. "The diaries were in a box in the attic. I sort of wish I had never found them," Whitlock said when this journalist caught up with him at his Austin, Texas condo.

The diaries Mr. Whitlock refers to belonged to an Eleanor Rosen, whose brother, Alton, Jr., left Rosen Ranch in hopes of beginning his own cattle empire. Alton, Jr., claimed an expanse of land even farther west in Texas, in isolated Gunpowder County. There Alton, Jr. discovered the remnants of an early settlement.

Many of the structures had decorative features created out of human bones. One structure, which seemed to be a meeting place, contained a lantern made from a human skull.

Despite his fear, Alton, Jr. tried to make a go of his investment. He used local stone to build a church, hoping the presence of the Holy Spirit would chase away any demonic entities. He named the town Pale Horse in loose reference to the apocalypse described in the book of Revelation found in the Holy Bible.

The text stopped to display a picture of a building built of reddish tan stones with the peaked windows and steeple seen on older churches. A second picture zeroed in on the building's cornerstone. It read "Erected in 1852" and had a Mason's symbol and another one that looked like a figure eight with an extra loop.

Alton, Jr.'s first letters after building the church reported more settlers had moved to Pale Horse and things were going well. But then a final letter arrived with the following message: "Sis, these people have been here before. They were the original settlers. They tricked me, and now all is lost. I'm sending this letter with a traveler passing through. If it finds you, and you haven't heard from me, know that I loved you and thought you a fine sibling. Tell Father I'm sorry for this failure and for the loss of my eternal soul."

"More than a century and a half after Alton Rosen, Jr. headed out to the wilds of Gunpowder County, Texas to find his fortune, Dane Whitlock did the same. Unlike Mr. Rosen, Dane Whitlock had modern technology on his side.

"He used satellite photos to find the town of Pale Horse and had hired guides to help him find his way to the town."

The text stopped to show a picture of downtown Pale Horse, which wasn't more than a few sun-warped, dilapidated wooden buildings with tumbleweeds stuck between them. The caption read "Pale Horse as it looked the first day Dane Whitlock laid eyes on it."

Whitlock wanted to make Pale Horse a destination for young hipsters and immediately began pumping money into the site, arranging for modern conveniences and turning Alton Rosen, Jr.'s church into a saloon, which he named the Pale Horse Saloon.

But Whitlock's dream was short-lived.

"Everything went wrong," Whitlock says. "The

appearance of the skull lantern mentioned in Alton Rosen, Jr.'s letter to Eleanor seemed to make matters worse.

"We put the creepy thing in the saloon. That's when things really went south. We began hearing hoofbeats nearby. We'd go check, and nothing would be there." Dane Whitlock has never been back to his ghost town and says he'll die before he returns. He says anyone interested in purchasing Pale Horse, Texas should contact him.

The text broke one last time to show a cleaned-up Pale Horse, Texas downtown with a large realtor's sign in front of the first building.

But the story doesn't end there. Legend trippers who have made the arduous journey out to Pale Horse, Texas report meeting a variety of odd people, some of whom sound like something out of a horror movie.

When this journalist put out the call for experiences of people who have journeyed to Pale Horse, she got reports about people with glowing eyes who chased intruders, foaming at the mouth.

Note from Louisa: Please remember that Pale Horse, Texas is private property and visitors are technically trespassing.

A chill crawled up my back as I finished the article. Pale Horse didn't sound like the kind of place I wanted to visit. I handed the phone to Tanner and tried to walk off the odd details I'd just read about.

Tanner read for a few more seconds after I finished. "Despite what this article says, it looks like someone's settled out there. If you want to get the skull lantern back, we'll have to pay them a visit."

I didn't want to visit Pale Horse, Texas. It sounded like one of those creepy places I always ended up having to go to. But Tanner was right. This was the only way to get the skull lantern for Miss Ugly. "Fine. Let's see if we can figure out where it is."

———

Within thirty minutes, we'd talked to Cecil and told him our plans so someone would know where we'd gone in case we never showed up again. Shelly had gotten Kenny and his wife, Anita, to watch my tent. They grudgingly agreed to close up both Tanner's and my tents and take all the valuables back to camp.

Tanner did a little more research on Pale Horse, Texas and learned Dane Whitlock had spent millions to put in a passable road between Pale Horse and the nearest town. He thought we could make the trip in less than two hours.

That put us at the Pale Horse Saloon before two a.m., closing time for most bars. Not that people running an illegal business on land where they were trespassing kept regular business hours.

"Let's take my truck." Tanner walked past my much newer truck to his beat-up jalopy.

"Think it'll make the trip?" I put my hand on my ride.

"It made it all the way from California." Tanner straightened and fixed me with his intense stare.

"How many times did you have to stop and look for a mechanic?" I had no intention of antagonizing Tanner, but the way he stiffened let me know I'd crossed some line. "We get out there in the sticks, and there won't be anybody to help us."

Tanner crossed his arms over his chest. "I've been to Death Valley. I know more about isolated country than you can imagine."

I threw out what I hoped was the winning card. "In that truck?"

Tanner slumped, and I knew I had him. I unlocked my truck and started climbing into the driver's seat.

"Can I at least drive?" His voice came from right behind me. He'd snuck up on me again.

I didn't like handing over control to Tanner and wasn't sure why he'd expect me to. Then I thought of all the sadness surrounding him, how grateful he'd seemed when I gave him the salve and the white willow bark for his wound. Maybe he needed to feel in control of his fate. I handed him the keys.

"If you get sleepy, let me know. I don't want to end up in some hundred-foot ravine with a rattlesnake all coiled and ready to bite me. " I raised my eyebrows at Tanner, and he gave me a sheepish grin and nodded.

I climbed into the truck and watched as Tanner settled

into the driver's seat, plugged his phone in to charge, and started the directions. After the hours of running back and forth, of fighting demons both figurative and literal, the fatigue I'd been ignoring came back full force. My eyes drifted closed.

I woke when the truck ran over a rough spot. The dashboard clock showed I'd been asleep an hour and a half. I glanced over at Tanner. He had both hands on the wheel.

"Sorry that woke you up. We just left the main road and crossed onto the road Whitlock had built. The entrance has been torn up. Wouldn't have known had it not been for your GPS." I rose in my seat and twisted to stare behind us, but there were no lights. The only thing visible was a cloud of white dust burned red by the truck's taillights.

"You think Whitlock tore up the road to keep squatters out?" I wanted this to be a normal case of squatters taking over any place where nobody was there to stop them, but I had a bad feeling. Especially after Louisa Mora's comments in her article about things legend trippers saw out here.

"I don't know," Tanner said. The spirits of his wife and kids swirled around him, very visible now that I knew to look for them. They feared what Tanner would do to himself and stayed only to comfort and protect him. But their presence created a link between Tanner and his sad past, allowing him to hold on when he really needed to let go.

Curiosity about what had happened to them churned in my brain, but I'd never ask. It wasn't my place or my business. All it had to do with me was a warning that maybe I didn't want to pursue Tanner Letts romantically. No matter how hot he looked in his tight T-shirt and jeans, no matter how intense his green eyes were, no matter how there was just something about him that touched me deep.

Tanner had slowed the truck considerably. He leaned forward, staring at the road ahead with an intensity that looked exhausting. Maybe he was tired.

"Want me to drive the rest of the way?" My nap had refreshed me.

"I'm good. In L.A., where I lived before, there were always streetlights, no matter where you went. It's dark out here. If there are deer, we won't see them until it's too late."

I sat up in my seat and stared out into the darkness ahead, hoping I'd get a flash of the headlights on the deer's eyes before they darted out. I could scream at Tanner to brake, but we'd probably still hit them and possibly make the truck undrivable.

"I thought you said you'd been to Death Valley, and it was more isolated than this would ever be. Surely you're used to darkness." I stole a glance at Tanner, gauging his reaction to the light jab.

He snorted. "I went there once with some buddies in college. Bunch of scared city boys."

We both laughed. I kept a careful eye on the darkness for moving shapes. In the distance, a few lights flashed. I silently pointed. Tanner slowed almost to a stop. "That's gotta be it, and it's obviously occupied."

"You ready for this?" I stared at his shadowed face.

"Ready as I'll ever be." He took his foot off the brake and started us moving again.

A few minutes later, our headlights flashed over a large sign. It read "Pale Horse, Texas." Then underneath, "Population: To Be Determined." It should have been cute, but it wasn't.

The town, unlighted, was a flat expanse of shadowy, dark buildings sticking up like tombstones. The only light came from the Pale Horse Saloon. We drove toward it. As we neared, so did the frenetic beat of heavy metal music. The screams of the lead singer sounded like someone was castrating him with a pair of pliers and a cutting torch. *Those screams might be real.* I cut off the thoughts. It wouldn't help to imagine what I'd find inside the Pale Horse Saloon.

Tanner parked my truck in front of the stone building I'd seen on the website. It sat in a bed of loose looking sand that seemed to be piled higher on one corner than the other. He took a deep breath and opened his door. I did the same, hurrying to his side of the truck so I didn't have to walk into this weird place alone. Not that I was scared. Because I'm too tough to be scared. And there's flying pigs on Sunday.

Tanner opened the door. A roar of music blasted out, so loud I felt the bass against my skin and rattling against my eardrums. I stepped inside first, ignoring Tanner's effort to get around me and play alpha male. It was a decision I regretted almost immediately.

All conversation stopped, and every head in the saloon turned to face me. Tanner shut the door and hurried to my side, putting one arm around my waist. Despite my fear, the sexual charge between us hummed a little harder. He pulled me toward the bar and sat on one of the new, made-to-look-antique stools that Dane Whitlock must have left behind.

A huge man wearing a black leather vest over his bare chest sauntered toward us. In one hand, he held an object I couldn't quite identify. The other hand held a dirty towel he was using to polish the object.

Rather than speaking to us, he spoke to the room. "Fresh meat, folks." Nobody answered. He set whatever he'd been polishing on a shelf and walked the rest of the way to us. "What can I get you folks to drink? It's all luke-warm, but it gets you where you want to go."

"Water," I said and pulled out my wallet.

"Whiskey," Tanner said and pulled out his wallet, which I knew was just for show, because it was empty, except for his lucky two-dollar bill.

The man behind the bar scoffed. "Free for newcomers. We're trying to build our brand." He cackled at his own words.

I didn't get the joke, and the intensity of his laughter set off warning bells inside my head. *Deep breaths. Stay alert. Sit still. Don't let him know you're scared.* I'd been to my share of backroads taverns and ice houses. Some of them seemed like portals into Hell. This one was no different.

The bartender set a short glass in front of Tanner and poured brown liquid from an unlabeled bottle. That was when I noticed the tattoo on his hand. It showed a horned ram, set over a point-down pentagram.

The bartender reached underneath the bar and came up with a smudged glass, which he set in front of me. Next to it, he placed a dirty, unlabeled plastic bottle of water. I nodded my thanks but didn't bother to pour the water into the glass. I had no intention of drinking it.

I leaned close enough to Tanner's ear to see where he'd had it pierced and whispered, "Don't drink it."

"You think I'm crazy?" He whispered back, picked up the glass, and swirled the liquid around. Specks of unidentifiable material floated inside it.

I leaned back on my stool and surveyed the bar's interior, running my gaze along the stone walls for the skull lamp. I'd brought all the cash I could rustle up, about two thousand dollars, in the hopes it would be enough to purchase it from a bunch of squatters. Now that I was here, felt the atmosphere of the place, I knew we'd have to fight for it. I suspected we'd have to fight to get out of this place alive.

An obese man with greasy, black hair and a tattoo matching the bartender's wandered over. His black vest hung open, displaying a chest covered with whorls of black hair stretching over a beer gut so huge I couldn't believe it was real. "Looking for the bathroom, pretty girl?"

He reached for my hair with one chubby hand and had his fingers wound in it before I could stop him. He proceeded to stroke my hair the same way he'd pet an animal. He smelled like meat right before it goes bad.

I nodded, too repulsed to form words. Directions to the bathroom would give me leave to look for the skull lantern and get me away from my admirer.

"All the way at the back. Left corner." The bartender's voice said from right next to my ear. I spun around, heart thundering, and found his face an inch from mine. He grinned, and it wasn't a nice grin.

Tanner had his arm around me again. "Want me to go with you?"

Hell no, came to my lips, but I pushed it back. He was trying to help. I smiled and shook my head. Tanner pressed his lips together and gave me a solemn nod.

I pushed myself off the stool and hurried away from the bar. Coming here had been a mistake, but I wasn't sure what else I could have done. Passing the tables, I became aware something was wrong, but I couldn't quite put my finger on what it was until I got almost to the back of the saloon.

None of the bar's patrons had even looked up as I passed their tables. Even the people sitting alone, many of whom were male, did not seem to notice me passing by their tables. Apprehension built in every muscle of my body, urging me to take some kind of action, until I was almost running by the time I got to the little inlet in the back.

The skull lantern stood right next to a cutout in the wall. One side had a sign that said "hombres." The other sign had a sign that said "señoritas." Making a point not to look at the skull, I hurried into "señoritas." These weirdos didn't need to know what we'd come for, not until Tanner and I were ready to make a move.

The women's restroom was obviously new construction. Even the wood smelled new. Light came from some indiscernible source and cast the room in a deep orange glow. The toilets were behind stalls with closed doors. I had no intention of pulling my pants down to sit on one of those toilets, so I approached the sink and twisted the knob on the faucet, intending to splash water on my face. Reddish brown water gushed out, bringing with it the smell of rotten eggs. I turned it off without even letting it dampen my fingers.

How were Tanner and I going to do this? He wasn't afraid to fight, no matter how scary the opponent. That was a plus. But there was something wrong, big wrong, in this place. Not knowing what it was put us at a great disadvantage.

If these were just a bunch of human assholes, I could do a little sideshow magic and scare them out of bothering us. If they were supernatural—either boogers or humans under the control of boogers—we had a hell of a fight on our hands.

Tanner's angry shout pierced the silence. A drawn out, agonized scream followed. The opportunity to plan lost, I turned toward the door and marched out.

12

I emerged from the restroom expecting to see a brawl. What I saw instead scared me worse. The bar's patrons sat at their tables, still drinking as though nobody was screaming their lungs out. And the scream. *Jeez Louise.* It droned on and on like the hum of machinery or the buzzing of a mosquito. I ran to the front of the bar, expecting to find Tanner missing a limb.

The fat guy who'd been fondling my hair stood holding the hilt of a knife, the one Tanner took off my asshole ex-husband, sticking out of the center of his chest. By all counts of logic, the knife was lodged in his heart. He should have been on the floor gasping his last.

Tanner saw me and rushed to me, pointing at the screamer. "He tried to bite me. Just leaned over and opened up."

The guy turned his considerable beer belly toward me, still bellowing, and belched a gout of black blood toward my face. I backpedaled, shaking the thick, and surprisingly cool, mess off my hands. I didn't have time for fear. My stomach had other plans. My last meal raced up my throat. I let out one sour burp and projectile vomited all over the fat guy. He screamed louder, eyes beginning to glow fiery red.

The terror came then, crawling over my body with sharp claws. My heart slammed hard against my ribcage. Exactly how bad was this? If the drama was isolated to the screamer, Tanner and I might be able to get out with the skull lantern.

I looked for the bartender. He stood at the other end of the bar, a bowl of something in front of him. He stuck in his fingers, pulled something wiggling out of the bowl, and stuffed it in his mouth. He didn't seem to hear the screaming man.

My plans for a speedy getaway ground to a halt, and the gravity of the situation, the truth about what Tanner and I had bumbled into, hit me hard enough to make me dizzy. This place felt just like the lost church of St. Augustine, where I'd encountered the freaks singing religious hymns backward. I hadn't seen the signs I'd come to associate with a thin place, two columns or posts, maybe a doorway. But that meant nothing. I learned about some new horrible thing every day.

I cut off the increasingly hysterical train of thought. However we'd gotten here, we were now trespassing in the some outpost of the damned. We needed to get the skull lantern and get out. Fast. I gripped Tanner's arm, too freaked out to enjoy the feel of his bicep.

"The skull lantern's at the back near the restrooms. Let's get it and go." I gave him a tug.

We hurried to the back of the room, the guy Tanner stabbed still screaming bloody murder, the other patrons and the bartender still ignoring him.

I snatched the skull lantern, having to pull it upward out of a base set into the wood plank floor. Magic shot through my arm, pinged my black opal, and settled against my magical core.

Its power burned, almost too much for me. Had I not already had the mantle, the power would have hurt me. Bad. My hand that held the skull lantern emanated pure, white light. The corners of my vision lit up with this power.

The fat guy's scream cut off as though someone had flipped an off switch. The murmurs of the bar patrons ceased. Busy marveling at the lantern's power, the danger of the sudden silence didn't register.

"Watch out." Tanner grabbed my arm and jerked me into the alcove where the bathrooms were.

The white bowl I'd seen the bartender eating out of hit the wall right where my head had been and shattered. Baby snakes hit the floor with a meaty splat and began writhing, trying to get away.

My stomach lurched again. I clapped the hand not holding the skull lantern to my mouth. One of the baby snakes slithered over the toe of my cowboy boot. I did a wild little dance, the motion of the snake seeming to wiggle through my body.

"Come on." Tanner led the way out of the alcove.

We'd only been in there a few seconds, and we hadn't heard a peep from the people inside the bar. But they'd somehow moved to the back of the bar and gathered, forming a stinky, greasy wall while I'd wigged out over the baby snakes. The bartender stood at the front of the group.

He opened his mouth, revealing a top and a bottom row of teeth that had been filed to points. Or maybe they just became that way after he got here. The roar that came out of him rattled over my skin and shook the building's floorboards.

His bellow somehow flipped a switch in his friends. They broke their silence and answered his howl, some throwing their heads back like wolves. Their eyes glowed with feral light that flashed red every few heartbeats.

Jumping beans bounced around in my tender stomach. My bowels went loose and hot. There was nowhere to run, no way out. The collective outcry went on and on, so long I had time to think of all the ways I'd fucked this up. I grabbed Tanner's hand, as though touching another person would act as a talisman against the hell about to erupt around us. We clung to each other and waited to see the reward of our stupidity.

They stopped yelling as one and advanced on us. Tanner let go of my hand and bellowed a war cry. He was right. The time to be scared was over. Now it was time to fight. To the death if necessary.

I pushed the panic to another part of my mind and called to the mantle. Its comforting veil slipped over my vision. The things in front of me wore red skins that moved like fire. Smoke rose off them. Their eyes, which had only looked a little crazy with my regular vision, now glowed mad and hungry.

One of them grabbed me, opening his mouth wide, saliva dripping in long, stretchy strands. Terror locked my muscles, and I could only watch, heart thudding dully, sluggish thoughts clogging my brain. The thing's spit hit my skin and sizzled like hot bacon grease. That broke me out of my stupor.

I channeled the mantle and sent it to the surface of my skin where the man-thing's hand clutched me, expecting it to burn him. But the white light from the skull lantern married itself to my magic at the last second. I lost control.

The combined magic flowed into the man-thing, pumping him full. He jittered in place, making a sound like a motor burning itself up. Spit flew from his mouth. The sharp smell of urine drifted to me. The man's movements reached a fever pitch, and his eyes burst, spraying me with warm, sticky liquid. His skin began to smoke, then to peel off his face. Light, the same white light I'd seen coming from the lantern flowed from his skin and back into me. My head ached the way it did when I took too big a sip of milkshake.

The man dropped to the floor in a pile of smoking, bloody rags. Another lost man grabbed me by my hair, pulling my head back to expose my neck, bowing my back in the process. His mouth opened, displaying those sharp-pointed teeth. *For tearing, like a dog's,* my mind babbled. He bent toward me.

I sent the mantle out at him, but it couldn't connect. His skin wasn't touching mine. I pushed it between us, but the effect was weakened. He only jerked as though he'd gotten a handful of static electricity.

Another set of rough hands grabbed one arm, yanking, presumably getting ready to bite a chunk out of it. It didn't matter if I killed the one trying to bite my neck. Melting that first one had taken a lot of juice. I could give maybe two more that treatment. What then? I had to figure out another plan of escape.

I glanced at Tanner, thinking maybe he'd help, but he had his nine irons amulet in one hand and was slamming one of the pieces into the monster's faces. They fell away when the iron touched them but came right back in twos and threes. One took a nice, healthy bite out of Tanner. He winced but spun and slammed the iron into the thing's face. Soon they'd overwhelm him.

I thought fast. Going for the skull lantern seemed to have mobilized them. That was what they'd protect, not each other. Hot breath tickled the skin on my neck. Shit. I was about to get eaten alive if I didn't act.

So I did the only thing I knew to do. I threw the skull lantern like a javelin over their ugly heads. It arced up and over them. A dirty hand reached up and grabbed it midair. The other monsters crowded around the one who'd retrieved the skull lantern.

Tanner turned to me gaping. "Why'd you do that?" Blood steamed from no telling how many bites on his arms. There was a scratch oozing blood on his neck.

"There were too many of them. They were just going to eat us, drink our blood, whatever." I gasped, leaning against the wall and trying to catch my breath.

"But how are we going to get it back now?" Irritation flashed in Tanner's eyes, bright as any emotion I'd seen there so far.

"I don't know." I put my hands on my knees, wheezing, and watched the not-quite-men gibber and slobber over the skull lantern. "But we're going to use it to kill them."

Tanner faced me, frowning.

"When I picked up the lantern, its magic mixed with mine. I melted that dude there." I pointed at the pile of smoking clothes. It didn't even look like something that used to be sort of human.

"I'll ask again. How do we get the lantern back?" Tanner watched the knot of humanoid creatures. Soon, they'd turn back to us, either wanting revenge or wanting to initiate us into their weird club.

I noticed Tanner's bites again and leaned closer. The edges had already turned red and puffy. But the bite on my arm looked like an old wound that I had used a hot iron to cauterize. The white light from the lantern must have done that. We had to get the thing back.

I regretted my decision to throw it. It had been spur of the moment, and it didn't play well in the chess game of this situation. But there was a way to turn things around. I just had to get my mind calm enough to think.

The big-bellied guy Tanner had stabbed came shambling around the idiots as they fought over the lamp. His eyes had turned solid black and now fixed on us.

"Intruders," he grated. More black blood dribbled from the corner of his mouth. "Intruders." This time he said it louder.

Tanner took my arm and leaned close to my ear. "Five more seconds, and he's going to have the whole gang of them on us. They get us down, it's over."

I glanced back at the bathrooms but couldn't remember a window in the women's. If I went in there, I'd be trapped. But we were also trapped in this little corner of the Pale Horse Saloon.

"Intruder." The guy tripped on one of his friends' feet and went down face first, right onto the knife. He rolled on his side and began trying to regain his feet.

"The iron was working on getting them to move." Tanner still had it in his hand. Gore and charred skin stuck to the amulet. "I'll start hitting them with it, and you make a grab for the skull lamp. What are you going to do?"

"In that folktale, Vasilisa somehow let the lantern burn her wicked stepmother and stepsisters to ashes." I tried to reason out what I was going to do as I said the words. Tanner shifted impatiently, throwing glances at the freaks a few feet away. "Somehow I've got to keep the power of the lantern with the lantern and project it outward."

Tanner nodded. "Fine. Let's do it." He held up his fist for a bump, eyes fierce, kissable lips pressed into a determined line. Dorky, but hot. I bumped with him, and he turned away, starting toward the monsters, shoulders squared like he accepted his mission, whatever it brought. I grabbed at him.

"What I did earlier took a lot of energy. If I do a mass burning, I might collapse." I paused. Tanner would have to get me out of the Pale Horse Saloon, but explicitly telling him this made me feel all squirmy and embarrassed.

"I won't leave you, okay?" He gripped my arm with one hand and gave me a light pull toward the men.

Tanner marched with his nine irons amulet held high, the cross stuck out. He clapped it against the sweaty head of one of the men. I gripped the guy's arms and slung him out of the way, ignoring the too-hard pull in my muscles and back. He staggered from us, holding his hand to his head.

Tanner repeated the exercise on three more men before we got close to the lamp. By that time, the men we'd already burned with the iron were staggering back toward us, hands covering their wounds but mad as hell and ready to take a bite out of our asses.

I grabbed for the lamp, felt a brush of its magic, but the men held on tight. Tugging at the thing, desperation building, the lantern's magic fluttered against mine again. There was no way I could wrench it from them.

Tanner couldn't help me. He was busy planting his iron cross on the skin of our enemies. If he stopped, they'd be on us like a flock of ducks on June bugs.

I held on tight to the lantern, its magic still ebbing at the edge of mine. Could I send magic through it even if those things were holding on to it? I didn't know, but I had to try. Otherwise, we were about to become monster chow.

Trying to block out the gibbering and the growls, I latched on to the mantle, concentrating on the magic around me. Magic is everywhere. It's in lights in the form of electricity. It's in wood that carries earth magic. It's even in the air, just a little charge most people don't feel. And magic is part of fire.

I called to the fire inside the lantern, letting its magic flood into me. It swirled around my magical core again. This time it made itself at home, slipping through the hole in the scar tissue and teasing against the power of the mantle.

Slippery, sweaty fingers closed around my neck. It was one of the monsters getting ready to take a bite out of me. The thing let out a howl and dropped away. Tanner must have given it a shot of iron.

Begging the universe for just a few more seconds, I gathered both the mantle and this sharp, white magic from the lantern together and pushed them back through me. It was like forcing rushing water to turn and go the other way. I strained, pressure building behind my eyes, body shaking with the effort. Sweat popped out on my body.

It went on so long, my energy flagged. I couldn't keep this up much longer. Once I let go, that would be it. I was too exhausted to do this again. I searched deep, looking for my last bit of stubbornness, found it, and pushed at the magic one last time.

The energy flowed down my arm, found the old wood of the stick, and raced to the skull. The skull's eyes lit up, bluish white, the hottest of flames. Realizing what was about to happen, I tried to let go of the stick on which the skull sat. My fingers wouldn't move.

Fear pulsed just as strong as the magic. When this thing started burning stuff, it would likely burn off my arm. I tried again to let go, but it was as though invisible fingers held my hand fast to the wood.

The other men holding the stick began to do a weird

one-handed dance that got faster and faster until they vibrated. They didn't so much scream as they howled, teeth popping from their mouths. One by one, their eyes blew out. White light streamed from the eye sockets, spreading over them and consuming them. By the time each one dropped to the floor, he was nothing more than a pile of ash with red embers glowing inside.

Light beamed from the skull's eye sockets. It landed on the head of one of the not-quite-men. The man's greasy hair began to smoke, conjuring an odor of unwashed, burning hair that I would never forget as long as I lived.

The man danced foot to foot to music only he could hear. A guttural sound came from him, growing higher by the second. His head exploded, sizzling pieces of it landing everywhere, including on my skin where they burned. I brushed them off. They kept burning all the way to the wood floor where they landed as ash.

The skull's eyes found man after man, the horror repeating itself until I was almost numb to it. It drained me of energy. By the time the last man fell, and the light inside the skull faded, I could barely hold myself upright.

I staggered a few feet away from the piles of ashes and pieces of sizzling skin and slid to the floor, fingers still wrapped around the skull lamp. Tanner stood pressed against a far wall, eyes wide, chest rising and falling with his rapid breaths.

"I think I want to go home and to bed," I said and collapsed on the filthy floor, not even caring how nasty it was.

"You're going." Tanner trudged toward me and lifted

me off the floor. He carried me out of the bar the way a groom carries his bride over the threshold of the honeymoon suite. The skull lantern bumped against the floor, my fingers still locked around it in a death grip.

———

Tanner propped me and the lantern against the bed of my truck. He left me to dig around inside and came back with a bottle of water and a granola bar.

I sipped the water. It stayed down, so I nibbled at the granola bar. It gave me a second wind. Using my free hand, I pried my fingers off the skull lantern's stick and shook feeling back into them.

"Is it okay if that doesn't ride in the truck with us?" Tanner came close but wouldn't touch the thing.

I nodded and placed it in the bed of the truck. Sides heaving from the exertion of the activity, I grabbed the bed of the truck and gasped for air. Tanner stood a few feet from me.

I held out one hand. "Give me my keys."

He pulled the keys out of his pocket and jingled them. "Sure you can drive?"

No, but I want to drive my damn truck myself. Sluggish, heavy fatigue fuzzed my head and blurred my vision. I wanted to drive, to be in control, but could I keep my eyes open until we got out of this pocket of hell? While I thought it over, my eyes drifted closed. My knees buckling woke me. Tanner grabbed my arm to keep me from falling down.

"Let me help you." He slid one arm under my legs, carried me around to the passenger side, managed to open the door one-handed, and stick me in my seat. He kept his arms around me longer than he needed to, his face barely an inch from mine. Then the moment passed. He let me go, shut the door, and walked away.

My head lolled against the headrest while I waited for him to get in the truck. Thoughts of what Tanner's lips would feel like on mine clouded my head. My inner voice of reason pushed them away.

Tanner had damage, the kind that burrowed so deep into the heart it never saw the light of day again. Together we had enough wounds from the war of love and loss to start our own hospital, the kind where nobody ever got better and ghosts haunted the halls forever.

The driver's side door opened, and the overhead light came on. I tilted my head to look at Tanner as he crawled into the truck.

He gave me a little half smile. "That was pretty impressive back there. You saved my ass."

"And a nice ass it is," I mumbled. My cheeks heated, but the words were already out there, and there was nothing I could do but give Tanner a sheepish smile. There was something about this hot, broken man that drew me in, no matter how bad I knew he'd be in the long run.

He bit his lower lip, seemed to think something over, started to speak, but then stopped. He put one hand on the steering wheel and took it off. He shook his head and let out a deep sigh. It was like watching a seesaw.

"Never mind that," he mumbled to himself and leaned

toward me, lips parted. I closed the distance and put one hand on his cheek. Our lips barely touched.

Tanner scooted toward me and slid his hand behind my neck, his movements fluid and powerful. I'd like to say I pulled away, told him this was a bad idea for both of us, but I gripped his T-shirt in both hands and met his lips.

I'd based my lust for Tanner on the intensity caged in his jewel-toned eyes, in his careful movements. Both hinted at sweaty, midnight passion. Whatever I'd seen hadn't prepared me for Tanner's kiss.

His lips pressed against mine, insistent and all-consuming, stealing my breath. Dizzy, body tingling, I kissed back. The sweat on Tanner's lips from our fight in the Pale Horse Saloon stung salty and hot. His lips felt every bit as good as they looked.

I forgot where we were and all my crazy problems. I cared about nothing but Tanner's lips and tongue and his smell, musky and primal, invading my senses. His hand gripped the back of my neck tighter, late-day whiskers rasping against my upper lip.

His tongue touched mine. My body jerked, and I moaned. Desire opened up its petals and stretched. Tanner used one trembling hand to trace my jaw with his thumb. He trailed it down my neck. A shiver ripped through my body. Were we going to do what I thought? He was just as nervous about it as I was.

I drew back to look at him, to make sure. What I saw was as effective as a cold shower in terms of killing the mood.

The spirits of Tanner's family swirled around his head.

Without me using the mantle, they weren't more than a soft breeze, a wisp of displeasure. But I felt them and knew they saw me as a threat to Tanner, someone who might hurt him. Any hurt at this stage could prevent him from ever getting past their loss.

Tanner broke away from me, flopped back in the driver's seat, stared straight ahead. "That was wrong. I'm sorry," he mumbled, the sexy purr of his voice nothing more than a hoarse croak.

"It's okay." I reached out to touch his arm, almost hit one of the bite marks, and drew away. "Is it the bites? They're hurting?"

But I knew it wasn't the bites. Those spirits circling Tanner's head hung over him like storm clouds, same as Wade's memory in the back of my mind kept me from going forward. The funny thing was, we both chose to keep the hurt of our losses with us. We imprisoned the ghosts of our pasts and forced them to haunt us.

Tanner started the truck. Of course he wouldn't want to talk. Path of least resistance. Drive me back to Summervale, pretend this never happened, maybe slip away when he got back on his feet.

Would that really be so bad? *Maybe not.* I wouldn't let Wade drop out of my head, even though I wouldn't start anything with him now if he begged. I loved him too much to play a part in the story Desiree told me.

Cigarettes. I needed them now. They'd make me feel better. I dug in the console, took out a new pack, slapped it against my palm a couple of times, and opened them.

Tanner took his eyes off the road to watch me get one out of the pack.

"All right?" I asked as I lit it. It was my truck. I'd smoke if I wanted to, but I would give Tanner a chance to voice his displeasure.

"I didn't quit until I ran out of money." He kept his eyes on the white sand in front of us, his voice back to his normal one. I held the cigarettes across the truck.

Tanner glanced at them and shook his head. "I can't afford them now any more than I could when I quit."

Holding my cigarette between my first and middle finger, I lit Tanner a cigarette and held it to his lips until he took it. He clamped down on it and drew deep.

"You can smoke mine." That must have been some kiss. I never offered to give someone access to my cigarettes. But there was something about Tanner. I wanted to help. And deep down, I wanted more.

"I can't agree to that." Tanner took the cigarette out of his mouth and cocked it between his fingers on the steering wheel.

"Why not? You've saved my life once, and you helped me fight my way out of that hellhole back there." I jerked a thumb over my shoulder and glanced out the window.

Next to the truck galloped a white horse. The man riding it glowed like the noon sun. Both man and horse were transparent. As I watched, the man turned to look at me, and they both disappeared. I turned to Tanner to find him watching with wide eyes and an open mouth.

"This country's haunted," he muttered and faced the road again.

I nodded. It was. But so was the rest of the world and me along with it. No point in worrying about it. We'd been talking about cigarettes, and that was good enough for now.

"So it's settled. You'll smoke my cigarettes," I said with finality.

Tanner needed a friend whether we hooked up or not. The reason the spirits of his lost family hovered over him, the reason they were so protective, was that he thought about them constantly. He depended on them to get through the day. They'd never leave if he didn't let them go.

Not unlike the spell keeping me from my full power. What Hannah and others had said rolled around in my mind. I saw the logic in letting go of the scar tissue myself. But I just didn't know how to do it. Hurt holds pretty firm to history. Together they built a wall that was almost impossible to tear down. I let go of the thoughts, knowing they'd come back sooner or later.

I watched Tanner in the dashboard lights, trying to figure out what I found attractive. His features, if examined one at a time, weren't the stuff of male models. That had been Dean.

Tanner's high cheekbones and small, intense eyes gave him the look of a strong, fast animal. Having seen him fight, I knew his appearance fit what he was. Unwelcome lust heated my body at the memory of his hand on the back of my neck, his lips on mine. I shook it off.

"Did you box in high school or college?" I'd pretend nothing happened between us. Acting otherwise would be an echo of what I'd done with Wade and now regretted. Tanner and I could go right back to an unspoken attraction and pretend our kiss never happened. No matter how many times I called up the experience on lonely nights.

Tanner, focused on the swirl of dirt and the narrow road ahead of us, didn't answer for so long I thought he'd decided to ignore me. When he spoke, a hesitation weighted his words, as though he was going to be very careful about what he told me.

"Junior high. I was one of those runty, skinny kids. Always getting my ass kicked." He glanced at me, an impish smile curling his lips.

I laughed and nodded. "I was the outcast at school. Didn't know to keep my mouth shut about seeing ghosts. They let me know I was different." The memory heated my cheeks as though it had just happened yesterday rather than years ago. Just like Tanner, I carried my ghosts.

Tanner clamped his cigarette in his mouth and took one hand off the wheel. Gently, the way a lover would, he touched my knuckles on the hand nearest him. "I noticed that. My dad had boxed in the Army. He got me started. I was fast, liked the competition, even though my mom hated it."

"She afraid you were going to get hurt?" Tanner wasn't runty now, but if he had been, I could understand the fear.

"No. Mom was born and raised in California. Different culture. She saw boxing as barbaric." He stopped speaking. I glanced over to see him frowning. Was he considering telling me something big? I sat as still as possible as though moving might jinx his decision. Finally, he slumped.

"After high school, I did some amateur boxing matches. It paid more than retail or fast food, and I had a family to support." He took his eyes off the road and spoke directly to me. "I got my girlfriend pregnant senior year. Her parents wanted her to have an abortion. My parents wanted me not to get tied down so early. But I knew she was the right one. I married her the week after we graduated, and we had a baby a few months later."

I tried to imagine a young man so determined, so sure of what he wanted. And to know he still loved his wife deeply, would take his family back in a second, touched me. My eyes burned, and a sadness opened up, almost as strong as the desire I'd felt a few minutes earlier. I envied anybody who got to enjoy their true love.

Tanner let out a loud breath. "Earlier when I kissed you, it was just the intense situation. Coming down from it, you know?"

I agreed, even though I'd hoped he found me as attractive as I did him. Men turned my head every day, but liking one versus liking to look at one were two different things.

"Losing my wife and daughters ripped me apart." He gripped the wheel tight. "I'm not looking for a relationship." He glanced over at me, his meaning louder than if he'd said the words.

Laughter tightened my chest, but I held it back. Instead I said, "I understand. I went there after my divorce."

And I had. I alley catted around for several years after I divorced Tim the Asshole. My poor choice in men had led to me losing the only child I might ever have. Trying to choose the right man after that felt impossible.

Even after I started really dating again and fell in love with Dean, I still picked wrong men. Both Dean and Wade had been wrong men. I still wasn't sure I wanted to try for another relationship after the heartbreak of losing Wade before it ever started. But the feel of Tanner's lips on mine had gone a long way toward convincing me I might need to reconsider.

Tanner glanced at me. "I like you. A lot. But starting again with another woman, especially after the way my wife and daughters died, feels wrong, like a betrayal."

"Your family died in a car accident?" I watched Tanner's posture. Had he been drunk? Or a road rage incident? I couldn't see the latter at all. Tanner would fight if provoked, but he seemed even-tempered otherwise. The drunk driving was another matter. The level of his guilt suggested there was something.

Tanner nodded. We'd reached the little town nearest Pale Horse. Tanner pulled onto the deserted and dark Main Street and parked the truck on the side of the road. I tried to hide that I was dying of curiosity.

"I told you my wife got pregnant with our daughter when we were seniors in high school. I was barely nineteen when Maya was born." He pointed at my cigarettes and raised his eyebrows. So it was going to be that kind of story. I tossed the pack in his lap.

"You don't owe me an explanation of your life," I told Tanner.

"No, I want to tell you. Because that kiss was...well, it

was what I wanted right then." He lit his cigarette with smooth, practiced motions. "So there I was, thirty-five years old, with a sixteen-year-old daughter. Maya wanted to get her driver's license with the other kids. Both Bea and I were more worried, but we signed the consent forms."

My imagination went wild. I knew the end of the story, just not how it happened. The big mystery was how the mother and other daughter got in the wreck.

"Maya passed everything she needed to, and her driver's license came. One of our rituals as a family was to eat out every Friday night at this little Italian restaurant not even a mile from our house." He smoked in silence for a while. A tear streaked down his face. When he spoke, his voice wobbled. "Maya wanted to drive. Bea didn't want to let her. It was Friday night. Traffic would be worse. I argued with Bea, told her this would be a good learning experience for Maya, and we'd be there to help her if something went wrong."

My shoulders tightened as my imagination zeroed in on the right story. Tanner had been with them, had seen the whole thing happen. As a man who could fight his way out of a situation, not being able to save them had to be unreal. Worse, he now blamed himself for allowing his daughter to drive.

He started the truck again, and I thought he'd decided not to tell me the rest of the story. He drove down the deserted street, stopping at the red light even though nobody was there.

He spoke, and his already raspy voice was raw with unshed tears. "Bea and I thought Maya would make the mistake. But we never saw him coming." Tanner drove, focused on the road ahead. "The police said the guy had lost his job and was angry, yelling on the phone to his wife. He ran a red light going sixty miles per hour."

The particulars of the story formed in my mind. Tears tightened my throat. I wanted to reach out to Tanner, but doing so would likely insult him or make him uncomfortable. So I said nothing and kept my hands to myself.

He swallowed hard. "The other driver plowed into the driver's door on our car. The impact knocked us into another car, and the pile-up started there." He blew a hard jet of smoke from his nose and stubbed out the cigarette half smoked in the ashtray. "My wife and younger daughter died before they got to the hospital. Maya arrived in a coma from which she never woke. I walked away with a broken leg and a broken arm." He choked. "But I died that day too."

I wanted to tell him he hadn't, that he'd have to let go of his grief in order to start living again, but saying that would be hypocritical. Wade, the desire of him, grief over the connection we'd had, still plagued me. So did many other sorry events in my life. Who was I to judge Tanner?

I reached one hand across the truck and held it out, offering him some kind of human contact as comfort. He took my hand and squeezed it. We drove that way through the darkness. My mind drifted. Maybe I even fell asleep. The next thing I knew, Tanner jammed on the brakes, and the tires started to squall.

"Shit. Shit," he screamed. "It's her."

Miss Ugly stood in the middle of the road, arms out.

13

The bright beam of my truck's headlights didn't do Miss Ugly any favors. It made her shiny skin look green and her nose look like it actually touched her chin.

"Want me to run her over?" Tanner took his foot off the brake.

"No. I'll give her the lamp. Maybe that'll be enough to send her away." I opened the truck's door.

Tanner grabbed my arm. "Wait. You can't face her by yourself."

I turned to stare at him, wondering why he'd bother to risk himself for me. He stared straight ahead, unbuckling his seatbelt. His face, impassive if a little tight, gave away no reason he'd do such a thing.

Tanner and I climbed out of the truck together. I pulled the skull lantern out of the truck's bed and walked to Miss Ugly holding it aloft. Tanner hurried to my side.

She narrowed her eyes at us, head cocked. "My lantern."

I held out the lantern. She approached, holding out one of her long-fingered hands. The memory of those claws tightened my skin. I swallowed the urge to back away from her and held as still as I could.

She took the lantern from me almost gently and rubbed her hand over the skull's head. The eyes lit up. Tanner and I both scuttled backward to avoid the burning death rays.

She saw us and chuckled. "It will act as a light for me since I am the one who made it." She took a closer look at me. "You recharged it with your magic. Now you are tired, empty."

I did an inward assessment and realized she was right. I didn't have a bit of magic left to lend to any situation, not even to protect myself. Fear spread through me, stinging my nerve endings. Whatever Miss Ugly wanted to do to me now would happen. *Please let this satisfy her*, begged a childish voice in my head. But I lived in the real world. Things never worked out the way I wanted them to.

"Now it is time to meet your fate. Come without a fight." She crooked her finger at me.

I backed away until I bumped into Tanner. He put an arm around me, pressing himself against my side. His body shook.

"No, no, no," I said. "You promised to reward me if I gave back your lantern." I forgot to phrase this as a question to weaken Miss Ugly until the words were already out.

Miss Ugly considered me. She came forward and gripped my arm as though testing it for muscle. I stiffened at the slimy feel of her cool fingers.

"No. Your meat is ready tonight. Must go so I can prepare the meat and the fire." She gave me a tug toward the side of the road.

The moon beamed down on the huge, endless pasture stretching out from the road. In the darkness, two tall columns, stone with carvings at the top and bottom, rippled in and out of reality. That was where we'd cross. Once I left this world, I might as well sign my death warrant.

"That sucks," I yelled and jerked my arm. Miss Ugly pulled back, suddenly very strong. I fought for all I was worth, but only succeeded in twisting my own arm. "Where is the kindness you promised?"

This time I had remembered to phrase my comments in a question, but Miss Ugly didn't shrink at all. My magic. There wasn't enough left to work against hers and draw her power. I slumped.

Miss Ugly turned back to me. "What sort of kindness would you like?"

"For you to let me go." My voice came out hoarse and trembling. Miss Ugly cocked her head at me, and I hastened to make my case. "You came after me because you thought I stole the lantern—which I never did. Now I've gotten it back for you. Call our business done and let me go."

"Thieves must be punished even if they return what they stole." Miss Ugly tightened her grip and began walking, dragging me toward the two columns.

"I didn't steal your sorry-assed lantern," I yelled.

She ignored me and kept towing me. Tanner gripped

me around the waist, pulling the same way he had back in the tent.

"Where's your honor?" he grunted at Miss Ugly.

Miss Ugly stopped so quickly, I fell against Tanner. We landed on the pavement in a heap.

"You talk of honor? The man who was too afraid to let his daughter move on to the next plane of existence? The one who kept her alive on machines?" Miss Ugly leaned toward Tanner.

He shrank away, emotion twisting his features, and let go of me. Miss Ugly snatched my arm and started walking again. I dug my boot heels into the pavement. It didn't do much good, but it slowed her progress. I glanced back at Tanner. He knelt on the pavement with both hands over his face, mourning the day his life had turned to shit.

My life had turned to shit many times. This one was by far the worst. Talk about a disappointing way to end things. Magic all used up, emotionally preparing to be Miss Ugly's picnic ham. She kept pulling me toward the columns. My boots left the pavement and cut ruts in the sand along the roadside. The posts marking the thin place were less than three yards away.

Running footsteps slapped the ground behind me. Tanner pushed past me, his nine irons amulet held out. He slapped it to Miss Ugly's face, the same way he'd done before. She howled but tightened her grip on me and kept walking. Tanner ran around in front of her and gave her a hard push. He barely moved her, but she did stop.

"Do you want this to be your fate as well?" She leaned

into Tanner's face. His features pinched in disgust. He must've gotten a whiff of that breath.

"Reward Peri Jean Mace by letting her go, or I'll speak of your lack of honor to everybody I meet." Tanner stood stiff, shoulders squared, feet apart. He was ready to whip some ass, even if it wasn't with his fists.

Miss Ugly slowly turned to face Tanner. "How dare you speak to me as though you're as great as I."

"I'm better." Tanner raised his chin. "I reward people when they do the right thing."

Miss Ugly threw her head back. "Hoooooo." In this open space, it sounded like an air brake on an eighteen-wheeler. Some poor animal crashed through the bushes, trying to save its own life from whatever thing could make such an awful noise.

My black opal gave a weak ping. My magic was replenishing but not fast enough. I aimed what I had at Miss Ugly and threw out a question. "Why won't you reward me?"

The hand holding me shrank, but nothing like I'd made it shrink before. But I was more afraid this time. I'd done what she asked, and it hadn't helped. I twisted in her grasp. Miss Ugly readjusted her grip and grabbed me with the other hand as well, nasty fingernails biting into my skin.

"This fate is assigned to you now. You must follow the thread of your fate until it runs out. But I do have a small kindness for your hard work." She leaned toward me. I craned away, revulsion overwhelming my fear. Miss Ugly used one of her nasty fingers to prick my forehead in the same spot she'd already hit. The already tender skin flinched at the new injury. She drew back. "You have until tomorrow night to make peace with your fate." She turned toward Tanner. "Perhaps that will make me a more honorable being."

Without waiting for either of our responses, she walked across the pasture, footsteps crunching in the grass and gritting in the sand. The moonlight glowed on her skin. She reached the columns, passed through without hesitating, and disappeared.

I picked myself up off the ground, brushing at the grime on my clothes. *One more day to live.* Something like sadness pooled in my chest. I'd thought I would live to see how things turned out, regardless of how ambivalent I sometimes felt about it.

Tanner came to stand next to me. "You all right?"

I shrugged. "As all right as I can be in a situation like this."

"She's not taking you tomorrow. There *is* a way to get rid of her. We just haven't figured it out yet. But we will." He marched back to the truck and got in the driver's side.

I followed, too tired to try to explain to him that it was over. There was nothing left to do. I got in the truck and buckled my seatbelt. Facing death, buckling my seatbelt felt trivial and foolish.

My phone began to ring. I glanced at the caller ID. Dillon. "What's going on?"

Harsh pants came over the speaker. Had she butt dialed me?

"Dillon?" I yelled. "Did you need to talk to me?" I figured she didn't and got ready to hang up.

"Yes. Yes. Come back now. Something bad's happened." Dillon paused as voices raised in conversation behind her.

I strained to understand what the voices were saying. "What's going on?"

She sighed. "Go to the carnival. Hannah'll be in your tent waiting." She hung up before I could ask any more questions.

———

The minutes crawled by as Tanner sped through the darkness. My job was to watch for deer on the roadside and warn Tanner to stop before they made a suicide run under the truck's tires. Hitting one would break my heart *and* cost us valuable time.

To pass the time, I tried calling Dillon back. Her phone went straight to voicemail. She'd either turned it off or was declining my calls. Hannah's did the same thing.

Worry twisted my guts. I sat on the edge of my seat, glancing at the speedometer. Tanner drove the big truck like a Baja buggy, scaring even me. I couldn't yell at him to hurry.

Finally, we roared up in Summervale Carnival's parking lot. Empty again. All the fun-seekers had gone home for the night.

I climbed out of the truck and took off running. Tanner caught up and grabbed my hand. My impulse was to jerk away. I didn't need him leading me. But the comfort of another person, one who'd seen me receive my death sentence, helped just a little.

We turned the corner onto the midway off the thoroughfare where all our tents were. I'd expected to see family members waiting for us, but everything stood quiet and dead.

"It's like a ghost town." I let go of Tanner's hand and raced toward my tent. His footsteps pounded behind me. I burst through the flap and faced the worst mess I'd seen in a long time.

Junk lay scattered everywhere. I couldn't tell with a glance where it had all come from. The séance table sat in its usual spot, the only orderly thing in the room. Hannah sat at the table, a spread of three tarot cards in front of her, her tarot journal at her elbow. She raised her head at my commotion and let out a relieved sigh. Tanner crowded in behind me.

"What's going on?" I nearly yelled.

"Don't get too excited." Hannah stood from the chair, smoothing down her expensive pants. "We had a little incident. Your ex-husband burst in here and robbed your tent. Cecil tried to stop him and ended up having a spell with his heart. We had to let the ambulance come get him."

The edges of my vision went gray at the announcement. Panic took over my mind, making it run a hamster wheel of doom. Cecil was the elder of our family, the person who knew all the good stuff. He took care of the day-to-day minutiae of running the traveling community of Sanctuary. People brought their complaints and worries to him. He made the decisions of which way we'd travel and which jobs to take. He always knew the right thing to do. If he died, I'd lose my advisor and a good friend.

"How bad is Papaw? Did Tim hurt him?" The pain in my throat was the only way I knew I was yelling. Tim had certainly hurt me, nearly beat me to death. He was capable.

Hannah patted my arms. "Settle down and listen to me." She took deep breaths until I did the same. Then she started speaking again. "I called Tim a bug fucker. He hit me in the stomach."

Tanner shifted on his feet eyes narrow and glittering hate. He muttered, "Cowardly asshole."

Hannah nodded her agreement. "Cecil and Tim scuffled. I don't think either of them got in any blows. But Cecil's heart started acting up. I swear, his face was the color of oatmeal. Tim grabbed the runes and something else out of your trunk and ran out. I called an ambulance."

I flinched. No matter how bad things got, we only called in the authorities when absolutely necessary.

"Oh, I got chapter and verse from Shelly." Hannah's face reddened. "By the time the EMTs got here, the story of your sorry ex robbing us had turned into him being an irate customer who kicked over your buffet."

"Dillon didn't explain when she called..." I began.

Hannah cut me off. "I told Dillon not to call you, that making you hurry wouldn't change any of this. Cecil isn't dying, not right now."

I trusted Hannah's word on this and relaxed a tiny bit. But my muscles still ached with tension. "You could have told me not to worry any of the times I tried to call you. Why didn't you answer?"

"Huh? You called?" She took out her phone and clicked the side button. The screen stayed dark. "Son of a damn bitch," she said through her teeth and threw the phone against the tent wall. It bounced off and fell to the dirt. "It started acting up this morning. I'd thought once we hit a big enough town, I'd buy another one. I didn't realize..." She hugged me again. "I'm sorry."

I shook my head and walked around the room, surveying the damage. My shabby chic buffet, the one I'd restored and painted so carefully, had been busted into small wood splinters. I squatted on the dirt floor and picked through the mess. "You said the official story, the one you told the authorities, turned into Tim breaking this. What really happened?"

Hannah squatted next to me. "That thing exploded about ten seconds before your ex walked in."

"Tell me what happened from the start." I sorted through things, making one pile for ruined items and another for things we could keep. Tanner knelt next to me and helped. Every once in a while, his hand brushed my leg or some other part of my body. The contact sent electric pulses of lust into my brain and made it hard for me to concentrate. I settled my gaze on Hannah and waited for her to start talking.

"Cecil and I were looking at the tarot cards. All of a sudden, your buffet started shaking. Even I felt the magic coming off it." She licked her lips. "It exploded. Wood splinters, and your stuff went everywhere." She held up an arm to show me a few shallow cuts shiny with some kind of ointment. "Your ex-husband burst in. He had a gun."

Tanner stopped picking stuff up and glanced around as though the gun might still be there, waiting to shoot him. I grunted in irritation. Neither Tim nor his gun scared me. Anger and a general apathy over death fueled bravery that bordered on foolishness.

Hannah continued. "Tim said, 'The Coachman wants his runes.'"

The pronouncement made my head spin. I'd suspected Tim and Oscar were somehow working together, but I still couldn't figure out how it had happened. "I don't understand how they're..."

Tanner had his arms crossed over his chest, one hand cupping his chin as he thought. "I might."

I gestured at him to spill it.

"I've been puzzling over how awful that magic baking off those runes felt. Now I think I've got it." He tucked one lock of hair behind his ear, so excited about what he'd figured out he was almost smiling. I resisted the urge to rush him along. After what seemed like an eternity, he continued, "Your magic charged Miss Ugly's skull lamp, right? What if your magic charged Oscar's runes?" He raised his eyebrows.

I nodded. Despite the dire circumstances, I couldn't help but notice how impossibly cute Tanner was when he did the raised eyebrows thing. Stupid of me to even notice. This was the wrong time for both of us. *Focus on the here and now.*

The here and now was Tanner had made a good point.

I could have unknowingly charged the runes and given Oscar enough power to blow up the buffet.

But this was the third time Tim had come to my tent. The first time, he'd gotten into Oscar's runes and scattered them. The second time, I'd caught him in here snooping around, and Tanner whipped his ass for it. Now he'd come back and stolen the runes, saying the Coachman, Oscar, wanted them. The two of them were working together.

"Tell me what you're thinking." Tanner licked his lips, and I remembered our kiss.

"I agree with you about charging the runes. I probably did it unknowingly, and it allowed Oscar to make the buffet explode. But how did Tim get involved? I haven't spoken to him in years."

Tanner shrugged. "The way those runes emanate evil like they do makes me wonder if they're some kind of doorway."

A doorway. It hit me then. I felt more stupid than I had in a long time. The answer had been right there in my memories of my first encounter with Oscar Rivera, but I'd been too busy horn-dogging after Tanner and missing Wade to see it.

A few months ago, a misguided young man had found one of Oscar Rivera's runes. I had seen the finding of the rune in a vision. In this vision, Oscar had been right on the other side of this rune like someone looking through a window. Oscar had watched the rune be found and reached out to encourage this young man to help him find a way to be summoned back to the land of the living. Then, when Oscar was summoned back to this plane, he had come out of the runes. The connections flashed in my mind like lightning before a storm.

I put my face in my hands. "Oh, no."

"What?" Hannah gave me a light kick. "I'm lost."

"Oscar can see through the runes. He can be contacted through the runes. I knew all that going in. I thought it was harmless because Oscar had no access to power, that he was trapped where he hid his soul." I rocked back and forth, wanting to scream from the frustration of what my ignorance had allowed to happen. "But like Tanner pointed out, the runes are like a doorway. Evil comes out, other stuff goes in. When Tim came in the other night, Oscar somehow connected to him, convinced him to work for him." The weight of all that I faced pressed down on me without quarter. I couldn't push forward anymore.

Out of the corner of my eye, I glimpsed my cedar box. It stood open. I went over and knelt in front of it. I'd been so busy trying to catch up that I'd not really paid attention to what Hannah said about Tim getting into the cedar box. I didn't have to ask what he'd taken.

Hannah spoke in a low, ashamed voice. "Tim knew exactly what he was looking for. The leather bag with the gold disk in it." Her voice barely rose above a whisper. "By that time, Cecil was in distress. I was more focused on him than I was stopping Tim." She gave me a guilty shrug.

I shook off her apology. It was done now. Oscar had the runes and the wheel. He also had Tim as his henchman. He could create havoc beyond what I wanted to think about. And here I was farting around with Miss Ugly, who'd promised to come back tomorrow night and take me with her no matter what.

Hannah seemed to read my mind. "Did you find the skull lamp?"

I nodded and continued sifting through my scattered belongings. I'd have to leave them to someone. Zora was the most logical choice, though she was too young right now. Had I accepted my death so easily? I saw no way around it.

Hannah squatted next to me and began gathering things. "At least that's one good thing."

I turned to give her an incredulous stare. *Wait. She doesn't know.* I didn't want to tell Hannah my fate, but she had to know. "Depends on what you think good is." I told her about giving the skull lantern back to Miss Ugly and what she gave me as a kindness.

Hannah slumped. "Cheating old bitch."

Tanner continued brushing sand off items and putting them in piles for me to examine. "I can't quit wondering what Oscar would want with the wheel. I think it's the answer to some of our problems."

"Maybe he thinks he can crawl through it. I've seen boogers do that before." I smiled at Tanner as I used his word for chthonic beings.

He smiled back but shook his head. "Oscar'll come through the runes. You said so yourself." He put the last of the stuff back in the cedar chest and wiped his hands on his jeans. "Think about it. Miss Ugly keeps mentioning your fate. That wheel governs fate."

I cocked my head at him, still not getting it.

"That wheel might be able to change your fate, divorce it from Miss Ugly's." He squatted next to me, eyes boring into mine.

I focused my mind on the game. "So we need to find Tim and get that wheel back now."

"I think I've got an idea how to do it," Tanner said.

———

Tanner said he needed some things from his truck and left before Hannah or I could ask what. She minded her own business for about ten seconds.

"What happened between the two of you?" She twirled a strand of red hair around one finger and fluttered her eyelashes.

"Why don't you tell me about the tarot spread you were doing when we came roaring in? Thinking of adding tarot readings to your face painting?" I sat on top of my séance table, a cigarette between my first and second fingers.

It distracted Hannah. "Maybe. I've been studying. Before y'all got here, I had a three-card spread, just past, present, and future. The reading was for you."

"What'd you draw?" If I kept her talking about tarot, she wouldn't ask about Tanner.

"Three of swords, the lovers, and ten of cups." Her lips quirked into a smile, and her eyes sparkled. "The three of swords is your broken heart. The lovers represents a special bond and a deep connection between two people. The ten of cups is a happy family who has a loving home. Now let's talk about you and Tanner. The two of you can barely look at each other, and when you do, you blush like teenagers." She took out her long, skinny femme cigarettes and lit one.

I didn't know how to answer that. I'd been playing it as cool as possible with Tanner. No reason not to. Nothing needed to happen. He was still clinging to his family, and they were haunting him in an attempt to get him to break through his grief. He wasn't ready.

I wouldn't ruin what might be a good, mutually beneficial friendship by playing hot pants. I hoped I'd learned that lesson with Wade Hill.

Hannah snorted at my silence. "Oh, don't be a prude. There's something about him. If he wasn't so obviously interested in you, I'd take a run at him." She thought about that, frowning. "Maybe."

Hannah hadn't dated anybody since her runaround with King Tolliver. I couldn't say I blamed her. King Tolliver was enough to put any woman off men forever. But men still noticed her, especially Leon Blackfox. She noticed him too. But I still couldn't tease her about him. Not while she still radiated so much vulnerability.

"Spill it." Hannah came close and nudged me.

"We kissed," I said in the same tone I'd have accused Tanner of being a closet axe murderer.

"No good?" She dropped her jaw in surprise. "No way. The way he moves. The way he stares at you like a big cat waiting to pounce."

"Oh, it was good." I told her about his wife's and children's ghosts swirling around him, about his guilt over their deaths. I finished with, "He's not ready to let them go."

Hannah smoked, staring at the dirt floor. "The old me would have argued with you until the end of time. But look how I handled my romantic affairs." She made a sick face. "Don't give up on him completely. He looks very worth it. If you know what I mean." She lowered her voice and raised her eyebrows on the last sentence.

I agreed but said nothing. In the face of death, whether or not I had a romance with Tanner didn't seem to matter so much. It was a nice little mental vacation from reality, nothing more. I had bigger problems. "If you don't mind changing the subject…"

Hannah shook her head. "Not at all."

"Even if we get the wheel of life back, I have no idea how to use it to get rid of Miss Ugly." Spending my last day alive fighting to get it back might not be the best use of my time.

"But you still have to get the runes back and do something about your ex." Hannah turned down one corner of her mouth. "Otherwise, you're going to be dead, and we're going to be dealing with Oscar."

She had a good point. To protect my family and friends, I'd fight to get the wheel back, but I'd probably have to kill Tim to accomplish my means. I felt no guilt at planning my ex-husband's murder. The world would be a better place without him.

Tanner picked that moment to come back into the tent holding what looked like a stack of maps. "I'll need the table."

Hannah and I scattered. I got out my cleansing supplies, but Tanner shook his head.

"We don't need much ceremony for this." He dropped the maps on the table, unbuckled his belt, and slid the nine irons amulet off. He flipped past the charms until he got to the shovel head. "This one is for helping to find stolen items. Last time I used it was to find a car stolen from me back in California."

"Find it?" Hannah peered at the shovel.

"Yep. But it was in gang-banger country. I was too afraid to steal it back." Tanner dropped the amulet on the table and spread out the Texas map. "All right." He turned to face me, staring intently into my eyes. My stomach jumped. He held out the nine irons amulet. "From what I've seen, you're a really powerful witch, so I'm hoping this'll work."

I nodded and took the amulet.

Tanner said, "Hold the shovel in your hand. Envision the items, think of your claim to them, and why you need them. Think it as hard as you can. Then back up three steps from the table and toss the nine irons amulet onto the table."

I gripped the amulet in my left hand.

Tanner shook his head and reached for my hand. "Use your right hand since these items belong to you and Tim stole them."

"The runes were stolen." I let the amulet dangle from my fingers. "My great-great-grandmother stole them from the Coachman the day she killed him."

"But the wheel..." Tanner did that raised eyebrow thing

again. I smiled, and he smiled back. The air around him grew cold as the ghosts of his wife and daughters circled him protectively. Now that they'd left the living realm, their perceptions had changed. They had no perspective on Tanner's attachment to them, and they'd hurt me if they thought it helped Tanner. I had to tread carefully.

"The same great-grandmother gave me the wheel to use." I felt the stupid grin still on my face and tried to get rid of it.

"Use your right hand and think about the wheel. It's yours." Tanner took the nine irons amulet from my left hand, touching me way more than necessary, picked out the shovel, and placed it in my right hand. He even closed my fingers around it.

I held my hand at waist level and let my focus soften. I reached inward, feeling for my magic, hoping we hadn't exhausted it by sticking that cross to monsters' faces all evening.

For a second, it seemed we had. But then I felt the fire that had forged the amulet. My black opal flashed power in response. The blacksmith who had made this amulet had power of his own. He had infused elemental magic into the metal, given it his principles of protection and justice.

The mantle swirled inside me, somewhat rested and ready for action. I released it. The mantle, which seemed expert at calling fire magic, rolled itself into the fire magic of the amulet. A hot wind picked up in my tent, and all my candles lit at once.

Tanner spun in a fast circle, as though looking for

intruders. I didn't bother to tell him it was okay. Instead I kept my focus inward and called up my memories of the wheel. I thought about the soft, velvety feel of the metal, as though many hands had touched it, rubbing it smoother than any polishing ever could. The way the metal always felt skin temperature like something living came to me. I imagined running my fingers over it. Then I called to memory what the wheel could do.

The amulet twitched in the palm of my hand. A blast of magic heated my bones. It was ready. I backed up three steps and tossed it onto the table. The amulet landed in the upper right corner of the map, more miles away than my jerk of an ex-husband had had time to run tonight.

The amulet jittered against the table. It slid backward, to the center part of the state, and then down, down, down. The shovel came to life and moved just a tad. Then the amulet was still.

Tanner hurried forward. "It's pointing right at Austin." He picked up the amulet and unfolded the Austin city map on the table.

"I can't believe you have paper maps." Hannah touched her finger to it. "I just use my phone."

"I haven't had a phone that would do that in many months," Tanner mumbled. "It was the first thing to go after I decided to keep my oldest daughter on life support and insurance told me how little they'd pay."

Hannah blanched and stuttered out an apology. Tanner ignored it.

"I'll get you a new phone that does that." I took the

nine irons amulet out of his hand, ready to get back to business.

"You're not taking me to raise." Tanner leveled his intense gaze on me. Hannah's careless words had brought back the hurt.

"But I'll get you a phone anyway in case I need you to have those features." I held up the amulet to stop his argument. "Do I go through the whole ritual again?"

Tanner nodded, his pretty lips set in a sad line.

I relaxed my muscles and let the magic flow. In this state, the ghosts circling Tanner's head, emanating worry for their husband and father, were more clear than ever. I let my gaze slide off them. Another time. When he was ready. After I let go of the distraction, the mantle and the amulet rolled their magic together. I called up the memory of the wheel, this time in even more detail, even thinking about how I'd use it to save my own life.

The nine irons amulet must have liked that. It heated up instead of twitching. I took the three steps backward and tossed it onto the table.

The amulet went in circles around the map, reminding me of those old videos of satellite radar. It slid toward the middle of town. The shovel twisted a bit and stopped.

Tanner went forward and used a pen off my table to circle a small area around the tip of the shovel. He turned to me, eyes still dull from whatever the phone argument had reminded him of. "Want me to go with you?"

He was upset, and I hated to make him help me any more than he already had. Each time he helped me risked his life. His luck might run out. "No. Tell me what to do to narrow down the address, and I'll go alone." I didn't give him a chance to answer and turned to Hannah. "Get to the hospital and tell Cecil that I'm coming to see him as soon as I get back to town. I'm going to go back to my camper, sleep, and…"

"To hell with that. I'm going." She grabbed her purse from somewhere on the floor and hiked it up on her shoulder.

Tanner closed his eyes and shook his head. "You stay. I'll go."

"We'll all go." Hannah's voice got all snippy. I knew this tone of voice well and had quit arguing with it a long time ago. Dressing up a pig and trying to teach it to sing was a better use of my time.

I turned away and began gathering what I could salvage of my witching supplies, ears pricked up for whatever was going to happen next between Tanner and Hannah.

"You don't need to go." Tanner said the words like Hannah was a three-year-old who'd been asking the same question for forty-five minutes.

"But I'm going to go. This is my best friend, and I…" She cut off her words. "This is about the phone thing, isn't it?"

I shoved a mass of junk into my cedar box to sort through and turned around. This ought to be good.

Tanner put both hands on his hips, dropped his head, and let out a sigh.

"I'm sorry, all right?" Hannah, about the same height as Tanner, got right in his face. The muscles in his jaw worked. Hannah softened her voice. "I said the wrong thing because I don't know you well. I'm sorry for any hurt it caused you. That was not my intent at all." She took another breath to spill out more words.

I interrupted the whole fiasco. "Hannah. Let him be."

She spun, red-faced, to glare at me. Hannah meant well, but she had a whole dictionary's worth of self-help expressions. Sometimes they made people, meaning me, want to whip her ass.

"You can go," I said. "Tanner knows you didn't mean anything. Ignore him until he gets over it."

For some reason, I felt the same way I felt when I babysat my little cousins.

Tanner stomped out of the tent with, "I'll meet you back at camp."

I spoke to Hannah. "Help me get all my magic stuff together. Seems like closing the gate after the horses done got out, but I can't quite bring myself to leave it here."

14

After only a couple hours' sleep, we got up, drank coffee, and sped toward Austin, the sky already graying with the coming dawn. The short drive passed quietly.

Tanner, angry that I insisted on driving my own damn truck, slammed into the backseat, crossed his arms over his chest, and sat there looking like sex on a cracker. Hannah shrugged at him and got into the front seat. She wouldn't apologize again, so he'd better not be expecting that.

As we got into Austin, dawn faded into a deep blue sky scattered with puffs of cloud. The morning rush hour had already started. I wished we'd driven in last night and slept in the truck until dawn. The traffic flowed in a start and stop pattern. We'd get caught at a red light, wait, and then race to the next red light and stop.

"Isn't there a faster way?" I asked Hannah. She'd spent some time in Austin.

She snorted. " If you think this is bad, wait until we get downtown."

By the time we got downtown, I regretted not letting Tanner drive and glanced in the rearview mirror only to find him watching me. His eyes blazed with some unreadable emotion, and he glanced down at his lap. "We'll have to walk and use the amulet to find the exact address."

Hannah tapped my arm. "Park in the next pay-to-park lot or parking garage. We won't find curbside parking."

I did as she said, again berating myself for not coming in the middle of the night. But the sleep had done me a world of good. My magic tingled just under my skin, showing me an underworld of horror lurking right next to us, and ready to do more.

We parked and locked up. I slung my witch pack onto my back. Tanner came around and pulled the backpack into place. I tipped my chin to thank him but said nothing.

"You really think you'll need any of that?" He tried to smile, maybe to show he was past his dark cloud.

"I'd rather have it and not need it than need it and not have it." With that, we set off walking, Hannah reading the map on her phone.

We found the street the nine irons shovel showed us on the Austin map. Tanner took the amulet off his belt and handed it to me. "You'll have to picture the item again. You should feel the pull of the shovel in your body. Like a magnet."

I did as he said, closing my eyes to concentrate, too emotionally whipped to give a shit who thought me a weirdo. The routine of picturing the wheel of life, of imagining the soft feel of its worn metal, came easier this time.

The shovel jumped in my hand. I closed my fingers over it. A feeling, not electric like my usual magic but more of an ache, crept up my arm. As Tanner had promised, it pulled me down the street.

We walked in silence, all of us smoking. It drew glances. We were probably breaking all kinds of no-smoking laws. None of us stubbed out our cancer teasers. The shovel kept pulling me, and I kept walking, holding on to my concentration as best as I could amidst the noise and distractions. The pull stopped in front of a fancy-looking restaurant.

This couldn't be right. I walked a few more feet, but the shovel pulled me right back where I started.

"This is it, but I can't imagine Tim McSwain anywhere within a mile of this place. Unless he was here to burgle or rob it." Revulsion at who I'd once been married to crawled over me.

Hannah marched to the door, cupped her hands around her face, and peered inside. "Nobody. Not even a cleaning crew."

I slumped. All the way to a big, loud city to run up against a brick wall. I glanced back at the building. Or a stucco and glass wall in this case. What next? I lowered my head to stare at my black cowboy boots.

Magic in the form of electric prickles rushed over my skin. I stood still and pushed all thought from my mind. The black opal heated on my chest. Faintly, almost beyond what I could hear, came a woman's scream, high and full of animal terror.

"Did you hear that?" I asked Tanner and Hannah. Both shook their heads. I walked back to the building and peered inside. Nothing.

"What is it?" Hannah followed after me.

"I hear something." I walked around the side of the building to see an employee's entrance, a delivery bay, and a dumpster.

The scream came again, this time a little more clear. I walked to the edge of the narrow lane behind the restaurant and stopped, listening. Nothing.

I walked alongside the building, running my hand over the stucco, searching for the evidence of something otherworldly. Again, nothing.

I turned to Hannah and Tanner, ready to tell them we had to make another plan. My phone rang, and I pulled it out of my pocket.

Mysti Whitebyrd requesting a video call. Ignoring it ran through my mind. I didn't have time for this. But Mysti might have some ideas. I accepted the video call.

Mysti's smiling face appeared. She took one look at me, and the smile faded. "I called to see if you'd gotten rid of Miss Ugly. But things aren't going well, are they?"

I shook my head, my failures tumbling out before I could stop them. Once I finished, I realized I hadn't even asked about her and Griff. Their case had sounded like a dangerous one. "How are things going for y'all?"

She shook her head. "Just another day for Reed Investigations." Disappointment deepened her normal chipper voice.

I asked, "Are you okay?"

She tinkled a sweet laugh at my concern. "Neither of us is in actual danger. Let's talk about what's going on with you."

An almost shameful relief spread over me, and I nodded.

"First, who's there with you? I hear voices. Is one of them this Tanner Letts I've been hearing about?" Her eyes flicked to a spot near me.

I made Tanner and Hannah come over and speak to Mysti. She wiped the worry off her face and said charming things. Finished with the pleasantries, she got right down to business. "Tanner, I think you made a good call on the runes. I wish I had thought of it and warned Peri Jean to get rid of them."

Tanner wiped some of the sulk off his face and stood a little straighter. "Sure doesn't help now."

"No," she agreed. "All that matters now is finding Peri Jean's asshole ex and getting both the runes and the wheel back. Peri Jean, you said you heard screaming. Is it possible there's a thin place there?"

I shrugged. "I didn't see anything, but I can feel magic."

"And there's no way he's in the restaurant or whatever is behind you?" Mysti frowned as though she already knew the answer and the question was just for form.

I turned away from the cell and stared at the building, searching. "I don't see how or why... Wait a minute."

I took the nine irons amulet out of my pocket, went

through my ritual, and held it in midair. It pulled me toward the dumpster. The smell threatened to knock me out.

Still staring at the nasty thing, I said, "The nine irons amulet took me to the dumpster, but he's not in with all this trash."

"Perfect," Mysti grumbled. I turned back to face the camera again. Mysti frowned. "Come closer so I can see you."

Confused but knowing I couldn't win an argument with her, I did as she asked. She directed me until only my forehead was in the camera.

"What are those marks between your eyes?" Her voice had sharpened.

The sound of it made my nerves tighten up. She always sounded this way right before she made a new discovery. I reached up to touch my forehead and felt the scabs. The memory came back. "Miss Ugly pricked me there. I figured it was just part of her signature."

Mysti shook her head. "She sees something within you that she thinks she'll enjoy eating."

Hannah made a disgusted noise. "Ugh. Prime Rib of Peri Jean."

Mysti made a face and nodded. "To a being like Miss Ugly, someone as powerful as Peri Jean would taste extra good." She frowned. "Do you know what a third eye is?"

Jadine's weird vision again, that light coming from my forehead. Shelly's story. My short-lived research expedition. I'd meant to do more thorough research, but I'd been on the run since Miss Ugly made her first appearance.

"Only that it lets you see beyond what the human eye can perceive."

Mysti nodded. "Close enough. Have you ever had any experiences of seeing things that you didn't know were there?"

Coolness spread through my body. This was it. This was the new thing, and I already knew I didn't want it. "Sometimes. When the magic is really strong. Or when Oscar Rivera's followers blew that dust in my face. Remember that?"

Mysti swallowed. "What did you see?"

"I could see stuff like faces in trees, these huge animals that weren't there, people within people. After Sol ate the hole in the spell covering the mantle, I started seeing this vibration, like I'm seeing the earth's power." Dread pounded with every heartbeat.

I glanced at Hannah, then at Tanner. I didn't want them to see me discovering a new superpower. Hell, I didn't want a new superpower. I turned my attention back to Mysti.

"It's time to activate your third eye." She had that no-nonsense tone in her voice. I groaned and slumped anyway. She stiffened. "Wipe that damn pout off your face. You have mere hours to get this straightened out. Get with the program."

My cheeks flamed with her rebuke and maybe a little shame at the way I was acting. But I never asked for this, dammit.

"I see you have on your witch pack." Mysti gave me the kind of smile that let me know she wasn't angry with me.

I nodded and hooked my thumb underneath one strap.

"There's a secret pocket inside. Have you found it yet?" Her smile turned sly.

"No." The news worried me. Mysti had loaded my witch pack with all sorts of supplies she used regularly. My magic didn't call for the same supplies as Mysti's, so as I needed more space I took out the things she'd included and stored them. Now I worried that whatever she'd left might be in the cabinets in my little RV. But nothing had been in a secret pocket. I hoped.

"Give the phone to Hannah and open the pack," she said. I did. "Unzip the compartment that rides nearest your back." I did as she said. "Feel around the edges for a thick spot." I walked my fingers over the padded material. Mysti kept talking. "Near the bottom, right at the edge, is a tiny spot held closed with Velcro."

My fingers found it, but I didn't open it. Each time some new gift manifested itself, I got a little farther from the normal girl I'd wanted to be all my life. Deep down, I knew normal didn't exist for me. I was a freak, destined to live a freak life. Most days, I made peace with it. But on the days when new stuff cropped up, the little pang of loss came back.

"Do you feel it?" Mysti's voice came out of the speaker.

"Yep." I pulled open the Velcro and reached into the padded pocket. Out came a tiny plastic tub, about the size of a thimble, with a screw-on cap. I pinched the tub between my fingers and showed it to Mysti. Hannah held my phone so Mysti got a good view of my scared face.

She nodded. "That's your flying ointment. There's a

long history of witches and flying ointments that I do encourage you to read, but for now just understand that it's going to help you open your third eye."

I stared at the small tub, more wary of its contents than ever.

"It does contain things that would be poisonous to ingest. Never eat it or let it get in your eyes or mucus membranes." She paused. "Some witches disagree with me on this. But this is potent stuff, not to be played with."

"Did you make it?" I still wasn't sure about this flying ointment.

Mysti shook her head. "A witch from Oregon makes it for me. Are you ready?"

As ready as I'll ever be.

Mysti barreled on, probably aware of my hesitation, but not caring. "Put a tiny amount on your finger and dab it on the place where Miss Ugly pricked you. The open skin will allow it to soak in faster, so beware of using too much."

I couldn't quite make myself do it. "After that?"

"Then wait. The door to the thin place should appear. You won't need a spell or an invitation to get through." She smiled.

I held the tub in the palm of my hand, wondering if there was any other way.

Mysti interrupted my thoughts. "Peri Jean, you have a gift. Appreciate it and be grateful."

I nodded, knowing better than to argue.

"You want me to wait while you try it?" She had that teacher look on her face, curiosity mixed with authority and a little pride. The look said, *This is my witch, the one I taught. Look how far she's come.*

I shook my head. "Tanner and Hannah are here to help me figure it out." I paused, trying to think of the right way to say the next part. "Mysti, thank you for everything you do for me. Even though I drag ass and complain, you make a difference in my life."

Red rushed up Mysti's neck, over her face, and disappeared into her hairline. She pooh-poohed my compliment. "All in a day's work. Helping you is my pleasure."

"I'll call you after it's done and let you know how it goes." My finger hovered over the end call button.

"Part of the reason I called is to let you know we're flying into San Antonio late tonight. I'll be available to help you early tomorrow morning." The pleasure fell off her face. "Which I realize now will be too late."

"It's going to be fine," I told her, even though I didn't believe it.

"Love you, sister." Her voice cracked. "Call me if there's any way I can advise you."

I nodded. "Love you back." The call ended. The black screen somehow fostered an emptiness in my chest. I wanted to scream and cry, but it wasn't worth the energy.

I took a deep breath and twisted the cap off the tub. Inside was a shimmering translucent paste. I dipped the tip of my pinkie in it. It felt cold and oily on my finger. My black opal pulsed.

"Here." Hannah, out of patience, grabbed my finger and rubbed it on the spot Miss Ugly had marked.

Once the flying ointment was on my head, I rubbed the tip of my pinkie on my jeans, thinking about Mysti's warning not to get it in my eyes. Then I waited.

"You feel anything?" Tanner crowded near.

"Not yet." My heart was beating too hard, making blood rush under the skin. Whatever was going to happen would likely happen fast.

"We're right here," Hannah said. Next to her, Tanner nodded. The spirits around his head came into sharper focus, their presence a ripple in reality. They curled over Tanner's face protectively.

"I've heard this stuff can get you sort of high, sort of make you trip." The green of his eyes seemed to sharpen.

In them, I saw hurt, shame, and regret over his wife and daughters. Underneath all that, I saw a desire to start again. One of the spirits flashed out at me, teeth bared in warning. They'd eat me down to nothing if I came near him. Tanner felt shame when he looked at me. That made me a threat.

Numbness spread outward from the spot where I'd dabbed the flying ointment, cooling my skin as it went. The mantle woke, watched the spreading coolness, and went out to meet it. My vision flashed, turning the world black and white, then right back to color.

The screams came again, but this time they weren't faint. They sounded like they were right around the corner. I followed the sound to a clump of trees separating the restaurant from the next property, which happened to have a very old house set right in the middle of downtown. Tanner and Hannah crowded behind me, almost fighting each other to be the one closer, the one who'd help. The door leading across the veil flickered right in front of those trees.

On the other side stood a house painted light blue with white gingerbread trim. The scream came again. In it was that kind of animal fear people get when they realize there's no hope left, just the promise of death and the great unknown. The sound of running footsteps pounding on the house's floorboards reached me. So did Oscar's familiar evil. It rolled off the house like cartoon stink waves.

I turned back to Tanner and Hannah. "They're in there."

"We'll come too." Tanner started toward me, already reaching for me.

"No. If I don't come back, explain what happened to my family, and warn them about Oscar. Tell them he's coming for them." With that, I stepped through the door. It closed behind me. Tanner shouted in frustration on the other side.

Now that I had crossed, the entire world around me changed. The huge buildings of downtown Austin faded away, replaced by houses, many of which had barns behind them.

I climbed the steps onto the porch, energy flowing into my hand from the spired wooden railing, and walked toward the white front door. The numbness had spread down my body now, and my heart beat too hard. The stained glass windows around and above the door seemed to undulate and breathe.

The scream came again.

"Come back here, you dumb bitch," Tim yelled.

A cold laugh, one I recognized as Oscar's, followed Tim's order. Footsteps pounded through the house, shaking the windows in their frames.

I stopped with my hand on the doorknob. Even over here, I could out-magic Tim, maybe even kill him. But Oscar too? His power would be strongest this side of the veil. This was the realm of the dead, and Oscar was one of them. He'd had Tim bring the runes here, thus allowing him to manifest here, for reasons that probably gave him some other advantage. Fear ached at the center of my chest. There was no way I could win this fight. I glanced around, looking for Priscilla Herrera and some tough love. Nobody came.

Digging for courage, I turned the doorknob. A woman ran toward me, mouth open wide to scream. A gash had opened one cheek, and blood covered that side of her old-fashioned floor-length dress. She passed right by as though she didn't see me and ran into the next room.

I watched her in disbelief. She was the same woman I'd seen when I'd touched the rune back in my tent. One of Oscar's victims. My chest tightened. I didn't want to see this.

A figure rounded the corner behind her, axe held in one hand. At first, I didn't recognize Tim. He'd somehow stuck Oscar's runes all over his naked body. Every visible piece of skin was slicked with blood, and he left bloody footprints.

His eyes settled on me. "You. The biggest bitch of them all."

"She's a thief as well," came Oscar's voice. It seemed to originate at the same place Tim's did. Was Oscar talking through Tim? One way to find out.

"What do you think I stole from you, Oscar?" I'd expected a little mouse squeak to come out of my mouth. Instead, I sounded big and bossy, just like Priscilla Herrera.

Oscar's voice came right back. "You stole my runes. You stole my grand re-entry into the world. You fouled my plans. And you've robbed me of valuable time." Sure enough, his voice was coming from somewhere within Tim, maybe the runes. Heaven only knew how much power he'd stolen from me.

"But you no longer have a place in the living plane," I said. Oscar's determination to return to life baffled me. He couldn't possibly think he could come out of nowhere and rise to any kind of power. It was Monday morning quarterbacking. No more.

"I can make a place. Take the turmoil in your world and cause apocalypse. Then I'll rise as a king—a god!— once they see what I can do." His voice had risen with excitement as he talked, and the last word boomed around me as though the world was already crashing to its end.

"You won't have any power once you get back." There was no way he would. He'd use it all getting himself reborn.

"I'm glad I met you, Peri Jean Mace." Now Oscar's

words came out of Tim's spit shiny lips. "You're the one who taught me how to siphon power. I'll never be without power as long as I exist."

"You will once I get rid of those nasty damn runes. I'm going to drop them down the deepest, darkest hole I can find, and that'll be the end. You'll never be able to contact anybody else through them." And that was exactly what I intended to do, right after I got hold of the wheel. Which I had no idea how to find.

Oscar didn't reply. Tim's eyes, which had gone dull while I argued with Oscar, came back to life.

"Where'd that cunt go?" His eyes, completely free of sanity, darted around the room. They settled on something near the far wall.

Tim's face changed. A little sanity flickered back into his eyes. He lowered the axe, sides heaving, and dropped his head to stare at his bloody bare feet.

I backed out of his path and quickly glanced into the corner. The wheel of life lay in the middle of an ornately drawn pentagram, the style of which I recognized from some of Mysti's older books on magick.

Tim and Oscar must have tried merging their considerable evil. It seemed to me the experiment had failed, driving Tim mad and leaving Oscar contained in the runes.

I crept toward the wheel. If only I could get it, half my reason for coming here would be finished.

Tim's head snapped up. The insanity crackled in his eyes again. He gripped the axe in both hands and ran toward me. My muscles trembled, begging me to run for my life, but I stayed in Tim's path just long enough for him to think he had me.

A mad grin stretched his lips back, revealing teeth covered in blood. My muscles jerked to get away. *Wait, wait.* Tim raised the axe over his head. *Just another second.* His wild yell filled the room. He reared the axe back to strike. I dove out of his way. The axe whistled through the air and lodged in the wall.

A scream came from behind us. The injured woman stood at the edge of the room holding a butcher knife. At least she'd found herself a weapon. She launched herself at us.

Tim struggled to get the axe out of the wall, muscles bunching underneath the runes.

"Hurry up," came Oscar's voice. "This is where you kill her. Then you can do it all again."

The axe came out of the wall with a screech. Tim spun around in time to meet the screaming woman. He raised the axe over his head and swung downward. It buried almost to the hilt in her skull. The life drained from her eyes, and urine pattered the floor as her bladder let go. Her knees buckled, and she slid to the floor.

Dizziness made my head float. The scene horrified me, but I was too stunned do anything but stare. Hadn't Oscar said they'd do it again?

Tim wrenched the axe out of the woman's skull. Her body lay still for a second, but then she picked herself up. Her dress, which had been stained with every kind of blood and grime imaginable, was stain-free. She smoothed it down, not seeming to see the naked madman in front of her, and walked to the front door. She patted her hair and opened it, already smiling.

"It's so good to see you this evening. Won't you come in?" She held the door open as nobody entered.

"Kick him out," I yelled from my place on the floor. She never even looked my way.

Tim left me and went to stand near the woman as though he'd just come in from the outdoors. She smiled at him, not even seeing that he was naked, bloody, and covered in bone runes.

Tim said, "Why, thank you, Sister Samuels."

The black opal gave me a particularly sharp jolt. I jerked and took my gaze off Tim and Sister Samuels, trying to figure out what the black opal was showing me.

The wheel of life lay only a few feet away. I glanced back at Tim and Sister Samuels. Could I get it while Tim and Oscar were going through the first act of their murder spree? None of them were paying me any mind.

"Would you like a glass of lemonade?" Sister Samuels clasped her hands in front of her floor-length dress.

"That would be wonderful." Tim actually smiled, showing off his bloody teeth again.

I reached for the wheel of life. My hand knocked against something cold and hard, jamming the fingers into the knuckles. I gasped and jerked back. The circle Oscar and Tim had made around the pentagram somehow kept me out. I tried again. The magic cramped in my hand. I drew back with a yelp.

"Be good, Peri Jean," Oscar's voice came from the runes. "Unless you want to fight for your life right now."

"Please sit in the parlor while I get your lemonade." Sister Samuels motioned Tim/Oscar into the parlor with me and hurried into another room, presumably to get the stupid lemonade.

Tim walked over to me, junk dangling, and reared back his foot to kick me. I gathered the mantle and shot fire magic into him. It rebounded and hit me, waking up my numb skin with the feeling of pins and needles. I yelped and rolled to my feet, backing away.

Tim walked toward me, but Oscar's voice came out of him. "This is my place, dear, and your magic won't work. I've taken life here. Miss Samuels, her maid, and her sweet baby daughter, and this memory belongs to me. You're a guest."

I backed away from the monster I'd been married to, not sure what to do next. Using my magic to scramble Tim's brain might simply rebound it onto me. I might kill myself. The circle around the pentagram was as good as a steel wall, so it was lost to me for the moment. Maybe I should go back to my world and regroup.

I glanced at the door. Ten steps tops. Once I got outside, I'd likely be okay. Oscar had driven Tim mad. He was now useless unless being controlled by magic. He'd hinder Oscar more than help him outside this house. Which left Oscar trapped here. If he left, it would cost him whatever spell he was using to control Tim. Oscar would have no choice but to go back where he'd hidden his soul and wait for another chance. He wouldn't want to do that.

But if I left, I'd be leaving without the wheel of life.

Miss Ugly would come for me when it got dark, and I'd have no way to fight her. I had to do what I came to do.

Possibilities raced through my mind. None sounded like they would work. I counted the steps to the door again. Something new hit me.

I could get Tim to leave the house. Oscar had said my magic wouldn't work in here. This was his memory, and he was in control. But he wouldn't be in control outside the house. I could get the wheel of life and then figure out what to do about Tim and the runes. I turned my attention back to the horror movie playing out before me and began to plan my move.

While Sister Samuels prepared the lemonade, fresh-squeezed no doubt, Tim crept to the fireplace. Someone had left an axe lying on the brick hearth. Tim picked it up and went to stand next to the doorway Sister Samuels had gone through. He put his finger to his lips for me to be quiet.

I shook my head at him, walked to the front door, and opened it. Sister Samuels's footsteps rang on the wood floors.

"Be right there," she sang.

"No problem," Oscar/Tim sang back.

I pulled the nine irons amulet from my pocket and crept toward Tim, using my fingers to find the cross. Just as Sister Samuels reached the doorway and her mouth opened to scream, Tim swung the axe. She ducked away, but the axe caught her cheek, laying it open. Blood gushed down the front of her dress. She spun on her heels and ran. Tim took the first step to chase her.

I slapped the nine irons amulet onto a bloody patch of exposed skin. Smoke rose from the contact, along with the smell of cooking skin. Tim, still holding the axe, let out a howl that was half him, half Oscar. I shoved him toward the open front door. It was like trying to move a piece of dead meat. Even skinny, he outweighed me by no telling how much. I pulled the cross away from his skin, leaving behind a raw, bloody spot, and stuck it to another exposed piece of skin. Tim spun, trying to get away from me. I gave him another hard shove. He tripped toward the front door.

Oscar must have caught wind of what was happening. "Don't go out the door, fool," he screamed.

But Tim had an exposed circle of skin on his ass cheek. I stuck the cross there. The sizzle and sudden pain goosed Tim out the door. An oscillating wall of reality appeared, and I shoved him through it.

The house changed. I had broken the cycle of Oscar's memory of the havoc he wreaked in this place. Now the final result of his visit faced me.

The bodies of Sister Samuels, a baby, and a woman wearing a black and white dress lay on the floor, hacked to bits, sightless eyes staring at nothing. In seconds, the bodies disappeared. The pools of fresh blood where they'd lain dried and then faded in the blink of an eye. The walls of the house aged and buckled, the flowery wallpaper peeling off in great long strips. The windows broke out, and phantom balls and rocks hit the floor around my feet.

I jerked into action. Without Oscar here to hold together the illusion and replay the memory of the day he murdered Miss Samuels and everybody else in the house, the house's future was happening in fast forward. I doubted I had more than a few seconds before it burned or a wrecking ball came to make room for progress.

I raced for the pentagram drawn on the floor. It was now nothing more than a few faded chalk lines. Gingerly I reached forward, expecting Oscar's circle to throw me back, but my hand went through where the circle had been. Tim taking the runes, and Oscar, out of the house must have broken it.

I grabbed the wheel of life, held on tight, and ran for the door. Just as I crossed the threshold, the first wisp of smoke rose in one corner. I dove for the billowing wall of reality.

"There she is," Tanner yelled and ran toward me. Hannah followed close behind him, her face white with shock.

Beyond them, Tim swung the axe and screamed. The runes that had covered him lay on the asphalt at the spot where he'd crossed back to this side of the veil.

"Get the runes," I yelled into Tanner's face. He and Hannah knelt with me and gathered the pieces of bone. At first, evil emanated from them, but then it flattened out and left. Good. Oscar had used up all his power.

Bare feet slapped the pavement, coming toward us. I glanced up from shoving the last of the runes into my pockets just in time to see Tim bearing down on us, axe raised. Tanner stepped aside, and I dragged Hannah and myself out of the way. As Tim raced past, Tanner delivered a punch to the back of his neck. Without a sound, Tim fell on the asphalt with a meaty splat.

"I'm calling the police," a woman standing in the open back door of the restaurant screamed.

Tanner, Hannah, and I ran for my truck. I tossed the keys to Tanner at the last moment, and we all piled in. Tanner burned rubber getting away from the scene.

Three blocks later, I remembered my witch pack. "We gotta go back. My witch pack." I poked Hannah in the arm.

"Right here." She patted it. "We put it in the truck after you'd been gone so long."

Sirens started up nearby. Tanner, who'd been leaning over the wheel driving, stopped the truck at a red light. We watched them speed toward the restaurant where Tim must have still been.

Tanner turned to look at me. That mind-altering lust passed between us again. I turned away and began getting the runes out of my pockets, determined not to have them touching my skin.

<h1 style="text-align:center">15</h1>

Despite a brief text message from Finn saying the hospital was keeping Cecil another day and telling me not to bother coming, that's where I told Tanner to take us. The hospital turned out to be nothing more fancy than the kind of country hospital I grew up with in Gaslight City. Tanner drove with maddening slowness around the parking lot, the midday sun blindingly bright through the windshield, only to finally back into a spot away from all the other vehicles.

I climbed out of the truck and into the scorching sun before Tanner even shut off the motor and then set off across the parking lot at a near run. The heat from the concrete at my feet turned my boots into a sauna and my feet into slippery little fish inside them. Ignoring the discomfort and Hannah's calls to wait up, I picked up my pace.

I needed a break from Tanner. The tense silence set my nerves on edge, made the back of my neck ache. This lingering attraction between us had to end. Maybe I could quit shaving my armpits and switch to sleeveless shirts. That ought to do the trick. I snickered.

Better to laugh about it than sulk. The latter wouldn't change where Tanner was with his grief right now. I sympathized, but I didn't want this to become another Wade Hill situation, wanting a man I'd never have, regardless of the reason.

The glass door leading into the hospital slid open, and I ducked inside, checking my phone for Cecil's room number. The hospital was so small that it really wasn't much more than a clinic with the patient rooms down two wings on the first floor. The sliding door opened behind me. Tanner and Hannah were catching up. I sped down the hallway toward Cecil's room without looking back.

I came first to a glass-walled waiting room. Dillon saw me and rushed out of the room, her youngest child, Zander, hanging on her hip. The poor kid's big, brown eyes drooped, but as soon as he saw me, he sat up straight and held out his hands, clasping them and opening them for me to take him. I held out my arms, put on a happy face, and let him slide into them. Dillon moaned with relief and shook her arms.

Finn came out right behind his wife, his daughter Zora's hand clasped in his. The little girl zeroed in on me and began trying to yank her hand out of her father's.

He glanced down at her. "Stop it, Zora. You set off the fire alarm last time I let go of you."

"I want Peri Jean to hold me like Zander." Zora turned

her eyes on me, big and mournful as though only I could make her happy.

Her father frowned at her and shook his head. Zora stuck out her lip. Finn ignored her pique and spoke to me. "I told y'all not to come."

"I'm not going to stay away with Papaw in here. How is he?" I took shallow breaths, not wanting the hospital smell to soak into my sinuses. Bad stuff always happened in hospitals.

Zora used her free hand to pull at my jeans. "Pick me up. Now."

Finn shook his head at her but spoke to me. "Papaw seems fine. Don't know why the doctors are making him stay."

Zora began to tap my leg. "Pick me up. Now. I want to tell you a secret."

Zora's secrets scared the hell out of me. I pretended not to hear. Finn shushed her.

"I guess I'll go on in and see Papaw." I pushed Zander back at Dillon. He gave a warning wail, only half the volume of a real one, and grabbed a fistful of my hair. I hissed at the pain.

Dillon reached for Zander. He pulled my hair harder and wailed louder. Zora yanked on my jeans, hard enough to pull them down, chanting for me to pick her up. I grabbed the belt loop with my free hand. Between her and Zander making angry baby sounds, it was like being under siege by an army of Lilliputians.

About that time, Tanner and Hannah came rushing down the hallway. Hannah gave me a red-faced glare and wiped the sweat off her upper lip. Finn stuck out his hand for Tanner to shake. The two men gave each other those mysterious male nods. Zora forgot about me and zeroed in on Tanner.

"You're the new guy. My mommy said I have to be nice to you." Being a kid, Zora yelled the words.

Tanner squatted down and solemnly held out his hand. "I'm Tanner Letts from California. What's your name?"

Zora, who'd recently learned about handshaking, gave Tanner an overly enthusiastic handshake and shouted, "I'm Zora Kaye Gregg."

Dillon giggled and glanced at her husband. They exchanged a smile, the glue of their bond showing. Despite their grifter lifestyle, they'd found something lots of people, including me, never did. True love. A little twinge formed in my chest.

Finn spoke to Zander. "Let's go for a walk."

Zander tightened his grip on my hair and shook his head.

"I want to go for a walk, and I want him to go." Zora quit yanking on my pants and grabbed Tanner's hand.

Seeing this, Zander held out his chubby little hands to Tanner. Tanner raised his eyebrows at Dillon. She nodded with a look on her face that said, *Anything to move this forward.*

I handed the kid over to Tanner, surprised at how Zora had just influenced him out of both his stubbornness and his natural mistrust of strangers. Tanner, Dillon, and Finn walked off with the kids. Zora's voice floated back to us, announcing her desire for ice cream.

Hannah leaned into my face. "What'd you run off for?"

I shrugged.

She glanced in the direction Tanner had taken Zander. "Oh good grief. The two of you need to get over yourselves." With that, she marched into the waiting room and sat down next to Jadine.

My jaw dropped at who was sitting next to Jadine. None other than Brad Whitebyrd. Could he possibly have worse timing? He ought to be in Canada helping Mysti and Griff. I grabbed the doorknob, ready to go in there and tell him off, but then let go. Maybe I'd mind my own business for once instead.

I marched down the hall, searching for Cecil's room number. I found the room and stood outside, staring at the slip of paper on the door that had his name and age scribbled on it. Eighty-one. Close to fifty years older than I was. How much trauma could a body that old take? *Sooner or later, he'll be gone just like Memaw.* I swallowed panic and lightly tapped on the door.

Shelly opened it, looking fresh in a brown sleeveless blouse and yellow slacks. Boy, I hoped my upper arms looked like that when I was her age. She smiled. "Come on. He'll be thrilled you came."

I crept into the room, memories of Memaw's final months spinning poisonous webs in my head. Cecil lay on the bed staring at the TV, playing with the sound off. Without looking at me, he said, "It isn't over, is it?"

I sat down next to the bed. "Nope. It ain't. But I got the

wheel and the runes back." I launched into the explanation for how Oscar had tricked me and continued siphoning off my power to use for his next attack. I took the wheel of life out of my bag, where I'd returned it to its leather case. "Worst part? We think this would help me get rid of Miss Ugly, but I don't think I have the power."

"That damn power-blocking spell again?" Cecil's voice, thin and weak, rose.

"Stay calm, Papaw," Shelly said. "Unless you want the nurses to come back." She pointed at his heart monitor. For the first time, I noticed it was beeping slowly, had been since I walked in the room.

"I am calm." Cecil frowned and stuck out his lower lip. Then, to me, he said, "I've not seen the first sign of the man who could help you remove the spell. But believe me, I am asking around, putting out feelers."

"It's okay." I told him Hannah's idea about simply letting go of my bad memories, stripping them of their importance. "But I don't know if I can. Who I am is all wrapped up in that stuff. It's how I learned to be me."

Cecil nodded at what I said, deep thought darkening his expression. "Hannah might be onto something, but I think it'll take more than just letting them go. Keep rolling it over. You'll come up with a plan."

But before tonight? I didn't say that to Cecil, of course. No need to stress him over something he couldn't help with. I decided to change the subject. "Have the doctors talked to you yet?"

Cecil made a face and talked through his nose with no Texas accent. "'Well, Mr. Gregory'—that's who I am today

—'it would help if you didn't smoke as much as you do. Every time you light a cigarette is fifteen minutes off your life, and you're running out of fifteen-minute increments.'" Cecil's dark eyes burned. "I was smoking cigarettes and serving this country before that kid was even thought of."

"But you do need to quit smoking," Shelly said. Then to me, she said, "The doctor told Papaw that if he didn't quit smoking, he might have a year left. They're doing a heart catheterization today to see how bad the blockage is."

Cecil and I stared at each other. He held out his age-spotted hand, and I took it. He smiled at me. "Long life for a Gregg, ain't it?"

I gave him a squeeze but didn't answer.

"You know the worst part of all this?" Cecil changed the subject smoothly.

I shook my head.

"When people think you're on your death bed, they want to get all the loose ends tied up." He pointed at his water. Shelly got up none too happily, put the straw to his lips, and let him drink. He cleared his throat. "Jadine brought that boy she's seeing to ask me if they could be married. You go to all the trouble to raise a child, to teach them your ways, and then they come to you holding hands with an ass-clown they want to marry." The blips on Cecil's heart monitor sped up. Shelly cleared her throat. Cecil shot her the finger. She sent it right back.

I bit my lip hard to scare away the laugher. "What'd you tell Jadine?"

Cecil put his palms up and shrugged. "What the hell could I say?"

"You lying old man. You tried to run him off." Shelly crossed her legs, smiling at Cecil. It was the same kind of smile Dillon had given Finn. *We're thick as thieves, this old man and I. What we have goes beyond a few finger gestures and a little name-calling.* Soulmates. That stab of envy came back.

"How'd you try to run Brad off?" I hoped Shelly and Cecil would act up more. Seeing them made me feel less lonely.

"I told him he'd have to take the Gregg name." Cecil raised his shaggy eyebrows, making it clear he'd have never agreed to changing his surname to be married to any woman.

"Hell, you lost before the game started," I told Cecil. "Mysti chose her and Brad's last name after they got out of foster care. I think the original is White."

Cecil nodded sourly. "Yeah. That's about what he told me."

"I hate to see her get married so young, but my daughters from my first marriage did the same thing." Shelly shook her head. "I was only seventeen the first time I got married. Who am I to talk?"

"Brad's an okay guy. Just lazy," I said to nobody in general.

"He'll get along fine with Finn then." Cecil rolled his eyes. Suddenly, the bad-tempered joking went off his face, and he turned to me, serious. "I want to apologize to you, Peri Jean."

I flushed. "What for?"

"The way I talked to you about why you need to have a child. The way I pushed you at Tanner embarrasses me now." He licked his lips and swallowed hard. Shelly got him another drink of water, eyebrows raised in command for me to tell Cecil it was all right.

"Don't worry about that. I do like Tanner…"

Shelly cut me off with a whoop. Cecil shushed her.

"But he's broken," I said. "Did he tell you what happened to his wife and kids?"

Cecil nodded. "If Tanner had a dollar for every pound of guilt he's carrying around, he'd be rich. But who knows? Maybe he'll let it go. Sometimes you do find a way to shed the past."

The expression made me think of the ouroboros Tanner wore around his neck. A snake shedding its skin was another form of renewal. My tattoo twitched, and I thought of the wheel sitting in my purse. My brain had that fluttery feeling, like I was right on the edge of an epiphany. Then Cecil spoke again, and it slipped away.

"We've put a lot on you from the second you walked into our lives. If you've been made to feel like there was some kind of test to pass, I'm sorry." Cecil chuckled. "Talk about death bed loose ends. I'm as bad as the rest of them."

Cecil and my family hadn't made life easy for me, but I'd never doubted my place among them. That was worth all the trouble. I cast off his apology with a flick of my fingers, but he shook his head and kept talking.

"Once I started getting to know you, it felt like you'd been one of us forever." He stared into my eyes.

"I feel the same way." I put my hand on the bedside rail. Cecil put his over it. Tears stung my eyes and my sinuses. I didn't want Cecil to be coming to the end of his life. The idea hurt.

"Aww, not you too." Cecil lay back with a drawn-out sigh. "You know, I've been sitting in this room seeing my wife's scared face, knowing my family's right down the hall worried, but I'm sort of on the fence."

I drew back, too surprised to speak. "You don't want to stay with us?"

"Well, sure I want that." Cecil widened his eyes, incredulous again. "I want to be with y'all forever. But this old body is getting tired. The day's coming." He pointed one finger at me, the way Memaw had always done when she was dead serious. "Don't think I'm not grateful to see all I've gotten to see. I'm seeing my parents' beloved Sanctuary being reborn with new, talented young people. Seeing my daughter get married, which is a kind of rebirth for her. Seeing you birth yourself, painfully sometimes, into your destiny as the bearer of this family's power." Cecil's chin wobbled, and his eyes brimmed with tears. "Not so bad for an old ex-con."

I got up, kissed his whiskery cheek, and put my forehead to his. "I love you."

Cecil said, "I love you too, baby."

Two sharp raps sounded on the door. A nurse wearing purple scrubs with green lobsters on them came in and said, "We need to get Mr. Gregory ready for his procedure."

I kissed Cecil again and stood. "I'll see you tomorrow." I couldn't tell him things would end one way or the other with me and Miss Ugly tonight. Not in front of an outsider. He seemed to understand anyway and gave me a grave nod.

I walked out of the room but didn't go straight back to the waiting area. The image of the snake shedding its skin, of Cecil's talk of rebirth, kept coming back to me. It played over and over. Then I'd see the wheel of life in my mind.

I went outside and found a table with an ashtray next to it. A man with gray hair wearing a white doctor's coat sat, holding a cigarette between his fingers. He took urgent drags, eyes fixed on a blank wall. Not wanting to interrupt, I lit up my cigarette a few feet away and leaned against a sign that said "No Smoking within Twenty-Five Feet of Building."

The doctor finished his cigarette and crushed it under his polished black shoe. He walked to the door, turned back to me, and said, "Across that threshold lies a new, smoke-free existence." We exchanged smiles, and he went inside.

The idea of a threshold added itself to the carousel of ideas revolving in my mind. Rebirth, threshold, wheel.

The wheel of life controlled fate. My fate was connected to Miss Ugly's. What if I could rebirth myself to a new fate?

I took out my phone and called Hannah.

16

Hannah and I spent most of the day researching rituals that represented death and rebirth. I had the formula now. I must die in order to be reborn to a fate without Miss Ugly.

Although it would have been the simplest to pull off, we quickly nixed baptism because it just didn't feel right. And who'd perform the baptism? Certainly none of us. But it was more than that.

The spell surrounding the mantle was made up of all the bad things I'd experienced in life. The stuff that marked me. I believed in learning from my mistakes, even those perpetrated on me by others. But the scar tissue had helped me hang on to it far longer than was helpful.

Since I was the one who'd done the hanging on and picked what to hang on to, I was the one who needed to cleanse myself of it.

By mid-afternoon the search had become frustrating. I went into my camper's tiny bathroom and dragged my long, sweaty hair into a ponytail on the top of my head, longing for the convenience of short hair again but liking the way I looked.

Hannah watched me from the table. "I saw a taqueria in town. Let's go get some real tacos, come back here, and settle on something."

By real tacos, Hannah meant the kind served in a soft corn or flour shell rather than the hard shell served in the American version. Hannah meant the kind of tacos garnished with hotter-than-hot salsa, fresh cilantro, and sliced avocado if we were lucky.

I grabbed my purse, we got in my truck, and I drove us into the tiny town near the RV park.

The taqueria was so authentic that the counterperson didn't speak English. Hannah and I struggled through broken Spanish to order beef tacos and the kind of green salsa that started a fire behind your eyeballs. We ordered tall glasses of *horchata* served on ice and sipped the sweet, cinnamon-flavored drink while we waited for our food.

The earthy smell of cumin and the sweetness of frying onions had my mouth watering by the time they called Hannah's name. I snatched the tray, and we hurried to a booth and sat down.

The tacos came with a bowl of Mexican white cheese, tiny paper cups of crema, and two plastic cups of the hot green salsa. I put a little of everything on my tacos and bit into the first one, chewing slowly, and waiting for the burn of that green sauce to hit my tongue.

When it did, sweat popped out on the back of my neck and forehead. I imagined myself descending to the underworld, the common perception of Hell, letting it engulf me, and arising without my baggage.

"I'm going to do what Inanna did," I said around my food. Hannah and I had read about Inanna during our research. The Sumerian goddess was the subject of a famous death and rebirth myth.

Hannah chewed thoughtfully, swallowed, and wiped the sweat off her forehead with a rough paper napkin before she answered. "Descending into the underworld and dying to be born anew is pretty powerful. How do you want to do it?"

"Before Inanna could complete her journey into the underworld, she had to give up her jewels and fancy clothes." I took a bite of my taco.

Hannah began speaking while I chewed, swallowed, and sipped *horchata* to soothe my tongue. "Those fancy things were her confidence, the things she believed showed her power. She had to strip something off at each of the seven gateways."

I dipped a crisp tortilla chip in the hot red salsa at the center of the table while she talked. When she finished, I said, "Inanna had to do these things to make herself vulnerable and open so that she could die and be reborn. I'm the same as Inanna, only my earthly accoutrements are the bad things I've endured." Tears stung my eyes. "Deep down, I think if I hold on to it, I'll be immune to more bad stuff happening, or at least tough enough to withstand it."

"You're never immune." Hannah leaned forward to whisper, her food forgotten. "And your strength comes from you being you. Not that stuff."

She was right, but up to this day, stripping myself down to an open canvas had been scarier than holding on to the poison. Hannah and I stared at each other for several seconds in silence, then began eating again.

Between bites, I said, "I may not be able to do seven stations, but I think I can find something tangible to symbolize the big hurts. I'll get rid of each one, then die and be reborn. What do you think?"

"I think if it works for you, I may try it." She winked and took a huge bite of her taco, extra-hot green sauce dripping to the plate.

We finished our tacos, got a refill on the *horchata*, bought two concha pastries with yellow icing, and went back to the RV park. Tanner was sitting in front of my camper at the picnic table. I tossed my cigarettes and lighter down on the table in front of him, tore off half of my concha, and gave it to him. He wanted to refuse, I could tell, but he ate the pastry and lit a cigarette.

"What are you going to do?" He held his smoking hand in front of his face, almost as though he was hiding behind the smoke.

I lit my own cigarette because I couldn't stand not to. "I'm going to make my own version of Inanna's death and rebirth."

Recognition flashed on Tanner's face. "I know this story."

"I can't recreate the doorways, where you leave behind things or the climbing out of the underworld, so I'm going to have to improvise." And I had no idea what I was going to do.

Tanner stood and motioned Hannah and me to follow him. He walked to the edge of the RV park's property. The property didn't end at a fence. It ended at a steep drop-off into a deep crevasse. From far below came the sound of rushing water.

"Been down there?" Tanner gestured at the drop-off.

"Hell no." The descent was so steep I'd never make it back up. My smoker's lungs would strand me down there, and I'd have to start my own new civilization. Live on bugs and dirt.

"I went down there and came back up. This is nothing compared to the mountains I used to hike all the time in California. You saying you can't?" Tanner's lips, which I remembered vividly on mine, quirked into a sly smile.

Did he just challenge me? Really? Time to pull out my big guns. "Liar."

"No. The lady who works the desk in the office told me about it. It's an area attraction. I hiked it while the two of you went to out to eat."

I rolled my eyes. "Go on then, mountain man." I gestured at the drop-off. "Show us how it's done."

Tanner nodded. "Okay. Get the stuff for your ritual, though. It's about three-quarters of a mile both ways. You won't want to come back up and go back down."

I glanced at him, looking for a twinkle in his eyes, even a smirk. Nope. He was serious. I swallowed hard, not looking forward to eating my dare.

Hannah and I went back to my camper to gather up what I needed. Choosing items that I thought represented the contents of my scar tissue proved more difficult than I thought. In the end, I guessed and hoped it was enough.

Tanner led Hannah and me to another area of the RV park. We passed a swimming pool full of screaming kids. The people who knew us yelled our names. We waved. Behind the RV park's office, Tanner gestured at a set of steps.

I narrowed my eyes at him and turned down my lips. "You acted like you climbed down that steep hill."

"Did not." Tanner started down the steep, stone steps.

"Did too." I followed him, still having to pick my way down, despite the footholds. I wished for a railing, something to hold on to and steady my descent.

"Fine, I did." Tanner stopped and turned around. "Let's stop joking. You wanted to emulate Inanna's journey. These steps are your descent into the underworld."

I nodded my understanding. As I picked my way along, I imagined myself leaving the known world. In a way, I was. I had no idea what was at the bottom of this ravine, only that it was wet and that water was a source of cleansing and rebirth.

"These steps really are old," Tanner said. "The lady in the office said these current steps were put in by the WPA during the Great Depression. But they were put on top of steps already here. Nobody knew how long those first steps had been here or who put them here."

We walked in silence. I concentrated on the roiling mass of scar tissue, on all the disappointments in my life, all the heartbreak, all the stuff I'd done wrong, all the people who'd let me down. I thought about the contents of the little bag I'd packed and hoped again they were enough.

The descent got steeper as we went. The punishing sun beat down on our backs, and a painful burn built in my thighs as they strained against the sharp angle. The sounds of the water splashing came nearer bringing with it a mist of humidity to steal my breath. Sweat slicked my skin. Just as I decided I'd have to stop and catch my breath, the land leveled out, and we stood on a slight rise overlooking a briskly moving stream. We walked to the edge of the water and stared into it. My black opal gave me several sharp, warning pings. *This place is haunted with magic or ghosts. Beware.* The steps took a sharp turn to travel alongside the water.

"Hannah and I stop here," Tanner said. "If you want to be like Inanna, you go the rest of the journey on your own."

I walked to the steps and stared down, unable to see where they ended.

Tanner came to stand next to me. "The water flows over several natural levels of rock. Wait till you see what's at the bottom. The path gets harder and harder. It's slippery in places. Be careful." He gave me a light push to get started.

I glanced back at Hannah, wanting some kind of reassurance, but her face was fixed and serious. Heart pounding in my throat, I took the first step into the underworld.

———

The steps went straight down. On one side was a moss-covered expanse of rock. On the other side, water rushed past me. After ten or so steps, the land widened out to a steep drop-off of three or so feet. Below that, the water splashed down, and the steps started again.

The black opal pinged on my chest. It was a signal. I didn't have instructions for this journey, so I acted on instinct. I took out the little bag of things I'd brought from my camper and drew one of them out.

It was a picture of me with my mother, Barbara Mace. The picture was a cheap studio shot taken at a discount store a couple of years after my father died. It was the only picture I had of us together. I had carried it in my wallet or on my person all my life. At one point, it had been in hopes Barbie would feel my love for her and come back. In later years, it became a symbol of rejection. In a sick way, I had relished the hurt it caused. *If I can survive being shunned by my own mother, I can take anything.*

In the picture, Barbie wore perfect makeup, a revealing top and a miniskirt. I had on regular kid clothes, a shirt with cute designs on it, baggy little jeans, and dirty sneakers. Unlike most mother and daughter photos, Barbie and I sat a few inches apart. She smiled as though her life depended on looking pretty. I looked uncomfortable and maybe a little scared.

A tear tickled on my lashes and burned down my cheek. I set the picture on the ground next to the stream. "I'm sorry you hated me, Mom." It was the first time in a long time I remembered calling her that. "I wish you'd had a happier life, and I'm sorry you died the way you did. Now I have to let you go."

The mantle shifted around inside me like a huge serpent whipping its tail. A couple of wisps of smoke drifted up from the picture. The paper curled, and the image of me and Barbie turned black and bubbled. A pain flared in my chest, in a place too deep to soothe. The picture burst into flames. Soon nothing was left but a piece of charred paper and some bits of ash. A wind whipped through and blew away the whole mess.

I watched it go. My chest gave a particularly sharp throb. I raised one hand to massage the spot, regretting the very spicy lunch I'd had.

The pain lanced deeper. I pressed harder and moaned. The discomfort increased to agony, to the point where I stood with my hands on my knees gasping, a line of slobber between my mouth and the ground. Then, just as quickly as it had come, the hurt went away. I fell to my knees with relief.

Ideas flooded my mind. My mother had hated herself. Maybe she'd hated me, but she'd hated herself more. It didn't excuse what she'd done or how she'd treated me, but I understood now she'd been unhappy too. I could pity her. I could forgive her.

And with forgiving the woman who'd abandoned me, my hate for her lessened until it was no more consequential than a spill that needed wiping up. I accepted that I'd never change the way she'd felt about me, that I could only change how I reacted to it.

My chest hitched several times, and I realized I was

crying. Not just crying, but sobbing, arms clutched around myself. I cried myself out and looked for the way forward.

I crouched on the edge of the drop-off. Just a few feet to my left, water rushed over the edge and splattered on rocks, creating a rainbow mist that drifted onto the steps. I'd have to be careful. I let myself drop. My feet hit the first step and almost flew out from under me.

Panicked grunts escaping me, I grabbed for a root sticking out of the embankment beside me. A set of tiny black eyes stared out at me. A snake. I jerked back. The snake, just a water snake, flicked its tongue out at me.

Keep going, said a voice that came from all around me. The snake meant no harm. He was only there to remind me that this process was one of rebirth.

I did what it said, reaching the next riser with a little more bravery. Now that I knew my routine, I didn't have to dig through my bag of things to let go.

I took out the picture of Felicia Brent Fischer Holze I'd printed off the internet. My old enemy had a new last name but seemed to be up to her old tricks of swinging man to man to get what she wanted out of life.

My business with Felicia was over, had been since she and her awful family burned down the house I was raised in and I beat their asses for it. But Felicia represented all the malicious bullying I'd endured growing up. She represented every bloody nose I gave and got. All the negativity and mistrust I felt when I met someone new.

A flash of anger lit my emotions, and my fist curled as though I was being called upon to defend myself. I took a deep breath and let the anger go as best as I could and set the picture on the muddy ground near where the water washed over the slight drop-off.

"I'm sorry I took the way they treated me so personally. I'm not sorry for being different. I still hate them all."

A crackle answered my words. The snake had followed me down here and now lay in a lazy curve, watching me. A wind shook the trees. The noise seemed to say, *rebirth.*

Staying mad wasn't any kind of rebirth. And it wasn't letting go either. I tried to look on the situation from a different angle. After a few seconds, I found it.

Kids are mean to each other. It's how they learn about the world. I hadn't always been Miss Nicey-Nice myself. What we'd done to each other was done. It was time for me to let it go.

Letting go didn't mean I had to be asshole buddies with any of those walking turds or that I had to slow down if they crossed the street in front of me. It just meant I needed to be kinder to myself.

The piece of paper with Felicia's ugly mug printed on it crackled and burned without any encouragement from me. I leaned over it and blew the ashes into the wind.

"Go away," I whispered.

The fire of hate that never stopped burning at the pit of my stomach blazed high, the way fires always do when the oxygen is cut off. Awful images ached behind my eyes. Every awful emotion I'd felt at the hands of those people came out for one last hurrah. Then I let my mind blow it all away into the void where memories go to die.

I didn't cry the way I had when forgiving Barbie. Instead, an emptiness opened where the old hate had been. The snake flicked its tongue at me and slithered away. I'd have to grow to fill that emptiness with good things.

The trail went on in front of me, another drop-off looming a few feet away. I squatted there, this time more careful to find a way to let myself down easy instead of jumping. My feet slid on the narrow step, but I was ready and just took the next step down. That's what life was about after all, riding out the bad shit and moving forward.

I took the steps to the next riser and pulled out the next picture, this one ripped from one of the home decorating magazines I secreted away in the cabinet next to my bed.

They all ran features on quaint houses surrounded by white picket fences, with an abundance of sunlight flooding into them and colorful accents bringing the house to life. In front of the houses were always flower-choked arbors and white rocking chairs just waiting for someone to sit in them and watch the lightning bugs float around the yard.

I laid the picture, my favorite out of all the magazines I had right now, on the ground, knelt next to it, and waited for the emotion to come.

It did, in the form of deep hurt and loss opening up in my chest. It went so deep I couldn't find the beginning or the end. This picture represented my image of normal, and normal represented happy. When I tore this picture out of the magazine it came in, I threw away all the others, vowing not to buy another.

"I'll never have you," I whispered at the picture.

"Maybe I'll have something equally desirable. Maybe I won't. Life will be good, and I'll find things to be happy about either way."

Anger flared inside me over the loss of normal. I let the fire roar, stoking it with self-pitying thoughts. Then I let it go. The mantle lashed out at the picture as though it hated it. The picture bubbled and flames licked around its edges. In seconds, there was nothing left. The wind came again and blew it away.

I walked forward on my journey. This drop-off was much greater, at least ten feet. There were no steps at the bottom. It landed on a muddy bank next to a pool of water roiling from the force of the waterfall rushing into it.

I took a deep breath, squatted, and slipped over the side as gently as I could. The impact still landed me on my ass in a wet splat. Dampness from the mud soaked through my jeans immediately. I climbed to my feet, brushing uselessly at the mud, and took the last item from my bag.

I set the black and white picture on the ground, hand shaking. It was a picture of someone's ultrasound. Not mine. That picture burned up with Memaw's house, thanks to Felicia and family.

Next to it, I dropped the cheap, plain gold-plate band Hannah and I had bought in the costume jewelry section in a discount store before we came home from lunch. The one my ex-husband gave me the day we said our vows also burned up or melted when Felicia and her awful family burned my house to the ground.

It wasn't so much the failed marriage or even the beating that resulted in the miscarriage of my only pregnancy. It was what the failure represented. Me not liking myself enough to make good decisions.

"I treat myself like worthless junk." Tears sprang into my eyes at the truth of it. I treated myself no better than my mother, the Felicias of the world, and my ex-husband had treated me.

"I'm going to do better." My voice quaked. The fire in my chest came back. This time so intense, I could do nothing but clutch at it.

The mantle coiled inside me, ready for action. But I needed to make the first move on this one. I flicked my fingers at the mound of broken dreams. It burst into hot blue flames, burning only for a few seconds, and disappeared into the earth.

All I'd seen and done as I traveled alongside this water welled up, and I cried like a tired child. The emotions hurt more than any fistfight I'd ever gotten into. The tears slid down my face as a final goodbye to it all.

The mantle flared, moving more freely than it had before, but not completely unleashed yet. I'd have to do this again. Possibly more than once. Maybe each time would be easier. I laughed at my own naivety. Stuff that was worth having scratched and kicked the hardest.

I stared at the drop-off I'd used to get down here, trying to figure out how I'd get back up. Tanner, if he even came this far, had probably climbed back up with no problem. Could I do it? Only one way to find out.

I took a running start and managed to jump high enough to get my hands over the drop-off. But the ground was soft. I just pulled off two hands of sod and landed right back on my butt. I sat next to the pool of water, watching the way the waterfall constantly renewed it.

The mistake I'd made hit me. I had come to the underworld, but I hadn't died. Without death, I couldn't be reborn. Staring out at the pool of water, I thought again about baptism, the symbolic death and rebirth I'd so quickly rejected.

It would be a way to die and be reborn, my mind whispered.

I didn't want to get in this pool of water. No telling how deep it was. What if I got caught up in roots on the bottom? And that snake I'd seen earlier. There were more of them somewhere.

But the water called to me, dark depths inviting. Maybe I'd never come back up. If that happened, I'd win. Miss Ugly wouldn't get to kill me. I smiled at the childish thought and got to my feet.

A row of boulders stretched out over the water. Had they been a bridge for whoever built those older steps Tanner had mentioned? Maybe.

I walked out on the first one, arms waving to keep my balance. Maybe I could make myself jump in. Three boulders out, I hit a slick surface. Fate made the choice for me.

My feet slid forward. I did a wild, arm-waving dance. Then I remembered what I'd come to do and dove face-first into the water. Cold, winter cold, seeped into my clothes and shocked my heart. Rather than floating to the top, I sank, some invisible force pulling me under.

The mantle heated inside my chest, burning with a hotter fire than the one I'd conjured to burn away my past.

The stress on my body made my lungs scream for oxygen. I struggled to rise to the top, but I only sank deeper. My feet hit bottom.

The need for oxygen beat at my chest like wings of a frantic bird. The mantle answered with its white fire, which brought an ache so intense, so awful, I forgot to fight. My muscles went loose. I accepted my death.

Whatever force had held me down let go, propelling me at the water's surface. The light came closer and closer. I broke the surface with a whooping gasp. It sounded not too different than Miss Ugly.

I swam to the shore opposite where I'd started, weak muscles shaking, and lay in the sun on the muddy bank, trying to catch my breath. With each lungful of oxygen, more of the mantle escaped the scar tissue. It stung like acid as it seeped into my muscles and nestled deep in my brain.

Shadows descended over my vision, the entirety of the earth moving and shimmering around me. The black opal heated. Somewhere, very far away, I heard Orev's cry.

The scar tissue spell still hadn't gone. Not completely, but my magic had strengthened. It prickled over my skin and whispered in my mind. Had I strengthened myself enough to get the wheel of life working and save myself from Miss Ugly? I hoped so. Because after that, I still needed to do something about Oscar.

I opened the dorky hip pack I'd strapped to my waist and took out the last item. The satisfaction of having done something right for once welled up inside me. When I'd put the wheel in the hip pack and strapped it to my waist, its color had been dull, the metal well-worn and soft but cold. Now a sunny nimbus glowed around it.

"Give me another fate, one without Miss Ugly," I whispered at the wheel, no idea what else to do. I put all my concentration into the command and held it until the light around the wheel died. Then I replaced it and began looking for a way to get back to Hannah and Tanner.

Back across the pool waited the ten-foot rise that was too steep for me to climb. The shadows of the mantle darkened my vision again. My third eye spot ached, and tears blurred my vision.

A nearby rock sparkled in the sun, so bright it could have been a diamond. I stumbled to it, dug it out of the mud, and found it was a hag stone, one where the water had worn a hole in the rock.

Mysti loved these and collected them. The legends surrounding hag stones claimed peering through the hole in the center let you see into the other world. Feeling inspired, I fitted the hole over my third eye. The world shimmered, and the sound of the water frogs calling grew louder. In front of me, an overgrown path became clear. It was a trail, old and deep, ascending upward, back to the topside. I started walking.

17

───────

The path I took somehow looped me around behind Tanner and Hannah. Despite the emotional exhaustion from my ritual, it was satisfying to outsmart Tanner after all his bragging about his stupid hikes. Plus, I got a good look at his muscular butt from this angle.

"Hey," I said to their backs.

Hannah let out a little scream and spun around, tripping over her own feet. She ran at me, and we hugged. She never jumped up and down anymore when she hugged. The bad stuff she'd been through had taken it out of her.

Tanner marched past me to peer down the trail. He turned to me frowning, as though I'd cheated. "I didn't know that trail was there."

"It was on the other side of the pool at the base of the big waterfall. There's some rocks crossing it if you walk a little way through the woods." I tried to sound casual, as though it had been easy.

Tanner nodded, then smiled a little. "You couldn't lift

yourself back up the drop-offs. Plus, you're wet. That means you fell in the water."

I stuck my tongue out at him and turned to say something to Hannah. She faced the huge crevasse created by the ravine. Sunset glowed salmon and peach with a little dab of turquoise at top. Above it, the darkness ate the light, getting closer and closer to snuffing out the last of it.

"Maybe Miss Ugly won't come." I stared out at the darkness, waiting for that awful, moaning howl.

"Don't worry about that old monster. You changed your fate down there." Tanner pointed into the deepening night in the direction of the rushing creek.

Hannah stood a few feet away from us, arms crossed over her chest. I walked away from Tanner to see what she thought. She ignored my approach. I leaned out so I could see her face and found her bug-eyed with her fists clenched.

"What is it?" I put one hand on her arm.

"You're going to die." She let out a shaky breath.

"What?" I tried to laugh.

She took a breath, probably to repeat herself, but she never got the chance.

"Hoooooo." It echoed in the ravine, floating up to us like a foul odor.

I grabbed Hannah. "Run. Go back to camp. If I don't come back, gather the runes, take them somewhere bottomless, and drop them in." I knew bottomless sounded crazy, but this land was full of caves and caverns. There had to be a place.

"Hoooooo." This time it was closer. We had only seconds.

I turned to Tanner. "You go with her. Help her."

He shook his head. "I'm not leaving you here."

"If my ritual didn't work, she's going to take me." I grabbed his shirt and shook him.

He shook his head again. "I won't leave you to face her alone."

"Run," I said again to Hannah.

She stared at me, eyes wide, teeth chattering. She ran to me and hugged me. "I love you," she whispered in my ear. I squeezed her back.

"Don't say goodbye yet. Your death visions aren't always right." I winked.

Miss Ugly rose over the edge of the drop-off. She had a broom clenched between her legs. It should have looked ridiculous. Instead, the sight of her floating in midair, riding a broom, scared me more than just about anything else ever had.

A scream rose up my throat, and I swallowed it down. I would not show fear or act like a sissy. I marched toward her.

"It is done. You are mine." She floated toward me.

"Nope. I went down into the underworld and let go of my bad shit. Then I told the wheel to divorce my fate from yours. We're done." I shot my arms out like an umpire calling safe in baseball with a confidence I didn't feel. Something was wrong. Miss Ugly wouldn't have bothered to come across the veil unless she was sure of a free meal.

But still I held out hope she'd ride off into the sunset and we'd never meet again.

Miss Ugly flashed her rotten teeth and lowered herself until her nasty, long toenailed feet touched the ground. She let the broom drop. Crushing tension built in my chest as she walked toward me. "You might have changed your magic, but you did nothing to change your fate."

My heart thudded hard enough to jar my vision. The sour taste of bile rose up the back of my throat and jumped into my mouth. No. This wasn't right. I'd died and been reborn. I'd changed my fate.

Before I could present an argument, Miss Ugly launched herself at me, threw me to the ground, and ripped open my still-damp top. She finished scratching her signature in my chest. A lethargy heavier than I'd ever felt sat on me. I couldn't even raise my arms to ward her off.

Tanner rushed forward, grabbed me under the arms, and began dragging me away. I glanced at his face, expecting to see a fierce warrior. But he looked as terrified as I felt, eyes wide, gasping in horror.

Miss Ugly stood with her gigantic feet crushing my chest, making it impossible to breathe. She shoved Tanner with both hands. He flew backward and landed hard enough to elicit a pained grunt.

He bounced to his feet and came back with his fists up. Miss Ugly stalked toward him, both long-fingered hands raised with the claws splayed. I tried to move, to go help Tanner fight her, but I couldn't move.

"Run," I tried to yell. My voice came out in a sluggish mush as Miss Ugly's final dose of poison worked its magic.

Miss Ugly advanced on Tanner. "Leave now with your life."

"I'm already dead. I died with my wife and kids." Tanner darted in, threw several jabs at Miss Ugly's face, and ducked away when she tried to claw at him.

Miss Ugly held both arms out straight. She drew in a breath. The air around me changed. She was accessing her magic. Her arms grew by many inches. She slashed one out at Tanner and caught him across the face. He staggered away from her, hand held to his cheek.

The initial torpor of Miss Ugly's poison lessened. I couldn't move my body yet, but my mind went into overdrive.

Even if my silly little ritual hadn't changed my fate, it had changed the scar tissue blocking my full use of Priscilla Herrera's mantle. I turned inward and probed at the scar tissue. Now, rather than being hard like armor, it felt softer, maybe looser. Good enough to put up a serious fight. I drew on the mantle, calling to the magic of all the elements, and pleaded with them to help me.

Earth responded first, sending a little ping of an answer to my black opal. The ground trembled beneath my back. The grass rippled, and a ripping sound came from it. A bulge rose out of the grass and headed straight for Miss Ugly.

My third eye spot burned, and I turned my attention to it. It let me see a man made of grass grow out of the ground and tower over Miss Ugly. I lay drained from the effort but filled with foolish, childish hope. The grass man tried to cover Miss Ugly.

"Hoooooo," she screamed. The force of her howl blew him over the side of the ravine. He lost form, and a clutch of torn grass floated down.

Tanner had regrouped and advanced on Miss Ugly again, fists in a boxing pose. Again, I tried to get to my feet. My legs did nothing but twitch. Despite my increased mental acuity, Miss Ugly's poison still pumped through me, seasoning my meat for her to dine on later.

"Come on, bitch," Tanner spat at Miss Ugly. My third eye showed me his family, swirling around him, trying to offset his foolhardy actions.

They didn't matter to Miss Ugly. She circled around Tanner, swinging with her extra-long arms.

Wait a minute. I could help. Tanner needed to ask Miss Ugly a question to make her shrink back to normal size.

"Ask her a question," I tried to yell. My words came out in the barest of whispers.

Tanner danced around Miss Ugly. She stood very still while he did this, every once in a while darting forward to slash at him. Tanner's reddening face told of his flagging energy. He wouldn't last forever.

Then I saw the nine irons amulet dangling from one hand. He'd made me give it back as soon as we got home, and now I was glad he did. Miss Ugly swung at him again. He jerked out of the way at the last second. Her arm arced around her, the force of her strike carrying the momentum. Tanner darted forward and pushed the nine irons amulet against her ear.

"Hoooooo." Miss Ugly's howl of pain hurt my ears. She

clapped one hand over Tanner's amulet. He danced away, ran to me, and pulled me to a sitting position.

"I'll pick you up now." His chest rose and fell with harsh breaths. Sweat beaded his face. He didn't have enough strength left to carry me back to camp. And even if we made it, what then? He tried to roll me into his arms, but I was limp with no control over my muscles. I slid right out.

"Just go. Get out," I whispered.

Tanner clenched his jaw and shook his head. "Can't just leave you to die. Not like my girls."

Miss Ugly, apparently having gotten over her injury a little, stalked up behind Tanner. Despite my vow not to scream, I did. It didn't make any sound, but there was enough force behind it to make it feel as though it was stripping my throat raw. She grabbed Tanner's shoulder and spun him around.

"Go now. Peri Jean Mace wants you to let her go." This must have been Miss Ugly's idea of fairness.

"Never." Tanner shook his head.

Miss Ugly cocked her head at him, bug eyes getting even wider. "You are serious."

Tanner widened his stance.

Miss Ugly slowly nodded at me and touched her finger to her third eye spot. I opened mine again, but it did nothing other than show Miss Ugly as a huge monster towering over a fragile mortal.

She leaned down to speak to Tanner. "I only kill for food." She moved so fast she was a blur, tearing Tanner's shirt open and making her mark on his chest. Tanner fell limp just as I had.

"Dummy," I tried to scream at him. He'd sacrificed himself for nothing. Now we'd both die.

Miss Ugly tucked me under one arm and Tanner under the other. She straddled her broom, and we took off, jetting through the night sky.

In this state, with my third eye active, the columns marking the entrance to the underworld appeared as solid as the boulders I'd used to cross that pool. The human skull sitting on top of each column marked this as the private entrance to Miss Ugly's domain.

I felt a lot of things at that moment. The strongest one was horror that tonight's fun would end with Tanner and me getting served up as a meal for Miss Ugly. We passed between the columns, and the world flashed black and white for just a second. The poison in my system pulled a dark curtain over my vision. I passed out.

———

I woke with a start and stared into darkness. A dank, earthy smell surrounded me, and frogs sang somewhere nearby. The smell of woodsmoke tickled my nose. How I'd gotten here came roaring back. Miss Ugly had me and planned to do away with me for good. Oscar had won.

My hate for him seeped over me, hot and pure. I'd get him. Even if I had to do it as a ghost, I'd get him. The anger gave me enough energy to move.

I pushed myself to a sitting position, marveling at the

nubby hardness of the floor I'd been lying on. My fingers couldn't figure out what it was made of. Jadine probably would have been able to reason it out, but I was glad she wasn't here with me, mentally preparing to be eaten.

My eyes adjusted to the darkness, and I could now see stars above me, multicolored, bigger and brighter than on my side of the veil. I watched a streak of red shoot across the sky. The earth rumbled with it.

Whatever I was inside swayed back and forth, bumping against something. Each time the structure hit, grains of sand hissed against a hard surface. Where the hell was I? And where was Tanner?

I concentrated on the stars, searching for the power of the mantle. It came back to me, weaker than usual. No matter. It was enough for what I wanted to do. I pulled the light from the stars toward me. The enclosure brightened. It took me a couple of seconds to focus on the details, to realize what I was seeing. What I saw made me wish I hadn't bothered.

Above me, starlight glowed on a dull white crosshatch grid. I could have told myself it was just de-barked pieces of wood, but I could see the knuckles and joints of human bones. At each corner was a half skull, the bones fused to it by some means I couldn't detect. The sides of the structure came into focus. More bones tied together with something leathery and white. Steeling myself, I lowered my head to see what I sat on. The rounded humps of skullcaps made up the floor of the cage.

My eyes pulled in more light, and I made out a still form on the other side of the bone cage. The broad shoulders rose and fell with deep breaths. Tanner. Still alive.

But for how long? Miss Ugly was stumping around somewhere nearby preparing to cook and eat us. Or maybe make some sort of human sushi out of us. My skin tightened at the thought.

Tanner turned and moaned in his sleep. "No, no. My baby. No, no." He began to sob.

I crawled over to him, aware of the bone cage swaying with my movements. The cage was suspended on something. I could still see stars above us, but from the sides of the cage came only pitch blackness.

Tanner's sobs picked up in intensity. I hurried to his side. I held my hand over him, suddenly afraid to touch him. The ghosts of his wife and daughters might see my efforts as a threat.

I searched for them. They hovered protectively around Tanner, ready to fight for him. I'd always had a talent for feeling the emotions of the dead but had learned to separate myself from it. Now I opened myself to the ghosts and sorted past their desire to protect Tanner. Next to me, Tanner bawled like a kid, reliving the wreck that had claimed the lives of his family.

The ghosts' emotions came to me in a tangle. Desire to move on. Worry about Tanner. Fear he'd join them before it was time.

The intensity of their love for him welled in my chest, almost too big for me to take. It both touched me and made me scared for Tanner. He was destroying himself piece by piece every day he refused to move on. His wife, the beautiful Bea, moved toward me.

Save him, she whispered in my head. I sent back a message of comfort but knew only Tanner had the power to save himself. But I could wake him up.

I gripped Tanner's shoulder and gave him a hard shake. "Wake up. It's not real." He wept on. I had to repeat the exercise several times to get him to wake up. When he did, he jerked into awareness with a harsh inhale. He lay still for a few moments and then curled away from me. I scooted back and gave him space. As I did, my hip pack bumped against the rounded skulls making up the floor.

"Dorky damn thing." I moved to take it off. Dead, I wouldn't need it. The wheel of life, my last chance to save myself, was in the pack. I zipped the pack open and removed the wheel.

It still felt warm to the touch, and my black opal jumped on my chest. It had power. Why had my ritual not worked?

I'd let go of all the injuries I held dear. The hurt my mother caused by hating me, the hurt my true nature caused, which led to me wishing for normalcy, and the guilt I felt over letting a jerk like Tim McSwain into my life, which resulted in the destruction of the only pregnancy I'd ever had. Then I'd almost drowned in that pool of water but fought my way back to the top. What else was there? I caressed the wheel with my thumbs, searching for the answer.

Across the cage, Tanner spoke in a near whisper. "What is this?"

I slipped the wheel back into my hip pack and crawled near him. "It's a bone cage." I echoed his whisper.

Tanner let out a disgusted moan and shifted around, making the thing rock. "Are we suspended?"

"I think so, but I don't know where. Look up." I followed my own command, fascinated by the multicolored stars. One of them fell and left a streak of red in the sky.

Tanner did as I asked and let out a horrified gasp. "What is that?"

"We're on the other side of the veil. Miss Ugly's taken us to her lair to cook us." I scooted closer, wanting the comfort of another person.

Tanner stared at me, whites of his eyes glittering in the murky light, but didn't shoo me away. I settled into a sitting position and leaned against the wall. The long bones pressed hard against my back. I tried not to think about what they were, that they had once been part of someone living and breathing.

Tanner brought his knees up and put his hands over his face. "I should have never come to Texas. My mother always refused to come here when Dad wanted to go with Grampa to visit old friends and places. She said it's like the Old West, full of outlaws and bad people."

I bristled at the implication but let it pass. Knowing you're going to die soon really highlights what's important and what isn't. "Coming here wasn't all bad for you. You're going to rejoin your family."

"Huh?" Tanner slowly lowered his hands and fixed his

gaze on me. Even in the darkness, I sensed that primal nature of his, that caged beast pacing.

I didn't answer right away. The swirling ghosts around Tanner's head weren't my business. But Bea had asked me to save her husband. That meant convincing Tanner to let them go. I wasn't sure how much good it would do him in the last hours of his life, but it's always wise to honor a ghost's request. Especially one that benefits the living.

"What did you just say to me?" Tanner moved closer, got in my face.

I gave his shoulder a hard shove. "Don't fuck with me."

He raised on his knees, gripped my shoulders, and drove me to the cage's floor. The rounded skullcaps jabbed painfully into my back. I strained against Tanner, stomach muscles trembling. His weight gave him the advantage. I was trapped.

Tanner hovered over me like we were about to play a violent round of hide the salami. Fury filled me, pounding against the backs of my eye sockets, turning the world red. I was pissed that my whole life had brought me to this end, pissed that I'd never had a real chance with Wade, and doubly pissed that Tanner thought he could overpower me and bully me with no consequence.

I brought one knee up, aiming for Tanner's nuts. He shifted his weight and used his legs to hold mine down. "What did you say about my family?"

I took my hand off his wrist, where I'd been trying to push his hand off me, and made a fist. I let it fly and slammed it into his ribcage.

Tanner jumped and grunted in pain but didn't let me go. "Say it. Now."

Other than sparing Tanner's feelings, there wasn't any reason to keep what he was doing to himself a secret. Why spare his feelings? "The reason you feel like shit every day of your life is that you're forcing your wife and daughters to haunt you. Their presence keeps the grief raw. You might as well die tonight because you're not going to have any kind of life if you don't let them move on. Plus, they're ready to go."

The ghost swirled faster around Tanner's head, sometimes stopping to whisper to him. He didn't want to hear it.

"Liar," he growled.

"No," I grated through bared teeth. "When I woke you, I did it because you were dreaming of their deaths and crying. Let them go, or you're going to burn yourself to the ground."

"Liar. You just want me to feel like shit because you feel like shit every day of your life." He gave me a hard shove. Pain shot down my arms.

I'd had enough. I began to gather the mantle. Bea was wrong. I couldn't save Tanner. Sorry as I felt for him, I wouldn't let him hurt me. I'd scramble his brains and be done with him.

The power swirled inside me, pulling on the energy left in the bones and from the dank smelling earth surrounding us. My third eye opened, and I saw inside Tanner. Hurt roiled red and ugly. Underneath that was uncertainty. He almost believed me.

If only I could make him see. I had made other people see before, but how could Tanner see without a mirror?

I poured my power into Tanner, shaking with the effort of trying to control it. He jerked against me when it hit him, the movement primal and erotic. My body responded immediately, reminding me how I'd wanted Tanner.

"See them. They want to go to the next plane, but they want you to be happy first. Bea wants to save you," I whispered and closed my eyes to concentrate on what he needed to see.

Tanner stiffened against me, setting my nerve endings on edge even more. I tried to ignore it and concentrated fully on him seeing what he was making his loved ones do to him.

Tanner raised off me, breaking the connection. He stood, clunking his head on the roof of the cage. He doubled up one fist and smashed at the bones, making the cage jiggle wildly.

"Don't." I stood but kept my distance. "We might fall, and I don't know where we'll end up."

Tanner's shoulders shook, and he clapped his hands over his face again so I wouldn't see him crying. I moved toward him, unsure if I was walking into the jaws of a lion, but coming anyway. I slipped my arms around his waist and pulled him close.

His sobs rose in intensity, garbling the flood of words coming out of him. I could only pick out a little. "I want them back. I want to change that day."

"You can't. I'm sorry." I stroked his back, waiting for

him to push me away, maybe give me a few punches for good measure.

Tanner cried himself out like a fire burning. First it flamed hot and wild, then it dimmed until only a few embers crackled. Finally, he said, "I'm sorry I pushed you down and hurt you."

"I antagonized you." I kept stroking his back "Just because I'm a girl doesn't mean I get a free pass."

Gently, he detangled himself from me. I moved away, but he gripped one hand and squeezed it. "Thank you for letting me see the truth. I wish I had seen it sooner. I guess I'll be with them soon."

I shook my head. "I have to get out of here. People are depending on me. You have to get out of here so you can live your life."

"But how?" Tanner nearly shouted.

"I'm going to figure out why the rebirth ritual didn't change my fate. You're going to help me. Then I'm going to do whatever it takes to change my fate." I leaned into his face and said the most important part. "We're both going to live."

18

Tanner sat on the floor, motioning me to sit with him. Tears streaked with the neon of the stars shone on his face. He scrubbed them away. "Let me see the wheel of life."

I took it out and handed it to him. He weighed it in his palm, tracing one finger over the top of it. "What you did had no bearing on fate or the wheel. Maybe you didn't let go of the right thing so you could access its magic."

And maybe I still didn't have enough access to the mantle. I let out a frustrated grunt, took the wheel from him, and laid it on the floor of skullcaps. We both sat staring at it.

"I don't know what else to let go of." In the myth, Inanna had let go of her worldly treasures. She'd given away everything she was proud of, everything she felt she needed to retain her dignity. Then she'd died and was reborn. What had I not let go of?

I raked through my mind, digging for ideas, but couldn't think straight. My upcoming fate at Miss Ugly's hands fractured my thoughts into nonsensical shards. This sucked. I had all the tools I needed but couldn't figure out how to use them. *Think.* But I couldn't. A sense of deep loss, a feeling I'd missed out on something big and important, blocked out my ability to focus.

My hand rested close to Tanner's, and I thought of taking it for the comfort. And to touch him again. I had to be honest about that. Seeming to read my mind, he took my hand, threading my fingers through his.

"I wanted you so bad back in Pale Horse. But I couldn't even give you a proper kiss." His teeth flashed in the dimness. I thought he'd done a pretty good job of kissing me but said nothing. It was over. He rubbed his thumb over the back of my hand. "I'm sorry, because I like you. Life is sort of fun again when I'm with you."

He thought my life was fun? I turned to stare at him. Our eyes locked, and my desire for him writhed, begging to be allowed to do something embarrassing and stupid.

I shrugged, pretending nonchalance as best as I could. "Your love for your wife and kids, and theirs for you, the intensity of it, is what most of us want and never get."

"But our fates went in different directions," he said. "Keeping them around has kept me from giving myself a second chance. I wasted the time I had left living in the past." He let out a sad chuckle. And now it was too late. The words hung between us, unspoken but loud as a tornado. He faced me. "We've still got some time left. Would you let me kiss you again?"

I didn't answer. I just leaned toward him. He bent his head with maddening slowness. Each second elongated, stretching to the point of madness until finally our lips met. We'd already gotten past that shy hesitation, the dance of figuring out what was too hard and what was gentle enough. Our tongues touched, and my pulse stuttered. Tanner moaned deep in his throat. I trailed my fingers down the side of his neck. His heartbeat throbbed against my fingers, proof we were both alive and real in this moment.

Was I really about to make out with Tanner on the bones of Miss Ugly's victims? It made a weird kind of sense. We were celebrating life with death surrounding us and death waiting on the other side.

Tanner gripped my hips and slid me out from the wall. Eyes locked on his, I let him do what he wanted. He braced his hands on either side of my head and lowered his body to hover over mine. His lips teased against mine, and our breath mingled.

A tickle started at my center and spread, fighting the part of me that didn't want to let Wade go. Moving on, living in this moment, was the right thing. So why did it feel so disloyal? I wasn't the only one with baggage to shed. The spirits of Tanner's family beat at my skin. They wanted out before he moved on.

Tanner stopped kissing me. "I feel them here. I feel like I'm cheating on Bea. I never did that, and I can't start now."

I let go of him, trying to hide my disappointment. Bad timing. The story of my life.

The voices of Tanner's wife and daughters rose in a mournful howl. He'd almost let them go but chickened out. The force of their cry rocked the cage back and forth on whatever it hung from. Dirt sifted to the floor and into my face.

I began trying to get out from under Tanner. He blocked my escape and kissed me again, but it was half-hearted. I put one hand on his chest to push him away.

"You're not ready to let them go. That's why you feel guilty." I said the words as gently as I could. Sex often meant nothing, but this time it meant everything.

"I want this with you. Without feeling guilty." His voice rose in frustration on the last sentence.

"You can't have both." My own words hit me like a blast of cold water. Who was I to talk? I pretended to accept that Wade and I would never be. Yet I trotted out the memory of him every time I tallied up the wins and losses of my life. Maybe there *was* something I hadn't let go of in my little ceremony.

Tanner frowned at my pronouncement. His wife's spirit swirled the strongest around his head. She tried to comfort, but she also pleaded with him to let them go. Maybe she saw this as a final opportunity. I didn't have time to wonder why because Tanner picked that moment to take action. He pushed himself off me, stood as much as he could, and turned his back.

"Bea," he whispered, as though I wouldn't be able to hear. "You will always be my first true love. I'll cherish you every day."

Bea's spirit whipped faster around Tanner, almost a cyclone. She sent her love, her devotion, but then she pleaded with him to release her and their children.

"I wish things were different." Tanner choked on the

words. Then he swallowed and seemed to regain control. "Go with my blessing."

Bea gathered her two daughters to her. The spirits moved faster and faster in a whorl of blinding light. At the last second, the older daughter leaned in and whispered something in Tanner's ear. Then they blasted between the bars of the cage, finally shooting red against the dark sky. Tanner watched them go. When their light faded, he spoke.

"All this time, letting go felt like a betrayal. But holding on to them was the betrayal—to them and to me." His voice broke.

"The way to honor the dead is by living our lives to the fullest." The words were just as much for me as for Tanner. Wade still lived, but clinging to the idea of him was a dishonor to both of us. A weight I hadn't even been aware of carrying fell off my shoulders.

Tanner turned back and crouched in front of me. "None of us knows how much time is left. Each moment needs to count."

I nodded, heart too full to speak.

"Let's make it count together." He held out one hand, and I took it.

Tanner had the right idea. I didn't want to lose another second to what might have been. Tanner lowered his mouth onto mine again and pushed me gently onto my back. I hooked my legs over his hips, and we twined our bodies together, hearts beating harder.

The wheel of life lay next to my head. Something came from it, not quite heat, but more like a wisp of magic, tingling over my skin. Tanner shivered against me. He felt it too. The power of it rose, and the nimbus of light appeared around it again.

Had making out with Tanner given me another chance to change my fate? It didn't make sense. And yet it did. Sex was another ritual of death and rebirth. But it wouldn't work unless I accepted that Wade Hill wasn't the great loss of my life but instead the loss that opened the way for good things to happen.

Tanner trailed kisses over my jaw, calloused fingers drifting over my neck. My body, starved for attention, responded to the point I could barely think. He raised his head and crushed his lips against mine, moaning.

His smell drifted into my nostrils. Turned earth, primal, full of energy. The thrumming of his heart against mine.

In the back of my mind, I saw Wade. The ghost of my failed love life. Perfect because he was untouchable and untested. We hadn't had to weather life as lovers or part-ners. It was easy to say he was the great lost love of my life, my only chance at true love. It gave me the perfect excuse not to give anybody else a chance. That had been fine until I met Tanner and felt that odd, consuming connection. Things had changed. Now I had to let Wade go and face the future.

Tired of the pain, I was willing. But I didn't have a symbol of Wade on my person to destroy. Then it hit me—I did. The mojo bag I'd created from what he left in the hospital room after he'd been shot.

But I had to act fast or lose the opportunity. With only

a torn shirt between us, Tanner had already unhooked my bra, pushed it aside, and began teasing his thumb over my nipple. Soon, I'd quit thinking, and I wanted this to be right before I did.

"Just a minute," I mumbled against Tanner's lips.

"What? Did I do something you didn't want?" He raised himself off me, voice raw with disappointment.

"The opposite. Just give me a second." I slid out from under him, dug in my pocket, and came up with Wade's mojo bag. Tanner craned to see what I had. I held my hand open so he could see. Stretching as far as I could I dropped it out of the side of the cage, expecting it to fall. It rolled to the end of my fingers and hung there. In a hurry to do with Tanner what I'd wanted to do since the first second I saw him, I gave my fingers an impatient flick. The mojo bag stayed where it was.

Wade's smell overwhelmed me. Wind from long-ago motorcycle rides whipped across my face, and I heard his laugh. But then it faded until nothing was left but a scared girl-woman trying to let go of the past. The mojo bag clung to the ends of my fingers as though it knew I hadn't quite closed the door on all that could have been.

But was the past so golden? In all my mourning for days and loves gone by, I had forgotten the truth. The past was nothing but ashes and broken dreams.

Everyone I'd known and loved in Gaslight City had either died or moved on. Even Hannah, after all she had been through, was a different person. Wade was just someone who reminded me of a time when I had Memaw, and the appearance of controlling my own life. Things look better, happier in a rearview mirror, even though reality is often far different.

Reality didn't dress up and play sweet-sweet. That bitch was a glowing bed of coals banked by bushes with poison-tipped barbs. There were quicksand, minefields, and sheer drop-offs of hundreds of feet. Monsters with names like guilt, regret, and sorrow lurked int the shadows.

I had learned about the landscape of reality by the virtue of sweat, failure, and bad decisions. My reality had become a game of weighing consequences and deciding what I could live with.

According to Desiree, the reality of Wade and me ever getting together was his death. I loved Wade too much to be the cause of his death. Would I always love him? Probably, in some part of my heart. But I had to love him enough to let him go; to love myself enough to move on to whatever happiness I could find. I deserved that much.

Wade's mojo bag slipped off the ends of my fingers and dropped into the endless darkness.

"What was it?" Tanner had himself braced over me with one arm. Our bodies still touched, but we'd almost lost our connection. The dulling nimbus around the wheel of life said so.

"We both had ghosts to let go of so we could change our fates." I traced one finger down the side of Tanner's sweat-slicked neck, gripped his shirt in one hand, and pulled him to me.

He held back, lips smiling, eyes intense and serious. "You using me to change your fate?"

"Only a little. I wanted this the second I saw you. Even if it doesn't work…" I shrugged.

He nodded. "Seeing what happens is worth whatever I lost. I want this too." He shifted on top of me so I could feel how much he wanted it.

We moved our bodies together, staring into each other's eyes. The darkness hid a lot of detail, but the intensity that had so attracted me radiated off him. It channeled between us, wrapping around us, pulling us tighter together.

Tanner dropped his lips to mine, devouring me. It was another first kiss, the one where both of us didn't have the past hanging over us. The wheel glowed brighter than ever.

"Take off your shirt." I tugged at the stretchy T-shirt material, which Miss Ugly had left in shreds. "I want to feel your skin on mine."

Tanner raised onto his knees, jerked his shirt off, and began tugging what was left of my clothes. I let him pull the ruins of my top over my head and push my bra down my arms.

His hands slid up my ribs, the touch leaving trails of fire. My body throbbed, begged for more. I pressed toward him.

The wheel of life glowed brighter, sending a warm glow through our cage and into my body.

Gazes locked together, Tanner and I peeled off the rest of our clothes. Bathed in the golden glow of the wheel of life, Tanner's muscles stood taut on his body, as though carved in marble.

I let my fingers trail down his chest, through the crisp strip of hair in its center, over his navel, and wrapped them around his smooth, throbbing hardness. He moaned, eyes fluttering shut. A wave of desire crested and slammed through me.

"No, baby. Look at me." My breath came in quick pants.

Tanner opened his eyes and pushed me onto my back. When our faces were less than an inch apart, so close his breath whispered over my tender skin, driving me almost over the edge, I guided him into me. We both groaned and stiffened.

"Not yet, not yet," Tanner chanted, his whispers like caresses on my overly sensitized skin.

I kissed his lips light as a feather. We moved together, hips rocking in a rhythm as old as time. The wheel brightened to the point that it could have been daylight. Its magic caressed that of the mantle, driving the sensation of Tanner's body moving against mine to heights I'd never felt before.

Our bodies bucked together, and my fingernails dug into him. We stared into each others eyes, breath mingling, lost in each other. He touched me deeper than I'd ever expected. Tanner's and my souls, our destinies, joined, and we moved forward in life together, the dark past a few steps behind.

The scar tissue surrounding the mantle thinned even more with the scar of Wade becoming less important to me. This time I felt it for sure. Rays of the mantle, bright and pure, began to seep through the membrane, still stunted, but stronger than ever before.

It quivered, titillating, maddening. It spread through my body, part of this ancient ritual of death and rebirth. Tanner, seeming to feel it too, quickened his movements, eyes still on mine.

Our bodies slapped together. My legs squeezed around his hips. His arms tightened under my shoulders, and our movements reached a hard, desperate pitch.

The light from the wheel took on weight, encapsulating us in a bubble of gold.

Tanner moaned deep in his throat. "Now?"

"Now," I said against his lips.

We stepped over the edge together, eyes making love just as much as our bodies. My vision grayed out. I heard a woman scream. It was probably me, but I didn't care. Then I came back to myself, alive again.

The wheel opened up and took me in. A million neon threads zipped in front of me, electricity running down each one of them, taking it to its final destination. Tanner and I had opened up fate by trusting one another, by giving one another a chance, and I wouldn't let it go to waste.

I looked down at my naked, love-slick body floating in the sphere of light and shining energy and found my fate. It stretched out from me, a line of neon sunshine.

Tanner spoke next to my ear. "That's the one you keep...if you're still willing to give me a chance. The one you want to cut's behind you." He slipped his hand in mine and turned me.

I twisted my body and saw the line of fate stretching out behind me. It glowed black with infection. I leaned down and picked it up with the hand Tanner wasn't holding.

"I don't have anything to cut it." My voice sounded so calm, like a goddess out on a casual walk, not like someone desperate to escape the worst fate had to offer.

"Bite it." Tanner kissed my cheek and then moved onto my neck, his hands already tracing fire down my body.

I lifted the thick cord to my mouth and bit into it. Sour, spoiled life force filled my mouth. My mouth drew up. Repulsed, I let go of the cord. It flopped to the ground at my feet.

Don't quit. It's not finished. I picked it up and bit again, hard as I could. The cord crunched between my teeth and shot more sour awfulness into my mouth. I chewed like it was the best damn steak I'd ever had because this was my last chance.

Finally the cord broke, spilling its blackness into the sphere, where it turned to bright, gleaming light again and drifted away. The discarded line of fate lay in lazy squiggle on the floor, like some child's abandoned toy.

"*Adios*, motherfucker," I muttered. The sourness in my mouth left as though it had never been there.

Then Tanner turned me to face him. With one finger, he teased open my folds, stroking until I moaned. His lips met mine, and he eased me onto my back, sliding into me like we'd been doing it every day for the last ten years. We moved together, and my new thread of fate filled with life.

———

When I woke up, sun blazed into the cage from above. Tanner and I lay naked, bodies tangled together, one of his legs resting over mine. For the first time, I saw the dirt walls surrounding us, confirming my suspicion that we'd been dangling over a chasm no telling how deep.

The cage moved again. I realized what had woken me. We were being hoisted out of the pit. I nudged Tanner awake. Even the small movement irritated my sex-sore muscles and reminded me how many times—and ways—Tanner and I had enjoyed each other before the sun came up.

"Get up. She's raising the cage." I tried to pull myself from underneath him.

Tanner put one hand behind my neck and kissed my lips gently. Then he let me up. We both yanked on our clothes and prepared to find out if I'd succeeded in changing both our fates.

The cage jumped up maybe a few inches at a time. From somewhere above came the sound of gears turning slowly. I slipped the wheel of life back into the hip pack and clipped it around my waist.

Tanner came to stand behind me, arms encircling my waist, and nuzzled my hair aside to kiss my neck. "You sorry?"

I curled my fingers around his wrist. "Not a bit."

The night before had freed us both from some demons. What lay ahead didn't matter as much as the journey of getting there. Leaving my old fate behind felt like shedding a dirty, dead skin.

The top of the cage broke the edge of the pit where it

had hung. Daylight gleamed dull on the bones, making them appear bleached and dry. I couldn't wait to be out of the cage and back to our side of the veil.

A few more cranks, and Miss Ugly's face appeared. Daylight didn't make her any prettier, not even the daylight of her side of the veil. It brought out the greenish cast of her skin and made visible ropy veins just below the surface of her skin pop out.

She smiled at Tanner and me, a thin line of saliva snaking from the corner of her thin lips. "Did you enjoy your final night?"

Tanner and I exchanged a horrified glance. My chest tightened. No. This was wrong. I'd escaped my fate. My business with Miss Ugly was finished.

"That's not right. I cut my fate." My mouth puckered with the memory of the sour taste of it in my mouth.

"You cut your fate line, but someone else must take your fate for you." She untied a strip of thick white tendon and let the cage's door swing open.

"That's not fair. You didn't tell me that." Frustration chased out the horror of having made a simple, stupid error out of ignorance. I was sick of operating on only half the information I needed, sick of stumbling around in the dark.

Miss Ugly's crazy eyes settled on mine. "Fair is a lie."

Bullshit. I grabbed at Tanner's hand and tried to run around Miss Ugly. She caught me, yanked me away from Tanner, and swung me around. The bones making up the cage slammed against my face. Tanner shouted something. The hanging cage rocked with the force of my blow and pulled me off balance. My foot hit the edge of the pit and slid in the dirt.

That got my attention. Heart thundering, I tried to backpedal, but my foot kept sliding forward. Tanner yelled at me to stop, not to fall. I wanted to snarl something smart-assed at him, but I was too damn scared. My other foot got into the slide. I began to fall fast.

Miss Ugly caught me by one arm, pulled me away from the edge, and whispered in my ear, "No. I've worked too hard for this meal."

Her foul breath turned my stomach. I struggled against her, elbows flailing. But she was strong, too strong for me on this side of the veil where she could walk in daylight. She used the length of her arm to hold me away from her and snatched Tanner out of the cage. He threw punches that landed but did no harm.

Miss Ugly dragged us through a little stand of trees and back into the clearing where she'd brought me the first night we met. I tripped over one of the skulls lining the clearing and let myself fall, hoping it would knock Miss Ugly off balance.

No such luck. She gripped my arm tighter and yanked me along like a tired mom wrangling a toddler in the throes of the fifteenth tantrum of the day. Tanner kept punching her in the head, his face set in a fierce grimace.

She dragged us to a bone sticking out of the ground, one from a creature so huge I didn't want to imagine what it was or how Miss Ugly had beat it. Because if she could beat this thing, there was no way Tanner or I could physically best her.

Coils of the white line, which had to be tendon, lay at the base of the bone. Miss Ugly nodded at the stuff and said, "Secure them," then shoved us at the bone.

The line slithered toward us with lightning speed, wrapped itself around both us and the bone pole and began tightening. I locked my legs to resist the pull, but the cord of tendon only pulled tighter, digging into my skin.

I held my ground, but the tendon dragged me against the bone, tightening even more. Fear wrapped freezing bands around my chest. The idea being eaten, even if I was dead when Miss Ugly did it, made me dizzy.

Tanner slammed into the pole next to me, struggling so hard, his head whipped side to side. Then it was over. The cords quit moving and held us fast against the pole.

Miss Ugly picked up a dirty, wickedly long knife and ran it across a flat stone to sharpen it. Muscles working underneath her thin shoulders, she began to hum. Next to her sat a huge club. It occurred to me that she'd probably club us so she could cut us into pieces without us resisting. I kicked my feet uselessly against the ground, skin tingling as it went numb.

"Stop," Tanner whispered out of the side of his mouth. "Connect with the wheel of life again and give your fate to someone else."

I concentrated on the wheel, hidden in the ugly red canvas of my hip pack. It lay dormant. The chatter in my mind rose, a cacophony of screams, fears, and regrets.

"Let it go. Be here now." Tanner's voice next to my ear lent the only sanity I had in that moment.

I tried to relax my shoulders, tried to let go. But it

was like asking a person on fire to forget the pain. Something cool touched my quickly numbing hand. I cut my eyes as far as possible because I couldn't even move my head and saw Tanner's fingers touching mine. I concentrated on the brownness of his skin, the way the yellow undertones matched mine, and the shape of his fingernails.

The wheel hummed to life. My black opal jolted in response. I connected with the new level of power from the mantle. It had a deeper, fuller feeling. It crackled over my skin, almost electric, then climbed its way up my arms, crawling over my face, and seeped into my brain.

Motes of light filled my vision. The world around me turned to a blur. The wheel of life's ball of energy hung only a few inches away. I pushed my mind toward it, the power of the mantle thudding stronger with every beat of my heart. I stepped into the wheel as I had before.

The lines of fate went out in every direction, the neon of life energy cracking through them, running at light speed. In front of me stretched the new brilliant yellow fate I'd created for myself. I turned back and saw the dead, black line of fate I'd cut off the night before.

I picked it up in one hand, and my skin began to turn black. It was infecting me with its deadness. The black necropsy spread up my arm. *Fast. I had to find someone fast.* I could have kicked myself for not planning this, for not figuring out who I was going to give it to ahead of time. But I hadn't known what to do.

I stared at all the lines of fate. Who could I damn to a death more horrible than anything I could imagine? And why? Nobody deserved this, except maybe me, and only because it was my fate.

I glanced through the fates connected to mine. They were all people close to me. Cecil, whose line still burned bright despite his failing health. Shelly, whose line looked as young and vibrant as mine. Finn and Dillon. Their children. Hannah. Even Kenny, who I disliked, still had plenty of adventures ahead of him.

Then I spotted the black line writhing amidst all the colored ones. I didn't even have to stare into it to know who it belonged to. My ex-husband's essence came off it like stink off shit.

I picked up the line, and a picture formed in my head. Tim rode in the back of a car, head lowered and moving with its motion . He wore the kind of jumpsuit I associated with someone enjoying a nice stay in jail. A metal mesh grate separated Tim from the uniformed driver, who wore a gun at his hip. Some kind of cop probably.

The police must have finally picked up Tim's crazy, naked, screaming ass. He deserved whatever they had in store for him so much that I almost hated to give him to Miss Ugly.

Then Tim raised his head, mad eyes darting around the car. His nostrils flared. How could he sense me? I wasn't even with him, not even in spirit. Something flashed behind his eyes. Tim's small, sharp features gave way to Oscar Rivera's smoother, more rounded ones.

"You can't. You're not strong enough," Oscar growled in Tim's voice.

"Wrong again, asshat." I married my old, dead cord of

fate to Tim's dying one. Maybe we'd once had some kind of a future together. The only thing left now was death. My old fate came back to life, the black regaining its luster, and pumping Tim full of the poison my fate still needed to pass along.

Tim screamed, and Oscar screamed within him. The cop driving glanced into the rearview mirror and yelled, "Shut up back there." Tim acted as though he didn't hear.

The cop wouldn't have to listen much longer. I had to bring Tim back to Miss Ugly, back to my fate. I gathered my power and reached for Tim. He stopped screaming. Oscar Rivera's eyes looked out of his, and a smile hovered on his lips.

I froze. Oscar wanted me to touch Tim so he could access my power and create havoc I didn't even want to think about. I drew back my hand. How could I do this? I had to touch Tim to drag him into the wheel of life, but I couldn't touch anything Oscar had control of.

Easy answer. I had to expel Oscar from Tim. I groaned, remembering how hard it had been to get rid of Oscar a few months ago, how weak it had left me. I'd had to be carried afterward.

No matter. It had to be done or Miss Ugly would kill me, and she'd kill Tanner, and neither of us deserved it. Besides, Oscar had caused this whole shit show just so he could chase some asinine dream of world domination.

Oscar began to laugh through Tim's mouth. Finally he said, "You're still too weak to control me, aren't you? Still too backward and afraid to embrace your power. Such a pathetic excuse for a witch."

The cop glared into the rearview mirror. "Mister, you're gonna shut up back there. I promise you are." Then he muttered, "You're not as untouchable as you think you are."

My eyes opened, and I saw the situation for what it was. I'd moved forward in my life, let go of the past, received even more of the mantle's power. Oscar was dead. He'd never move forward. All he could do was live in the prison he'd created for himself or move on to the realm of the dead, where he actually belonged.

All those racing lines of fate came back to me. Oscar's dead fate was somewhere in there. If I could send him back down the line of his fate, he'd be trapped in his own bad decisions, back in the place where he'd hidden his soul.

One problem remained. How would I do it without lending him power? I couldn't. But I could let Oscar think he was taking my power and then use it against him. I had enough power to do that now.

The mantle strained against the weakening scar tissue, trying to work its way into the rest of my body. To get started, I just needed to get Tim's sorry ass out of this police car.

I stared at the cop. He didn't deserve what was about to happen to him, so it needed to be not too bad. I sent out my usual fire ants and aimed them right for his family jewels. He squirmed in his seat a few times, trying to adjust his pants.

"What is that?" His voice rose several octaves. He swerved to the roadside, tires crying out, and slammed to a stop. He glanced back at Tim, shook his head, and got out of the car, patting his crotch and dancing around.

I grabbed Tim by the shoulder. In my current state, that of spirit, he was no heavier than a pencil. I kicked the car door open a little too hard, and it blew off the car and tumbled into the ditch.

The cop spun around, red-faced and sweating, one hand holding his dick through his pants. The surprise on his face would have been comical had he not been reaching for his gun.

I opened my third eye and looked for the place where I could step back into the wheel of life's highway of fate. A little dab of the neon sunshine of my fate line flashed near a culvert a few feet away. I focused on it, pulled Tim out of the car, and dragged him toward it.

Tim, or maybe Oscar, kicked and screamed, gibbering curses. Oscar's power pulled at mine, teasing at first, then gobbling it like a man starving. I ignored it. Let him hang himself.

The first bullet whizzed past me and hit dirt about a foot from Tim's kicking legs. I moved faster, strength already flagging. I dug deep and pushed with all I had, heart throbbing in my neck, exertion aching deep inside. Another bullet hit the dirt right next to Tim. The yellow dot of fate was only a few feet away. I yanked Tim the rest of the way and let us both fall into my new fate.

We stood in the sphere, Tim and I. The madness fled from his eyes. It had been wiped away when we passed between worlds.

"What is this?" He looked around. "Where is this?" He

leaned close, staring at my face. "Are you an alien? I could always tell something was wrong with you, Peri Jean."

His words killed any guilt I felt. I stared deep into his eyes, searching for Oscar. My enemy had turtled down inside my ex-husband for safety. But he'd forgotten something. Or maybe didn't realize it. I could track my own magic now.

I followed the glow of the mantle through Tim, chasing it down to its source. Tim's soul was colorless and pitted with the scars of a wasted life. He'd never once cared about anybody but himself and even now thought he'd escape unscathed.

I slammed my fist into the ugly, parched surface of Tim's soul, making a hole big enough to pull Oscar out. Oscar scuttled backward, tried to send magic out to shock me away from him. I opened myself, opened my third eye, and let my own power absorb back into me. Then I used it to pull Oscar out of Tim.

Tim convulsed, and his eyes rolled back in his head, the experience too much for his fragile body. I kept pulling until I had Oscar out of Tim.

Oscar grappled to get control of the power he'd stolen from me, by now understanding I was using it against him. I kept my third eye open, calling for the line of fate that had once been his. I found it, dead and rotted, buried under more vibrant lives.

I struggled with the power Oscar and I now shared, straining so hard to control it that my eyeballs bulged and my head pounded. Sweat dripped from me, but finally I wrangled it into a force not unlike a catapult.

I pulled back on it, letting it gather momentum, and then released. Oscar, now nothing more than a sliver of light, rocketed toward his fate and hit it with an earth-shattering boom.

Next to me, Tim had fallen. His body bent with tremors. Reaching into his soul had done something to his brain. His body stilled, and his eyes opened.

He smiled at me. "You really are an alien, aren't you?" Tim smiled. "You can tell me."

I gripped his arm, pulled him up, and marched him into the line of my fate and back to Miss Ugly's lair. I found her standing over my still form, her club held aloft over her head.

Tanner strained against his bonds screaming, "No. No. Just give her a minute."

"Hey!" I yelled at Miss Ugly's back.

She turned, club still held up to strike, and saw my spirit form bringing her Tim in the flesh.

Tim's eyes widened at the sight of Miss Ugly. He let a little giggle slip from his lips. "The fuck is that?"

"Mine," she whispered and came toward Tim.

I let go of him and leapt back into my body, horrified at my numb hands and fingers. Miss Ugly pointed behind her. The ropes of tendon binding Tanner and me fell off and snaked toward Tim.

I climbed to my feet and almost fell right back down. Icy needles prickled through my arms and legs as feeling tried to come back.

Tanner wobbled to me and grabbed my hand. "Let's go, right now."

I shook my head and pointed. Miss Ugly had backed Tim against a huge, ancient oak tree and slashed her mark into his forehead. The cords of tendon wound around him so tight that they'd embedded into his skin. My ex-husband's eyes rolled to me, pleading.

The magnitude of what I'd done washed over me, hot and ugly. I'd condemned a man I'd once loved to death. It didn't matter that his line of fate had already been terminal. I'd chosen to give him to a monster to save myself.

Miss Ugly raised her huge club over her head, arching her back as she prepared to bring it down. Tim's scream intensified, turned into the terrified wail of one doomed. The club came down with a sickening crunch. The tendon cords dropped from Tim and arranged themselves back into a neat pile.

Miss Ugly gripped Tim's ankle and dragged him to the bone where Tanner and I had been bound. One side of Tim's head was caved in, but his sides moved. He was still breathing. Miss Ugly's pet tendon cord bound Tim to the bone post.

Sickening understanding hit me. She'd let Tim season before she finished killing him and butchered him. The meat would taste better that way.

Tanner tugged my hand again and whispered, "Let's go."

I'd thought Miss Ugly would have a parting shot for us, but she no longer even seemed to know we were there, now that our fates were no longer connected. Tanner gave me another gentle tug, and I let him lead me back toward the two columns that marked passage across the veil. Over here, they were easy to see. Not so much on our side.

Ashamed as I felt, I still gave myself a little cheer for surviving. Letting Oscar beat me would have been worse than letting Felicia beat me. Or Michael Gage. Or anybody else whose ass I'd had to kick in my history of ass kickings. And I'd gained something more with this victory.

I glanced at Tanner out of the corner of my eye. He still looked like sex on a cracker. The final battle with Miss Ugly hadn't dampened my anticipation for the next time we took our clothes off and pressed our bodies together. It might not be love, and it might never be. But anything we had together would happen in the present moment. That was a hell of a lot better than living for a memory.

19

─────

Tanner and I crossed into our side of the veil between dark and light right where we'd gone in, behind the RV park. The heat punched into us like an invisible fist. Sweat popped out all over me. Tanner groaned.

"The humidity. It's like a wet towel over my face. I can barely breathe." He let go of my hand and marched toward the campers and air conditioning.

I followed, not willing to spare the energy to speak. This kind of heat didn't allow for mistakes. Before I'd gone ten feet, a sheen of sweat covered my body.

Caw. Caw. Cawww.

Orev flapped toward me and landed on the ground at my feet. He opened his wings as though in greeting. I knelt in front of him and gently patted his sides. The bird, whom I'd seen attack and try to put out eyes, made a cooing sound.

"Where did you go?" I whispered.

A picture took form in my head, one of Sol and his goat

friend Bub sitting at a table, hunched over a chessboard whose pieces were made of tiny, hideously deformed humans. While I watched, Sol touched the head of one of them and spoke. It moved across the board. Another piece proceeded to hack it to death with a sharp weapon. Sol and Bub laughed together.

The image faded. Why had Sol and Bub taken Orev? I rummaged through my exhausted mind until I realized Tanner had squatted next to me. He stretched one hand out to Orev, who drew his head back in warning.

"Let him," I told Orev. "He's our friend now."

Orev let Tanner stroke him, but I could feel his indignation. I ignored it and rose. Orev flapped to perch on my shoulder. I walked into camp, exhaustion aching in my legs.

We'd only gotten about halfway to my camper when Hannah came running up to us, sweat rolling down her red face. Rather than speak, she ran at me and grabbed me in a hug.

She tried to jump up and down a little and almost made it. That made me smile.

"I knew when you changed your fate," she panted, fanning her face. "I knew. The vision of your death just went away."

"Did you take the runes and dump them like I said?" If Oscar had any power left, down in the dungeon of his soul, he'd be trying to reconnect to them. I didn't want him anywhere he could use them to siphon my power or to spy on me. That was exactly how he'd found a way to sic Miss Ugly on me.

"When I knew you weren't going to die, I waited." She walked alongside Tanner and me, glancing between us, probably trying to figure out how far things had gone.

I sure wasn't going to tell her, not after all the naysaying I'd done over Tanner. Instead I voiced one of my bigger worries. "How did things go for Cecil at the hospital?"

Hannah twisted her lips and stared at the sand clouding around our feet and sticking to the sweat on her bare, whiter-than-white legs. "They put in a stent, I think you call it. He'll be home later today. But..." She turned to me and said, "Shelly seemed upset."

"Do you see his death yet?" I put on the face I used as Sanctuary's second in command and locked my gaze onto hers, something I never did with Hannah.

Shock widened her eyes. "N-n-no. But I've never seen a death more than a few days out."

I nodded, and we neared our campers. Tanner slid one arm around my waist, kissed my cheek, and said, "I need a cool shower. This humidity has me soaked. But I'll help you do whatever needs to be done with those runes."

My face heated. Hannah stopped walking and turned to stare at me, mouth open. "You were naked with him. I can tell."

Tanner's face turned dark red. He hunched his shoulders and shuffled to his camper, slamming the door behind him. A lock clicked.

I tried to play it cool. "Do you have a cigarette? Mine got wet."

She took the pack out of her pocket but held it out of my reach. "You have to spill at least a little."

I led the way back to my camper, went in, and got out my own cigarettes. Lighting one, I gave Hannah a smug smile.

She rolled her eyes. "He's probably as fantastic as he looks."

"Twice as fantastic." I put a saucy lilt in my voice, not willing to tell Hannah that it had been more than just sex. No need to push things.

Tanner had a long way to go before he decided what he wanted out of a life without his wife and daughters. I had a long way to go before I knew if Tanner was anything more than Mister Right Now. But it was good so far, and I was glad I'd turned the corner.

"How do you get all these men?" Hannah frowned at me, as though she didn't turn heads everywhere she went. Men like Leon Blackfox, men who owned things and didn't have a zillion problems, glommed onto her way before they would me. She was classier and didn't look like she might give them a black eye.

"I'm a charming sumbitch." I grinned and jetted cigarette smoke out of my nose.

An SUV crept through the RV park. I recognized Griff's stiff posture behind the wheel. I stepped out into the lane and motioned to him. He saw me and sped toward us.

Both Griff and Mysti clambered out, looking as though they hadn't slept in a day. I ran at them, and they wrapped their arms around me.

I hadn't yet changed out of my ruined shirt, and my

wounded chest was on full display. Griff zeroed in on it.

"This is the mark? It's complete." His eyes widened. "Holy shit. You escaped after she'd completed the mark?"

Griff's reaction brought even more pride in what I'd managed. I let him take pictures of the mark with his phone and beamed at his praise.

"Tell us how you won." Mysti's eyes sparkled. My win equalled a win for my mentor.

I spilled the whole story, excited words running together. Mysti stopped me at points to clarify. Her eyebrows raised when I got to the part about the death and rebirth ritual that finally let me use the wheel of life for its true purpose. Hannah rolled her eyes at that part.

"But I'm so exhausted now I don't even think I could call a circle," I babbled.

"You need rest." Mysti had said these words to me so many times she could have saved herself energy by printing them on a card and just holding it up when needed.

"You do too." I pointed underneath my eyes to show I'd noticed the dark circles under Mysti's. "I hate that you came rushing over here."

"Our purpose is double-pronged," Griff said.

Before he could continue, Tanner banged out of his beat-up old camper, hair wet. He'd dressed in olive shorts, a brown tank top, and flip-flops. He glanced around the group, saw the knowing looks, and flushed.

"Hot water heater doesn't work. I've learned to shower fast." He shoved his hands in his pockets with the pronouncement.

Griff strode to Tanner, hand out. "I'm Griffin Reed, Tanner. You don't know me, but I've heard of you. Are you still dealing in..." Griff thought for a few seconds and said, "Special items?"

"That's my real job." Tanner relaxed and smiled at Griff.

Griff took out his card and handed it to Tanner. "Maybe we'll find a way to work together when the time's right."

"Is this why y'all came rushing over here?" I muttered to Mysti.

She shook her head. "Brad and Jadine are getting married tonight."

"That was a quick engagement." I glanced at Hannah, eyebrows raised. What had happened while I was gone? Before Hannah had a chance to answer, Mysti pulled me aside.

"You need to do something with those runes, like yesterday." She'd turned back into my teacher. It was a good thing because I'd almost forgotten about them in all the hubbub.

"I told Hannah to drop them somewhere deep where nobody would find them. You got a better idea?" I watched Tanner talking to Griff.

His demeanor had changed. He stood straighter, more confident, and talked like an expert. I truly didn't know him well. Perhaps feeling the weight of my gaze, he turned and gave me a little smile and a wink. But we knew each other well enough for a start.

Mysti watched the direction of my gaze with none of

Hannah's teasing lasciviousness. When she spoke, it was with concern. "So no more Wade?"

I shook my head. "I told you about Desiree's visit."

Mysti's gaze scanned over my face, sadness evident in her soft eyes. "If Wade believes in Desiree's prediction, it's true. We create our own reality." She stepped a little closer. "But I'll tell you something about Tanner. I sense that one mates for life. Watch yourself." She tipped a nod in Tanner's direction.

If that was the case, I was too late. The future pressed down on me, filled with worries about wasting my time with Tanner. I shut it off with a click. Enjoying life with someone you liked was not a waste. Especially not when they looked like Tanner Letts.

"Now about these runes," Mysti said. " Do you have any potions or herbs to ward off interest?"

We exchanged a smile. I had tried out a lot of the recipes Samantha had in her grimoire. Most of them were in the tradition of root work and scarily effective. "Come on in my camper."

Mysti grabbed her witch pack out of the SUV and followed me inside. Hannah trailed behind us, so curious she almost climbed up our backs to see what was going on.

Inside, I dug through the items that weren't destroyed when Oscar blew up my shabby chic buffet. I found myself bitching to Mysti about the loss of the buffet as we searched through my magical arsenal.

"At least you figured out what he was doing," said Mysti, the queen of silver linings.

Hannah got the runes out of the camper's tiny freezer

where she'd put them in a plastic freezer container, the kind usually used for food.

Evil rolled off the runes, ominous as the heat waves that rise off blacktop in the summer. Oscar knew I was up to something. He wanted to scare me away. Too late now.

"We might want to work a little harder to seal this box airtight," Mysti said.

Hannah found a roll of silver duct tape and started to tape the box shut. Mysti stopped her.

"We'll pack this with agrimony." She withdrew breathable packets of herbs from her witch pack.

"What do those do?" Hannah leaned close.

Mysti went into full teaching mode. "Agrimony sends negativity back where it came from."

I held up a little brown vial of oil I sold to people in my tent at the carnival. "I'm going to anoint the runes with Althea oil to persuade anybody who finds the box that it's nothing of interest."

Mysti nodded and packed the agrimony around the runes, whispering, "Do not let this evil touch others."

The fork I'd left lying in my sink began to rattle. "It won't work." Oscar's voice filled the camper. We ignored him.

I anointed the runes with the Althea oil, eyes closed, calling the mantle to bless it. "Nobody who sees this box wants it. They don't want to know what's in it. They will forget they even saw it right away."

Oscar rattled the fork in my sink some more. Finally the fork rose and flew at me. I batted it out of the air and said, "Close it, now."

Mysti snapped the top on the runes. They rattled inside, popping the lid like bugs hitting a light after dark. Hannah covered the box with duct tape. The runes kept rattling. Mysti reached back into her witch pack.

"I think it needs more." Mysti dug through my pack and held up a can of flat black spray paint.

I nodded my agreement, picked up the box, and walked outside. I dropped it on the ground next to the charcoal grill provided by the campground.

"Why are we doing this?" Hannah followed close behind.

"Black soaks up nasty energy and dissolves it." Mysti shook the can several times and began spraying the box. When she covered the top side, we sat down at the picnic table to wait for it to dry.

Griff and Tanner still stood in a huddle, talking intently. Brad and Jadine had wandered over.

Brad threw his arms open. "Sis!"

Mysti got up and hugged him but without her usual sparkle at seeing her beloved brother. She hugged Jadine as well. "I can't believe someone as pretty as you wants to marry my scalawag brother."

Jadine gave her a shy smile. I knew her well enough to know she was capable of her own shenanigans.

"Who's marrying y'all?" I asked.

"Finn," Brad said.

I raised my eyebrows at Hannah. She put her hand over her mouth. The idea of Finn marrying someone made me want to bray laughter, and I couldn't in front of Mysti. This was her brother.

Mysti got up to turn the box and spray it again. I followed to find her squatting, with tears streaking down her face.

"What is it?" I whispered. Mysti had always been such a comfort and help. She deserved the same kind of friendship from me.

"Brad and I have been together since our parents died, except for the three years when I had already aged out of foster care and couldn't get guardianship of him." She bit her lip. "Now he's moving on. I can't be there to watch and make sure everything goes well for him, that he's treated fairly."

I bit my lip. Brad could use a little real world experience. Mysti had him spoiled. He considered most mundane tasks beneath him. That didn't fly in Sanctuary. I didn't let it. If Brad wanted to thrive here, he'd learn exactly the kind of lessons Mysti wanted to shield him from. But I could keep a watchful eye on him.

"I'll make sure he's treated fairly." I didn't promise he'd get his way all the time or that he'd be farting "If You're Happy And You Know It." But nobody would crap on him.

She nodded, and another tear leaked down her face. "Griff's glad he's moving out."

I laughed and gave her a one-armed hug but dropped my arm when I got a whiff of myself. "We've got time before the wedding to get rid of these runes. What do you say?"

"I'd like nothing better." Mysti put on a brave smile, but sadness still clouded her usually sparkling brown eyes.

"Let me get a quick shower." I hurried into my camper

and washed both the sex and the fear sweat off my body. Just as I got out, my phone rang. The number showed up as unknown. I answered. "Hello?"

Silence on the other end. Then a click as they hung up. I took the phone away from my ear and stared at it. The smell of Wade—sunshine and gasoline—filled my senses. Had it been him? Didn't matter. Good or bad, it just hadn't worked out.

I let the loss of Wade well up in me and spill over. I sat down on the edge of my unmade bed, put my hands over my face, and wept. The proximity of people who'd be upset if they knew I was crying convinced me to keep my sobs as silent as possible, but I let myself hurt over the loss of Wade.

It wouldn't be the last time I cried over Wade. Healing takes time. That's why I could anticipate that things might change between me and Tanner. All I had, all any of us ever have, is the one moment in which I existed. So I let myself feel the way I felt.

The sobs died down on their own. I got up, washed my face, and put on makeup. Someone rapped on my door.

"Come in," I yelled, still smearing eyeliner on my lids.

Hannah climbed into the camper, her phone in one hand. Had she gotten the strange hang-up? Maybe Wade had talked to her. If he had, I hoped she kept it to herself. It was past time for me to let go of the whole thing. I stiffened in anticipation of whatever she had for me.

She put her face next to mine in the mirror. "That the eye shadow I bought for you?"

"Tantalizing Taupe in the flesh." We both snickered at

the silly name. "It's good stuff. Thanks for getting it for me."

"You need to buy better makeup and clothes for yourself. You're worth it." She winked in the mirror.

Hannah's friendship made me feel like I could face anything. I tipped my head at her phone. "What you got?"

"While you were missing, I looked for places to get rid of the runes. Mysti and I were just discussing which would be best, and I wanted to run my idea by you." She held up the phone. I clicked off my makeup mirror and faced her. She held the phone where I could see. "This place is only an hour away. It's a hole over one-hundred feet deep, and public spelunking is not allowed."

I stared at a deep, dark hole that looked wide enough to be a small pond or lake. The deep blackness of the hole made the hair stand up on the back of my neck.

"We'll have to invent a ruse to get in." Hannah gave me a wild-eyed smile, another little remnant of her old self. She loved shenanigans. "It's only open to the public when tour guides bring people into the park."

I returned her smile. "Sounds like a winner to me."

———

The drive out to this deep, deep hole felt as though it took forever. Tanner sat in the back seat next to me, his arm over my shoulder. I let his smell, soap with a hint of wild musk, push away the memory of Wade. A weight lifted off me. We smiled at each other. He gave me a light kiss.

Mysti's words came back. *That one mates for life.*

The thought of all that could mean rose up, threatening to destroy the inner peace I was working so hard to find. *Not the time*, I reminded myself and settled into Tanner's side, watching the landscape get more and more sparse as Griff's fast driving ate up miles of parched highway.

When we got to a place where there was more sand and short trees than anything else, Griff told us to look for signs of a state park. We found it and pulled off on the roadside.

"Someone get my briefcase out of the back." Griff's eyes met mine in the rearview mirror. Paying me or not, Griff was still the boss, and I was still the employee. I ducked out from under Tanner's arm, climbed into the scorching heat, and opened the SUV's cargo doors.

Beneath heavy luggage, I found Griff's scuffed, black leather briefcase. I dragged it out, got back into the car, and gave it to him. Griff took out a wide wallet, the kind I associated with law enforcement, and tucked a laminated card into it. Then he started the car and drove down the narrow lane into the state park. A vehicle marked with an official seal had parked across the road to block our way.

A skinny guy wearing a khaki uniform climbed out of the car. "You folks want to visit the park, go back into town and look for the park visitor center. You'll buy a ticket, and they'll drive you out here for a tour. That's the only way the State of Texas can allow you out here. Too dangerous otherwise."

Griff showed him the wallet and badge. "Griffin Reed, deputy chief. Our agency is considering doing a geological study on the area. My team and I were assigned to assess our interest level."

The park ranger leaned into the car and looked us over. Between Tanner with his long hair, funky jewelry, and shorts and Mysti with her hippie wear, we didn't look the part at all.

Griff said, "My crew is made up of freelance archaeologists and geologists."

The park ranger handed back Griff's fake ID and put his hands on his hips. "Well, I suppose since this is what the US government wants, I've got no choice but to let you pass. But I'll just say I'm not happy about you people coming out here like you own the world. This is Texas. We take care of our own business here."

"We understand, sir." Griff put the car in gear and waited for the park ranger to move his car. When he did, Griff drove past, following signs directing us to the sinkhole.

The desolate, open land, so different from the lush pine forests of East Texas, had its own kind of beauty. The sun made the dull-colored rocks and sand blaze like white fire. The thorns on the scattered cacti looked like a thin, wiry coating of hair. Animals raced in the distance. I first thought them deer, but closer inspection revealed they were large goats. The largest ones I'd ever seen.

I thought of the place as desert but knew we'd not quite reached the Chihuahuan desert of Texas. This was just the prelude.

We finally found the sinkhole. On one side was a fair-sized asphalt parking lot. On the other, stark wilderness with heat ripples floating over the sand. A thick metal guardrail protected the sinkhole, warning people not to get too close. At over a hundred feet deep, if someone fell in, they were done in this life.

Griff took the plastic ice chest where we'd put the box containing Oscar's runes out of trunk. I held out my hand. Griff cocked his head at me.

"You sure? I'll do it." He held the ice chest just out of my reach.

"Oscar's my problem." I leaned down and grabbed the ice chest, pulled it from his grasp. The evil of the runes, blunted by the protections and wards Mysti and I had put on them, still crawled up my arm. I steeled myself and walked toward the huge hole.

When I got close, I set the ice chest down and removed the box of runes. A cloud raced over the sun, and a chill wind sent sand to pepper my face. I put my arm up and staggered backward. Rocks slid under my cowboy boots.

Remembering how close that long, dark drop-off was, I panicked. An arm slipped around my waist, and Tanner pulled me against him.

His deep purr was hard with panic. "Careful."

I opened my eyes. Nobody was there but Tanner, eyes bright and concerned. Hannah hovered nearby, pulling on her fingers, one after the other. I gathered myself and gently pushed Tanner away.

"It's okay. Almost done." I reached for the mantle, letting its power flow through me. The box trembled in my hands, trying to get to the mantle, but now I knew what was going on. I held the mantle just out of reach and shaped it into my will. In a loud, clear voice I said,

"I call on the elements

Earth, air, fire, and water."

Here I paused and let the energy from each element manifest. The earth beneath my feet charged, sending its renewal through my boots and up my legs. The wind picked up, ripping through my hair, caressing my face, carrying energy on its infinite wings. More renewing energy came from beneath my feet, from an aquifer, deep below the earth's surface. And the fire came from within me. A bolt of heat lightning flashed in the distance.

"Bind this box

Bind the runes within

Block its evil from without

Make it invisible to curious eyes

Make it repel and revolt

By the power within

By the power without

Blessed be."

I got a good, tight grip on the box and reared back my arm like a softball pitcher. My arm flew forward. At the apex of my pitch, I tried to let go of the box. My fingers were stuck.

My heart jumped in fear. The momentum from my throw carried me forward. Tanner pulled me back from the edge again. This time, Hannah grabbed him, bending her knees to get leverage. Griff and Mysti crowded in, Mysti with her wand grasped in one hand and Griff holding her back from the edge.

"I command you to release." She hit my hand with her wand. "Release."

I concentrated on my fingers, begging them to let go of the box. The black opal pinged on my chest, and Orev appeared. Wings flapping, he hovered in front of me and latched his beak on to the box. The mantle swirled between us. I used it to push the box away from me.

My fingers let go. The box fell, disappearing into the darkness faster than I'd thought it would. For a long time, no sound of impact followed. I imagined the box suspended in midair, maybe about to expel itself. Then the faint splash of water came.

I relaxed and backed away from the sinkhole. My legs trembled, and my head spun from relief. I sat down hard on the rocky soil. It hurt my behind, but I didn't care. It was over for now.

I'd still have to find where Oscar's soul was hidden and banish him, but he could no longer draw power from me. I hoped I hadn't shot myself in the foot by getting rid of the runes, but they were too dangerous to keep.

Priscilla Herrera's form appeared across the sinkhole from us. She acknowledged me with the barest of nods and faded from sight. So she was back too.

My friends and I climbed into Griff's SUV, all of us exhausted.

"I guess we have a wedding to go to." Mysti tried for a brave smile and almost made it.

Griff drove us back to the RV park, smiling ear to ear.

20

Brad and Jadine's wedding was a hurried, thrown together affair.

The owner of the RV park lent us use of the park's community hall. We grouped as many metal folding chairs as the small room would hold in front of the slightly raised stage.

A nearby craftsman brought over an arbor for Brad and Jadine to stand beneath. Finn, who'd gotten his minister's license online sometime back, helped the guy carry it in. Hannah sat off to the side picking out a pretty tune on the new guitar she'd bought recently.

Then it was magic time.

Brad, wearing one of his expensive suits, probably purchased by Mysti, walked to the front of the room and shifted foot to foot, his face tense. Finn, wearing nothing fancier than a pair of cargo pants and a thin button-down short sleeve shirt, stood next to Brad, dark eyes glowing with mischief. The sight would have made me laugh had it not been for the stricken look on Mysti's face. She leaned against the wall near the stage, chin trembling. She needed me. I left my post at the back door and walked to the front.

I passed Leon Blackfox and a group of performers from Summervale Carnival sitting along the back row. Leon watched Hannah, his dark eyes mournful and longing. I gave him a nod and kept walking past a mish-mash of campers from the RV park and members of Sanctuary sitting closer to the front. I reached Mysti and held out my hand to her.

"Come on. We'll sit on the front row." I led her to a pair of chairs occupied by a thirty-something couple who'd been staying in the RV park. "This is the sister of the groom, and I'm the cousin of the bride. Do you mind if family sits in the front row?"

The female hipster huffed but dragged her male companion out of his seat and moved to another row. Mysti and I sat down. Shelly, face tight but dressed in a gorgeous light blue suit, sat down on the other side of Mysti. The two of them exchanged understanding nods.

Tanner hurried down the aisle and sat on the other side of me. His white shirt and light tan pants set off his dark skin and green eyes. He gave me a smile and a wink, leaned over, and kissed my cheek. We joined hands.

Finn straightened and said, "Would everybody stand for the bride?"

The room rumbled as everybody stood. Hannah began picking Canon in D on her guitar, the notes ringing beautiful in the small room.

The back door opened, and the room rustled again as everybody craned to see Jadine. I stood on my tiptoes.

Jadine, arm through Cecil's, walked down the aisle in a white dress she absolutely had not just had hanging in her closet. She and Brad must have planned this coup for weeks, maybe thinking surprising everybody was the only way for it to happen. Or maybe they just wanted to live for today and get on with the good stuff as fast as they could.

Cecil walked with his shoulders stiff, staring straight ahead, all signs of the old community leader gone. He was simply a man facing the heartbreak of giving his only daughter away to her husband as best as he could.

Finn took out a white sheet of paper and studied it. By the time Cecil and Jadine got in front of the podium, he set the paper aside. In a better speaking voice than I'd have given him credit for possessing, he said, "Who gives this woman in marriage?"

Cecil stood a little taller. "Her mother and I." His voice trembled only a little. Cecil passed Jadine's hand to Brad and came to sit with the rest of us in the first row.

Finn cleared his throat. "When you know you've met the right person, you don't want to waste another minute of your life without them. You want to face whatever life has to offer together, starting right then."

Tanner squeezed my hand. My throat tightened. *Maybe. Just maybe.*

Finn continued. "So when Brad and Jadine said they wanted to get married today, not tomorrow or next week, I said, 'Let's make it happen.'"

Several people giggled, including me.

Finn smiled and stood a little straighter. "Let's all join this couple in celebrating as they embark on the greatest journey there is: that of partnership, family, and togetherness. Bradley Jamison Whitebyrd, do you take Jadine Gregg to be your lawfully wedded wife?"

Brad, who looked like he might faint, said, "I do."

The remainder of the ceremony went off flawlessly, and when Finn told Brad he could now kiss his bride, the room broke into applause. People formed a line in the front of the room to congratulate the bride and groom.

The rest of us cleared the chairs, let in the caterers, and got ready to party. Cecil and Shelly had arranged for the taqueria where Hannah and I had eaten to cater the after-wedding supper. The taqueria brought in a group of traditionally dressed guitarists who began playing Mariachi music. When Brad and Jadine joined the party, the band cut off a lively song and announced the bride and groom would dance their first dance.

The guitar players launched into a fiery song full of fingerpicking and haunting highs and lows. Jadine and Brad danced their first dance. Cecil and Shelly joined in about halfway through.

I watched, fascinated at the juxtaposition of the older couple and the younger couple, both following each other's cues, smiling at each other. A lump rose in my throat. This was the wheel of life. Old, young, up, down. To be lived for whatever moment you found yourself living in.

Tanner came to stand next to me. He held out one hand and raised his eyebrows. Would I dance with him?

The wheel of life spun on, ready or not. Go forward or get left behind. I sure didn't want that.

I took Tanner's hand and kissed him. Then we got on the dance floor and had a good time.

Shelly and Dillon drank a few too many margaritas, got the band to play "Sweet Caroline," and drunk-shouted the words. It was a scene too awful to ever forget.

Leon Blackfox spent the time sitting next to Hannah and talking, his expression grave. She listened with her brow furrowed and her hands clasped between her knees. At least she didn't tell one of the men of Sanctuary to throw Leon out.

I gorged on tacos, chips, and rich *tres leches* cake and danced until my stomach hurt. Tanner stuck to my side. We exchanged steamy glances, each touch supercharged and more intense than the last. Finally, we slipped away from the party. I took one last look over my shoulder to see Leon Blackfox hold his hand out to Hannah. She stood, and the two of them glided onto the dance floor. I closed the door with a feeling of relief and practically ran with Tanner through the park to my little home on wheels.

Once inside with the door locked, we peeled off each other's clothes. Lips and tongues tasted each other's bodies. Lights dim, we caressed and explored until our bodies quivered, covered with sweat, and finally made love. After, we lay on the bed facing each other, arms and legs entwined, not talking, just enjoying each other's presence.

I jerked awake sometime in the night, not sure what had disturbed my sleep. Tanner's leg rested over the top of mine. He slept still and sound. Deciding I needed the bathroom, I disentangled myself and crept across the silent camper to the tiny restroom.

A dog barked somewhere near, the sound not quite muffled in these tin can houses. The dog had probably woken me. I peeped out the tiny window next to the toilet and saw the red cherry of a lit cigarette. Looked like the dog had a good reason to bark.

I snuck back toward the bed, naked, and picked around as silently as I could for my clothes. I settled for the long skirt and black tank top I'd worn to the wedding with no underwear. The person sitting outside my camper wouldn't care if didn't have on underwear. He might get a thrill out of it.

Tanner moaned and rolled over. I froze. Too much more fiddling around in here, and I'd wake him up. Then I'd have to explain. I didn't want that.

I palmed my cigarettes off the counter by the sink and stepped out as silently as I could, sliding my feet into the flip-flops I kept near my steps. I lipped a cigarette out of the pack, lit it, and walked toward the picnic table.

"What are you doing here?" I said.

Wade Hill turned around, drew on his cigarette, and crushed it out in the ashtray. "Less than you. Sure didn't take you long to move on after Desiree talked to you the other night."

So he had known I was at the carnival that night. I smoked in silence. Wade had walked away from me. His sister had told me to stay away, that I'd get him killed if I didn't. There was no way I'd let him shame me for moving on. "Did you sit out here and watch Tanner and me?"

"No." He said it the way a sullen teenager does, with two syllables. *No-wuh.* His teeth flashed in the darkness in more of a sneer than a smile. "But it was impossible not to hear the two of you."

"And you listened." This seemed like something I should be embarrassed about, but I couldn't quite work up the energy to give a shit. The way things ended between Wade and me didn't leave me a lot of tolerance for scene like this.

"Some." He shrugged his huge shoulders. "I'd come here to talk, to tell you something. Then I saw you and Mr. Grunge-Rock Nineteen-Ninety-Nine hanging all over each other at the wedding."

"Grunge-Rock?" I said the words without inflection, really focused on the other part of what Wade said. He'd come here to talk to me, to tell me something. It must have been important.

"You know...your new guy's got that long, straight hair. The stubble. The tan. The tight jeans. The wanna-be badass jewelry." Wade rolled his eyes and snorted.

I let the dig at Tanner pass. I'd never win. "What did you come here to talk to me about?" Right away, I wished I could take back the question. Whatever Wade had to say would only shit on my newfound happiness.

Maybe what I had with Tanner was not forever, but it was something enjoyable for both of us. A nice friendship and more. I was ready to make peace with the present, to learn how to dance with change. If Wade said he'd changed his mind, was willing to risk the consequences of being with me, what would I do?

"It doesn't matter now." He lowered his chin and looked at me from underneath his brows, pouting.

That pout threw cold water on any misgivings I had. I would not play this game with Wade. I had a soft bed and a willing man in my camper. Tanner might be complicated, but at least he was willing to take a chance on leaving his grief behind to seek out happiness.

What was I doing? I couldn't compare Wade and Tanner tit for tat. Wade had special circumstances. He carried a curse when it came to me. If he hung around too long, it would kill him.

I thought about the wheel of life inside my camper. Could Wade's fate with regard to me be changed? Maybe. Maybe not. The price of it not working would be death for Wade.

He couldn't risk that for me. If Wade died because of me, I'd have to kill myself. Because I wouldn't be able to stand the guilt. So it was over and done with. Forever.

Giving up on Wade broke my heart into a million jagged, howling pieces. But the last few days had taught me one important thing. Life went on.

I had to live it the best I could and find my own happiness because there would not be a do-over. I wouldn't get a special medal at the end for spending my life pining over the big love that never happened.

Wade sat across from me, watching me think. This was the first time I'd noticed how intently he watched and wondered how much he intuited just from body language. Against my better judgment, I reached across the table and took his hand. "How are you?"

He nodded. "Good. Got a decent job doing factory work. Pay tops out at more than I've ever made in my life. Got a couple of women who don't mind my company."

His dark eyes searched me for a reaction. There was no way I'd give him one. It wouldn't help the situation.

I let go of his hand. "You take care of yourself, you hear me?"

"That my invitation to leave?" He stood, stepped out from behind the picnic table, and held out his arms. I went to him and let him hug me, inhaling the scent of sunshine, of open road, and of gasoline. I closed my eyes, drinking it in like it was the last time. It probably was.

Wade let go of me and dug out a slip of paper about the size of a business card. "Desiree asked me to give you this. It's her address and phone numbers. She said if you ever need help, her door is open."

Wade didn't wait for me to react, to say yes or no. He took off walking into the darkness. I watched him until he faded from sight and listened for his motorcycle.

But then I remembered he'd blown it up the last day he spent in the Six Gun Revolutionaries motorcycle club. Somewhere in the distance, a loud motor started. Not a motorcycle. Maybe a truck or an old car with a nasty muffler.

I slipped back inside my camper, set my cigarettes back on the counter where I'd found them, and began undressing.

Tanner's voice came out of the darkness. "That him?"

"Who him?" I stripped down and crawled into bed with him.

"The guy who broke your heart, the one you didn't want to let go of." He moved his hands over my body, light and teasing.

I pretended to ignore or forget the question and tried to pull him on top of me.

He shook me off. "Tell me. Was that him?"

"It was him." I took my hands off Tanner and scooted away.

"I saw him earlier tonight at the wedding. Finn told me who he was." Tanner didn't sound jealous, but he didn't sound happy either. The dim light hid whatever emotions I might have seen on his face. Defensiveness pricked at me.

"Okay. I was outside talking to a guy I used to have a thing for. What do you want to know about it?" I tensed, ready to get up, get dressed again, and tell Tanner to get the hell out of my home.

"I know everything I need to know. You came back in here with me." Tanner scooted closer and caressed my face with the tips of his fingers. My eyes had adjusted a little more to the dimness, and I could see amusement sparkling in Tanner's eyes. It almost buried the spark of fierce possessiveness. But not quite.

"Then why question me about it?" I held my body stiff, still not sure if he wanted to fight. A lot of men would have.

"I wanted to make sure you're okay. It hurts to lose somebody when you think it's forever." He let out a sigh.

I scooted closer and wrapped one leg over his hip. "I'm

okay. It doesn't matter. He doesn't matter." That was a lie, but what was that silly saying of Hannah's? Fake it till you make it. That's what I was going to do. I kissed Tanner's lips and spoke against them. "The important thing is that he's gone, and you're here, and we're both awake."

I trailed my fingers down Tanner's chest and touched him in a place that made his legs stiffen and his breath catch. He made a low sound in his throat, a growl. I kept my hand moving and pushed him onto his back.

Neither of us spoke the rest of the night. Instead, we made up for lonely nights and lost time.

Sometime in the complete darkness before daylight, I lay staring at the ceiling, listening to Tanner sleep. Though I'd put away the wheel of life, its magic thrummed hard, all those lifelines racing forward like a freeway at rush hour. Time passing. Life changing. Every day, every second. And we were no more than travelers tossed between paths dark and light.

Dawn crept through the blinds, playing over Tanner's tawny skin, underlining the point of it all. Be happy when it's good.

Smiling, I lit my first cigarette of the day.

21

———

The box of runes still sat at the edge of the lake where Peri Jean Mace had thrown it several hours earlier. The sight of them haunted Oscar Rivera, drove him mad with desire. And there was nothing he could do but sit in his stupid soul box staring at them.

The real shame was Oscar hadn't been able to pull Peri Jean down with the box. She'd been right at the edge when that stupid man, the one still grieving his wife and children, had pulled her away.

If only Oscar had been able to isolate her and make her fall. Then he might have been able to siphon her dying power into him, pull the runes to his soul box, and resurrect her dead body. Peri Jean's body thrummed with untested power. Oscar's soul shivered at the thought of it.

At least he had another chance. He'd lived in this cave many, many years. People came down here more often than Peri Jean thought. Oscar only needed a chance to make one of them curious enough to touch that box of runes. Once they did, all the black paint and flowers and prayers wouldn't make a bit of difference.

Once he got topside again, Oscar would relieve Peri Jean Mace of her power. She didn't even know how to use it. Then he'd resume the plan he started so many years ago. This century was so much better suited for it.

Keep reading for a sample of the next Peri Jean Mace Ghost Thriller.

WRONG TURN (EXCERPT)

PERI JEAN MACE GHOST THRILLERS #10

CHAPTER 1

The house, a white brick ranch with pretty turquoise shutters, didn't look like a witch's house. But the hemlock and henbane growing in the flower beds hinted we'd found the right place. I parked my truck a little way down the block and left the engine running. Too hot to do otherwise.

Tanner, sweat beading his forehead, fiddled with the truck's air conditioner until he had it running full blast. He gave me a smile.

I smiled back, but fatigue wavered behind my eyes. I took a sip of Vietnamese-style coffee. It was sweeter than I liked, but I hoped the combination of sugar and caffeine would keep me rolling just a little longer. The two days spent driving from Archer City, Texas, to Natchitoches, Louisiana, had me whipped.

It wasn't just the drive that had kicked my ass. My hot boyfriend had kept me awake most of the night. I reached across the truck and tucked his hair behind his ear. He grabbed my hand and planted a sweaty kiss on it. I took another sip of the sweet coffee mixture. Come to think of it, it was a nice change from my usual strong, bitter coffee.

Summervale Carnival had a yearly engagement here. They had invited Sanctuary to join in as long as we kept it on the down low. Nobody else wanted to come to humid north Louisiana at the end of August, but Cecil voted us all down. Sitting in front of this witch's house, I suspected his ulterior motive for this visit to sportsman's paradise.

Across the truck, Tanner held his condensation-beaded plastic cup of Vietnamese coffee to his forehead. "Why are we here?"

"Cecil didn't say any more than I told you—this Queenie woman might have a solution for getting rid of the scar tissue spell." The scar tissue spell had been placed on me in infancy. It kept me from accessing the full measure of my witching abilities. Eventually, it was going to get me killed.

"What are we waiting for?" Tanner adjusted the air-conditioned vent until it blew directly in his face. The livid red streaks decorating his broad cheekbones worried me. The humidity in this part of the Southeastern US didn't agree with my California-born boyfriend. He'd already puked once.

"Cecil said he'd be here at one." I lit a cigarette and picked at the lighter's safety label with my fingernail.

Tanner put his hand over mine to still my restless fingers. "Look at me."

I blew out a long breath but did what he said. More than just my lover, Tanner had grown into my closest confidant. We talked naked in the dark of night. We spent the miles driving from place to place talking on phones. Hours-long conversations about everything and nothing. Now Tanner fixed me with his gaze. Jewel green, sexy, and wild.

"Whatever Queenie the Witch says won't be all bad. If it is, you and I will find another way."

I wanted to believe him, but nothing ever came easy for me. There was no reason to believe this would be any different.

Someone tapped on my window. I turned to see my great-uncle Cecil wiping sweat from his face with a plain white handkerchief. He motioned me to follow him and walked toward the witch's house.

"You can stay in the air conditioning." I opened my truck door.

Tanner grabbed my arm. "How could you think I'd want to stay?"

As close as we'd gotten, I didn't feel comfortable having Tanner hear me get bad news. One day he'd get tired of the bad news and head out for greener pastures. I wanted to put that off as long as possible. There was no way to tell Tanner that without making him mad, so I shrugged and said, "Come if you want."

He reached for the door handle, and the relief I felt shamed me. How had I let myself turn into such a wimp? Cecil raised his eyebrows when he saw Tanner trailing behind.

"I didn't tell Queenie there'd be three of us," he said in a low voice when we reached the porch.

"Do you think she'll be upset?" I had never even heard of Queenie until Cecil told me I'd be meeting with her.

"Hell if I know," Cecil stage whispered. "Last time I spoke with her, she and her husband were running house repair scams in the Deep South. That's been thirty, thirty-five years ago."

This visit with Queenie the Witch was beginning to worry me. "Why do you think she can even help?"

"Because Queenie always knew where to find the Wanderer." Cecil spoke out loud now, voice sharp with impatience.

Cecil hadn't yet explained who, or what, the Wanderer was or how he might help. When pressed, he'd only say, "The Wanderer just knows. If anybody can help, it's him." But what if I didn't want his kind of help?

Hinges whined as the front door swung open. "Cecil Paul, are you and these young folks just gonna stand out here and argue, or are you going to ring my doorbell?"

Cecil's lips cracked into a grin, spreading wrinkles across his face. He turned and held out his arms. "Queenie! Sugar, you look just the same."

The two embraced, laughing. I studied Queenie. Black hair shot with liberal white threads. Face as wrinkled as Cecil's. Crepey skin hanging off skinny arms. Either it hadn't been three decades, Cecil's eyesight was failing, or Queenie didn't look the same at all.

I pushed away the less-than-nice thoughts. Queenie had agreed to help, even though she didn't know me from a frog on the porch. Tanner took my hand, twining his fingers through mine. I glanced at him for reassurance. He winked and squeezed tighter.

Cecil and Queenie broke their embrace. Cecil, still squeezing her arms, said, "Thank you so much for making time for us."

Queenie mock frowned. "For you? Anytime."

Cecil gestured at me, pride shining in his eyes. "This is my great-niece, Peri Jean Mace."

"Leticia's granddaughter?" Queenie cocked her head and studied me like a cut of beef she might be considering in a butcher shop.

I nodded.

"I suppose you'll do." Queenie's dark eyes sparkled with humor, and she grabbed me in a hug and squeezed with a strength I hadn't suspected. She let go of me and took in Tanner.

"Tanner Letts, ma'am." He held out one deeply tanned hand.

Queenie stared at it for several beats, making no move to take it.

Cecil said, "Tanner is Peri Jean's...ah...friend. He's a trusted member of Sanctuary. He decided to join us at the last minute."

Queenie nodded and took Tanner's hand. Instead of shaking it, she turned the palm up and traced one of the lines. She raised her eyes to Tanner's. "Passion. Loyalty. You're a catch."

His sun-browned cheeks flushed, and he cast his eyes down. Queenie let go of Tanner and held open the door for us. We filed inside and stood in the entry hall. An old wall mirror threw my reflection back at me. I winced. The humidity had turned my black hair into ropy clumps that looked like something out of a painting of Medusa.

Queenie closed the door and led us through a spacious living room where a huge TV showed a peaceful ocean scene. The plain beige carpet and tasteful furniture could have been in anyone's home. Not what I expected at all.

Queenie motioned us into the dining room. "This is where I work."

She went straight to the oblong dining room table and straightened the black tablecloth covering it. A tuxedo cat jumped onto the table and meowed. Queenie gave the cat a pat and went to a shelf of different colored candles.

I took one step into the room. Queenie's considerable power rushed out in warning. It swirled around me, testing, probing. My black opal necklace, which magnified my gifts and warned me of magic nearby, shot painful electric jolts into my chest. I stopped right inside the door. Cecil, oblivious, sat at the table. The cat hissed at him.

Tanner stopped next to me. "What is it?"

I shook my head, keeping an eye on both Queenie and the cat. She turned, holding a virgin purple candle, and gasped. She spoke in a harsh, unfamiliar language to the cat. It jumped off the table and came to rub against my legs. The black opal's pings softened to a bearable level. The magical force lost its menace and welcomed me inside.

"Faustus thinks every person of power is a threat. He likes us to have all the power." Queenie sat the purple candle on the table and two vials of oil next to it. "Since we're working for you, dear, you'll need to dress the candle."

I moved to the table, taking slow steps to keep from tripping over Faustus, who trilled at me. I'd spent enough time with my raven familiar, Orev, to understand Faustus was laughing at me. Little rat-turd muncher. I held my left hand over each of the two vials of oil, testing to see which one had the magic that fit mine, and picked up the one on the right.

"We're contacting the Wanderer?" I needed to know so I could set my intent before I rubbed on the oil.

Queenie nodded. "I'll contact him on your behalf."

I picked up the candle and the oil and walked to a table that had several animal skulls on it. Placing my hands on the table, I drew on the energy of the bones, the wood, and the magic of the beeswax Queenie had made the candle from. The lights flickered. Intent set, I cleared my mind of everything else and rubbed the oil from top to bottom to draw things to me instead of push them away.

"Someone taught her well," Queenie said to Cecil.

"It wasn't me." But the pride on his face said he took credit for me anyway.

"Oh, I know that. You were always too busy chasing women to learn the old ways." Queenie took the candle back to the table and motioned me to follow.

For the first time, I noticed only three chairs around the table. Suddenly I understood Queenie's reaction to Tanner. She'd set up the table for three participants. Three as a number held great power. Now she'd have to add a fourth person. It might throw off the balance of what she had planned.

"Queenie, Tanner won't be upset if he can't participate in the ritual," I said quickly. "He knows he's gate-crashing."

Queenie gave me a wink. "No, sweetie. If I understood Cecil Paul correctly, this is serious stuff we're discussing. Your lover needs to hear whatever is said."

My cheeks flamed because Queenie had hit on why I almost didn't want Tanner here. Letting him in on too much personal business solidified his spot in my life. And I wanted to keep it loose and easy. Every little merge tangled things further, made it harder and more painful for one of us to change our mind and leave. But Queenie was already dragging a chair away from the wall. Tanner hurried to help her, placing it exactly where she told him.

She took an object covered with black lace out of a cabinet behind her chair and placed it on the table. Next to it, she set the purple candle and motioned for me to light it. Queenie and I sat at the same time.

She pulled the black lace away to reveal a black crystal ball. "My power is much like what I feel coming off you, Peri Jean. By that, I mean I won't be conducting a traditional ritual. Instead I'll use both your power and mine to tell me what you want to know."

I nodded to let her know I understood and agreed.

Satisfied, Queenie turned to Cecil. "I'm afraid I'll need you to explain why you need the Wanderer. He doesn't like being disturbed for frivolous reasons, and if I facilitate such a thing, the responsibility will fall on me."

Again I speculated on who this person—or creature—was. And I questioned the wisdom of hunting him down.

Before I could tell Cecil we needed to get out of this place and leave this nice lady to her TV programs, he launched into the story of how I came to have a spell covering my magical core. Queenie listened with her faded brown eyes fixed on Cecil's face, nodding every few sentences. When he stopped talking, she sat in silence, her wrinkles arranged into a frown. She started to speak a couple of times but shook her head.

"So Leticia is the one who chose this for Peri Jean?" Queenie looked me over again, as though seeing me for the first time.

I nodded. "From what I understand, yes."

Queenie nodded again. "I'm sure she had her reasons. Why don't you tell me your reasons for wanting the spell removed."

"Two different times I've dealt with a spirit called the Coachman. In life, he was a man named Oscar Rivera. " I paused to take a calming breath. Just thinking about Oscar made my chest tighten.

Queenie drew back from me, face set in distaste.

"You know him?" I asked.

"Heard of him." The distaste stayed on her face.

"Both times, he almost killed me because I couldn't access my full power." I stopped because I wasn't sure what else to say.

Cecil spoke up. "This is her destiny, Queenie. The challenges intended for her will come whether or not she's ready." He leaned forward. "In addition, she may not be able to pass our family's power on to the next generation without full control of it."

"And that's the really important thing." Queenie raised what eyebrows she had left and gave Cecil a not-very-nice smile.

He leaned back in his chair. "This power has been in our family for millennia. It's important that it continue. Is it not important to you that your family's power continue?"

Queenie appeared to think that over, but she wasn't really considering. She was gathering her energy. It moved in the air, cooler and sharper than my power. Reality rippled around Queenie. Tendrils of it moved near her sagging ears. She put her hands on the black crystal ball and took a deep breath.

"Put your hands on the ball, Peri Jean." Her voice had gone guttural.

I leaned forward and did as she asked. Soon as my fingers touched the black sphere, Queenie's power sang in my fingertips, testing me, pressing against what little bit of Priscilla Herrera's mantle I had access to.

"Now Cecil Paul." Her voice rang deeper with more power.

Cecil wiped his hands on his dress pants and put his fingertips on the ball. He closed his eyes and breathed deeply. The power stabilized to a low hum.

"Now Tanner Jackson Letts," Queenie commanded.

Tanner jerked next to me. Queenie knew his middle name. He took a deep breath and put his fingers on the ball, throwing me a nervous glance. Power vibrated around the woman's little old lady shell, greater and more terrible than anything I had in my arsenal. Just went to show things aren't always what they seem.

Queenie's strong voice cut into my thoughts. "Cecil Paul, join me in thinking of the Wanderer, in remembering all we know of him."

Both elders leaned their heads forward in concentration. A low hum came from Queenie.

Threads of bright light shot through the black sphere like rainbow lightning. Different colored threads touched each person's fingers. When it got to my fingertips, a light shock carried through my body. It tried Cecil again, but came back to me. The shock grew more intense.

"Don't pull away," Queenie said. "Just let it test you."

The light shot power into my fingertips over and over again until an ache spread up my arms. My black opal grew warm on my chest, then hot enough to burn. It would leave a red mark. My raven familiar, Orev, cawed outside Queenie's house. Faustus hissed in response. I opened my eyes to find Queenie staring at me.

"You are the one," she said and took her fingers off the black sphere. The rest of us followed suit. Queenie picked up the swath of lace and draped it back over the black ball. She stood from her seat and blew out the candle.

Finally I could stand it no more. Patience had never been my strong suit. "Did you find out anything about the Wanderer?"

Cecil blew out a breath and shook his head. "She means no disrespect, Queenie. She's young and impatient."

Queenie barely acknowledged either of us. "You're not ready for contact with the Wanderer. He'll only help you on the last leg of your journey. You have at least several more trials to complete. More to discover about yourself. Keep your mind open."

I leaned back in my chair and tried to keep the disappointment off my face. Pissing off Queenie might create an ass whipping I didn't want to experience. But I was disappointed. We'd come all the way to Natchitoches, Louisiana, for nothing.

"If you want to move forward, stop living in your own life like a ghost." Queenie pointed one arthritis-warped finger at me.

What did that mean? I couldn't keep from frowning as I puzzled over it. Meanwhile, Queenie stood and walked us to the front door. Remembering the customs of our kind, I dug in my pocket for the fold of cash I kept there.

"Do you take donations?" I asked Queenie.

She held out one hand and said her line. "Whatever you feel appropriate."

I put the entire wad of cash in her hand. Fear can motivate generosity as well as anything else.

Queenie made the money disappear. "Don't be so disappointed. Today was a success."

"How so?" I couldn't hide my incredulity. The money I'd given Queenie would have bought groceries for the month.

Queenie smiled as though she knew my thoughts as well as her own. "The Wanderer will meet with you when the time is right. He is now aware of your need."

She closed the door on any answer we might have made. The deadbolt clicked home. It was a clear message that we needed to go. Tanner and I followed Cecil to the economy car he and Shelly pulled behind their motorhome. He unlocked the door and stood back for the heat to boil out.

"Follow me downtown. We got in too late last night to get meat pies, and I'm ready for one or two." Without waiting for an answer, Cecil got in the car and started it.

"Are meat pies barbecue?" Tanner asked on the short walk to my truck.

I answered with a glare. Tanner's obsession with Texas barbecue—the culture and the food—left the permanent taste of smoked meat in my mouth. The only smoke I wanted to taste all the time was cigarette smoke.

The restaurant Cecil chose consisted of a long, narrow room full of tables for four. Despite the lunch hour being over, people jammed the place. The smell of frying food made my mouth water.

Cecil ordered a plate of corn fritters as an appetizer. Tanner had never even heard of the deep-fried balls of batter embedded with corn kernels. He wolfed one down and refused another.

"Too heavy," he said, face pale and beading with sweat.

I finished my corn fritter and reached for another. The food wasn't too heavy for me. I loved deep-fried anything. But worry churned in my stomach.

Cecil voiced my feelings. "Queenie scared me. What might be in store for you?"

"Nothing good." I had several pissing matches running in the background.

The threat of Oscar Rivera hung over me like a storm

cloud and would until I vanquished him from this plane. I'd destroyed the Six Gun Revolutionaries Motorcycle Club. And I owed favors to several chthonic beings who could choose to call in their markers any time.

Cecil pinched the bridge of his nose between his thumb and forefinger. "Other battles you've been through have lessened the scar tissue, yes?"

Yeah. And they almost killed me too. Cecil didn't like whiners, so I kept the thought to myself and just nodded.

"Then there's nothing to do but be careful." Cecil dug into his meat pie, which had come while we talked, and chewed with his eyes closed. His wife, Shelly, would have had a shit fit at him for eating so much fried food.

I finished my meal in silence, wondering how much more I could stand before I fell over from exhaustion.

Cecil went back the RV park to rest before the carnival started that evening. Tanner and I set off to see the sights of Natchitoches. Established in 1714, the city was the oldest permanent settlement in the 1803 Louisiana Purchase.

Guzzling cold drinks and pouring sweat, we explored the carefully preserved downtown buildings. Along the banks of the Cane River Lake, right off the downtown, Tanner pointed to a sign advertising the Christmas Festival of Lights.

"We should come back in a few months." He kissed me.

"I'd like that." It felt good pretending to be just another couple in the honeymoon phase of a relationship.

The day ended as most days did with Tanner, our clothes in a pile on the floor and our bodies tangled together. Had I known how much things would change in just a few hours, I'd have cherished it more.

———

I lay in the dark trying to figure out what had changed. Maybe it had been a nightmare, the kind waking up erases so completely you're left with nothing but an unsettled feeling. But I didn't think so. Something was different.

The shadows of my camper seemed the same. The basket of laundry sat on the table where I'd left it, silently scolding me for being too lazy—or horny—to fold it before I went to bed.

Tanner slumbered next to me, a heavy arm and leg thrown across me, pinning me to the bed. He slept the sleep of the dead, slow even breaths puffing against my hair. He hadn't woken me with a sudden movement. What then?

The air conditioner rumbled overhead, shaking my little camper with its noise. It may have woken me when it kicked on. The unit blasted cold air into the small space, but the late August heat and humidity still burned like fever under my skin. But it wasn't the only thing that kept me from falling right back to sleep.

Queenie had said I had more trials to face before the Wanderer would help me with the scar tissue. Trials, most of which turned out to be life-threatening, scared the pudding out of me. This trial would likely come at exactly the wrong time. But what could I do? My thoughts began to fragment as the languor of sleep slipped over them. My eyes drooped.

A shadow moved near the bathroom at the back of the camper. I sucked in a deep breath. My heart lunged into action, pumping blood and adrenaline through me. Someone was in here with us.

My body tensed. Had I left the door unlocked? No. I'd locked the door as Tanner tugged off my clothes a few hours earlier. The shadow slowly taking shape in the darkness belonged to someone who'd broken into my little home. I nudged Tanner. He responded with a sluggish grunt and tightened his grip on me.

Great. It would take force to wake him up, and right now I wanted to believe the shadow didn't know it had woken me. I reached for the mantle. Even though I didn't have full control of the power it contained, the few hours' rest had me fully charged. I gathered energy, pulling on everything in the room, even the electricity.

Once the shadow neared, I'd give him or her a blast of something they might not live through.

The bathroom light flicked on. I jerked with shock, eyes burning, and threw up one arm to shield my eyes, squinting at the blurry figure. There was something wrong with his head. It brushed the camper's ceiling and seemed to bend with it.

Next to me, Tanner's slow breaths stopped. He was awake. Good. At least he'd help me fight.

The shadow spoke. "Peri Jean Macccccce." He dragged out my last name, making it hiss. All of a sudden, I knew who it was. Mohawk. I couldn't mistake that voice.

His skinny body came into focus. Now I could identify his bleached blond Mohawk as the part of him brushing the ceiling. In spite of the heat, he still wore a leather jacket, ripped black pants, and heavy jack boots. Made sense. Aren't snakes cold-blooded?

Faster than my vision could track, Mohawk rushed at the bed. I let out a sissified scream, clawed at Tanner like a damn girl, and hollered, "Don't let him take me."

Tanner, with no regard for his own safety, rose to meet Mohawk. The covers fell off his naked body and puddled at his knees. Tanner drew back his fist. His back muscles bunched, and he let one punch fly at Mohawk. The creature from the dark outposts dodged Tanner's fist the same way he'd have avoided walking through a spider's web.

My hope sank. Of course Mohawk could counter any physical attack and beat it. He wasn't even human. My friend and mentor, Mysti Whitebyrd, called beings like Mohawk chthonic beings. The only way we had any chance of beating him was to use magic.

Shoving the covers off my naked body, I crouched next to Tanner, drawing on our combined magic, and let loose a bolt of electric fire. It slapped into Mohawk's chest and died there in a puff of smoke. The smell of singed leather competed with the being's swampy, snake stench. He opened his mouth, let his snake fangs show, and hissed. The sides of his neck flared out like a cobra's.

One skinny, long-fingered hand flashed out, grabbed my arm, and yanked me off the bed. Tanner let out a warrior's yell and leapt on Mohawk. The snake man held my arm so tight the bone began to ache. In a second, my lower arm began to tingle from having the blood flow cut off. With his free hand, Mohawk plucked Tanner off him like an errant kid and slung him back on the bed.

Tanner rolled to his feet and tensed to launch himself at Mohawk again. The monster held out one hand. A flash of light, not unlike the one I'd tried to blast Mohawk with, blazed into Tanner. He fell on his side, holding his chest and gasping.

I quit fighting to get away from Mohawk and launched myself at him, jabbing at his eyes with my fingers. He let go of my arm to fight me off, curled his other hand into a fist, and slammed it into my sternum. Pain bloomed in my midsection. My legs folded, and I sank to the floor of my camper, where I lay naked and curled into the fetal position, struggling to breathe.

Tanner, a red welt forming on his chest, got to his feet. He was ready to fight again. Mohawk pointed one finger at him. "Stop now, Tanner Jackson Letts, or I'll kill you."

No. I wouldn't let Mohawk kill Tanner. He didn't even deserve to be in the middle of this. I tried to draw breath to speak. My injured sternum spasmed, refusing to let me draw more than the shallowest wisp of oxygen. I held up one hand to Tanner and shook my head.

Tanner frowned and gave Mohawk a death glare. His battle-scarred fists clenched.

Mohawk flicked his forked tongue at Tanner. "One more attack, and I'll consider Peri Jean Mace in violation of our agreement."

"She'd never make a deal with a piece of shit like you."

Tanner's chest rose and fell with each breath. A vein throbbed in his forehead. He was ready to go to war.

Mohawk's woody brown eyes flicked over my naked body. His pupils expanded, and his nostrils flared. He chuckled. "If that's what you believe, you don't know this woman very well."

A chill started at the base of my spine and spread over my body. I shook my head again at Tanner, silently pleading.

Recognition flooded his face. The fury went out of his green eyes as though a switch had been flipped. Shoulders slumped, he dragged on his clothes, retrieved mine, and helped me into them. I had a hard time uncurling my body. Each pull on my abdominal muscles sent stabbing pain through my bowels.

Mohawk sat at my camper's table watching our progress. He drummed long, sharp fingernails on the table and checked the time on his phone every few seconds.

When I could speak, I said, "Why did you break into my home?"

"We have a bargain. I can tell you haven't forgotten. Did you think you could fight your way out of it?"

I shook my head. Tanner set a glass of cold water in front of me, face set in hard planes of anger. We exchanged a glance. I'd told him as little as possible about Mohawk and the deal I'd made. Some part of me had hoped it would just go away. I should have known better. Never taking my eyes off Mohawk, I sipped the water.

"I'm not a cheater. I do what I say I'll do. But you promised to contact me through the marble. I thought you'd changed your mind and come to just take me." If I failed to fulfill my end of the bargain with Mohawk, I'd forfeit my freedom. Become his slave. Bear his offspring. I shuddered at the thought.

"Then you *do* want to attempt to find the book?" Mohawk checked his phone again. Like he had anything more interesting to do than harass me.

"Anything to get you out of my life." I took my first deep breath, and then another just to make sure I could do it again.

"At the risk of sounding like a broken record, I want to remind you that coming with me voluntarily would satisfy all debts." Mohawk set down his phone and leaned forward. "I am willing to grant your freedom in five years' time. You only have to..."

"She's not going anywhere with you," Tanner shouted.

Nausea roiling in my sore stomach, I ignored Tanner and spoke to Mohawk. "No. I'll get the book. Whatever it takes, I'll get it."

Mohawk sat back in his seat and watched both of us for several long seconds. Finally, he heaved a deep sigh, reached into an inside pocket of his jacket, and withdrew an old, wrinkled photo. He set it on the table.

A young woman with wispy blond hair blowing in a long-dead wind stared out at a vista of tree-covered hills. A minidress with a geometric pattern showed off her shapely legs. The garment's cut suggested the picture might have been taken in the late sixties.

The young woman clutched a huge book to her chest. On the visible end of the book was metal twisted into a circles and dots pattern that raised the hair on the back of my neck. Even the years separating me from this book were not enough to hide the wrongness of it. It probably didn't help that Mohawk had already hinted at what it did to people who read it.

"This is the book? The one you want me to find?" I reached out to touch the picture with my index finger but drew it back. I didn't even want to touch an image of the nasty thing. Tanner crowded in for a closer look.

Mohawk nodded. "This human is the last one to possess the book." He slid out of the bench seat and took the few steps to the camper's door.

"Wait." I shot out of the bench seat, shoved around Tanner, and went after Mohawk. "I need more information. I don't even know her name."

Mohawk spun to face me. I halted in my tracks. He tilted his head, dead eyes boring into me. His tall, stiff hair scratched against the cabinet over my sink.

"Why would I help you? I've told you how I'd like this to end." He ran one skinny, cold finger over my face.

Cold horror radiated outward from where he touched. I backpedaled away from Mohawk and sat down in the seat he'd just vacated hard enough to jar the breath from me.

"You have..." Mohawk looked at his phone again. "Oh, let's make this fun. You have seventy-two hours from right now. Failure means you belong to me."

My lungs constricted, and my mouth dried up. A lifetime as Mohawk's consort would drive me mad. Blood roared in my ears. Mohawk smiled.

"This is your last chance to come with me voluntarily. As promised, I'd release you in five years. But if you play this out and fail?" He clucked his tongue. "You'll be mine for the rest of your natural life."

"Now wait a minute…" Tanner, who'd gotten control of his anger, took a step toward Mohawk.

The creature hissed and pointed one finger at him. "Interfere, and you'll die crying for your mother."

I grabbed Tanner's arm, sweat stinging my forehead and scalp, and pulled him close. Tanner put one arm around me. The three of us glared at each other, barely breathing. One drop of sweat rolled down the back of my head, down my neck, and left a cold trail down my back. Mohawk's pupils grew larger until they spread over most of his eye. A smile twitched at the corner of his mouth.

"Last chance." He sang the words.

I shook my head. "I'll find the book."

He laughed and stepped out into the night, leaving the camper's door hanging open.

Tanner walked to the door, closed it, and locked it. He turned to me, green eyes burning bright and intense. "All right. Time to come clean about that asshole and whatever he's holding over you."

I took a deep breath. "You remember me telling you about the hag that almost killed Hannah?"

"It attached itself to you, and to get rid of it, you had to buy it out of slavery." His face slackened. "That was the hag's owner? Sweetie, why did you…" He put both hands over his face and took deep breaths. Finally he dropped them. In a deceptively calm voice, the one he used before he started screaming, he asked, "What happens if you don't find the book?"

My voice trembled when I spoke. "He admires the line of witches I'm descended from. He wants to have a child with me."

Tanner's face fell in shock. "But I thought you were… couldn't have kids."

I shook my head. "It can be fixed by a healer. I've just never…"

Never what? Wanted to risk having a child? Wanted to see how badly whoever fathered it could screw up both our lives?

"But any child you had with him wouldn't even be human." Tanner's face paled, and he swallowed hard.

I imagined the result of a union between Mohawk and me. A sour wave of nausea shot up my throat. I ran into the bathroom, fell to my knees in front of the toilet, and barfed.

CHAPTER 2

Tanner held my hair while I called dinosaurs. When I was finished, he wiped my face with a cold cloth. I sat on the floor, eyes closed, leaning against the tiny door to the camper's only full-length closet space, too weak to move just yet.

Tanner ran more cool water on the cloth and wiped my forehead with it. I felt a rush of love for him. I opened my eyes to stare at his not-quite-handsome face and his brilliant eyes.

Sweet Tanner, so sincere and helpful. We exchanged a smile. With one arm, I pushed myself off the floor. Tanner pulled me to a standing position. I got out my toothbrush and brushed the awfulness out of my mouth.

He watched me. "Tell me about this book. What does it do?"

I spat out toothpaste and turned on the faucet to wash it down. "Best I can understand, it instigates murder and mayhem."

Tanner frowned in the mirror.

"Mohawk was once worshipped as a god. He compelled his followers to draw symbols on the walls of caves. These symbols drove his worshipers into a violent religious frenzy."

Tanner, who'd dealt in magical items all his life, thought this over. "The symbols probably created a mild hypnotism. So you're saying the symbols from the caves ended up in these books?"

I nodded. "There's three of these books. Mohawk wants this one back into play."

Tanner made a disgusted face. The gravity of my task hit me. I was going to release evil into the world to save myself from an awful fate.

I examined myself in the mirror. Could I really be so selfish? Tanner stood behind me in the mirror and put his arms round my waist.

"I know what you're thinking." His whisper sent a shiver through me. "You can't look at it that way. You have to value yourself enough to fight for your own survival. Whatever it takes."

He released me, helped me back to the table, and sat me in front of that creepy picture while he rummaged in the refrigerator. He was about to make me ingest some of the awful sports drink he loved. And I felt so bad I'd probably do it.

I studied the picture while he filled a glass with ice. The woman holding the book had a sweet face ruined by evil, dead eyes. Her fingers curled around the edge of the book possessively. Was she dead or alive? I concentrated on the picture. Sometimes I could tell if a person in a picture was alive or dead. But this time, I only got a whiff of dry, dusty air. I turned the picture over. Scrawled on the back were the words "Devil's Rest, 1973."

Tanner set my neon-colored drink in front of me. "Any ideas?"

"No." I hid the lie by putting the condensation-covered glass to my forehead. Tanner couldn't know about Devil's Rest or 1973. He'd only want to help, and it might get him killed. No. I had to do this alone.

A plan pieced itself together. I'd get in my truck and leave everything, including Tanner, here. My friends and family would be pissed, but they'd be safe.

Tanner watched me, brows drawn together. "You're lying." One hand flashed out and snatched the picture from me. He held it close to his face, studying it.

Don't turn it over. Please. I sat still as possible, as though that would make my hasty prayer come to pass.

Tanner squinted at me across the table. "What are you hiding?"

Not waiting for an answer, he put the picture close to

his face again, memorizing details. I held my breath and begged the universe to make him give it back. *Don't let him see the name Devil's Rest.* Tanner moved the picture a few inches away from his face, eyes moving back and forth. He turned over the picture. I wanted to scream at him to drop it, but Tanner had a stubborn streak.

Now he raised his eyes to mine. "What's Devil's Rest?"

I shook my head.

He pushed the picture across the table. "I see plans forming behind those dark eyes. Tell me."

"I'm leaving as fast as I can. Before anyone wakes up." I put my fingers on top of the picture.

"What? Why?" Tanner, always eager to involve others, never understood the wisdom of going the course alone.

"They'll want to help." I said the words as though my family's help came with cooties.

"The more of us there are, the faster we can get it done." Tanner drank down his own over-sweet sports drink.

"No way. Mohawk doesn't want me to find his book. He wants me to fail so he can make me his slave. If they get in the way, they're toast." I finished off my sports drink in three big gulps with a grimace and a shudder.

Tanner thought this over in his usual solemn way, head lowered, hair fallen across his face. After a few seconds, he nodded. "You're right. Let me go get a shower and pack. We'll leave a note for them."

This was the hard part. "You can't go either, sweetie."

He stood, came around the table, and shoved his way

into the booth seat next to me, crowding me in. "I go where you go." Before I could answer, he kissed me.

A few seconds later, I pulled away, heart hammering, body flushed. "I'm serious. You can't go."

Those eyes, molten green and hot as asphalt at the end of August, hardened. "Why not?"

"There are a thousand ways this could go bad." I cupped his face in both hands, hoping to soften the blow. "I need to know you're safe."

Tanner snarled and pushed my hands down. "You don't trust me."

I shook my head. That wasn't it. I trusted Tanner with everything I had. My body, my life, my belongings. The person I didn't trust was myself. Things tended to go wrong around me, and people got hurt. Like Wade Hill. There was one who'd never speak to me again.

An expedition like this could change everything. Tanner and I had gotten together in the midst of extreme danger. Another bout of extreme danger might be too much. I cut the thoughts off cleanly. What needed doing? Pack for Devil's Rest. Go talk to Hannah.

I climbed over Tanner to get out of the booth style dining table and went to my bed. There I lifted my mattress to access the storage underneath and pulled out both my witch pack and the traveling hatbox I used for a suitcase. The latter had been a gift from Hannah. She'd bought it in Austin from an artist who'd painted runes and ravens all over it. I hefted the hatbox onto the table, opened it, and began tossing in the freshly laundered clothes.

Tanner followed. "That Queenie woman was right about you."

"Huh?" Busy calculating what I'd need for three days—because nothing mattered after that—I barely heard Tanner.

"Look at me." He grabbed my wrist, hard enough to make me gasp at first, then loosened his grip. "Stop packing." He spun me to face him. His eyes burned into mine. "That woman said you live like a ghost in your own life. That's what you're doing right now by not wanting me to go with you."

"Hey, you're right. Let's all go. Go tell Dillon and Finn to get the kids ready to travel." I threw another handful of underwear into my hatbox. "No, wait. Let's go get Hannah first. She really needs some more fucking trauma in her life."

Face reddening, Tanner narrowed his eyes into angry slits. "Don't blow me off." His voice rose to a shout on the last couple of words. Someone's dog started barking. He took a deep breath and spoke nearly in a whisper. "Do not blow me off. You know exactly what I'm talking about."

I yanked my wrist away from him. "No. I most certainly do not. All I know is my whole life is a circus of tragedy and danger, and I don't want you dragged into it."

Maybe a quick session of mattress rodeo would soothe his hurt feelings. I sidled close to him and brushed my lips against his.

He wasn't finished saying his piece and talked against my lips. "Then let me go with you. Finding stuff like this book is what I do. I can help you."

I drew back to stare at him. What he said was true. But what else came with it? Danger for him. Maybe death. I shook my head.

"Let me go take care of this. I'll make up for it when I get back." I trailed my fingers down his bare chest.

He moaned and planted soft kisses along my jawline. "I know exactly what you're trying to do right now."

"Me too." I popped open the button on his pants and dipped my fingers inside, still thinking about the time and getting out of here before people started stirring, and tugged him toward the bed.

Tanner didn't let me pull him. He planted his bare feet and stood like a statue. "You're avoiding the subject. I said you live in your life like a ghost. In order to keep from thinking about it, you're trying to get me naked."

I glanced down at the front of his pants. "You want to be naked with me."

He put his arms around my waist and pulled me against him. "But I also want to talk to you about this."

"About what?" I let my chest rub against his.

His eyes slid closed, and he pulled me against him hard enough to make us both grunt. He shook his head and pushed me away.

"Listen, please." He held up one hand. "That lady, Queenie, said you walk in your own life like a ghost. I know what she's talking about. You tiptoe around like you don't belong here rather than just living. Not wanting me to go is part of it."

My face heated. "That's not true."

He rolled his eyes and huffed out an ugly laugh. "Of course not."

I closed the distance he'd put between us, pressed my lips against his hot skin, and slipped my arms around his waist. "I can't risk you going with me and getting hurt, maybe even dead. What if I lose and he takes me as his... concubine?" The idea made my mouth dry, and I swallowed hard. "He'll kill you if you fight him. Or he might kill you for fun. Or he might take you as well. This is no game."

"And what we faced together a few months ago was a game?" He cupped my chin and tilted my head to look at him.

I shook my head. "No. It wasn't a game either."

"I helped you then, and I want to help now." He slid one hand under my shirt and ran his fingers over my bare skin. I shivered.

"Not this time." I tugged him toward the bed, to make that the last thing we did together, rather than argue.

But Tanner pushed my hand away and stepped around me to open the door. The sound of frogs singing drifted into the camper. "I'm going to shower and pack my bag. If you're not here when I get back, we're done."

Knowing I was beat, I waited until the door slammed before I got up and finished my packing. I grabbed my bags and a wad of cash I kept for rainy days and slipped out of the camper.

Available now.
Order Wrong Turn from your favorite bookseller.
ISBN: 978-1-947462-18-2

Visit Catie's website:
www.catierhodes.com

Find Catie on Facebook:
http://www.facebook.com/catierhodesauthor

Follow Catie on Book Bub.
https://www.bookbub.com/authors/catie-rhodes

Join Catie's email list:
http://smarturl.it/lrdenewsletter

ABOUT THE AUTHOR

Catie Rhodes writes southern-fried urban fantasy with a strong dose of horror and a side dish of humor.

She is the author of the Peri Jean Mace Ghost Thrillers. Her short stories have appeared in *Tales From The Mist, Let's Scare Cancer to Death, and Allegories of the Tarot.*

Catie was born and raised behind the pine curtain in East Texas. She comes from a family of world champion liars.

Their tall tales molded Catie into a purveyor of her own brand of lies and legends. One day, she found the courage to start writing down her stories. It changed her life forever.

Catie Rhodes lives steps from the Sam Houston National Forest with her long-suffering husband and her armpit terrorist of a little dog.

Find Catie online:
www.catierhodes.com